# GUARDIAN DEVILS

A DIVINELY IRREVERENT NOVEL BY
REBECCA McELDOWNEY

WINDSTORM CREATIVE
PORT ORCHARD ☿ SEATTLE ☿ TAHUYA

Guardian Devils
copyright 2006 by Rebecca McEldowney
published by Windstorm Creative

ISBN 1-59092-320-0
First edition August 2006
9 8 7 6 5 4 3 2

Cover image by Erika McKinnis.
Cover and interior design by Buster Blue.

All rights reserved, including the right to reproduce this book or portions thereof in any form whatsoever, except in the case of short excerpts for use in reviews of the book.

Printed in the United States of America.

For information about film, reprint or other subsidiary rights, please contact Mari Garcia at mgarcia@windstorm creative.com.

Windstorm Creative is a multiple division, international organization involved in publishing books in all genres, including electronic publications; producing games, videos and audio cassettes as well as producing theatre, film and visual arts events. The wind with the flame center was designed by Buster Blue of Blue Artisans Design and is a trademark of Windstorm Creative.

Windstorm Creative
7419 Ebbert Dr SE
Port Orchard, WA 98367
www.windstormcreative.com
360-769-7174 ph

Windstorm Creative is a member of Orchard Creative Group, Ltd.

Library of Congress Cataloging-in-Publication data available.

To the Real French Hens.

Thanks to Erica Orloff and Pamela Morrell, the writer's group who laughed and criticized in all the right places, and to Arline Massey and Anne Siren for reading the first draft ten years ago and pretending it was good. Acknowledgements also to Kenneth L. Woodward, author of *Making Saints: How the Catholic Church Determines Who Becomes a Saint, Who Doesn't, and Why*, for his fascinating account of that process. Apologies to C.S. Lewis: Those familiar with *The Screwtape Letters*, and such lines as, "When you enter heaven, the sound you hear is laughter," will see his influence throughout the story. Thanks to Cris DiMarco, my editor, for knowing what to leave out, and to the whole wacky gang at Windstorm Creative for their continued support. Lastly, though none of the characters is in any way based on actual persons living or working within the Episcopal Diocese of Southeast Florida now or ever, thanks for the use of the locale as my imaginary playground.

# Guardian Devils

### A Divinely Irreverent Novel by
## Rebecca McEldowney

# Part One
# Saints Below

# Chapter One
## In Which Ferdy Gets a New Assignment

Ferdy didn't really hate being trapped in the Spitting Gargoyle of Notre Dame. The job was low stress, and he could imagine worse places to watch a sunset. Earlier in the day rain had pelted his parapet and given the stone surrounding him a nice sauna smell as it dried.

His attention drifted back and forth from the late afternoon light burning the Eiffel Tower black in the distance to the street vendors in the cathedral plaza far below him packing up their tiny replicas of the city's monuments. Ferdy had to lean to the right to see around the gun metal pipes of a repair scaffold erected for the latest round of cleaning. The scaffolding obscured his view just a little, but he couldn't complain.

Oh, what the hell.

*Maybe the job is getting a little old,* he admitted to himself, *maybe I'm getting a little burned out, but wouldn't anybody feel that way after six hundred and eighty-four...five years?*

Not that there hadn't been variety to the job, not at all. The Spitting Gargoyle was only a couple hundred years old. The gargoyle before that looked more like a monkey with fangs that had crumbled into an indistinguishable lump of stone. In time this one would crumble too. The time before the first gargoyle, and the time after this one, he tried not to think about. Being older than a rock gave you too much time to think. And when that happened his thoughts wandered back to that stupid, stupid foul-up that landed him here.

Happily, his focus turned to the sound of slow footsteps coming up the flight of stairs behind him. Yves usually didn't give tours this late in the day, and sure enough, he appeared alone to stand by Ferdy and gaze with him beyond the *Ile de la Cite*. Ferdy never tired of listening to Yves's lectures about the cathedral seven times a day (four times in the off season) since Yves had taken this job as a young man. Yves's passion for the structure made Ferdy proud of being part of it all, instead of always thinking about what a loser he was. The last thirty-two years had passed more quickly because of Yves.

Better than the lectures, though, was when Yves would come up to this parapet alone, watch the city with Ferdy, and sometimes talk to him like an old friend.

"It will be beautiful tonight, eh, *Monsieur Chimiere*? The sun will set long after I've gone home. It is nearly the longest day of the year." Yves sighed and rubbed his fingertips over Ferdy's pitted bicep, a gesture that always signaled some intimacy. "Marie finally left me for that painter, you know. She says she's tired of competing with a cathedral. I don't think that's so. I think she just wanted a younger man, and also a painter is much more romantic than a tour guide. I don't know whether to wring her neck or my own. What would you advise, *Monsieur Chimiere*?"

The gargoyle encasing Ferdy stared impassively, its protruding tongue, for which it was named, stone still.

Yves sighed again and traced through the graying hair around his ear with his fingers. "I may as well be married to the cathedral. My hair matches the stone, eh? Perhaps in time I may aspire to be a gargoyle like you." Yves leaned his elbows on the wall, cupped his chin in his hands and thrust out his tongue as far as it would go. "What do you think, *Monsieur Chimiere*? Do I have the job? Heh? What's that you say? Too ugly? Well, then I suppose I must finish out my ten years telling people about you."

He affected the drawl of a bored lecturer. "And here my friends we have the Spitting Gargoyle, the most famous of Notre Dame's *Galerie de Chimiere* erected in 1845 by the architect Viollet-le-Duc who engineered the restoration of the cathedral. You will notice that he spits in the direction of the *Tour Eiffel* which is an upstart when compared to the cathedral's life of eight centuries."

Yves pointed over the parapet as he spoke, then grasped one of the cross-bars of the scaffolding just within reach and stared at the back of his right hand. He examined the few white hairs, the blue veins straining against the papery skin, the thickened nails. Then he drew the hand down and sniffed at the palm. "She said I smell like an old man." The man's face wrenched into a sob. "Ah, Marie. I'm getting old but I swear I would have loved you as hard as you need to be loved."

Though Ferdy tried hard to listen carefully to Yves as he always did, his attention wandered to a time when Yves would be dead and he would lose the only connection with a sentient being he'd had in nearly seven hundred years. He felt a little heaviness about his insides, apart from the stoniness of the gargoyle, a feeling that might have been sadness, if a devil could feel. He wondered if this was how the tour guide felt.

When Ferdy brought his attention back to Yves he saw with some amazement and a little concern that the man had somehow maneuvered his way around the protective wire mesh arched over the parapet and climbed onto the ledge. Ferdy wouldn't have guessed he was that depressed—or that limber. He watched as Yves held his arms out for balance and stepped one foot in front of the other like a tightrope walker, slowly moving away from Ferdy across the narrow stone surface. Ferdy wanted to call out to the man to be careful, but even if he had been capable of sound he was stunned into speechlessness. Yves hadn't gone very far before he grabbed a vertical pipe from the metal scaffolding close to the wall and swung nimbly onto the frame like a child in a jungle gym. He stepped from pipe to pipe until he was back in front of the Spitting Gargoyle where he held onto the scaffolding with one hand and leaned down so that his face was inches away from the statue's. Ferdy stared hard into the mortal's face and saw what he had begun to suspect. This was no longer Yves. The cackling laugh he heard next confirmed who it was.

"Hey, Ferdo, you're one ugly ass son of a bitch! How you been, buddy?" said the creature.

"Gregory! What in hell's name are you doing here?"

"What, I can't even visit my best bud without a reason?"

Ferdy felt his emotions tossing like a salad. He nearly cried with the pleasure of talking to another being. At the same time he was a little worried about Yves's body hanging thirty meters above the plaza pavement. He recalled that Gregory always seemed to have this conflicting effect on him.

"Yoo-hoo! Come back, Ferdy! Come back!" Gregory jumped up and down on the stiff frame and shouted as if from a distance. "Focus on me, boy. Answer my question."

"What question is that, Gregory?"
"Can't I visit my best bud without a reason?"
"This is the first time you've been here, Greg."
"Been busy. There's a lot going on the Middle East."
"The Crusades, you mean?"
"Ah, no. Looks like you've been a little out of touch. No problem, I'll fill you in." The body of Yves leaned over a pipe and gazed at the ground far below while Gregory's voice spoke. "Hey, great view from up here. Those people look like cockroaches—but then I always think they look like cockroaches."

Yves/Gregory held onto the scaffolding with only one hand and swayed as gently as a contemplative chimpanzee. Ferdy felt his heart give a little fillip and hoped the rain had dried off the pipes.

"Say, Greg, why don't you get out of that guy and come sit on the wall. You're making me dizzy. You're also attracting attention."

Gregory looked down at a half a dozen early evening passersby who stared back and pointed at him. "You think this is scary? Look at me, I'm Quasimodo!" He grabbed the rounded pipe with both hands and flipped over it, looping repeatedly through the bars. The passersby applauded as if they assumed they were watching a better than average street performer. Gregory stopped to throw kisses with one hand. "*Merci, mes amis!*" he shouted, then more softly, "Whoops," as he lost his footing. Ferdy saw the fingers that had been Yves's frantically clutch at the nearest beam and miss.

The scaffolding made the thirty meter fall last a long time. In the first few seconds Yves reached frantically for bars to stop his plunge but slipped past them without gaining a grip. When his head hit a bar for the second time he stopped fighting for a hold. After that Yves's body thumped from beam to beam in a lazy descent. As jerky as an epileptic puppet, his body jarred each time it contacted with another cross bar, and his head wrenched from side to side, his arms flailing purposelessly in a mockery of trying to stop the fall. He came to a stop six feet from the pavement, like a toy with old stuffing bent in half backwards over a beam. Yves may have slipped as a devil, but he died as a man. Ferdy watched two people run off while the rest of the group converged around the body.

"Oh, Yves, I'm so sorry," he whispered in a sigh drifting out from his stone.

"You're sorry?" the voice said next to him. "You guys *friends* or something?"

A warning prickle went up Ferdy's neck and he used some sense. *For once,* he thought. "No, Greg. I hardly knew him."

"Looks like I broke him," said Gregory, glancing down at the still form below. "Mortal bodies feel so good, all those senses happening at once," he purred with a frisson of delight. "Not real durable, though. Oh well, he only had, what, twenty years left and he was pretty depressed. Probably would have ended it himself sooner what with all that talk about wringing his neck. You know how the French are about love. Now get out of that stupid gargoyle and come sit."

"It's not break time."

"Live on the edge."

Ferdy tore his gaze away from the scene below. He extracted himself from the stone, sat on the wall next to Gregory, and took a good look at a fellow devil for the first time in seven centuries. There were lots of similarities between them. Frog-belly white skin, pale gray wings, bony arms and legs ending in outsized claws. Gregory at six feet, though, was about twice as tall as Ferdy. And while Ferdy sported something like a beak, Gregory's nose was pushed so flat against his face that the nostrils formed perfectly round holes you could look into, like twin entrances to a cave. Stalactite fangs snaggled below his nose. But for Ferdy the really disconcerting thing about Gregory was his eyes. Or lack of them. They were milky white and that made it hard for Ferdy's own blackberry beads to ever see what was going on behind them.

"OK, I'll stop fooling around," said Gregory. "I did come here for a reason."

"Get to the point, Greg."

"Oooh, we're sounding a little testy. Did nasty ol' Gregums break Ferdo's playmate?"

Ferdy carefully covered his sadness—it was sadness, he was sure of it now—with a harsh veneer. Although Gregory had influenced the decision that got him this job instead of a stiffer punishment, he was never quite sure about the other devil's motivation. Gregory didn't seem like the kind of guy who'd do you a favor.

"I don't give a shit about the old guy. I just have low frustration tolerance. So get on with it before I lose patience and get back to my post." He stared hard into the white eyes hoping to detect a dash of respect there. Nothing.

"The point is...I got a new job for you. High five, boy!" Gregory held up a claw but Ferdy's tiny eyes only got smaller.

"Tell me about the job, Greg."

"Cream puff of a job. You'll be stationed in—yes, ladies and gentlemen—bee-yoo-teeful Miami Beach!"

"Where's Miami Beach?"

"Florida." He pre-empted Ferdy's next question with, "Never mind that, we'll go over the location later. Here's the good part. All you gotta do is guard an SIP."

"NO!" Ferdy yelled, tumbled backward off the wall and started to crawl back into his gargoyle.

Gregory grabbed Ferdy's leg as he scrambled away and wrestled him to his back on the stone floor of the walkway. He straddled him easily, pinning the smaller devil's claws with his own to keep him still. His fangs glistened over Ferdy's beak, making Ferdy hope he wouldn't get excited. Gregory always drooled when he got excited. Ferdy played dead, trying not to think about one of his wings bent uncomfortably under him.

Gregory raked one claw across his face to get his attention. "Listen, buddy, you can do this job. This babe is a long shot for sainthood."

"Then why guard her?" Ferdy whined.

"Because somebody back at headquarters heard that the Enemy had her on track. Just a rumor, but we have to follow up. I promise you, a few weeks of work to derail her and you're on to your next assignment. It's your time, boy. You don't want to stay here forever, do you? Till the spitter here crumbles like the last gargoyle did?"

"What about B-Becket, Gregory?" Ferdy voice went whispery on the saint's name as if he were afraid someone else would hear.

"Becket! You say his name the way mortals say herpes. Becket was just bad luck."

"I should have been at the cathedral that morning, but I wasn't. I wasn't even in Canterbury," Ferdy heard the whine in his voice but couldn't disguise it. He was almost glad Gregory had his arms pinned down so he couldn't punch himself in the forehead like he usually did when he thought about that time. "I was supposed to guard–"

"Stop obsessing. You were out of your league. You were up against Henry the Second for pete's sake. Okay, so you let him get martyred. So now he's one of the most revered saints in the Catholic church. So they made a movie about him..."

"Movie?"

Gregory paused and stared open mouthed at Ferdy for a moment. "You been out of the loop too long, buddy. I gotta get you some serious briefing."

"What if I fail again?" Ferdy motioned at the Spitting Gargoyle behind him with his eyebrows since they were attached to the only muscle Gregory didn't have pinned down. "This was only a reprimand. What will happen if I lose her? Layoff? Huh? You want to get me laid off?" He felt a whimper in his throat and loathed himself even more. Apparently for a devil there were no bottom limits to self-loathing.

"You *won't* lose her. I swear. Do you think I would steer you wrong?"

"Why are you doing this, Gregory? Why should I do this?"

"Because I told headquarters you would do it. Because I'll look like a fool if I go back and tell them you refused. Because you're so annoying I'm the only friend you've got and you owe it to me."

"Aw, man...."

"Jeesh, you whine even more than I remember." Gregory got up from Ferdy's body and dusted off his claws as if he wanted no particle of contact with the other devil to remain on him. "Okay, so I go back and tell them Ferdy the Wuss doesn't want the job. You want I should go back and tell them Ferdy *rejected* headquarter's assignment? That's what I'll do, kid, and if they ask why I'll just tell them to see you. I tried."

Now that he was free, Ferdy drew one of his feet close to his mouth so he could lick between his toes. Gregory wacked him again.

"Stop that. It's gross even for us."

Ferdy gave one last swab with his tongue and drew his foot away, rolling the jam into a ball between his teeth while trying to think.

"I don't want you to do that," he said, finally. "I don't want you to tell headquarters I rejected the assignment."

"Well, that puts us in a fine muddle, doesn't it? What *do* you want me to do?" Gregory drew back his left hand as if to toss over the wall the folder that had suddenly appeared in his hand.

"What's that?" said Ferdy, still stalling.

"This is Bishop Monica Laparro's dossier. Not that you'll be interested in it."

"She's a bishop? A woman bishop?"

"She's not Catholic, she's Episcopalian. Times have changed."

"A bishop. She's a bishop—aw, Greg, it's Becket all over again."

"He was an archbishop. Trust me, buddy, this broad is not Becket. Nothing like Becket."

# Chapter Two
## In Which the First Miracle Goes Unnoticed

As Yves would have said, the more things change the more they stay the same. Ferdy perched on an exposed rafter high up over the crowd which had come to see Monica Laparro be ordained a bishop at St. Stephen's Episcopal Cathedral. He was thinking this wasn't much of a change from the gargoyle post at Notre Dame. You find your rafter, you watch the mortals below. He told himself the tops of people's heads didn't look any different over the centuries, or from one continent to another.

On the other hand, maybe he was just trying to talk himself out of the jitters. He shifted his leathery buttocks from side to side, unsticking them from the varnished beam made tacky by tropical humidity. There actually were lots of differences here. For one, this narrow rafter was less comfortable than his stone parapet. And this tiny building that passed for a church was hardly what you would call gothic. Sure, the traditional stained glass windows took a shot at solemnity. But the hearty southern sunlight coming through them made even the depiction of St. Stephen's death by stoning look, well, kind of cheerful.

Ferdy contemplated the window showing a grim figure of St. Paul holding the cloaks of Stephen's murderers. *At least I wasn't the devil responsible for losing Paul to the other side.* He felt a chill up his spine remembering the screams of that fellow as he was laid off by The Boss. But that wasn't going to happen to him. No. Gregory had promised. Ferdy grabbed one of his feet and licked between his toes until he felt calm enough to go back to work.

The ordination hoo-ha was in progress in the sanctuary. Bored by that, he scanned the crowd for the other principals in Laparro's dossier. His roving eyes jerked to a standstill at the sight of one woman in a pew towards the front of the church. A real looker. No, that word didn't do her justice. To get a better look Ferdy swung down to hold on with one claw while the other absent-mindedly rubbed the vestigial appendage that mortals used to procreate. This woman was absolutely perfect. Short black hair, sculpted around her face like fingers cupping a chalice. Exquisite bone structure reminiscent of a goddess in carved high relief. A body with just the right amount of hills and hollows. She was draped in a black dress that didn't mean to be provocative but couldn't help itself.

Ferdy gave his wings an extra hard pump and pulled himself back up to the top of the rafter to check his guess in the dossier. He was right; this was Palma Blanco, one of Monica's oldest friends. First generation American, independently wealthy, currently unmarried.

He wanted her. He would have wanted her even if he'd had sex within the last six hundred years. Maybe this assignment wasn't going to be so bad after all if he could work in a little incubus action at the same time—or at least find someone to possess who could get into her—which was kind of like wearing a full body rubber but when you were a devil and horny you took what you could get.

A voice from the sanctuary broke his daydream and his hard-on. Ferdy looked at the tall, gaunt man dressed in bishop's robes who addressed the congregation from the sanctuary just behind the altar rail.

"—to serve in the Diocese of Southeast Florida. You have been assured of *her* (Ferdy noticed he said the word deliberately as if he had been practicing) suitability and that the Church has approved her for this sacred responsibility. Nevertheless, if any of you know any reason why we should not proceed, let it now be made known."

In the pause that followed, Ferdy felt vibrations of discord, like the shudder and groan of backed up water pipes, from the back of the church. He found their source in a nondescript woman of middle-age. Everything about her looked worn and faded, from her denim jumper to the careless pony tail pulled back from her face where the skin slackened into just a hint of jowl. She looked weary, too, except for her eyes. That was where all her energy seemed as concentrated as laser light. As if she had worn out her exterior long before her energy was spent.

Though she sat very still in the back pew, or rather on the back of the pew with her scuffed boots resting on the seat and her hands keeping balance on her own narrow perch, the negative vibrations were coming stronger. Ferdy was intrigued. He cocked his head and let his eyelids droop lazily, concentrating on her mind. Except for dabbling in Yves's thoughts from time to time he hadn't observed anyone's imaginings in six hundred years but found it easy. He joined her thoughts just as—

*She vaults over two pews in front of her and runs down the center aisle toward the altar shouting , "No, wait! Stop!" The faces in the congregation turn toward her as one. The Presiding Bishop's hand shoots up in an involuntary gesture of horror.*

*"What has she done that you should halt these proceedings?" he demands.*

*The woman marches rhythmically in front of the altar rail in a conga step, her denim dress twitching as she pops her hips, matching her words to the beats and kicking to the side with each grunt, "She isn't really good, uh. She isn't really good, uh."*

*First stunned, then mesmerized by the chant and the rhythm, the congregation sways hypnotically in place. When the chanting woman beckons, they slowly file out of the pews to fall in behind her until everyone has joined the conga line snaking its way around the cathedral aisles. As the end passes in front of the sanctuary the Presiding Bishop shrugs and joins in, chanting and kicking with the rest of them.*

*Monica Laparro, who has been watching in immobilized disbelief, falls to her knees sobbing, "Oh, God, oh my God, don't let it be true!"*

Ferdy pulled back into his own mind as the imaginings fragmented away into random thoughts. Who the hell was this? He flipped through the dossier and stopped at her picture. Ah, Adelaide Siren, another one of Laparro's long-time friends. Friend? He wondered, not for the first time, what The Enemy liked about mortals.

In the meantime the Presiding Bishop had continued reading from a red prayer book. "Let the whole world see and know that things which were cast down are being raised up, and things—"

"Yacka, yacka, yacka," thought Ferdy with a yawn but unstuck his buttocks once more to swivel around to the sanctuary which was as crowded with clergy as the church was with laity. Priests and deacons, their vestments showing varying degrees of splendor, hovered about the even more splendidly adorned Presiding Bishop and two other bishops who hovered about Monica, who was not splendid at all. She was dressed in a plain white alb and stood with her back to the congregation, facing the altar like a virgin eagerly awaiting her own sacrifice. Ferdy watched the priests solemnly cover her with gold embroidered stole and chasuble, lower the mitre onto her head and hand her the staff. Ferdy found some comfort in the familiarity of the age-old vestments, something that connected him to this strange time and place. Then he thought of the bloody chasuble covering Becket's body on the floor of the transept of Canterbury Cathedral and drove his tongue into the comfort of his toes once more. Two bishops from other Florida diocese placed their hands on the Monica's back while the Presiding Bishop spoke the words of consecration. The ordination was complete.

"Brothers and sisters, I introduce to you Monica Laparro, the Bishop of the Diocese of Southeast Florida."

The congregation erupted in applause while the pipe organ farted a triumphant blast. The new bishop finally turned to face the congregation and Ferdy leaned forward intently to get a good look at his Saint In Progress.

What a woofer.

She was short, but made up for it in expanse. Her face, and everything on it, was big, too. Ferdy was most fascinated by her eyebrows. Black and bushy, like acrobatic caterpillars they jiggled and bounced with a private enthusiasm. Pressing a ridge into her forehead the edge of the mitre squeezed out a bead of sweat that ran unnoticed into one of the eyebrows. Large silver earrings in the shape of dream catchers with purple feathers bounced while she swayed her head to the organ introduction to "The Church's One Foundation."

Ferdy leaned a little closer to look at her salt and pepper hair that grew down in front of her ears, enough for sideburns but short of a beard. This was a bishop? Let alone a potential saint? He re-checked the dossier to make sure he'd come to the right ordination.

The choir let fly with song, the bishops and priests in attendance processed down the nave followed by Monica, swaying in time with the music while her hand made imprecise signs of blessing over the singing congregation.

Nothing extraordinary here, Ferdy concluded. Maybe Gregory was right. Maybe this was a cushy assignment, a few months in a sunny climate, maybe even a chance to get laid. Laid. Reminded of Palma Blanco he focused again on the departing congregation, didn't spot her, and sailed down from his rafter through the open red doors to hunt her down.

☿ ☿ ☿

When she got to the green room behind the sanctuary, Adelaide found Monica already stripped down to a black skirt and episcopal purple blouse. Monica grinned at the sight of her.

"Hey, Del! No, don't hug, I'm sopping. Holy Mary, what a time for a hot flash. Did you like the ceremony?"

Adelaide hugged her despite her protest. "I laughed, I cried. It was better than Cats. Especially the conga line."

The blank look in Monica's eye only lasted a second. "Aw, you're just jealous–"

"The word is envy."

"Whatever— because I got applause."

Standing close by, the Presiding Bishop looked away as Monica took half a box of tissues from a nearby table and jammed them inside her blouse to mop between her breasts and under her armpits. She performed introductions with her arms held out like an anhinga drying its wings.

"How often do I get to introduce two such important people to each other?" she said. "Presiding Bishop Clarenton Roxbury, I'd like you to meet Adelaide Siren."

"Ah," he responded vaguely, and leaned forward to shake hands.

"I write plays," Adelaide offered.

"Yes, and Mother Teresa ran a dear little soup kitchen," Monica retorted, picking the wetter bits of tissue from inside her blouse. "Bishop Roxbury, Adelaide has won four Tony Awards for her plays. Last year she won for 'Human Resources.'"

Adelaide noted a lambent spark in his eyes, like a lighter low on fluid.

"Yes, yes, I remember it," he said, and stopped.

"It was best comedy," said Adelaide.

He disguised his struggle for words in a cough, then admitted, "I didn't see it, of course. I do live in the City, but I'm afraid I don't get out as much as I'd like to." He chuckled as if there were a joke in his remark. "Are you working on a new play now?"

"Why, yes," Adelaide replied. "I'm developing a show called 'How to Profit from Your Manic Depression.'"

While Monica laughed, Adelaide stared at Roxbury with a face as straight as his before the Presiding Bishop changed the subject. "So, Ms. Siren, what do you think of our new bishop? Only the second woman in the United States to be made a bishop. You must be very proud of your friend."

Adelaide turned to Monica with exaggerated disgust. "What? I came all this way for Second? You told me you were the first."

Monica laughed again while Roxbury's eyes shot open with an energy he had not yet displayed.

"Ignore her," Monica said. "It's just this thing we do. Can you stay a little, Del? Please let me see you over in the parish hall." She grabbed Del's wrist. "No, don't look at your watch."

Adelaide grimaced with the effort of ignoring time and nodded. She left the air conditioning of the church and picked her way through a steamy mass of pale green berries smashed on the uneven patio leading to the hall. The Cuban fig tree dropping the berries only succeeded in cutting the light, not the heat, on this mid-summer day. Though she was shy of crowds she was relieved to push through the red double doors into the promise of coolness. She remembered one of her character's lines; nature was something you had to go through to get to another building.

The crowd was as boisterous in the parish hall as they had been restrained in the church. Adelaide stood against the wall just inside the door to look around, taking in the scene as critically as if it were a stage set. Lavender crepe paper already wilting over fluorescent lights. Clusters of people holding plastic champagne glasses tilted at various angles depending on the intensity of their conversation. Tiny elderly women in bright dresses darting among the clusters like angel fish among coral heads. Near the kitchen a narrow table sagging under a silver coffee service, and a giant crystal punch bowl filled, presumably, with one of those creamy fruity fizzy compositions known only by church ladies.

A waspy group, Adelaide noted. There had been some street people clustered together at the back of the church who did not attend the reception. She wondered where the homeless got such an uncanny sense of protocol. *A great set*, she thought. *Now all we need is a problem. What kind of a problem in paradise...?*

"Stop writing, Adelaide."

The voice came from beside her. She slowly turned her head and focused on Palma. "Have you been standing there long?"

"Yes, and I got impatient waiting for you to come back. That denim smock is very youthful. It can't be easy for a middle-aged woman to look pregnant."

"Bitch. Episcopalians sure know how to party."

"I think they call it fellow shipping these days, but, darling, I missed sitting next to you during the service. Heaven knows we don't get to do this sort of thing often."

"Joe had to walk a dog. Did he come in here?"

"Yes, he's over there talking to some old dear about harnesses versus collars."

Adelaide followed Palma's discrete gesture to where Joe stood by a small woman with latte-colored hair who appeared to be conversing with his stomach. The best thing about having a six-foot-four husband was that you could always find him in a crowd. She met his eyes and wondered how long he had been staring at her. He seemed to take her glance as a summons and ambled towards her. Adelaide watched him move with the urgency of a manatee. He had added considerable bulk to his large frame over the years. Added to the weight, the silvery tufts of hair clinging to his nearly bald head gave him an overall grayish appearance that made him even look a little like a manatee. Adelaide smiled, knowing that at his leisurely pace it would be several minutes before he reached her side. So she focused again on Palma who was still speaking.

"...And don't forget you're coming over tonight to have the French Hen celebration."

"Palma, I really should go to rehearsal tonight. They're probably rewriting my play as we speak. I've got to stop them."

"Unacceptable, darling. Besides, I want you to meet Robert."

"Robert? What about Pablo?"

"That was Paolo."

"Jeez, Palma, you reject men faster than Martha Stewart goes through dinner candles."

Palma laughed good-naturedly. "Great line. You should use it sometime."

"I already did in *Eclair de Lune*. What happened to Paolo?"

"You're not keeping up. He flunked restaurant."

"What did he do, order a shiraz with the seared tuna?"

Palma gave an elegant shrug. "Much worse." Adelaide could smell her Joy perfume as she leaned forward to whisper the rest. "When it came time for the tip he pulled out one of those little plastic cards that figures it out for you."

Adelaide kept a straight face. "All I can say is Robert had better be the man because I've run out of space in my address book trying to keep up with the names of your boyfriends and I refuse to buy a new one. What's that?"

Palma took the copy of the Herald from under her arm and spread it open to show Monica's picture on the front page. "I brought this along to give to Monica. I thought she'd like to have an extra copy."

Adelaide frowned at the full color photo of Monica in her bishop's vestments. "She looks like she just swallowed a balloon. Look at her eyes."

"Her eyes are a little bulgier than usual in this one. Still, it's a big event, isn't it, first female bishop."

"Second."

"All right, second, but who would have thought—our Monica."

"And this is just the Episcopal church. Nothing new about female clergy. Now if she were a bishop in the Catholic church, that would be a really big deal. That would warrant front page."

"Del, don't be jealous."

"The word is envious, and I'm not. I couldn't be happier for Monica."

"You've been on the front page."

"Of the Arts and Leisure section."

"And the magazine insert. Remember that feature story they

did when you won your last thingy? Hello, darling!" Joe had finally reached Adelaide's side and Palma lifted a well-defined cheekbone for his kiss. "What a sweetheart," she added, pointing to a yorkshire terrier nearly hidden under Joe's forearm.

Joe stroked the shivering animal with a beefy hand. It's eyes bugged out with each pass of the hand over it's head, but it didn't seem to mind. "This is Gorgeous Alexander. A real flirt. I'm babysitting him while his owner's on a weekend cruise."

"May I?" Palma reached out and carefully plucked the dog from Joe's arm. Cradled in her own arms Alexander looked twice as big as he licked her well-manicured thumb.

Adelaide watched the dog succumbing to Palma's chemistry but any quip about another conquest was cut short by the entrance of Monica with the Presiding Bishop. Applause erupted once again and Monica's eyebrows leaped in appreciative response as two angel fish darted forward with champagne.

On the shoulder of the Presiding Bishop, Ferdy rode unseen into the reception. He clung there for awhile, giving his wings a flap for balance every time Roxbury leaned forward to shake another hand, and observed Monica work the room. She was a pro at this. Since the different parts of her worked independently contact with an entire crowd took twenty minutes. Pumping the hand of one person, she flashed her smile at another, bulged her eyes at a third, and jiggled her eyebrows in approval at some remark by a fourth, and all this while receiving a second glass of champagne from a fifth. Overall she lacked that standoffish quality that mortals called holy. Ferdy felt more and more at ease about his mission.

After watching Monica greet everyone, he wandered with her to the small group standing just inside the entrance to the hall. There was that playwright again, standing on the balls of her feet like she was preparing to bolt out the door. The man staring at her like an adoring spaniel was even bigger than Gregory, broad but rounded shoulders supporting red suspenders strained over an abdomen that got your attention. But harmless looking, even a little simple, maybe.

And there was Palma.

Ferdy felt himself becoming aroused again as he and Monica

approached the trio. Palma hugged her and said, "I can't believe the Presiding Bishop actually came to the ceremony. And stayed for the reception, no less! You really are an important girl, aren't you?"

Monica interrupted before Adelaide could get in a jibe. "Girl is the operative word, I think. He's making a statement to the Roman Catholics," Monica replied modestly. "So, Del. Do I win?"

"Bet you can't make Pope."

"Bet you can't win the Nobel," Monica said.

There was a silence while everyone smiled. Ferdy's attention was diverted from the silence by the sight of Palma gently stroking the terrier from the tip of its nose to the base of its tail while the dog nestled against her bosom. The front of her black dress flowed into a gentle drape half covering its silky back. In a blissful trance, the dog licked the inside of her wrist as she twisted its tail around her tapered fingers.

The sight made Ferdy's own tongue itch until he couldn't stand it anymore. *Sometimes you just have to work with what you have*, he thought. He had never possessed a dog before, but figured it couldn't be much more difficult than a gargoyle.

"Hello, Alexander," he said, focusing on the dog's eyes, drawing himself into them. Alexander was a young dog who had never seen a devil before, though he was familiar with a few angels. He sniffed curiously at the creature, drawn irresistibly to a stink that was part wet dog, part rotted sushi, with a dash of septic tank.

"Hello," replied Alexander. "You're very interesting. Are you dead?"

"Never mind that. I'm going to borrow you," said Ferdy. Before the dog could ask what that meant, Ferdy gathered up his spirit and poured himself into the dog's body. Alexander cocked his head and only had time for a tiny growl to form deep inside his gut before Ferdy was within him. The Yorkie showed no sign of devil possession beyond a slight jerk. Ferdy felt the beat of the dog's heart, twice as fast as his own, and his breath panting through his open mouth. He started panting faster with his awareness that Palma's left hand was supporting his tiny belly, the tips of her fingers close to his demonhood. That did it. He had to see what was behind the drape of her gown.

"I think Alexander has to go outside," Palma said, as the dog started to squirm. Ferdy leaped up, his back legs supported by her arms, and scrabbled with his front paws through the folds of her dress as though digging for a bone. The drape parted on one side to reveal a tan mound barely kept in check by a black lace bra. *Paydirt!* he yelped and jumped inside her dress, his hind legs flying over his head as he plunged. All this happened in a moment's time while the others stood immobilized, staring. Ferdy had just enough time to feel his cold wet nose slide against Palma's breast before Joe's hands seized him.

"Let me go, you son of a bitch!" yapped Ferdy in a high pitched bark.

"I guess we'll go get some punch," said Joe, restraining the thrashing dog whose legs were rotating like the paddles of a table fan. Palma rearranged the front of her dress, while Monica tried to act like a bishop and prevent Adelaide from pointing out the three inches of bright red erection that the terrier was now sporting.

By the time Joe reached the reception table he had Ferdy so firmly pinned under his arm that the devil could do no more than shiver in protest and stare fixedly at the table. An elderly lady sagged wearily by the silver coffee service, apparently holding her post though no one seemed interested in coffee anymore. She looked up at Joe expectantly and wilted again as he passed by. Only the punch bowl was still doing a thriving business. Joe and Ferdy had to wait while a grim-faced woman wearing a name tag that said "Melba" served several other patrons. With the precision of a military strategist directing munitions deployment, she snapped an order that styrofoam cups be brought from the kitchen after the crystal cups had run out.

A stack of cups arrived and the punch flew once more. When Joe finally got his turn and leaned over the punch bowl to take his cup from Melba, Ferdy looked at the small crowd slurping the punch and sniffed curiously at the bowl filled to the brim. Something was odd here. He strained toward the bowl while Joe concentrated on getting the tiny cup into his beefy paw. Ladle after ladle Melba slung the punch but...as Joe began to move away Ferdy gave one more wrenching squirm.

His squirm proved more effective than he expected. He found

himself airborne for a split second, then plunged through the icy ring floating in the center of the punch bowl. Surfacing with a curse at his clumsiness he tried to dog paddle out of the bowl but the slick sides prevented him from grabbing a paw hold. Punch flew in waves over the table.

Even in the midst of his quandary Ferdy was aware, as in slow motion, of the effect of his dive. The astounded Melba held a cup and the ladle in mid-serve, her lips quivering. The coffee urn lady was the first to respond, laughing raucously and nearly upsetting the cream pitcher over the tablecloth already saturated with punch. Her laughter sent out ripples of awareness through the crowd. Melba turned on her with the ladle raised but Joe reacted more practically, reaching into the bowl and swiping Ferdy out like a bear catching a salmon. Palma appeared with a dish towel to straight-jacket him. Bearing the dog at arm's length before her, Palma marched into the kitchen. Joe followed quickly with the punch bowl so no one would notice that a small Yorkie torpedo, probably launched in panic, was now floating inside the ice ring. He set the bowl down next to the sink while Palma gave the dog a quick rinse.

In all the commotion only Ferdy noticed that the suspicion that made him go into the bowl in the first place was correct. Despite all the serving, and his own belly slamming dive, the punch bowl remained completely full. It should have been nearly empty, but it was still full, as if it had kept filling itself. *Gratuitous miracles?* he thought with a trace of apprehension. *Not a good sign.*

# Chapter Three
## Joe

Joe felt his usual pang of joy as he opened the door of The Dog's Day Salon. Next to Del he liked being around animals best. They shared his sense of contentment. With this shop, and his old movie collection, and his wife, he had everything he ever wanted.

From their holding cages the other patrons set up a syncopated chorus of high yelps and low woofs. Mitzi, the taffy cocker spaniel, had her usually waggy lips pursed in the size of a cheerio through which she howled. Joe poked a finger into the cage and jiggled her chops.

"Doo yoo want yur baffy now? Huh? Doo yoo?"

He could sense the animals chuckling. Even the arrogant Saluki who occupied the cage next to Mitzi's, and who usually raised a disdainful white eyebrow at any undignified behavior, licked his lips appreciatively and shifted on his haunches. Joe went to the back of the shop and turned on the tape of Baroque harpsichord music that always calmed his customers, and focused his attention back on Alexander.

"Yoo were a vewy bad boy, Alexander," Joe mockingly reprimanded. "I've never seen you so bad."

Ferdy struggled to piece together the events that had landed him with an animal groomer. He had been busy pondering the miracle of the non-emptying punch bowl and found himself whisked out of the reception hall before he could collect his wits. Now he bared his teeth and growled at Joe, who looked questioningly back. "Never seen you so cranky...ah, I'll bet I know what's wrong." Joe hooked a small chain to the dog's collar while Ferdy tried vainly to nip at him.

"Naughty puppy-wuppy," sang Joe.

*Asshole-wasshole,* thought Ferdy, figuring the smartest thing to do was ditch the dog and go trail Monica.

Joe chose a metal comb from a rack on the wall and gave it a test run through the long fur on the dog's head and down its back.

Traces of punch still matted the fine fur, but the knots miraculously disappeared under Joe's gentle urging. Over and over the teeth of the comb ran over the dog's tiny ribs with just the right pressure, stimulating the tender skin while disentangling the feathering that grew from its chest. Ferdy gave an involuntary shiver of pleasure. He considered that he hadn't been touched this way in a long...well, ever. Feelings towards Joe mellowing despite himself, he decided to stick around just a little. It was unlikely that Monica would achieve sainthood within the next few minutes.

"Are yoo chilly, sugar babe?" Joe reached up to a rubber squeaky toy in the shape of a duck attached to the ceiling fan cord. It squeaked twice as he pulled it and the fan slowed down. The other animals rustled anew, sharing the office in-joke.

While the Yorkie waited contendedly on the bench, Joe turned on the water to fill the smaller of two aluminum tubs nearby. He rolled up his sleeve and tested the temperature of the water with his elbow before tossing in a capful of flea dip and a personal concoction of deodorizer and lanolin with the aplomb of an expert chef who scoffs at measuring.

The next moment Ferdy felt his body immersed in the perfectly warm water which stopped just below his chin. He heard the squirt of shampoo which rested coldly on the back of his neck until Joe's fingers gently spread it over his body. It felt like a massage by a giant who could touch every spot on his body at once. Fingers roamed around his ears and under his chin, down his belly and back and between the pads of his paws. The muck of eons of amorality slipped from him. In the bliss of the bath he forgot everything, Monica, Gregory, Palma, and the fact that he wasn't really a Yorkshire Terrier. He didn't even notice Joe's fingers mildly poking around his backside until a firm pressure and sharp release jolted him back into place and he whipped his head around to glare at Joe.

"Dere, dose nasty anal glands were annoying, weren't dey? That's why yoo tried to bite Uncle Joe." Joe pulled the stopper from the tub and rinsed the shampoo from Ferdy with a fine spray hose while the suds gurgled away. With his hands he squeegied the excess water out of Ferdy's fur and lifted him out of the tub.

"You look like something I pulled out of the drain last week,"

Joe chuckled as he toweled Ferdy vigorously. A warm blow-dry put him back into a contemplative state and he stayed there, wrapped in a pastel plaid baby blanket in one of the cages. Half dozing, he watched as Joe finished the business of the day and released the other animals one by one to their owners.

Ferdy woke up on the front seat of Joe's Mazda 323 on his way to where he didn't know. With as big a yawn as his little mouth could muster, Ferdy tucked his chin back between his paws, temporarily not much caring. He hadn't expected the fringe benefits of this assignment.

# Chapter Four
## Adelaide

Wondering how to kill the hour and a half remaining before she was expected at Palma's house, Adelaide pulled out of St. Stephen's parking lot. An hour and half didn't give her enough time to either stop in at the rehearsal or go home and write. She leaned over to open the glove compartment for something she could work on in a coffee house, found a pen but no pad, damned her lack of foresight.

There was only one thing she could think of to do although she tried to push it out of her mind. It kept coming back tied up with a ribbon of guilt. She sighed and turned off the exit ramp after crossing the Arthur Godfrey Causeway over the bay, heading south and then west from downtown Miami.

The part of Coral Gables where she had grown up was a middle class neighborhood with trees so huge it couldn't hide its age. Adelaide pulled her gray Volvo into a circular driveway shadowed by one of the larger banyan trees, stopped the engine and stared at the trunks of the tree twisting together and plunging root after root into the soil it held so fiercely. As she always did whenever she noticed the tree, she pictured herself as a child again, spreading a blanket over the bare ground where the tree allowed no grass to grow, and playing her games of "Let's Pretend" there even though the spanish moss overhead had a scary look to it. It reminded her of snakes and gnomes' beards. She watched the child in her mind for a moment, allowed herself one more sigh, and walked to the front door.

The curtains were drawn in the front bay window but the sound of a game show on television came through the door. That didn't necessarily mean that someone was home. When he was gone he always left the television on loudly enough to trick burglars. Adelaide opened the door with her key and stepped into the shrouded living room whose indications of life consisted of the vague smells of sweet medication, trapped flatus, and the breathings of an old man.

From where the man sat in his recliner he looked up at the unfamiliar crash of sunlight Adelaide let in when she opened the door. He moved a hand through a full head of white hair and shaded his eyes, one of which gleamed a creamy blue in the light, reminding her she needed to get him scheduled for his cataract surgery.

"Rose? Is that you?" he shouted over the television.

"No, Dad, it's Del," she shouted back.

"What are you doing here? Is it Monday already?"

"It's Saturday. I just came from Monica's ordination. Would you mind if I turned this down?" She moved to the television and turned off the sound without waiting for a response, but continued to speak loudly because he was growing deaf too. "I thought I'd come over today instead and leave the check for Rose. Is she doing okay? Seems like she could air the place out."

"She does. Not bad for a colored woman. At least she doesn't smell."

"Look who's talking," Adelaide said in a regular voice, wrinkling her nose.

"Eh?"

"Nothing. I'll write the check," she said, raising her voice to a near shout once more. Adelaide opened the top drawer of an old buffet and pulled out a check book with checks containing hers and her father's names. She sat down on the couch that ground into the rug precisely in the same spot it had thirty-three years before when she moved out. She looked across the room at the gristly man in his white undershirt and big old shorts, while she felt her years slip uncomfortably away. Struggling to keep from turning into a little girl, hoping to escape this time before she went too far back, she wondered how he could still emit that patriarchal power with all his senses failing. Maybe after all it wasn't he who caused it. Maybe she did it to herself, still hoping to give Dad what he wanted.

She focused on grown-up things. "A hundred dollars still good? Does Rose get you everything you need?"

"Yeah, fine. And what she don't get I get from the VFW."

"Jerry's still picking you up on Wednesdays."

"Nah, the bum wanted to switch to Tuesdays, something about

his wife and her mother, but I told him I was sticking to Wednesdays and he could kiss my ass. Told him it was my way or the highway." He laughed at the expression as if it were new, as if he didn't use it all the time.

"So did you find a ride for Wednesdays?"

"Damn straight. I'm a popular guy down there. Not like Jerry. You should hear what we say about him."

"You mean Jerry who picked you up religiously every fucking Wednesday afternoon for three years?" Although she kept her voice cool she cursed herself for responding at all.

"Hey, watch your language. Where did you learn to talk that way?"

"It's an acceptable word these days, Dad. Like "suck" used to be indecent but now it's not, as in 'the advertising for your play sucks and won't draw an audience.'" She emphasized each 'suck' like she was biting it out of her mouth, hearing herself speak like a rebellious teenager.

"So how is your play? Is it drawing a big audience?"

"Yeah, Dad, big audiences. I'm a real success."

"That's good. You know that I never graduated high school, that I wanted you and your sister to be more successful, even if you weren't sons. You know that your mother and I scraped together everything we could to give you a good Catholic schooling, though Margie's left the church, you still go to church, right?"

"Sure," she noted her lies came as regularly now as his family chronicles did.

"And what about that dog groomer? You still married to him?"

Adelaide only felt her jaw tighten and held her fire, back in control. She was prepared for this part. He had been asking that regularly for decades, never having become reconciled to his daughter marrying an Italian. Dad took a universalist stance when it came to bigotry.

"So you keep writing your plays, you keep being a success. Nothing succeeds like success. Win! That's what I always told you, right? Win!" He grabbed the large print TV Guide from the table next to his chair and waved it like a battle standard.

"Yeah, Dad, that's what you've always told me," said Adelaide, "just like you've always told me about your leaving school at sixteen to help support your family and how much you and Mom suffered so I could be raised by nuns. I'm slow but I think I've got it."

"Good," he said contentedly, making her wonder if he ignored her sarcasm or didn't get it. "And one of these days I'm going to get Jerry, well no, not Jerry, but somebody to take me to see one of your plays, even if I can't see or hear so good."

Adelaide finished writing the check and placed it on the buffet under a mille fleur paperweight, Margie's souvenir from her last trip to Venice. She lived in Jacksonville and only had to visit every other Christmas, and that was fine because Margie never stopped calling her Deli which made her as mad now as it did when she was five.

Loudly, she said, "You do that."

# Chapter Five
## In Which the Second Miracle Occurs and Ferdy Suspects He's Over His Head

Early next morning Ferdy huddled at the corner of Monica's bed watching her sleep under a thin flowered sheet, one arm thrown behind her head to expose a stubbly armpit. The celebration dinner party at Palma's the night before had been fun until he tried to hump her ankle and made Palma's date spew his brandy. Hump one ankle and you were labeled for life. He had left the body of the disgraced Yorkie shortly after Joe pried him from the gorgeous leg with apologies. The party broke up shortly after.

It hadn't been all bad, though. Sure, he'd struck out with Palma, but what could you expect from a Yorkshire Terrier? That had been a problem of species, he was convinced; there would be other chances with human males.

Then there was Joe's grooming. Ferdy turned to look at his image in the mirror over Monica's dresser and admired the sheen of his dark leather skin. The black curly hair creeping from his chest to groin and continuing between his tiny buttocks up his back into a mohawk on the top of his head was soft and clean. Even his wings, though murky and brooding, had an almost angelic fluff about them. So what if the feathers were thinning a little? Damned attractive, if you liked bats.

Still, it was time to get down to business. He pushed away the cherry print quilt turned down at the foot of the bed and opened Monica's dossier. "Subject's history," he said.

The voice he heard was, not surprisingly, Gregory's grating one. "Hey, Ferd-breath! Chances are you've waited till the last minute to do your homework and don't deserve this information, but here goes: The subject Monica Laparro is a mortal female of fifty-one years in time, second generation Italian born in Charleston, South Carolina, most of which probably means nothing to you. Parents Antoinette and Vincent moved the family to Miami when she was ten.

"At the age of seven she suffered a case of what her mother thought was pink eye but what turned out to be a large cyst pressing against her optical nerve. During a delicate surgical procedure to remove the cyst, Antoinette Laparro, a devout Catholic, offered Monica's life to the Enemy if she would be allowed to live. She threw in daily praying of the rosary for the rest of her life to sweeten the deal. Monica survived and her mother prepared her for life as a nun.

"Despite six children who came after, Antoinette's focus was on grooming Monica for the convent. While the others were hula hooping Monica was singing the *Tantum Ergo* at novenas. Our subject took to the whole idea without protest, even with enthusiasm. What her mother didn't know is that Monica had a small altar set up in her bedroom where she would pretend to be, not a nun, but a priest. She used Necco wafers and grape kool-aid to simulate the ritual of the Mass. Her brothers and sisters were enthusiastic communicants.

"Maybe it was the Anglican influence of the deep south in her early life, but Monica Laparro was no Catholic. She was able to keep her protestant leanings in the closet through college, but the doctrinal shit hit the fan when she was accepted after graduation to the Episcopal Sewanee Theological Seminary in Tennessee. Family legend has it that her mother set up a wail that was heard by the Vatican and startled the Pope at his breakfast. To this day Antoinette Laparro treats the family at least once a year, often on Easter Sunday, to the story of 'How Monica Left the Church.'"

Ferdy's attention was distracted by Monica's light snoring. She had forgotten to take off her dream catcher earrings and they were tangled in her hair. The mascara under her eyes looked like a cooled lava flow and some of her mauve lipstick was on her chin. More bad hooker after a good night than any saint he'd ever seen. He forced his attention back to Gregory's academic drone.

"...unstellar rise from deacon to assistant priest at Good Shepherd Church in North Miami, becoming a rector at Holy Redeemer in Lake Worth by the age of thirty-four, then on to Dean of—"

"Subject's spiritual life," Ferdy broke in.

"Hey, buddy, I don't like to be interrupted," Gregory's voice responded. "You sure you don't want to hear how Bozo the Clown got to be a bishop?"

"Nah, subject's spiritual life," Ferdy repeated.

"It's this kind of inattention to detail that gets you into trouble. Boy, if I was your supervisor...okay, suit yourself. Subject exhibits strong links to the Enemy Cause with frequent direct contact with the Enemy himself. Does not show extraordinary activity in most of the vices though occasional lapses into gluttony and impatience might suggest methods of derailment. Top virtues—"

"Gluttony," Ferdy said. "Tell me about the gluttony."

"There you go, interrupting again. We've not talking food, here, though from the size of her you can imagine she packs it away pretty good. Subject shows an obsessive tendency to engage in acts of charity. She's a glutton for goodness. You throw enough opportunities her way and she might either break down or find herself in a situation she can't handle. Just a suggestion."

"Give me an example."

"When Laparro was the rector at Holy Redeemer she noticed one of her parishioners coming to Sunday services looking kind of beat up. Her investigations landed her at the woman's front door confronting a six-foot- three beer swilling construction worker with a bat. The bat was raised but never came down because of the way she stood her ground. The man's wife lived with Laparro for a year while the woman got on her feet enough to raise her two children. Too bad. We've had moderate success with the construction worker, though. Want more?"

"This is a vice?"

"Can be. She tends to seize every opportunity till she's running like a gerbil in a wheel, like she doesn't want anyone else to have a chance at it."

"So lots of humans have a do-good compulsion. What are we worried about?"

"You gotta ask? I know you saw the punch bowl."

Ferdy felt his beak burn and his breathing go shallow. "You were trailing me yesterday?"

"I was told to check up on you, nothing serious. Look, I'll make you a deal. You stay on task with this assignment and I promise not to put the business about the Yorkshire Terrier in my report."

"You got it, buddy."

"Back to your question. We've never been able to figure out how the Enemy makes his choices, they all seem so random and illogical. But for some reason there's a power focused on your subject. The thing with the never-ending punch wasn't the first occurrence. We've had our eye on her for some time and reported a number of extraordinary signs that indicate the Enemy's particular approval. Nothing big so far, just small stuff that the mortals haven't noticed."

Ferdy understood that. Immortals understood that absolutely everything had meaning. Mortals, on the other hand, were always asking for signs and then ignoring them.

"Why didn't you tell me there were signs, Gregory?"

"I did. They're in the dossier you haven't read yet."

"I am not liking this, Greg. I am getting a bad feeling about this."

"Don't be stupid, and keep your feelings to yourself. You know The Boss doesn't have a touchy-feely kind of management style. Now what else do you want to know?"

"Nothing," mumbled Ferdy around his big toe.

Monica closed her mouth in mid-snore and ran her tongue around the inside of her mouth hunting for saliva, while wondering if she was getting too old for martinis. Then she opened her eyes and tried to figure out the time from the amount of light slipping through the cracks of the blinds in her bedroom window. Nine o'clock, probably. Del would have been up writing for hours, and Palma would have worked out with her personal trainer. Those two were morning people, and morning people always seemed so morally superior. Let them be; she had plenty of time to relax with a cup of tea and the morning paper before the eleven o'clock service at the cathedral.

She kept the air-conditioning cold, which did little to help her nightly hot flashes, so despite the summer heat outside she grabbed the maroon chenille bathrobe with a peacock on the back from the foot of the bed. On the way to the bathroom she stopped at a crucifix made from popsickle sticks that hung on the wall. She half touched it, half leaned on it and muttered with the habit of years, "Father, this day is yours. May each life I touch know your love through me."

Monica stopped at the bathroom sink to wash off some of the straying mascara and paused to look in the large mirror behind the vanity shelf. Unwrapping the belt of the bathrobe, she held it open and briefly examined her body, still covered by a sleeveless nylon nightie. Surprise, the belly's still there, she thought, having watched it slowly outdistance her breasts over the last five years. She turned sideways and tried to suck it in while lifting a breast in each hand but she couldn't make the proportions any more attractive. Did she think by some miracle her tummy might have disappeared overnight because of her ordination?

If she had had a different body, not to mention a different face, would there be a man in her life? Would she have had a chance at that man, or maybe a sip from the endless stream of partners Palma enjoyed? No, even if she had the right looks, how many men were hot to marry female priests? "Just you and me, God," she said, and sighed.

On the kitchen counter she found a glass showing a crescent of yesterday's lipstick on the rim. She poured herself a glass of orange juice to wash down some unpronounceable Chinese pills Palma had given her that were supposed to minimize hot flashes. She wondered when they would start to kick in as she stuck a cup of green tea in the microwave.

Prayer, toilet, pills, tea. PTPT. *Sounds like pity, pity,* she thought, and laughed silently at herself, a deep down chuckle that tickled in her gut and made her smile. She could only take herself seriously so long before she got bored. Did she really expect her whole life to change when she became a bishop? Well, she'd find out tomorrow; today was a day of rest, unless something came up, which it usually did.

She retrieved her cup of tea from the dinging microwave. The heat felt good on her hands. They'd been aching more and more lately. Maybe this week she'd find a natural product for her arthritis, but for the time being she might as well take some aspirin, too.

There was a tupperware container in the pantry cabinet where she kept the aspirin. The container had been left by the last bishop's wife, Marylin McKibben. Marylin probably used a lot of tupperware, Monica thought. She looked like a tupperware user. As a matter of fact, the house looked like it was decorated by someone who gave tupperware parties. Relentlessly charming, it was stiffened by enough wallpaper to withstand a hurricane.

She grinned at her own couch, a pattern bursting with lime green macaws in flight. Now that was style, she thought, and wondered what Marylin would say about the way it looked with the plaid walls.

The house was part of her stipend and she figured she might as well use all of it, so she took her tea out to the patio. She regretted her choice for two reasons.

One was the humidity that seemed to fill her lungs with more water than air as she took a breath.

The other was Gus, lounging in a chaise.

Monica could see the side of Gus's face, covered with a two days growth of white stubble from half way down his throat to just below his eyes. The eye she could see had a blue pupil surrounded by yellow, and was shrunken into his skull. His hair, as white as his beard, hung in dank strips to a point just under where his chin would have been if he had one. He wore the t-shirt he was wearing when he showed up at St. Stephen's a week ago. The t-shirt pictured a lime, an empty shot glass and a worm bitten in half with the advice, "Lick it, Slam it, Puke it," written over all. The shirt didn't quite conceal a pair of briefs with stains that told their own story.

Worst of all, he oozed. Not from any specific source, but in a general way. Every orifice, ears, eyes, nose and mouth, either had something trickling from it or promised a dampness. The old trails of body fluid had crusted, leaving a raised bed for the new moisture in the same way stalactites grew.

"Gus."

He didn't look up. "What?"

"You can't sit out here like that, go put your shorts on."

"Fuckin' A," he said. "I suppose you think you have to keep up appearances now that you're a hoity toity bishop. Next thing you know I'll be out on my ass. They'll suspect we're lovers." He belched and Monica wondered what it came from; she'd never seen him eat.

"I'm sure rumours will fly. Did you really take a shower yesterday and shave like I told you to?"

"Sure did."

"It's incredible that you could have become this filthy in twenty-four hours. Is it some sort of medical condition? Have you seen a doctor about it?"

"About what?"

"Never mind. Tomorrow I want you to go get a haircut."

Gus fingered the handles of two canes propped on either side of the lounge chair. "And just how do you expect me to do that?"

"I'll get somebody to take you. And then you'll go to social services to see about being put on some kind of disability. This is just a stopping place for you. I know you can take care of yourself, you're not helpless. You've just been through a hard time."

He swung his spindly legs around until they rested beside the chair and he was facing Monica who hadn't entirely moved from the doorway. A partially healed ulcer the size of a quarter shone on his left shin. "Hard time you call it? Sackashitcuntfuckpissin homeless is what I am! HOMELESS!" He was shouting now. "How would you know from a hard time you coddled—"

"That'll be enough, Gus." Monica wondered if the neighbors were used to hearing this sort of conversation wafting from the bishop's patio along with the scent of his frequent bar-b-ques. She admitted herself impressed by the seamlessness of his crudity, but thought it would not be widely esteemed. "I woke up in a good mood...well, I didn't wake up that way but I'm in a good mood now and I don't feel like putting up with you."

"I can leave right now, how about that?"

"You think that's a threat? You think I let you stay here this week because I find your company stimulating? Fine. Leave."

Gus reached for the cane nearest him but otherwise didn't attempt to rise. His fingers rapidly opened and closed on the handle like a motorcyclist gunning his bike. With his eyes slowly oozing something that had not been there before and that ran from his cheek down the curve of his frown, he stared at a spot on the patio several feet from the hem of Monica's bathrobe. His lips trembled in a soft muttering, but a gravelly "A-a-ah," was all Monica could hear him say.

She put her cooling tea on a nearby patio table and went to him. "Come on," she said gently, picking up his other cane. "Let me help you." With the help of the two canes and Monica's arm the two walked in the house.

Ferdy, watching the scene, had been temporarily immobilized in amazement at the aspect of Monica's house guest. Now he ripped open the dossier. "I thought I'd met all the players. Who the hell is Gus?" he shouted.

Gregory's voice didn't share his concern. It droned in the same dry way that it had about Monica. "A sixty year old Viet Nam veteran of three separate tours who should have been dead long ago. The fact that he lives must have meaning but we've been unable to decipher it. Formerly making his way through life as an Arthur Murray dance instructor, Gus suffered a reversal of fortune four years ago when the jealous husband of one of his students ran over his legs with a vintage Impala. He spiraled downward rapidly into the creature you see today, helped by anger, self-pity, and guilt, not to mention the old hootch. This guy is so low he has to reach up to tie his shoes."

"Guilt?"

"The youngest mortal he killed in Vietnam was nine years old." Gregory's voice trailed off in a satisfied pause. "Anyway, Gus appeared at St. Stephen's cathedral a week ago when the former bishop was celebrating his final mass before departure. Dressed in his obnoxious t-shirt and a pair of big old shorts, Gus made his way with the help of his canes down to the altar rail at communion time. The neatly groomed parishioners danced out of their places to avoid being the one to drink from the communion cup directly after Gus. Monica watched this happen and purposely knelt beside him at the rail.

"After church she saw him hanging around the parking lot. She didn't ask him if he needed help, or if he had a place to go. Instead, opening her car door, she said in her best Episcopalianese, 'I wonder if you'd like to join me for brunch?' Gus wheezed, 'Don't think I'll be grateful,' and got in the car."

Ferdy heard water running and turned off the dossier to see

what the mortals were doing. The front bathroom door was open and Gus was standing under the shower. Naked, he looked even worse than before. His thin chest sagged inward while his shoulders sagged out. There was no contour to his back; it flowed in a straight line from neck to heel without a break for a backside. His eyes and mouth were shut tight and he gripped a soap dish attached to the wall, exhibiting all the enjoyment of a wet cat while Monica shaved his face. Then she cleaned the crusted trails around his nose and ears with a hot wash cloth, and soaped his withered form. Ferdy recalled his own bath, and wondered what washing symbolized. Mortals wanted to do it so often for each other.

"Careful with that sore on my leg," Gus whined. "Last time you rubbed the scab off."

Monica sat back on her heels and stared at Gus for such a long time that Ferdy wanted to know what she was thinking. He was only mildly surprised.

*"Didn't I tell you I'm going through menopause? Didn't I warn you about that?" She calmly puts the soap down, rinses her hands in the shower, gets up and dries them on a hand towel. Then she opens the drawer by the sink. From it she draws a .45 caliber handgun, expertly throws off the safety catch and points it at his gut.*

*Gus puts his hands up, palms outward, in a futile attempt to stop her. "No, no, Monica, Madame Bishop, I didn't mean to be ungrateful. I don't deserve your kindness! I'm sorry!"*

*"Gus," she says, "you're a bum. You're totally self-centered, mean spirited, and you haven't shown a lick of appreciation for anything I've done. I don't love you and God doesn't even love you. Go see for yourself."*

*She pulls the trigger and blasts Gus gore all over the shower tile.*

Only mildly surprised. Unlike devils, in whom psyche and will were logically synchronized to the same end, mortals were capable of feeling one way and acting another. Ferdy was gratified that Monica was capable of hateful fantasies but did not imagine it put her anywhere near derailment.

Monica was on her knees washing Gus's legs. The lather worked up nicely against his remaining hair. She paused, and cleared away some of the soap to examine his left shin more closely. Her eyebrows crawled into a frown though she tried to keep her voice sounding unconcerned.

"Gus, I think we should think about getting you to a doctor. This ulcer has really started to bleed."

Ferdy looked, too. The soap lather was turning pink where she washed him. Gus opened his eyes and scowled at the rose colored water running down the drain.

"God damn it, that's all I need," he muttered. "You scrubbed too hard again. Why'd you want to go and do that, huh? It was starting to heal until you got involved. You could have left well enough alone, but no-o, you have to—"

"Shut up, Gus," Monica said gently. "Remember—menopause. I may kill without warning. Maybe it's not as bad as it looks. We'll leave it exposed to the air and see if it dries up. And if not, I'll have a doctor look at it tomorrow."

She grasped the edge of the tub to support herself getting up and reached for the detachable shower nozzle. As she stood Gus commented, "Wait, I don't think it's me. Look." Monica and Ferdy looked at the edge of the tub where Gus pointed and saw two red slashes of blood where Monica had pressed her hands. There was more blood there than on Gus's leg. Monica lifted her right hand directly under the shower spray to rinse the soap away.

The two mortals and the devil could all see in Monica's upraised hand a mark that was unmistakably a large hole. It was about the diameter of a pencil and when she turned her hand the same mark showed on the back, as if the hole went straight through. The blood seeping from it mixed with the water, spreading down her bulgy forearm in a sheet and converging at her elbow into a condensed pink stream.

Still holding up her right hand to keep the blood from getting all over the bathroom, Monica raised her left hand under the water to reveal an identical puncture. It wasn't Gus that was bleeding at all. It was her.

Ferdy watched recognition, surprise, and shock all wash over Monica's face as the blood washed down her arms. She half sat, half fell back on the toilet seat next to the shower, too weak to remain standing, though her hands were frozen in what looked like some gesture of supplication. She looked back and forth from one hand to the other while a tiny trail of blood, darker without the water to dilute it, trickled from each hole down the sides of her hands and spattered lazily on the white tile floor. If there was any pain she didn't seem to be registering it. Gus finished rinsing and displayed his leg.

"See, it wasn't me," Gus said. "That's a relief."

"I-I d-don't understand," Monica stammered, her eyes fastened on her hands and her face pale.

Ferdy understood, and felt a chilling tingle run from his scalp down to his toes as the horror of his situation hit him. Despite her denial, he knew from Monica's reaction that at some level she knew what was happening. Only the devil could understand why.

"Holy shit," said Ferdy.

# Chapter Six
## In Which Adelaide Hasn't a Clue

The only thing moving in the room was Adelaide's tongue. It traveled busily over the inside of her mouth, inspecting the layers of scar tissue left from years of nervous biting. Breathing so shallow she might have stopped altogether, the rise and fall of her chest was almost imperceptible. Her eyes stared unblinking at the screen saver on her computer terminal; William Shakespeare's face, with a scrawled inscription, "You win. Will," stared back. She had come to a momentary halt in her writing, and she allowed her mind to lose focus for awhile, let it scurry randomly down a thousand paths leading to other paths, knowing she could call it back like a well-trained dog.

The day had started like every other weekday. She awoke alone in bed around 8:00, Joe having been careful not to wake her as he left for the salon. When her eyes finally opened the first thing she saw was the white demitasse cup of espresso left on her bedside table. They had received the espresso maker as an anniversary gift from Palma ten years ago. Since then, Joe brought her espresso in bed every morning, waking her with it on weekends, or leaving it on her nightstand before he went to work during the week. In all the ten years he had never failed to do this, and in all the ten years Adelaide had never bothered to tell him that by the time she woke it was cold.

As she thought about the wasted espresso now her mind wandered off on a path of calculation. Cup of espresso times three hundred and fifty two days (no, not quite because she did drink it on weekends) so that was three hundred and fifty two minus one hundred and four equals two hundred and forty eight times ten years equals two thousand four hundred and eighty times roughly two ounces per cup equals four thousand nine hundred and sixty ounces. Her mind grew bored and stopped trying to translate to gallons, but she fantasized how much espresso it could be. Enough to fill a jacuzzi? Enough to operate a Gene's Beans Coffee House for a day? Enough to set off all the pace makers in south Miami simultaneously?  Hell, for all the high leaded coffee she'd poured down the drain the EPA might classify her property as a hazardous waste site.

She unhooked her bare toes from where they had crept to the top edge of the computer desk while her mind wandered.  A tap on a key dissolved Shakespeare's face into what she had just written and she read it hungrily, as if the words fed her.

Adelaide closed her eyes and breathed a long "Oh," more like a sigh than a sound.  Conscious that her teeth were chattering slightly, she held onto the rush of joy, enjoying the real reason for writing.  The scene needed a ton of work, she knew, but there was a play in it and her body trembled as with the aftershock of an adrenalin rush.  She wasn't kidding herself, she couldn't be kidding herself, this could net the Pulitzer and then, then she'd be on her way to being taken seriously.  After all, you couldn't get more serious than a play called "Sex and the Holy Trinity."

Her hand searched to her right, looking for the soup bowl containing a mixture of jelly beans and peanuts she always kept on the computer desk; the jelly beans calmed her down and the protein in the nuts kept her from getting the sugar shakes.  Instead of hitting the bowl she connected with her espresso cup, knocking it over and spilling the sludge left at the bottom onto some pages she had taken from the printer earlier.  She used the pages to blot up the coffee and and then found her original target.

The jelly beans and peanuts rolled sugar and salt around her mouth like pebbles plucked from the sea as she took her glasses off and laid them on the mouse pad.  There were no lenses in the glasses; she wore them, along with the loosely knotted man's tie dangling down the front of her t-shirt, because she thought they stimulated her creativity.  The tie she wore now portrayed the stoic characters of Woods's American Gothic.  A half dozen others with varying designs waited in the closet to be used in case of writer's block.

She cranked open the window next to her desk and lit a cigarette.  Joe's allergies reacted viciously to smoke in the house, but she didn't have time to go out onto the back porch so she cheated by exhaling the smoke with her lips pressed tightly against the screen.  Alternately holding the cigarette dangerously close to the screen and taking drags she let her mind run off again, this time further into the past.

She could never remember actually believing in God. From the time she had to go to confession at the age of seven she had made up increasingly absurd sins, just this side of unbelievability. She knew she couldn't say she'd murdered her sister, they'd never buy that one. No, at first it was something like, "I painted our refrigerator orange." In time she got more adventurous, pushing the priest's credulity with, "I crucified a lizard on a plastic straw cross." Later she wondered if the priest, who she heard smothering giggles in his side of the confessional box, would regale his colleagues back at the rectory with the sins, or whether he would maintain the confidentiality of confession. Once she was in high school she returned occasionally, long after anyone checked to see how often she confessed, to try her hand at pushing the limits of the envelope. "I...I have these feelings about our Maltese." The confessional box was her earliest theater and the priest the unwitting critic of her material. You don't have to believe in the Father, Son and Holy Spirit to write a play about Him.

Adelaide pushed her cigarette through a slit in the screen where it joined a pile of butts collecting near a hibiscus shrub. The stillness outside matched the stillness of her room and the air conditioning gave way before creeping heat and the smell of wetly baking vegetation in the unkempt yard. From just the few moments by the open window she felt a bead of perspiration slide between her breasts. She sat, or rather angled nearly horizontally, in her computer chair and pushed it several feet away from the desk, munching on jelly beans and peanuts and shrugging at her computer monitor as if it had spoken.

Sure, she was the bad daughter in the family, but she was smart. She skipped grades, studied Greek instead of the typical Spanish, and read untranslated Chaucer in high school. After college it had taken her five and a half years to get her first show professionally produced, at a studio theater in Miami. She made sixty-five dollars for the two week run, but miraculously the play was seen by someone who knew someone and she was Off Broadway the next season. At twenty-six and a half she was the youngest professional playwright in New York with so much drive Monica had quipped even her blood type must be A. Since that time she'd written one play a year, and gave it to her agent Harvey Kalman, who found backers. She had won four Tony awards. *I'm really smart,* she assured herself for the millionth time. *I've succeeded.*

Monica was the good one. When she was a kid she probably listened to the stories of the saint having her breasts ripped off by a lustful pagan king and envied the saint. So now she was a bishop. So what? *I wonder how many bishops there are? Of course, there are only two female bishops in the country right now, that counts for something. But where does she go from here? Archbishop? Presiding Bishop? God? And how did I get to thinking about this crap instead of writing?*

She knew very well why. Monica's crack about the Nobel Prize at the ordination reception two days before got to her the way those cracks always did. Sometimes the competition with Monica was the impetus that propelled her forward—and sometimes it stalled her, like now.

Tires crunching on the loose gravel of the driveway drew her attention to Palma's white Mercedes. She watched Palma emerge in a cream tennis outfit and take a small picnic basket out of the back seat. *This must be Monday,* Adelaide thought. *She always plays tennis on Monday.* Her tongue ran instinctively over her front teeth, aware that the espresso had left a film on the unbrushed enamel. Her breath must be foul; *oh, well, serves Palma right for just showing up.* She pulled herself up from her chair and had the front door open before Palma could ring the bell.

"Hello, darling!" said Palma brightly, kissing her on the cheek without letting on if she could smell last night's dinner. She touched a finger lightly to Adelaide's temple. "Your eyes are watery. Have you been crying?"

"Allergies."

"Ah. I assume you haven't troubled to make yourself lunch."

"Sure, I was just having the usual."

"How many times have I told you jelly beans and peanuts are not nutritious?"

"And how many times have I told you they're fruit flavored jelly beans? One hundred percent of my RDA, whatever that is. What did you bring me?" she asked, not hiding her pleasure in the anticipation of Estella Too's delights. Estella had been Palma's duenna in high school. The French Hens had added the "Too" onto her name when she became Palma's housekeeper.

"I have an arugula and curried shrimp salad with yogurt tossed pineapple on the side."

"Okay, you can come in." She followed Palma into the kitchen and opened the cupboard door. "Are you having some. . .oh, there aren't any clean plates. We can eat from the containers."

"Unacceptable." Palma opened the dishwasher with the intimacy of one grown comfortable in another's kitchen, took out two plates and quickly scrubbed them in the sink. "Do you have clean forks this time at least?"

Adelaide opened a drawer and triumphantly brandished two forks as if they were trophies. "Ha! And you thought I was a slob."

Palma didn't comment but took woven grass placemats out of the basket, set the small kitchen table and gestured for Adelaide to sit down. They both began to eat, Adelaide wolfing hers down with one elbow resting on the table while Palma dined at a more leisurely pace and pretended as always not to notice that Adelaide quietly hummed while she ate.

"Did I ever ask you why you do this?" Adelaide asked, having swallowed most of a mouthful of the salad.

"Yes, you just like to hear it again. I do this because, when you're receiving an award I can sit in the audience and think, these applauding crowds don't know it, but without me she'd be wasting away with rickets or pelagra or something and the world would never see her plays. Attractive tie, by the way."

"It goes with what I'm working on. Country motif and all."

"Are you happy with it?"

"Yeah, it doesn't show stains."

"You know I mean the play."

Adelaide could feel the trembling start again, this time a slight tremor of her head, so she rose from the table to disguise the emotion she wanted to hide. "I want to show you something. No, stay there, it's not the play." She went into her office and picked up the pages on the computer table, still stained brown from the coffee she'd spilled, but nearly dry.

"I did a web search on the Nobel Prize," she said, back in the kitchen, forgetting the lunch that had delighted her. "Look at this, these are some of the people who...don't try to read it through the coffee stains, I think I can dope it out for you. Look, here's Andre Gide, it says 'for his comprehensive and artistically significant writings, in which human problems and conditions have been presented with a fearless love of truth and keen, etc.' I can do that—and here's Selma Ottilia Lovisa Lagerlof, how's that for a name, Swedish, 'in appreciation of the lofty idealism, vivid imagination and spiritual perception that characterize her writings.' I can do that, vivid imagination, I have lofty ideals, I think, and what I'm working on right now shows a lot, you know, a lot of spiritual perception. Selma was only fifty-one when she got it which shows that it's not just the old farts who get it."

Palma put her hand over Adelaide's which was moving over the brown dappled papers like a squirrel in leaves. "Adelaide, slow down, please, and tell me what this is all about?"

"Okay, I'll get to the point. I researched it, and there have only been seven women who won the Nobel Prize for Literature. And no playwrights. Playwrights have won, like Beckett, Sartre, O'Neill, but they've all been men—no women. If I can win the Nobel Prize I'll be the first woman playwright. There."

"But Adelaide, is the Nobel Prize something you 'go after?' It seems more lofty than that, somehow, a recognition of more than just really good writing, some contribution to the betterment of mankind."

"Whatever it is, Palma, I think I have it in me. Like Monica says, this Tony Award business is getting old. Like being a bishop is such a big deal—it's just another church job—all she's done is get herself into a society of good old boys whose first names are interchangeable with their last names like...like Griffin Thomas. There's nothing Monica could do to top the Nobel Prize."

"You really let Monica get to you, didn't you? Why do you do this to each other?"

"A little healthy competition is good."

"You're obsessing."

"I have high goals."

"Look at you. You think this is healthy? You look like a nervous wreck. And you're proposing to win the greatest literary prize just to show up Monica. I love both of you but sometimes I think you need some therapy. Here you are, a famous playwright, probably a millionaire, though you wouldn't know it to look at this house. When are you going to do some decorating?"

"Don't rush me, we've only been here twenty-six years." Adelaide looked around at the bare white walls of the kitchen. "You know I'm co-dependent. I'd rather decorate your house."

"Stop feeding me one-liners from your plays and treat me like more than just a straight man for once. Why don't you ease up on yourself? Do you think Monica became a bishop just to compete with you?"

"You can't know that she didn't. And maybe she doesn't even know."

"Really, darling. I can't imagine Monica doing all this just to best you. Do you think that's why she offered her life to God? Do you think that's why she takes homeless people off the street into her home?"

"What homeless people?"

"She told me about some dreadful man who can hardly walk, who's living with her. He apparently has open sores and she's actually bathed him. For all we know he could have AIDS. I tell you, I don't know what her motivation is, but the woman is a living saint. She's a saint and you're a great writer, and I'm so proud to call you both my friends. Can't we just be happy with that?"

Adelaide picked at her pineapple, as if she were searching there for her appetite. "Have you seen this guy?"

"I haven't been over to her new house since she moved in. I stopped by St. Stephen's this morning because I wanted to have breakfast with her and I knew she was saying mass. Come to think of it, I wanted to tell you."

"About?"

"Only if you keep eating."

Adelaide reluctantly jammed a large forkful of salad into her mouth and spoke around it, which made Palma grimace. "How's this?"

"You're such a child. There was just a small group of us in the church, and a couple of those homeless people who always seem to be around these days. Monica was preparing the bread and wine for the consecration when I caught a movement out of the corner of my eye. I looked into the aisle, and there was this dove walking toward the altar."

"Walking?"

"Walking."

"You sure it wasn't a pigeon?"

"No, it was definitely a dove. It caught Monica's eye too, so she stopped what she was doing since there was no one there to speak of and we just watched it take its good old time marching up to the altar."

"Was it a white dove?"

"No, just a plain old brown one." Palma took Adelaide's now empty plate, rinsed it, and put it back in the dishwasher. She found the detergent under the sink and turned on the machine so there would be clean dishes to use later. "I've never observed a bird walking for such a length of time. They're very slow. This one finally made it all the way up the aisle, hopped up the three steps in front of the altar, and just stood there. Monica leaned all the way over the altar—it was hard to see the bird way down on the floor—and said good morning to it."

"This is so sweet I'm feeling a carb high."

"It really was cute. The dove finally flew up on the altar and sat down, kind of like in its nest. Monica let it sit there during the rest of the service."

"Then what?"

"That's all. After the mass it jumped off the altar and walked back out of the church. If the altar guild ladies she talks about ever hear that she let some filthy bird sit on their pristine altar cloth they're liable to call for impeachment."

"So the dove didn't whistle 'Amazing Grace' or anything? Didn't peck a happy face in one of the hosts?"

Palma laughed, then grew serious again. "There was another thing, though, that troubled me a little. Monica was wearing a pair of brown leather gloves. When I asked her why she just changed the subject. Isn't that strange? She's never been one to hold back anything. You've heard the way she talks about—"

"Menopause?"

"—right in public. If there's something wrong with her hands, like fungus, or something, why wouldn't she say so? I'll think I'll make an appointment for her with my dermatologist."

The phone rang and Adelaide got up once more to check the caller identification panel in her office. "It's my father. I'll call him back."

Their eyes locked briefly before Palma deftly turned the subject to her plans for the Spay Your Cat fundraiser dinner. They could talk about anything, almost.

# Chapter Seven
## In Which Ferdy Gets Advice From Gregory

Two women dressed in sports bras and biking shorts sat at a table placed out on the sidewalk in front of Chez Rocky's restaurant in a busier section of the South Beach strip. Rocky's, like the rest of the buildings on the strip, showed the art deco style of the forties. The plaster facade was bevelled in a geometric pattern and painted in different pastel colors; the powdery effect of the paint on plaster made it look like large sticks of sidewalk chalk standing on end. Even at noontime on a weekday the small-dog walkers and in-line skaters clad in thongs crammed the sidewalk. Through the passing throngs the women could look out across the avenue leading to the beach, traffic interrupted now and then and onlookers posing as a car slowly drove by filming the activity. The day was dryer than usual, so a table outdoors was acceptable as long as it came with enough chilled Perrier.

The taller, blonder of the women was complaining to her friend about her husband's latest infidelity. She couldn't know that her friend, lazily stirring the lemon twist in her glass with a long curved fingernail, had been possessed by Ferdy for the past quarter hour. He was waiting for Gregory to show up, and he was already bored by the blonde's ravings. There was such a 'sameness' to every act of adultery, he thought. Mortals seemed to think it endlessly fascinating, the theme of every story since Adam bit the old apple. But most of the time there was some positive aspect to sex of any kind, if only an illusion of affection. You could never get someone damned on the basis of sex alone.

This *was* where Gregory said to meet him, wasn't it?

"It used to be with liquor salesmen it was all guys," the blonde was saying. "You know, guys selling scotch to guys. Now they send out these little girls with skirts so short their pubic hair shows who'll do anything to make a sale. First thing you know, Jerry's started stocking weird brands of flavored vodka instead of the usual supply of J&B. That's how I know somebody other than Ben is selling to him, that he lets himself get talked into that stuff. I mean, it's not like his place is here on South Beach where the trendy stuff sells. It's a Big Daddy's in Hallandale, for pete's sake. Then, here's the real tip off, he starts coming home at five in the morning when he used to come home at three. I know it's one of those little cunts. Shit, look at me. I'm thirty-eight years old, I don't stand a chance against them. Look at this cellulite. And I know I'm a good two percent over on my fat ratio." The blonde pinched a one centimeter roll of flesh protruding over the top edge of her spandex shorts. Ferdy thought of suggesting sex, then figured she'd likely turn down overtures from her best friend. Besides, there was the business to discuss with Gregory if he ever got there. Focus...focus....

The blonde grew wide-eyed, had a brief if intense spasm, and leaned across the table to leer at Ferdy. "By the way, sugar, nice tits."

"Hi, Greg," said Ferdy, looking up from his lemon twist. Any passers-by continued to see two attractive women sitting at the table. From Ferdy and Gregory's perspective the image of themselves came and went across the faces of the women like two channels fighting for the same television screen. When Ferdy looked at his partner he saw Really Raisin lips waver and give way to a mouthful of drooling fangs. Blue eyes faded back and forth into white with no pupils. Ferdy found himself wondering again how Gregory managed to see. Then the image of the blonde returned. If anyone passing by noticed her drooling on her sports bra no one stopped—this was South Beach.

Gregory lifted his head and sniffed the air like a dog. This made sense seeing as how his nose was very much like that of a Pug. The smell of the heat mixed with sunscreen and sweat curled tangibly around them.

"Tell me, how you rate a cushy assignment like this?" Gregory asked. "You been blowing the Boss?" He pushed his tongue against the inside of his cheek to make it look like there was something hard in his mouth.

"You got me this job, remember? You could have taken it yourself."

"Got higher level things to do, Ferd-ball. I'm a young executive rising in the corporation."

"You're late," Ferdy added.

"Hey, man. You're lucky I'm here at all. I'm the only friend you've got."

Ferdy assented with silence and thought briefly that he had his doubts about Gregory, too, but let it go.

"I stopped to say good-bye to Al," said Greg.

"Why, what's up with Al?"

"He's getting laid off today."

"Bummer."

Ferdy hoped his mild reaction would disguise the thrill of horror he always felt at the mention of lay-off. Getting devoured by the Boss was the only way a devil could be really destroyed in the metaphysical sense. Being eaten meant eternal oblivion. Demonhood might not be the best way to make a living, but hey, it was better than nothing. If it really were nothing. That was just conjecture. Ferdy imagined Al living on powerlessly inside the Boss, watching through the other's eyes like a prisoner. He shuddered and wondered if the layoff had anything to do with Greg's drooling more than usual.

"So where are you posted?" Ferdy asked.

"Lebanon."

"How are things in Lebanon?"

"There was some sort of peace initiative all set to fuck things up, but I think I've got it under control," Gregory said, preening his dolphin-hide wings. "Before I left I heard some news commentator call it 'hell on earth.' Pretty cool, huh?" He was a cocky son of a bitch, thought Ferdy. Had every right to be. Gregory was rising through the ranks fast these days, word was out that he might even be made Supervisor of the Western Hemisphere North of the Equator. Ferdy should consider himself lucky that Gregory condescended to be here giving him advice. Then Ferdy wondered what was in it for Gregory. Then he stopped and paused to consider that he was wondering a lot more than usual. Typically, he hardly thought at all.

"So, how are things here?" Gregory smirked. He must have known there had to be problems for Ferdy to call him in.

Ferdy told him the whole story.

"No shit? That hasn't happened in what, fifty years or so? You think it's hysterical?"

"She doesn't seem like the hysterical type. More down to earth than any other SIP I've ever personally worked." Ferdy used the acronym for Saint in Progress hoping to look like he was cool and in control. If this guy was going to be his supervisor one day it wasn't too early to start sucking up.

Gregory cackled. "Oh, oh, you're fucked. That's the trouble with these mortals. Blood comes from their nose, they call it a nosebleed. Blood comes from their hands, they call it a handbleed? Oh no, it's gotta be The Stigmata. Got to make a big deal out of everything."

"But don't you figure it means something?"

"Like the Good Housekeeping Seal of Approval? Don't waste your time trying to figure out The Enemy. That's the trouble with you, you get off task when you start trying to figure them out. Concentrate: the only thing, and I mean the *only* thing it means for you is that you got your hands full with Damage Control, buddy. You've got to do something to slow this whole thing down—preferably before she goes public."

Ferdy's wings drooped as despondently as a wet canary's. This meeting was depressing him.

"And save that face for your next performance evaluation. It's time to focus on the job now. What's your goal?"

Ferdy recited the lines from the Complete Manual of Demonology. "CMD Code 7, article 666. To do everything within my means to cajole, disturb, or otherwise tempt the Saint in Progress to break contact with The Enemy with the result of ultimately rejecting The Good."

"That's right," Gregory nodded. "And this little stigmata thing could play right into your claws."

"Ready to order, ladies?"

Ferdy and Gregory both looked up to see an attractive young waiter, pen and pad poised in expectation of their luncheon choice. Neither spoke, so the man continued.

"I forgot to tell you about our specials today. We have grilled mahi mahi with a cranberry chutney, blackened shrimp caesar salad, and a portabello mushroom wrapped in prosciutto and grilled on skewers with red peppers. Everything comes with soup or salad."

Gregory winked at Ferdy. "Well, young man, that all sounds really good. You look really good, too." He opened his mouth, uncurled his tongue and slowly caressed his face with it. The waiter blinked as he saw what appeared to be a blonde woman licking her own eyebrows. He stepped back a foot.

"Let me give you a few more minutes." And he was gone.

"Like I was saying, before she goes public," Gregory continued. Ferdy averted his eyes.

"How long ago did this happen?"

"About forty-eight hours ago."

"Anti-Christ, you got to move fast. Who else knows so far?"

"Just that half-wit derelict who lives in her house. He was there when it happened. Seems his only reaction was relief that the blood wasn't coming from him."

"Hm, keep him in mind. Maybe you can use him." Gregory thought a bit while twisting a black claw around the blonde's gold hoop earring. "Say, what about assailing. Have you assailed her yet?"

"I only took the assignment a week ago," Ferdy heard the defensiveness in his own voice. "I was still, you know, trailing her, scouting around. You know, fact-finding to see what her strengths and weaknesses were." Ferdy felt himself stuttering, feeling unsure as he always had under Gregory's interrogation.

"Good, so while you're fact finding she's having doves nesting on her altar and nail marks appearing mysteriously in her hands."

"So you think assailing would do something?"

"Would I suggest it if I didn't? If you need help, I could get a few of the guys."

"No, no that's okay. I guess I'll go it alone for awhile." Ferdy knew if he let Gregory in on the job he'd end up looking like an idiot. "Waking or dreaming?"

"I'd go for the dreams, at least at first. Gives you more control over the reaction."

The waiter approached the table warily. Ferdy shook his head that, no, he didn't want anything. Gregory motioned the waiter to come closer. The waiter approached holding the pad like a shield.

"That caesar salad. Can I have blackened maggots with that

instead of shrimp?"

The waiter's patience ran out. "Look lady, I'm a second year pathology student at the U.of M. just trying to make ends meet. Do you want to order something or not?"

Gregory looked at Ferdy. "I gotta go, Ferbulous. If you need me I'll be in Beirut." Gregory stood up from his seat, leaving the woman behind. Ferdy watched the waiter look up at something looming about ten feet over him that would have been pretty gross even if it had skin on it. The young man dropped his pad and ran off screaming.

"Well, now I've seen it all," exclaimed the blonde. "Even the waiters are nuts here."

"Really," said her friend.

# Chapter Eight
## If Which Mortals Think They Have Control

While Ferdy was getting advice from Gregory at South Beach, Monica spent her afternoon in her office making up reasons why she had decided to add brown leather gloves to her ensemble in the middle of the summer, and otherwise trying not to think about the holes in her palms when they throbbed. Thinking about her hands caused a corresponding throb in the pit of her stomach that felt like fear. Without knowing what she feared, she didn't know what to do about it and hoped the whole event was temporary; maybe tomorrow morning she would wake up and nothing would be beneath the gauze pads wadded inside the gloves. At least she'd somehow been able to control the bleeding.

Gus sat on Monica's back patio where he had been sobbing over what he'd done in Viet Nam forty years before. There was a movie in his head that played over and over. It started with a sound behind him in the hut that was darkened with smoke and smelled of spiced blood. He whirled at the sound and fired at the form standing in the light of the doorway. He was the one left alive. The child must have been nine or ten. The safety catch was still on her gun. He was glad to be the one left alive. The movie ended, leaving him again to wonder if he meant to kill a child. He was glad to be the one alive. Then he stopped crying, suddenly aware of a pleasant tingle in his legs.

Palma worked out on the Boflex in her exercise room, perspiring lightly while listening to spec tapes of local bands. She was having trouble finding the perfect group for the black tie fundraiser she was underwriting to benefit the Spay Your Cat Foundation. About the time that Gus stopped crying, Palma began. Estella Too watched sadly, without Palma knowing. Palma never thought anyone saw her cry.

At the Dog's Day Salon Joe blithely spritzed a black cockapoo named Raven with *Chien de la Nuit* while thinking of Adelaide. Raven would have preferred *Road Kill No. 5* but a cockapoo had to keep up the right appearances.

Adelaide dangled her legs over the top of the seat before her as she sat in the tenth row of the Coconut Grove Theater to watch a rehearsal of her new play "Social Morays." It was having its out of town run in Miami which gave her an opportunity to do some more rewriting before it went to New York. Her mind hummed like an idling Maserati, and not just from the effects of caffeine and sugar. Her work on "Sex and the Holy Trinity" was coming along good, really good, and this play was looking good, too. She even had an idea for another drama that she might start working on right after "Sex," something even more serious. Everything was really, really good. Yes.

Melba McGregor, who had so expertly headed strategic command of the punch bowl at Monica's ordination reception, stood in the small office behind the sanctuary of St. Stephen's and discussed the flower delivery for next Sunday's service. She had been doing so for a quarter of a century. Seventy-two years old, head of St. Stephen's Altar Guild, and a bully, she ran the guild with the style of a South American dictator. The six elderly women reporting to her responded to her commands as if the continued safety of their families depended on getting the right amount of starch in the altar cloth. Melba knew what a liturgically correct service looked like, and she would give a correct service to the congregation or die.

"We've got a wedding here next Saturday, the flowers are already ordered, so we won't need any for Sunday. Are you doing the wedding? Okay, but they better be here no later than nine or I'm coming over there, and you don't want me to do that." She hung up on the florist and headed into the sanctuary. There, hands clasped behind her like a *generalissimo* surveying the troops, she examined the altar area while one of her tinier minions cowered by the sanctuary lamp. Melba herself was not a large woman, but her small frame was topped by a disproportionately large face which had the sheen and stillness of hardening clay. That, coupled with a rasping voice that could seize on you like a nail file against your cheek, accounted for the success of her intimidation. Melba kicked an embroidered kneeler into place, ran an imperious finger along the top of the tabernacle hunting for dust, and scanned the red carpet for candle wax on the chance she could have the pleasure of chastising some poor acolyte currently deluded into thinking that life was okay.

"What's this," she growled in her lowest tone.

The minion scuttled over to where Melba stood in front of the altar, looked where she was pointing and bent down to pick it up.

"It looks like a feather, Melba," she said with a slight head tremor.

"Oh, I thought it was a fuzzy grey cockroach," Melba's face remained impassive, but the minion knew her remark was meant to be sarcastic and she giggled in a way that indicated rising hysteria. "I know it's a feather. What kind of feather is it?"

"I c-can't tell."

"What's it doing in here?"

"Charlotte must have missed it when she was vacuuming. She's gone now," the minion said, immediately blaming the absent.

"All I can say is, there better not be a bird in here. Have you seen a bird?"

At a loss, the minion shook her head sadly and put the feather in her pocket, hesitating for a moment with it near her face as if she considered eating it instead.

"Do you know what that feather is? It's a sign, that's what it is. It's just another sign of the lax—of how lax the whole Episcopal Church is getting. It all started with them updating the 1928 Prayer Book, now we've got refugee Catholics coming to the services, and even our bishop wasn't born Episcopal." She jerked an invisible wrinkle out of the altar cloth and glared at the woman before her who stood quietly, having heard it all before, and only hoping that this would be the abridged version. "And an I-talian to boot. That on top of Ryan, a Catholic for pete's sake, who wasn't even ordained in the Episcopal Church." The Dean of St. Stephen's Cathedral was Brian Ryan, a former Catholic priest who had been received into the Episcopal Church sixteen years ago. "And now they're talking reunification. I ask you, what will happen if we get tied to the Catholic Church? I'll tell you what will happen, incense that will make you choke, Mary altars all over the place, and imported priests with accents so thick they might as well still be speaking Latin. Not that I'm old-fashioned, mind you, I'll still receive communion from a female priest, not like some of those die-hards who seize up at the sight of a woman at the altar, at least that separates us from the Catholics, but the problem with that is you don't get a clergy wife into the bargain."

The minion had been concentrating on Melba's tirade so she could shake her head yes or no at the appropriate points. She lost track near the end and Melba left her still standing before the altar, head cocked to one side, fingering the feather in her pocket.

Increasingly irritated thoughts acted as a kind of mental propulsion system that hurried Melba towards Monica's office in the building next door. She didn't stop till she hit the secretary's desk and leaned over it to get as close to the young woman as possible.

"Mornin', Mac," said Sharon, without flinching. Having a Jewish father and a Baptist mother had prepared her for Episcopalians; Sharon wasn't afraid of anything. Now she patted her well-groomed hair into place as if Melba's presence had somehow disarranged it, and leaned forward until she was inches from the older woman's face. "What can I do for you?" she asked.

"I want to see the Bishop," demanded Melba.

"She's got Dean Ryan in there right now. They've been talking awhile. You may not want to wait."

"I'll wait." Melba sat down in one of the comfortable chairs and continued on about how Father Ryan should have stayed in the Catholic church where he was ordained because he could never get a church to support itself without help from Rome. She muttered as if to herself, but loudly enough for Sharon to hear in case she wanted to join in, her volume swelling when she hit favorite phrases like "cradle Episcopalian" or "Anglo-come-lately." Sharon ignored the commentary and continued with her work, an effort akin to ignoring a sports bar on dollar draft night.

Finally the door to Monica's office opened and Dean Ryan

emerged laughing with Monica behind. Ryan's relaxed manner and easy smile shifted into a fight or flight stance when he saw Melba. He turned back so quickly that Monica ran up against his outstretched hand, making him blush at contact with the Episcopal breast.

Recovering, he said, "Now remember, Bishop Laparro, if there's anything I can do—"

"You can call me Monica. Thanks for the welcome, Brian." She ignored his hand and hugged him, after which he glanced at Melba and fled the office. Monica turned to Melba, whose presence could not be ignored, and grinned jovially. "Hello," she said brightly.

"Bishop, this is Melba McGregor," said Sharon, watching the two women, entertained by Monica's eyebrows twitching in recognition as one side of her grin drooped. "We call her Mac."

"Like the hamburger, or the truck?" Monica asked, while Sharon suppressed a giggle and bent over her computer keyboard. "We were, ah, just talking about...that is to say, Father Ryan was just telling me how well you run the cathedral altar guild."

Seemingly unable to communicate without being in close proximity to her target, Melba rose out of the chair to her full five foot three inches and stood close to Monica who only cleared her by an inch or two.

"Champs," spat Melba, and paused dramatically.

"Who?" Monica asked.

"Not who, what. They're those modern tennis shoes, you know. Bobby Glatzer was wearing them under his acolyte's robes last Sunday. I want you to talk to him. You know the regulation is a black shoe."

Monica shuffled, attempting to put some space between her and Melba without appearing to do so, and tried a placating stance. "Melba, I'm afraid I don't know who Bobby Glatzer is, but I sympathize with you. Kids these days show no respect at all."

Melba gave an approving snort so Monica kept on. "But it's so hard to get any kids to acolyte at all. It's not like the Catholic church where you have a steady stream of parochial school students to do the job."

Evidently no one had warned Monica against the use of the "C" word in Melba's presence. Melba leaned into the space that Monica had attempted to claim and snarled, "We don't need to be like the Catholics. All we need is two acolytes with some good—healthy—discipline." She punctuated each word with a jab of two fingers held together as if one wasn't enough to convey the gravity of her opinion. "I hate Catholics."

"Now, Melba, that's pretty strong. I don't think you mean what you say."

"Yes, I do. I hate Catholics. My late husband was a Catholic and I wouldn't marry him until he converted."

"Well, be that as it may, I'm not even the one to talk to. You should see Father Ryan about Cathedral matters. He's the Dean."

"Bishop McKibben used to deal with me directly. I don't have much to do with Father Ryan," she grimaced, pronouncing his name as if she were saying "sewer rats."

Monica's thoughts flipped between Gus at home and Melba at the office and she felt her patience slip. "Well, Melba, I'm learning this new job and I've got two committee meetings to prepare for. It was really nice meeting you."

"One more thing," Melba said, finally stepping back.

"Yes?" Monica said, growing weary with restraining herself from smacking the woman.

"What's with those gloves?"

# Chapter Nine
## Joe and Adelaide

Around 11:00 p.m. Joe was waiting for Adelaide to come home. He lay naked under a light sheet in bed, his head propped on a folded pillow, watching the scene from *The Fighting Kentuckian* where John Wayne presses his buckskin dangerously close to Vera Ralston's bosom and insists that he will have her no matter what. Joe loved to watch Ralston grow helpless under the spell of Wayne's gaze. Aware of the faint satisfying smell of his own heat, he felt the air conditioning kick on and creep gently over the surface of the sheet, cooling it and the corners of his eyes where the tears had pooled. Watching old movies was Joe's third favorite thing after Adelaide and animals.

He wiped his eyes on the edge of the sheet, pressed the rewind button of the remote control and looked around the bedroom, quiet except for the whirring of the VCR. It was as spartan as the rest of the house. Original paint on the walls, no pictures anywhere, no bedspread for the summer, and sheets so thin with washing Joe was certain they'd been a wedding present. Joe had no talent for decorating and if Adelaide did, she couldn't be bothered. But that didn't stop Joe from imagining the photos that other couples collected to remind themselves that they had a life together. Over there on the wall by the television stand would be the pictures from college, he in ridiculous bell bottoms and an already receding hairline. Maybe a picture recording the first adventures of the three friends, Palma posed as if for the cover of Vogue, Monica clowning, and Adelaide carefully looking like she didn't care. Adelaide.

Just thinking her name made his heart twist. He wondered when this initial infatuation would subside; thirty years was an unusually long first rush of love.

On the wall over the bed would be the pictures of the two of them as dressed up as they could get, Joe standing a little behind, watching her pose with her Tony award. There would be four pictures like that, taken over the years, the only difference in the clothes they were wearing and deepening lines forming a parenthesis around their mouths. Joe had always thought of Adelaide's success with pride, but lately with sympathy too. She didn't seem to love it anymore, and in his maturity Joe began to wonder if she ever had. It was always the next thing, and the next thing, greedily loving some place down the road that she never reached no matter how fast she ran toward it, or passing it with hardly a glance if she did. Years ago he had stopped wondering if she loved him, and had contented himself with his animals, and his movies, a half hour of her conversation almost every night, and sex on Saturday afternoons. Unlike Adelaide, Joe had hardly any expectations at all.

He reached under the sheet with his left hand to sooth the long, squirming thing moving impatiently against his thigh. It was a ferret he was babysitting for the evening. An apparently boneless musky smelling animal with coarse fur and a pointy snout capped by an ink spot of a nose, it had fallen asleep under the sheet when the movie started. In waking it had mistaken Joe's penis for another ferret and tried to strike up a conversation, then grown irritated when the penis remained coyly unresponsive. The animal nipped at the fingers coming towards him under the sheet and Joe decided to remove his penis from the bed before the ferret nipped at that too.

On the way to the kitchen Joe ran his hand over his sagging abdomen, felt the crease where it met his groin, and reluctantly decided on a low fat snack. He took his favorite mixing bowl out of the cupboard and filled it half-way with Coco Crunchies. Then he cut a hunk of non-fat angel food cake and plopped that in. Over the cake he threw a ladle of Guilt Free Chocolate ice cream big enough to bury the cake in a Coco Crunchie grave. Skim milk and a dusting of cinnamon finished it off. Joe was looking for the biggest spoon he could find when the lock turned in the front door.

Joe could always tell what kind of day his wife had had from the way she opened the door. If it was a dry day in which the computer had become the enemy and actors in her latest show had decided to have nervous breakdowns en masse during rehearsal the key turned wearily in the lock and the door opened with the slowness of a horror movie scene. If the day was good, the unlocking was brisk and the door flung open like the arrival of the good guys. Tonight the lock turned with one smooth click and the door flew open so hard it rebounded against the springy stopper attached to the wall. Adelaide passed over the threshold, caught the door triumphantly on the return, and closed it behind her in a single motion without slowing the door.

"Good day, sweetheart?" Joe asked, turning to her in his manatee splendor, the bowl of Coco Crunchies held nonchalantly before him, momentarily forgotten in the presence of her radiance.

Adelaide paused to howl the female version of Tarzan's cry and continued on to the bedroom to shed her own clothes in their customary heap by the side of the bed. Joe found his spoon, turned off the light, and ambled lazily after her. He got to the door just as she was getting into bed.

"Ferret," she commented, lifting the sheet.

"That's right," said Joe. "Cute, isn't he?"

"Does he use a cat box?"

"No, ferrets are even more independent than cats. You have to wait and see where they go the first time, then put paper in that spot. They always return to it."

"What spot did this one choose?"

Joe shook his head. "Regrettably, it's first choice was the middle of the living room couch. But we're in the process of negotiating for a strong second choice."

The ferret decided to go for a snack himself, shimmying down the side of the bed so Joe could take its place without fearing any attacks on his uncommunicative genitals. He eased himself in next to Adelaide, careful not to spill the cereal.

"Good day?" he repeated, knowing but wanting to hear her speak. The lines of their conversation would ripple over one another with the rhythm of small waves washing up on shore and receding, each one lapping over the last before the sound had subsided.

"Is the bear Catholic? Does a wild pope shit in the woods?" Adelaide squirmed in the bedding as if, yes, life was a bed of roses and the petals felt delicious on her back. "The play is coming along really—"

"Which one?"

"Morays. The one in production. Well, the director's a pompous asshole, Randy something or other. He spends a large part of the rehearsal telling anecdotes about his own career, and no sense of comedy. But," and here she gently put her hand on Joe's arm which sent a thrill through his body, "the words. The words are so good that no one can stop them. The actors seem to sense it and relax. Even the one who plays the mechanic who I figured we cast to type—"

"The one you said reminded you of me."

"Right. He was really intense at first."

"Not like me."

"No. Maybe he was nervous to be working with me. But he's fine now."

"And what about the one you're writing?"

Adelaide closed her eyes and moaned like she was approaching orgasm. "Oh, oh, that's what really has me flying, Joe..."

Joe. Hearing her say his name was enough to send him into a mystical realm where the whole earth gave one hard twist and dropped from sight. He could still hear her voice but for a few moments he let himself transcend and taste the goodness of her acknowledgment of his being. Then he put a spoonful of ice cream in his mouth to ground himself again.

"...the best work I've ever done. The premise is universal even though the concept is fairly parochial. It's an indictment of institutional religion. It's going to catapult me into fame and riches beyond my wildest dreams. It's the Pulitzer for sure." She laughed and rubbed his belly vigorously under the sheet as she were seeking luck from a statue of Hotee.

Joe licked his index finger after running it around the inside of the bowl, stared at the emptiness there for a moment, and put it on the floor beside the bed. "You're already famous beyond your wildest dreams. And you have so much money you don't even know how much money you have."

"It's going so fast I'm nearly done with the first draft."

"So let's take a vacation."

"I don't even anticipate a lot of rewriting."

"We could go down to Key West for a week. Celebrate

finishing it. Remember that bed and breakfast just off Duval that we couldn't find one night because we were drunk? And we hailed a taxi who drove us about twenty yards to the front door?"

"I can hardly wait to show it to Harvey."

"Okay, we don't have to go all the way down. We could go to Marathon, or Key Largo, even. When was the last time we snorkeled at Pennekamp?"

"He's going to be so surprised. I can see his face now."

"Harvey hasn't finished producing your current play."

Adelaide's focus wrenched away from her own thoughts. "Why are you nagging me? You never nag."

"Let it go," he said.

"Let what go?"

Joe wanted to talk about Monica, about how every time she accomplished something Adelaide slipped into sixth gear with her own work. How much of this had to do with Adelaide's usual drive and how much to do with the ordination of a bishop? But they had had that conversation enough times before for Joe to realize that it wouldn't get them any further than they were right now. Marriage seemed to him like an iceberg sometimes, the greatest part of it being the things that weren't said. Rather than speak his thoughts now he said, "Just stop. Wouldn't you like to get some rest? You've been at this pace for as long as I can remember, honey. You don't have to do this."

Adelaide grimaced and brushed his words away like cobwebs. She leaned over to turn out the light and Joe could only hear her whisper, "Yes, I do."

It wasn't one of her cleverer lines. He let her change of mood settle in the room, but the conversation continued briefly, their words drifting up from their pillows and mingling overhead, sound made more significant in the darkness.

"We got an invitation to Palma's Spay Your Cat Foundation fundraiser today. Black tie thing at her place," he started.

"She told me today she dumped Robert. A little effete, but I kind of liked him."

"Let's go."

"Oh, don't make me go. You know how I hate big groups. I don't even like to go to my own openings. And all those women saying things like, 'Darling—I love what you've done to your lips.'"

"It's a good cause."

"I'll send a check."

"It would be good for my business."

"You don't need anymore business. We have plenty of money, remember?"

"Hey, I got ambition, too. It's mostly dogs right now, if you don't count the ferret. Not a bad idea, cats. You know, diversify."

The darkness was silent for a moment. Then, "The vacation thing was just a throw away for negotiation purposes, wasn't it?"

"Yeah," Joe admitted, not adding that he could care less about grooming cats. He just wanted a night out with her.

"Okay. When is it?"

"Three weeks from Saturday."

"Okay." He could hear her yawning, feel her stretching beside him, then rolling over into her usual fetal position, her back to him. He remembered one more thing, and quietly got out of bed. In the kitchen he twisted the heavy metal grounds holder from the espresso maker and washed out the hard wet grounds from that morning's coffee. He opened the glass jar of coffee by the stove and breathed in the burnt chocolate aroma that gave him the same honeyed feeling as fresh garlic or a good Chianti. He scooped two teaspoons of coffee into the holder, tamped it against the compactor on the machine, and added another scoop. The few grains on the edge he smoothed away with his fingers and sniffed at his fingers once more before dusting them off over the glass container. Then he inserted the holder into its groove under the espresso maker. Lastly, he opened the lid over the water tank and filled it to the top. Now it was all ready for Adelaide's cup of espresso in the morning.

Joe turned off the kitchen light and felt for the switch of the nightlight by the sink. It cast enough glow for him to find his way back through the darkened house to the bedroom without stepping on the ferret, which was now in deep conversation with a rubber doorstop. Joe eased his bulk into the bed, turned on his side and very gently placed the cheeks of his backside against Adelaide's.

# Chapter Ten
## In Which the Fourth Miracle Occurs

Driving back to Miami along I-95 from Blessed Redeemer in Fort Lauderdale, Monica glanced at her gloved left hand resting at the top of the steering wheel. She couldn't tell if it was the angle of her hands or her thinking about them that made them bleed. While keeping up her speed to avoid being run over by a semi barreling along behind her she managed to dig into the glove compartment for a paper napkin to wipe up the trickle of blood that seeped from beneath the edge of the glove and nearly disappeared into her jacket sleeve before she caught it. She folded three fingers into the palm of the hand and gingerly pressed, feeling a slight squish. More than just a trickle crept out from beneath the glove. Three waves rapidly passed over her, one of panic, then nausea, then tears.

"Stop it!" she yelled at her hand, fighting back the tears so she could see to keep driving. "Can't you at least stop until I'm off the highway?" Monica raised the hand in frustration to bang it against the steering wheel, but stopped, afraid of what might happen. Instead she blotted her eyes with the dry corner of the napkin and shoved it under the glove, then let the hand dangle over the edge of the seat so any blood would stay in the glove.

Since her hands seemed to act up more when she thought about them, she forced herself to focus instead on the stained glass window she had just finished blessing at Redeemer. During the inevitable cookies and coffee reception following the service she listened while some of the parishioners praised the window excitedly, and heard others say how it had been a pity that the church had spent so much money on a "thing." Monica looked at the "things" about her. The left over coffee at the bottom of her styrofoam cup, jiggling gaily in the cupholder with the vibration of the car. The ratty novel on the floor by the passenger seat, a mystery which she had started six months ago and read only in traffic jams. The rainbow colored yarn crucifix that Palma abhorred dangling from her rear view mirror. If there weren't "things," what was there? She loved all the things about her because they told her who she was. And she loved other people's things. When she visited a home she greedily absorbed the things about her, looking, touching, sometimes wanting to taste their meaning. The photograph albums carefully decorated with padded gingham and eyelet ruffles stuffed with the record of a hundred Christmas celebrations, all blessedly identical. Grandpa's pipe with a nick in the mouthpiece that intimated a man biting down hard on life; she had wanted to take that pipe into her mouth and know him. A thousand beloved books that would never be read again but were kept around as friends, sometimes because of what was in them and sometimes as a way of holding onto the times in which they were read. An entire room preserved just as it had been the last time its occupant was alive.

*These things meant us,* she thought. *Hm, not a bad subject for a sermon if I can figure out what gospel to tie it to. Maybe for a finale I can rip off my gloves and show them my own things.*

There, she was back to it. Two days since the marks had appeared and she couldn't stop thinking about them, as if not thinking about them would make them go away. Should she go to a doctor, a shrink, a psychic or a priest for this problem? Though the bleeding was infrequent the pain was constant, and aspirins only helped a little. She flexed her fingers slightly and felt the nerve running up the inside of her wrist twinge in response. She wondered if the Neosporin she packed under the bandages was necessary. If you got the Stigmata did you have to worry about infection?

*Oh, my God, I thought the word.* Stigmata. There it was again. Her breath held onto the word and she waited, as if expecting something extraordinary to happen now that her brain had accepted full consciousness. She wondered if her hands knew what she was thinking, had heard the word, would react. The left hand dangled limply, quietly, while the right busied itself on the lower curve of the steering wheel, both oblivious to her brain which had come to think of them as independent creatures. She hadn't allowed herself to use the word even inside her brain, but now it had come in, taken up residence, and the hands didn't seem to mind.

Stigmata.
Fancy version of stigma. Stigmatize.
A mark signifying...what? *God, don't do me any favors,* she thought. *Just patch up these holes so I can go about my life. You know I'm no good to you this way. What will Mom say? She'll either say it's a judgment on leaving the True Church or a warning that I should return to it.* No, she wouldn't talk to her mother about this yet, she wouldn't talk to anybody.

As she thought about the singularity of her situation an unfamiliar feeling crept over her, something too cold to be sadness. What was it like? It felt like the air in the car had grown oppressive, heavier, and was both pressing in on her face and pressing out on the world around her forming a barrier to keep her apart. She glanced at the driver passing on her left, an urgent man so youthful he looked like he was playing dress-up in his dark business suit. He seemed to be moving in a different but parallel world on the other side of the air that kept her from him. Monica fought to keep herself from honking the horn to get his attention, to make him pull over and confirm her existence.

If this was loneliness she'd never felt it before. There was no such thing growing up in a large family. She had always felt connected to people, her energy growing in contact and conversation. Now in forty-eight hours she had become detached, and she didn't like it. It occurred to her that this might be how it felt when you were told you had AIDS. Like an alcoholic's need for liquor, her need for another soul was almost physical. She breathed in deeply, drawing in the air around her as if hoping to lessen its pressure, then releasing the breath in a prayer.

What she craved was the company of a listener to whom she could recite the events of the past two days over and over until they made some sense. She wanted to talk about how she had made the discovery, how the blood ran down her arm in the shower just so, and whether Gus had anything to do with it. Most of all she wanted to watch her listener's eyes and read there an affirmation that this was really happening and that everything would be alright. That's how she solved problems, by telling them again and again until the problems became boring or the solution became obvious. The French Hen Society was good for that. At least Palma was, Palma had always been the best listener. Del was different. Tell her any problem and before you had time to get weepy you'd find you were laughing instead. She could use Del's humor about now. So why hadn't she called either of them yet?

Monica noticed she had somehow gotten off the highway at the right exit and was already across the causeway to Miami Beach. The neatly landscaped avenue leading to the cathedral was lined with royal palms and spanish style homes with barrel tiled roofs the color of Georgia clay and wrought iron grates over all the windows as a reminder that Miami held the honor of being one of the crime capitols of the world. Then she saw St. Stephen's. For a moment her air lightened and she felt she was approaching "base" after a breathless game of Tag.

Her attention was drawn to a figure which looked like a giant fiddler crab scuttling from side to side and waving both pincers at once. The excited creature met her halfway up the drive of the cathedral. *Not him, I didn't mean him, Lord, when I said I wanted company. I had nearly anyone else in mind.* With a tremendous mental heave she pushed away the air and reluctantly rolled down her window letting the built up air-conditioning billow into the heat.

"Gus, what are you doing here?" she said.

"What d'you mean, what am I doing here?" he barked like a joyous seal. "Look at me! Look at me!" He did some more of his crab polka, this time rubbing his hands over his arms and legs at the same time as if he were being attacked by a nest of red ants. Monica watched his movements and finally understood.

"You aren't using your canes! What happened? Wait, let me park the car."

She pulled into a space with a sign that said, "Thou Shalt Not Park Here Unless You're a Bishop," and opened the car door.

"Not just the canes," he said, taking her hand and yanking her from the front seat, not noticing how it made her wince, how she looked alarmed and seized her hand back from him. "Look. All those nasty mother fucking sores are gone. I don't have a single one anywhere." Monica stopped him before he could pull down his shorts to verify the fact.

"Come into the office," she said hurriedly, and ushered him through the door where Sharon sat at her desk, looking gleeful.

"The Dean says the sexton quit," the secretary said before the door had closed. "Joined a Christian country band. Said sorry, but this was the break he was waiting for."

"Too bad," Monica responded instinctively, without really having listened. She was distracted by Gus who was doing a few steps he might have seen in a Fred Astaire movie and singing "You and the Night and the Music." It all seemed a little incongruous with his lick it, slam it, puke it t-shirt. Monica grabbed his sleeve before he could take a running leap onto Sharon's desk and pulled him into her office, shutting the door. Once there he made a few pirouettes around the room, then settled down, his jubilation having momentarily exhausted itself. Collapsing into a chair by her desk he rapidly transformed from hysterical joviality to gooey tearfulness.

"Ohmagod, ohmagod, ohmagod, ohmagod," he sobbed in rhythm with his perseverations on the edge of the chair.

"So. Gus. I take it you're pleased that you're feeling better," said Monica in a tone she had learned in a pastoral counseling class, hoping to stabilize him in a single emotion.

"It's you," he blubbered, spitting a tear on the corner of her desk.

"What do you mean, it's me?" she asked.

"I was sitting on the patio, and started to feel this tingle in my legs, like when you exercise and they get kind of itchy. I looked down and the hair was standing nearly straight up, all over them. When I reached down to feel it, I noticed that big ulcer on my shin was gone. Gone, just like that!" he snapped his fingers, and began to re-enact the moment. "I stretched out my legs, like this, gave them a couple of bicycle turns, like this, then just stood up." He fell to his knees and began to move towards her with his hands raised like a pilgrim approaching a shrine. "Oh my God, you healed me! I was washed in your heavenly blood and you healed me!"

"Gus, don't be ridiculous. Get up off the floor," Monica said nervously, hoping Sharon wouldn't choose this moment to come in.

Gus held his ground, and tried to kiss the tips of her gloved fingers which she irritably jerked away.

"I'll do anything for you for the rest of my life," he said, solemnly. "Just ask. Go ahead, ask."

Monica patted his head, feeling like she had just inherited an adoring mastiff. She leaned forward and sniffed him; he didn't even smell anymore. She felt her gray matter sparkle with inspiration.

"You know what you can do for me? You can be the cathedral sexton."

"What's a sexton?"

"Sort of a janitor—but a very special sort of janitor," she said brightly, hoping to cast a religious glow over the postion in response to his frown.

"I don't want to be a janitor."

"Sure you do. Just until the Dean can find someone else and you have time to find a job that suits you. It's a perfect set-up; the job comes with a little apartment next door. What did you do for a living before?"

"I was a ballroom dance instructor."

That took Monica aback a moment as she tried to picture it. Then she called Sharon's name loudly enough for it to carry through the thin door. In a second her phone rang and Sharon's voice was saying, "Is there something I may help you with, Bishop?" Sharon had apparently been trained by the last bishop to insist on professionalism.

"Yes. Tell Dean Ryan I've found a sexton for him. My friend Gus is going to do it."

"Ah-ha," Sharon said, her doubt coming through the phone. "Does he have a different t-shirt?"

"Good point. Can you take him shopping?"

Silence. Then, "I'm sorry, Bishop Laparro, there are some limits to my job."

Monica hung up. Is this really what bishops did for a living? Wasn't she supposed to be, you know, running the diocese? Doing really important stuff like parading around in her mitre blessing new pipe organs? She didn't have time for derelict makeovers.

Makeovers.

Makeovers.

Palma.

Well, it was worth a try.

☿ ☿ ☿

Monica heard the squeal of Palma's pearly white Mercedes sports car as it rounded into the church parking lot. If Palma had lights and sirens, those would probably be going too. She suddenly appeared in the office doorway like the head of the SWAT team for the fashion police. Her white linen slacks, her casual but crisp navy blue striped blouse, and her jaw all had a determined set to them. Monica loved to see Palma when she had a mission. Here was Palma the General, cool and courageous in the face of an outnumbering enemy. Here was Palma the Surgeon, with the patient's blood pressure plunging and a life hanging in the decision of the next moment. Here was Palma the Hero, leading the passengers of a plane crash downed in the Amazon jungles to... Monica shrugged. *So what if it was overkill?*

"Thanks for coming over, Palma," said Monica. "Could you just take him to a thrift shop and get him some jeans and a couple of different shirts?"

Palma strode across the room like Patton about to strike a shell-shocked combatant. Gus cowered appropriately in his chair.

"Hello, I'm Palma Blanco," she said, holding out a hand for him to shake. "How long have you been homeless?"

Monica watched Gus struggle for words, noting that what he finally muttered probably wasn't his first choice; it came out sounding something like, "Ch-ggg."

"This is Gus," Monica said. "He's been at my place the last week." Palma's right eyebrow shot up slightly, whether in shock, admiration, or disapproval, Monica couldn't tell. She continued, "Before that he's been out on the streets for about, what, Gus, four years?"

"Aug," said Gus, seemingly stunned speechless in Palma's presence.

"Up," Palma ordered, gesturing with her hand as if he might not understand the word.

Gus's skinny arms and legs came up off the chair like an unfolding lunar module. His head cleared Palma's by a good six inches.

"Stand up straight, please," she commanded.

Gus's spine lost its curve and he grew another two inches.

"He's awfully thin," Palma said. "What have you been feeding him?"

"I'm pretty sure his main diet has consisted of Marlboro's and cooking sherry," Monica said. Feeling suddenly as if she were in a veterinarian's office, and knowing that Gus could indeed communicate as a human, she addressed him directly. "Have you eaten much while you were at my place?"

"Shtin," he replied uncooperatively, while staring at the shadowy bottom of the V on the front of Palma's blouse.

"I'd say he's about six foot three, one-hundred-and-thirty-five pounds," Palma continued expertly. "Waist thirty, inseam thirty-four. Let's go, Gus. We'll stop and get him a haircut, too."

Gus finally smiled, showing yellowed teeth with brown grouting between each one. Palma lost her poise for a nanosecond.

"And let me borrow your phone. I'll make an appointment with my dentist." Palma turned away to place the call.

"Augustine," he said to her shoulder blade.

She turned around, phone still to her right ear, listening to him with her left. "Hm?"

"My name. My name is Augustine. Augustine Thomas."

"What a nice name," said Palma, then into the phone, "Palma Blanco...I have an emergency...terrific." Her nose quivered delicately over the receiver before replacing it. "Mmm, I don't recognize this perfume, Monica, but it's awfully pretty. What is it?"

Monica lifted her shoulders as if she were going to sniff her armpits, but only shrugged. "I haven't been wearing any perfume. Maybe it's my deodorant."

Palma looked mildly offended at the suggestion that she couldn't tell a good perfume from deodorant. "I don't think so. All right, Mr. Thomas, let's go."

"Have fun," said Monica, waving them off. She stepped over by the window to watch them, Palma marching ahead of Gus with her hips rolling like a seductive Napolean, while he spindled along behind, still a little too shaky on his legs to move as fast as she did. The last thing Monica saw was Palma's car turning out of the driveway with a giant hocker flying through the passenger seat window onto the lawn.

It was only then that her thoughts returned to her hands. She went into the grey and turquoise bathroom just off her office, flicked on the light over the sink and locked the door. From the cabinet underneath the sink she pulled out a container of surgical tape, a tube of Neosporin ointment, and the package of little gauze pillows she had bought at Eckerd's drugstore yesterday and secretly stowed here just in case.

Once these were set on the mica surface of the vanity, she turned her attention to the hands, hovering over the basin of the turquoise sink. The leather gloves resisted until she had picked at the tips of the fingers for several seconds. Then they began to slide reluctanctly away, exposing hands mottled with semi-coagulated blood except for the gauze pillows taped on either side of the wounds. The gauze was saturated evenly with a dark red stain.

She held the hands still a moment, not to examine them, but to identify the strong aroma which suddenly filled the room. It wasn't the usual burnt copper smell of blood, but some sort of flower. Was it roses? Less aggressive than that. Lilacs? She sensed a coolness in her nostrils as if the scent were coming from flowers poking up through spring snow. This must have been what Palma smelled. She went slightly dizzy, whether from intoxication by the smell or lightheadness from the loss of blood she couldn't tell.

First grabbing onto the faucet to steady herself, she turned on the cold water and backed the bulge of her stomach away from the edge of the sink to avoid the water as it splashed onto the gloves. She let the water run into the lining but though it bubbled up a lighter and lighter pink it never came clear so she gave up on the gloves and began to work on the hands instead, gingerly rubbing with her fingertips and a small piece of soap around the bandaging. Most of the blood came away, but she would have to wait until she got home to use a brush to get at the stain under her nails. The wet surgical tape lifted easily from her skin while still attached to the bandaging, a red glop which she left sitting like an animal's heart on the side of the sink.

She cupped her hands under the faucet; the cold water felt good on both sides. With her eyes closed she tried to imagine whether it was overflowing and washing over the backs of her hands or whether it was going straight throught the holes. Unable to tell, she opened her eyes and forced herself to examine the exposed wounds. On both sides of her hands the marks were still there, though no longer bleeding. She didn't think they looked anything but creepy, and they disgusted her. The unmarred tissue that she recognized as hers gave way in the center of her palm to a foreign ridge of whiter puckering flesh which descended into a darkened hole. She stared into the hole like a highway rubber-necker, wondering again if it really went all the way through the way it seemed to.

Her curiosity overcame her loathing. She might as well know. With a bigger sigh than before she quickly held her right hand up to the strong bathroom light and squinted. She didn't need to squint. Her palm was in shadow but plainly showing through the crater in the center was a point of light from the lamp behind her hand, looking like a super nova set against the dark side of the moon.

This affected her where all the blood had failed to and her knees buckled, making her crash against the back wall of the tiny bathroom. Before she could scramble up again Sharon was at the other side of the door.

"I'm sorry, Bishop, but are you all right?"

Monica softly tested her voice to see if it would crack before raising it loudly enough for Sharon to hear. Then she said from her seat on the floor, "Oh, I'm fine, honey, I just stumbled in this little box of a bathroom. Am I that fat you could hear me all the way out in the reception area?"

Sharon laughed. "No, it's just that this bathroom and the reception area share a wall."

"Well, thanks for checking."

"No problem."

She heard Sharon leave and heaved herself up as well as she could without relying too much on the hands for support. It hurt too much and she was afraid to do anything to start them bleeding again. New bandages were taped over a dab of antiseptic cream and the old bandages went into the plastic grocery bag used as a liner in the trash can beside the sink. The soggy leather gloves went into the bag too, after some consideration, and she pulled it out of the can and knotted it. It was only after checking the counter, the floor, and her clothes for traces of blood that she finally unlocked the door and went to her desk to retrieve the totebag which she used for a briefcase. Raising the flap of leather to open it she placed the the bag of gore inside and removed a pair of fuzzy woolen red gloves, amazed that she had had the presence of mind to take the precaution of having a second set with her. This was the last of her glove supply, though a drop of something clear fell on the gloves and she felt her stomach wrench in a moment of panic at this new phenomenon before she was aware that she had been crying.

She sat heavily in the chair behind her desk and stared at the red gloved hands propped up on her elbows. Okay, so she wasn't handling this as well as she thought she was. She wasn't staying cool under the pressure of it. But dammit, she was a bishop, with things to do. She couldn't stay in a locked office all day. And she was beginning to fear that she couldn't keep this a secret until it went away. That was why she was crying, she thought. Not from the sight of the blood, or having to change the bandages, but from keeping the secret. While there was no end to the secrets she had kept for others, she never remembered having one of her own. She didn't like it.

What would Palma do? Call a plastic surgeon? Then she thought about Adelaide. What would Del do?

"Would you like me to get you in to see my dermatologist?"

Monica didn't know how long Sharon had been standing at the door. She stared at the secretary and thought she could feel the secret showing in her eyes.

"Sorry," said Sharon, suddenly acting shy. "I just thought you had a little eczema or something. You know, the gloves."

Monica wiggled her fingers and focused on the red wool, tilting her head like a mountain gorilla discovering opposable thumbs. What would Del do? She looked again at Sharon who looked at her as if she really were a mountain gorilla sitting at the bishop's desk.

"Well, I guess I'll go to lunch," Sharon said, backing slowly out of the door.

Del would research it. Monica came back. "Do I have anything to do for the next couple of hours?"

Sharon looked more comfortable at hearing her speak.

"Preliminary diocesan budget meeting at three."

"Good. Would you bring me a sandwich?"

Sharon nodded and looked even more comfortable at the thought of Monica eating.

☿ ☿ ☿

The first known occurrence of stigmatization (she discovered when she Googled the word) was recorded in 1224 when St. Francis of Assisi received nail marks in his hands and his feet. Monica wiggled her toes gratefully under the desk. At least there was nothing in her instep, thank goodness—yet. She read on. Since that time three hundred people had been reported to exhibit bleeding marks in their hands, feet, side, forehead or, even more bizarre, their ring finger. This last seemed to have occurred exclusively in nuns who were said to be "brides of Christ." The Catholic church wrote off most of these events as having some natural cause.

Louise Lateau, a Belgian who died in 1883, had bleeding marks in her hands one inch long by half an inch wide. Dr. Warlemont of the Belgian Medical Academy enclosed her hand in a glass apparatus to show that the marks bled without any encouragement on Louise's part.

Teresa Neumann, a Bavarian who died in 1962, had marks which were sometimes square and sometimes round.

In 1923 Elena Ajello of Montalto Uffugo, Italy, experienced a vision of the Crown of Thorns. A doctor was called in when she started bleeding profusely from her forehead.

Most stigmatics were women given to mystical ecstasies and the only three men besides St. Francis to have the condition were reported in the twentieth century. The last known stigmatic was Father Pio Forgione, of the Capuchin monastery of San Rotundo near Foggia in Italy who acquired the stigmata in 1915 and died in 1968. While acknowledging that Padre Pio was not hysterical, the Catholic Church ascribed his stigmata to auto-suggestibility. All the investigations of this phenomenon had been conducted by the Catholic Church since Protestants were given to neither hysteria nor mysticism, let alone stigmatization.

Monica finished reading about the other physical phenomena associated with stigmatization. Could she look forward to incombustibility or levitation? Was the aroma of flowers that Palma had noticed, and which struck her so forcefully in the bathroom, the 'odour of sanctity?' The only information she couldn't find on the internet was when the whole business would just go away. Everyone else who was stigmatized seemed to enjoy it, something like having membership in an ultra-exclusive club. A new wave of loneliness swept over her as she thought of herself as the only, the last person in the world to experience this condition, like a surviving religious dinosaur.

Or maybe she was wrong; maybe there were others. She pictured herself in a cluster of people all wearing different colored gloves, people she could talk to about this. Why not? Everybody else was forming support groups.

*"Hello, I'm Monica, and I'm a stigmatic."*

*"Hello, Monica."*

☿ ☿ ☿

Monica's mind wandered in and out of the budget meeting that afternoon. Alternating with attention to a hot debate over medical benefits for clergy spouses were her visions of damp stone convents where pallid women dripped their way through bloodied cloisters. Once she caught the men and women seated around the conference table gazing at her expectantly, as if awaiting a response.

"Eczema," she hazarded. They glanced at one another and went back to the debate leaving Monica to return to her cloisters.

After the meeting she found a note on her desk from Sharon telling her that her editorial for the diocesan newspaper, "Acts," was behind schedule.

"How can I be behind schedule? I just started this job day before yesterday," she complained. "Why wouldn't McKibben have written this one?"

"He thought you'd want to do it, being the new bishop and all. I think it was real thoughtful of him," Sharon added defensively, with old boss loyalty.

Monica sat down to jot some notes comparing the beginning of anything to Genesis. Adelaide would call it cliché, but where there was cliche there was truth. It was seven-thirty before she walked through her front door feeling like she was moving through peanut butter.

As a matter of fact, she smelled peanut butter as she closed the door behind her. Peanut butter and men's cologne.

She followed the scents into the kitchen.

"Where the hell have you been," queried Gus jovially, who was seated on a stool at the pass-through. "Your satay will be dry as a bone."

Between her fatigue, the stress of her new position, what she had discovered on the internet, and the sight before her, Monica felt rushes in her brain like it was working double-time adjusting its perception of reality. She indicated the spread of styrofoam containers and tin foil on the counter.

"What is this?"

"Little strips of beef on bamboo skewers."

"I know what satay is. I mean what is all this food doing here?"

Gus unfolded his legs from around the stool and said casually, "Palma and I had dinner at the Black Thai restaurant and thought it would be nice to bring you some, too."

Monica turned her attention from the food to Gus. From the soles of his burnished Armani loafers to the collar of his Ralph Lauren shirt he reeked of designer label. In place of the big old shorts were a pair of khaki gabardine trousers with a crease that promised not to budge for a millennium. His graying hair was cut short and styled impeccably. His chin even looked bigger. The words *created in her image and likeness* flashed through Monica's frenetically sparking brain. In a single afternoon Palma had transformed Gus into a figure ready for any Coral Gables society function.

"Now quit fuckin' around and have some jumping squid salad."

*Well, maybe not quite ready,* Monica thought, as she pulled down a plate from the cupboard and served herself some pad thai.

# Chapter Eleven
## In Which Ferdy Attempts to Assail Monica, and the Result

The now-familiar perch at the end of Monica's bed made Ferdy think of his post at Notre Dame again. No matter what the job was, a devil spent a lot of time watching. He'd been watching her every moment except for his one visit with Greg at South Beach, saw her cleaning her hands in her office bathroom, reading about fellow stigmatics, and now falling asleep, the muscles of her face slowly relaxing. He closed his eyes and thought about the cathedral guide Yves, how much he had watched him, and how in all their time together he had never seen his old friend's face in repose, unless you counted that last time. A picture of Yves's battered face, perfectly slack and still except where a trickle of blood ran into his unblinking eye gave Ferdy an unaccustomed rush of sorrow and forced his attention back to his SIP. The last thing he needed to do right now was go soft, no matter how much this woman reminded him of his old mortal friend.

Nervously he gazed at the sleeping woman, and felt his heart warm again despite his best intentions. Most humans looked so different when they slept. He had noticed before how their eyelids grew soft, their lips relaxed as if they no longer had to guard their mouths. He pictured a tongue releasing its pressure against the roof of the mouth and sagging wearily into its own bed.

When they were awake most mortals looked like they were prepared to be hurt. Ferdy could see their defenses thrown up with controlled jaws thrust out like an advance army, warning other mortals not to hurt them. He saw muscles held taut over teeth fighting to contain their impotent rage against real and imagined injustices, and their eyelids, flickering the way a snake's tongue picked up danger signals. That's what Ferdy saw in mortals who were awake.

But Monica? That's where she reminded him of Yves. Monica's awake face failed to throw up the usual mask of muscles that barred connection to others. Her mouth invited the whole world in, and her eyes seemed on the look-out for any good joke, even at her own expense. He liked her plain talk and the way her eyes bugged out even more when she was amused. He liked the way she hugged people instead of shaking hands, and wondered how her embrace would feel. He liked the way she treated Gus, misfit that he was, and wondered—if she got to know him— whether she would treat Ferdy the same—

Ferdy jerked to the left as his right wing simultaneously wrenched upwards. Passing through the popcorn ceiling of Monica's room he found himself on her roof, feet dangling just above the barrel tiles. Gregory seemed a couple feet taller than before and had one claw wrapped around Ferdy's wing. The struggle to touch his toes to the roof's surface was futile so he finally went limp, and met Gregory's white eyeballs with his blackberry ones. The stench of gunpowder mixed with bowel wrenching fear told him Gregory had just come from Lebanon.

"What are you doing here?" Ferdy squeaked. "I told you I could do this alone."

"The Boss called me in for a special assignment. Told me to keep an eye on you. It's a good thing, too. I saw what you were thinking down there." Gregory gave the wing he held a playfully vicious shake. "Not doing a frozen yogurt, are you, Ferdbrain? Not dishin' us a soft serve?"

Ferdy was accustomed to conversations in which there was an "us" he was never part of. What he wasn't accustomed to was having those conversations while being hoisted like a recalcitrant puppet. "Greg, do you think you could put me down so I can really concentrate on what you're saying?"

Gregory tossed him as if he were a wet tissue onto the roof, and dropped onto his back with his elbows propping him up, uttering an elaborate sigh of disgust. Ferdy took a moment to stretch out the wing still twisted in the shape of Gregory's grip. Then he sat down cross-legged with a smile he hoped was sufficiently obsequious. "I was just observing her, Greg, trying to figure out what her weak spot was so I could, you know, attack it in her nightmares."

"And?"

"And?"

"And what's her weak spot?"

Coming from Gregory the ss's were a little too reptilian for comfort so Ferdy edged further away from him before continuing.

"Well, I hadn't quite found it yet," he confessed.

There was a pause, long enough for Ferdy to grow aware of the rough tile, still warm from the day, pressing against his bum. The tile contrasted with the cool offshore breeze ruffling through the line of fur down the center of his head. Except for the sound of Gregory's mouth breathing the night was so quiet Ferdy could almost hear the creak of his neck when Gregory turned his head to stare at him.

"You know," said Gregory, "I gotta ask this even though I'm afraid I already know the answer. Have you ever done this before?"

Ferdy felt his sphincter muscle seize up in dread of his own response. "No, but listen, Greg," he went on rapidly, "I got the manual, and you know I can read thoughts real good, so it shouldn't be much different—"

Ferdy found himself stunned silent before Gregory's stare. The mouth breathing came faster, before Gregory launched into, "Aw, man, oh, Enemy Incarnate, I've been set up, I've been fucking set up! First I'm given responsibility for an imbecile, then I find out the imbecile is totally clueless! Is this a joke or is someone out to get me? I recommended you for this gig, and do you realize what will happen to me if you fuck this up?" Recognizing a rhetorical question when he heard it, Ferdy leaped to his feet rather than come up with an answer, but Gregory was faster and had a claw around his ankle before he could get away. He jerked Ferdy down hard beside him and leaned close, his voice whispering across Ferdy's ear like a warm snake.

"When I find the angel fucker who got me involved with you again I'm going to chew him a new asshole and eat him from the inside out."

Ferdy wisely didn't remind him that pressing Ferdy back into service had been Gregory's own idea. The only other response that came to mind was to try to lick the toes on the foot that was free from Gregory's grip but Gregory slapped him to attention.

"Stop that. We have to think clearly now. So tell me again, you've never assailed before."

"No, but like I said, I've been going into people's thoughts a lot lately."

"That's different. You don't really go into minds when you read thoughts, you bring the thoughts out. You have no idea what happens when you actually let yourself go into a mortal mind, let alone manipulate his thoughts, let alone torment the hell into him."

"Her."

"Whatever."

"But I did read the manual."

"Shit, that's like trying to create life with a cookbook. I better do it."

Ferdy thought of Monica sleeping helplessly below him. "No! I mean, there's always gotta be a first time, right Greg? I bet there was a first time for you. Just talk me through it. I promise I'll stay focused and on task and make you proud. This could mean some big points for you at headquarters, if you mentor Ferdy the Imbecile and he succeeds, eh, Greg, buddy?"

Gregory paused again, then nearly smiled. "You know, given your inexperience there's even a good chance you won't survive."

Ferdy felt a wad of saliva appear in his throat, wanted to gulp but didn't, wanting more to hide his apprehension. He felt his voice gurgling around the wad as he peeled Gregory's claw from his ankle. "There you go. You gotta keep a positive attitude."

☿ ☿ ☿

A few minutes after his briefing Ferdy reclined on top of Monica, the tip of his beak almost touching her nose, his skinny torso curving around the mound of her belly, the claws on his toes resting just above her knees. His wings spread like a greasy tarpaulin over their heads. Gregory had told Ferdy what to expect in Monica's mind; he'd also told him what to avoid, though he hadn't said why. Ferdy was more nervous than ever, but figured he'd rather take his chances inside Monica's brain than go back up to the roof. He deliberately slowed the rate of his breathing down to hers so that their melding wouldn't jolt her awake; then he softly blew his own breath into the tiny space between her lips as Gregory had taught him.

And he was in.

That part was easy, and he didn't see anything to be frightened of. Actually, he didn't see anything at all. Where before he had been in a small bedroom hemmed in by walls and ceiling, and even before that, on the roof looking at a universe hemmed in by dark and stars above, earth below, now his view was limitless, filled with absolutely nothing. All around him was whiteness. There was nothing of created nature here, just an unlimited paleness without variation, texture, or flaw. Gregory had described this unused part of the brain to him not as nothing, but rather as a magnificent capacity for something.

Ferdy looked around and thought about these mortals with pity and a little awe. In the time allotted to them they filled a miniscule amount of the space provided them in their brains, like a library of a thousand floors containing only one book. Gregory said The Boss loved this part of the brain. Mortals would like to think he'd prefer their brains filled with evil, but The Boss said there was often passion in evil, and where there was passion there was hope. "Nothing" was the surer way to despair. That's why The Enemy abhorred a vacuum. *But if that's the case,* thought Ferdy, *why did he create the mortal mind like this? Why take the risk of allowing all this capacity for nothing?*

Ferdy shook his head ruefully and forced his attention back on task. He was doing more thinking lately but suspected it would only get him into trouble. Focus...focus...not knowing how long it would take to find Monica's dreams, he figured he had better get started if the job was to be finished by morning. He gave his wings one brisk pump and shot a million miles through the white void with the ease of a baby's sigh. Two more pumps like the first and he thought he detected some color ahead.

One more pump and he broad-sided a red bicycle.

Carefully extracting his beak from between the spokes he sat down on what was now a firmer surface, somewhere between concrete and stale jello. This must be Monica's memory bank, where she stored everything that had ever happened to her, no matter how trivial. The bicycle had blue and white plastic streamers on the handlebars and training wheels and had been floating above the surface where he sat. Now the wheels started to turn again as the bike rode away. Ferdy looked after it and felt his jaw drop.

There were things as far as he could see. All kinds of things jumbled in odd combinations and everything in constant movement, a circus with countless rings. He wandered among them in fascination, momentarily forgetting both his apprehension and his reason for being there. A french provincial bedroom dresser swayed to a swing melody, its surface covered with fish swimming in an aromatic marinara sauce. A television showing a close-up of a carroty-haired woman with a ridiculous grimace floated by on the back of a strolling encyclopedia. Fifty decorated Christmas trees changed position like soldiers in a close quarter drill. The movement made the things seem alive, and Ferdy put out his hand to touch a red felt skirt with a large poodle applique as it jitterbugged past him, to see if it had the feel of a living creature. Instead of the softness he expected, the fabric felt stone hard. He turned back and touched other things to see if they were the same. Sure enough, the Christmas trees seemed to be made of glass shards with ornaments that wouldn't break no matter how hard he squeezed, and even the marinara sauce resisted his touch like dried paint when he tried to dabble his fingers in it. The memory of these things was somehow more solid than the actual things had been.

A raucous seagull flew by, smelling of warm salt feathers, and he grew aware of other creatures. Millions of people, some upside down but not seeming to mind, having the conversations of Monica's life. Millions of Monicas, at every age, distinguishable by her outsized face even as a child. Sounds of laughter and sighing. Smells of babies and the disguised formaldehyde of funeral parlors. No one took notice of him; this was all the past and couldn't be affected by the present. The way he was heading grew denser, and he carefully picked his way through the crowds and things, stepping out of the way to avoid a pack of racing children or a skillet sizzling by, pungent with sauteeing onions. Ferdy noted wryly that, besides people, food seemed to take up a lot of her memory. He headed on.

After a long while the memories thinned out and he looked around, wondering again where to look for Monica's dreams. But before he could decide on a direction, he heard something like wind and something like the buzzing pound of a downed power line. The hair on his back stood up as if air had crawled under his skin. A sudden breeze turned into a wind while the sound intensified into a heavy rhythmic beat so powerful it made his wings vibrate. The fear in his belly told him this was what Gregory had warned him about and it seemed to be getting nearer all the time. He thought of running, wanted to run, but didn't know which way to go because he couldn't tell where the danger was coming from. He pictured a giant Gregory, ten times the size of his cathedral, running toward him, the sound coming from the beating of his footsteps. His heart pounded with the beat and he planted his feet as firmly as he could against the expected onslaught because he sensed it was too late to run anyway. It wasn't Gregory.

Monica's imagination was coming to get him.

Within the next second he was torn from where he stood and swept into a tornado-like wind, totally powerless to resist the force of its crushing weight on his tiny frame. The whirlwind roared and turned in on itself like a wild animal biting itself free from a trap, as if desperate to escape the confines of this mortal mind, as if it were something too powerful to be trapped within a single being. Arms and legs helplessly stretched out as far as they could go, unable to even close his eyes, he cart-wheeled through the wind as it pinned him into itself and carried him swirling wherever it pleased. Ferdy's mind was trapped, too, all his senses violated, benumbed in the pounding churn of the tempest, unable to think, let alone react to the horror of what might happen next.

But slowly, slowly, as he tumbled and soared and plunged through the writhing blast, a part of his mind became aware of what made up the wind. It felt warm and wet as if he were an embryo encased in a furious womb. He glimpsed contrasting colors and smells and sounds all mixed together so that he couldn't tell where one sense left off and another began; he sensed a diesel fume sopranic C above high C in the violence of a rainbow. It was as if this was the exact opposite of the part of Monica's brain where there was nothing. Here there was everything, all at once, packed into one intense space like the universe just before the Big Bang. He felt his wings begin to spin in its churning and opened his mouth to scream. The noise around him was so loud he couldn't tell if he really screamed or not, but only felt his jaws held open wide, unable to close them again as his mouth filled with a magenta shriek, and then with all the colors of Monica's mind.

Gasping for breath, choking on what had slipped down his throat just moments before, Ferdy was suddenly surprised to find himself sitting in a quiet corridor with no sign of the imagination that had buffeted him. He simply stared and listened to his own panting for awhile before taking stock of his condition. Like Jonah spewed from the whale he partly sat, partly splattered against the wall. He lowered his foot from where it had been resting against the side of his face, pulled in his arms from where they had sprawled at odd angles on the floor, and examined his limbs with disgust. They were covered with something that could have been whale vomit if it had a bad smell, which it did not. His wings, one of which he had to peel from where it was plastered wetly against the wall behind him, were pitifully denuded of the thin ebony feathers they had sported before, and now showed only a leathery surface spotted here and there with a few stubborn fluffs.

The condition of his wings shocked him more than anything. Over his existence nothing mortal had been able to touch him, let alone harm him. Yet the few moments spent in the maelstrom of Monica's imagination damaged him more than the wear of countless depraved millennia. Then he remembered something that Gregory had mentioned.

The imagination was where The Enemy liked to come and rest.

Ferdy shuddered and hoped there was another way out of here.

Voices down the corridor trickled into his perception and brought his attention back to the mission at hand. Damn it, she was probably already dreaming and he was late, let alone in control of it. Now he'd have to improvise. Ferdy crept along plush red carpet to a set of open double doors and stepped just inside.

There was a play going on in a small theater. The house lights were dim but not completely darkened, so Ferdy could see the faces of the audience. They must have been people from Monica's memory bank, clergy and parishioners she had known, friends and acquaintances. Her family, all of them sitting in one row, arguing quietly. Her friends Palma and Gus seated together. And a stern looking Adelaide, standing up in front row center. Joe seated, holding an open book next to her. Monica was center stage, standing alone in a spotlight. She was dressed in a floor length white sheet, dampening under the lights like a snowman in the spring. White cardboard wings trimmed with silver glitter were fastened to her back. A halo, attached to a wire extending upwards from her head, perched precariously above her. She looked uncomfortable and stiff, only her eyebrows twitching uneasily, as if fearful that the halo would slip. Monica whispered a word over and over in Adelaide's direction. Ferdy cautiously walked up the side aisle and leaned forward to hear.

"Line!"

Joe looked expectantly at Adelaide, who irritably waved a hand in assent.

"Fear not," prompted Joe in a stage whisper, reading from the book.

"Fear not," Monica repeated, loudly enough for the audience to hear, "For...for..."

"Behold I bring..." Joe hissed.

"For behold I bring..."

"Oh, stop." Adelaide stood up. "Monica, if you want to be in the limelight, for god's sake do it with a little panache. You said you wanted to be in the pageant. You have a very important part here, albeit only a few terribly significant lines. What did I tell you about a few lines?"

"There are no small parts, there are only small actors," Monica recited.

"And for the last time, are you committed to this show or not?"

Monica nodded vigorously, and then stopped her head abruptly while the halo continued to tremble.

"All right, then." Adelaide started to pace in front of the stage.

Monica looked slightly alarmed and gestured discretely at the crowd in the theater.

"I don't care. We have to get this right and besides you don't know your lines anyway, so what difference does it make? Okay, let's go over the back story one more time. You are the angel announcing the birth of Jesus Christ. You have been waiting in the bullpen of heaven ever since your creation. This moment is your destiny and you are understandably proud and excited. You arrive effervescent with angelic ebullience. Are you with me so far?"

Monica nodded again, less vigorously than before, careful of her halo.

"So when you say, 'Fear not,' you have to imagine how much you're frightening those shepherds with your metaphysical power, etc., etc., by the way, where are the shepherds?"

"Here," came a voice from backstage with a small scuffling sound and a low current of "baa-as."

"You're just not convincing me that you're frightening," Adelaide continued. "Frighten me." She stopped pacing and stood with arms crossed, apparently in expectation of being frightened.

Ferdy was close enough now to see the perspiration building on Monica's upper lip as she stood stunned into immobility before Adelaide. It was now or never to take control of the situation. He thought a moment and then concentrated on Monica, beginning to mold her dream, changing it to a nightmare. Under his control the halo descended until it rested over her brow. The wire turned to twig. Small thorns jutted out and into her forehead. Monica raised a thumb to wipe a trickle running down the bridge of her nose and wiped it discretely on her angel costume.

"Good Lord," Adelaide said.

"What's wrong?" Monica whispered.

"What is that?"

Monica looked where Adelaide was pointing to a gash of red where she had wiped her thumb on her costume. She touched her forehead again and looked at the blood on her fingertips. Not knowing what else to do with the blood she stuck her fingers in her mouth and mumbled, "Nudthing, Del."

"This just isn't working," Adelaide said. "Maybe what we need here is more conflict. You."

Ferdy watched Monica turn her eyes to him. He broke concentration to see that Adelaide was speaking to him.

"Yes, you. The little devil thing over there."

Ferdy felt all the faces in the audience swing towards him in a single motion. He hadn't known that he was visible in Monica's dream. He smiled tentatively and waved, shy at being seen by mortals for the first time.

"That's right, you. I want you to enter stage right, say something evil and stab Monica."

"Stab Monica?" Ferdy raised his hands to show Adelaide they were empty and discovered a fine rapier in his right claw.

"No, sweetie," Adelaide said. "Stab Monica. Go ahead, cross left."

Ferdy advanced across the stage towards Monica in as menacing a manner as he could. He wondered on the way if Adelaide were as big a bitch as Monica painted her in her dreams. Monica still stood frozen on center stage gazing at him fearfully while trying to keep the blood trickling down her face from reaching her angel costume. She looked like she wanted to run, but couldn't; like a demon who was about to get laid off. Ferdy knew that this was just a dream, that he couldn't really hurt Monica. Just the same, the look in her eyes made it hard to keep advancing. It occurred to him suddenly that he had never, ever actually hurt anyone, even in a dream. Thinking of Gregory's comment about his going soft, Ferdy scowled to himself and stiffened his resolve.

"Good!" Adelaide yelled. "Now, say something evil."

Ferdy thought. "I am going to *kill* you," he declaimed as dramatically as possible.

"Hold it!" Adelaide allowed everyone to wait while she leisurely extracted an already lit cigarette from her blouse pocket and took a couple of long drags.

"I am going to kill *you?*" Ferdy tried.

"No, not evil enough." Adelaide continued to draw on the cigarette and watch Ferdy through narrowed thinking eyes. "Try saying, 'I love you, Monica.' Say that."

Experiencing humans at their dream core was more bizarre than anything Ferdy had experienced in hell. But he could think of no other alternative at the moment, so he raised the rapier, shouted, "I love you, Monica!" and rushed her. His progress across the small stage took much longer than he would have expected. As he ran he saw her turn to face him as if in response to his words, her arms raising in a gesture of welcome more than wide enough to take him in. The trickle of blood from her brow ran in a stronger stream not only down her nose, but down either side of her cheeks as well. Her white costume was reddening from the shoulders down as the cloth invited the blood through it. Ferdy noticed for the first time that her raised hands were gloveless. The blood gushed from her palms as well. It was, in fact, beginning to puddle messily on the stage and flow down over the footlights, sizzling as it made contact with the heat, thickening to the consistency of high grade motor oil, but with the smell of incense.

Ferdy hit the red gooey mess on the stage before he reached Monica, and felt his feet scrabbling behind in the stickiness to catch up with his body which was still in forward motion. He fell into her arms like a long lost love except for the rapier thrusting through her. Monica caught him in her arms at the same time. The now soggy vermilion sheet completely enfolded him, so that only his face was visible, pressed against Monica's bosom. The rapier stuck out behind her but she didn't seem to notice.

"I love you, too," she murmured into the top of his head.

"Can't either of you take direction?" Still embracing, Ferdy and Monica turned their heads to Adelaide who took a last disgusted drag on her cigarette and flicked it into the puddle of blood that had collected at her feet.

The two on stage watched the blood ignite where the cigarette hit. A little yellow flash and the fire licked out in both directions. Adelaide was the first to go up. She watched fascinated as her feet popped and crackled like gun powder which finally caught and shot her up into the sky over what had now become an ancient outdoor amphitheater. The audience screamed and scrambled over the tiered stone seats to escape getting torched while Adelaide exploded gleefully over their heads and rained down in little white sparkles that whispered, "I'm in lights! I'm in lights!"

The fire lapped up the blood in its path and molded it into a slowly growing ball of flame as it rolled lazily toward the two on stage. Remembering how the run-in with Monica's imagination had felt, Ferdy struggled to escape Monica's grasp. This had gone way out of his control; he hadn't expected to be sucked into his own assailing. But despite all his straining to push her away she clamped onto him tightly, ignoring the fire and the pandemonium of the crowd. "Fear not," she said. The flames crept closer while on the top row of the amphitheater a fat Roman emperor fiddled, "You and the Night and the Music." A short bald man dressed in a Roman tunic walked out onto the stage, stepped around the puddles of burning blood and began to orate.

"Men of Athens, I see that in everything that concerns religion you are uncommonly scrupulous. For as I was going round looking at the objects of your worship, I noticed among other things an altar bearing the inscription "To an Unknown God." What you worship but do not know—that is what I now proclaim."

"It's—it's..." gasped Ferdy, his attention temporarily ripped away from his impending *auto da fé*.

"Yes, I know. I always seem to dream about Saint Paul," said Monica blithely, and kissed the top of his beak where it met his eyes.

The small fire ball rolling towards them finally hit their feet and twirled up around their bodies like a frozen yogurt swirl. Every muscle in Ferdy's body clenched with anticipation of pain while he made a promise to himself to never assail anyone again if he survived this. But rising out of his fear came the awareness that he felt absolutely delightful. The fire was as soft and nurturing as the bath Joe had given him, only more playful. Rambunctious puppy flames tongued his ears and giggled against his skin. The smell he recognized now as lavender. He relaxed, and could have stayed in Monica's arms forever except that she was suddenly spoiling the moment, raising her head and shouting, not in fear, or in pain, but in frustration.

"HOT FLASH!"

☿ ☿ ☿

At the sound of her own cry Monica awoke, the sheets and her nightgown soaked with perspiration. She was used to the hot flashes, but not to the accompanying nightmare. Well, not a nightmare exactly—she didn't remember feeling very scared—but a whole lot more bizarre than a dream. And she didn't need a Jungian analyst to interpret for her that enough was enough. Throwing off the sodden sheet she rolled out of bed without waiting for the air-conditioning to dry her sweat. It was six-thirty in the morning but daylight savings time provided at least as much light in the room as in a movie theater before the feature attraction. She peeled off her nightgown like a wet sausage casing and, using her chenille bathrobe from the foot of the bed, swabbed the sweat from her body. Jerking open a dresser drawer she grabbed a pair of shorts and t-shirt at random, pulling them on without noticing either her arthritis or her lack of underwear. This was no time to worry about appropriate attire. This was a showdown.

Seventeen minutes later she unlocked the door of St. Steven's Cathedral. Monica walked down the center aisle which was dimly illuminated by the sunrise coaxing its rays through the heavy stained glass. She moved with icy calm like a gunfighter meeting her nemesis at high noon. Only her eyebrows, pulled together so tightly in a frown that they almost met, betrayed her anger. Hanging tautly at her side were her fuzzy red gloved hands, fingers curved slightly inward as if ready to go for a gun.

Ferdy had followed along and watched curiously from up on his rafter in the darkness where the sunrise couldn't reach. He had no idea what Monica was up to, but he knew she looked pissed. If she was about to reject the Enemy he guessed he could take some credit. A little thrill of triumph rippled between his shoulder blades and mixed unexpectedly with a thump of sadness deep in his gut. When Monica was derailed he wouldn't be seeing her, or Joe, or Palma anymore. He thrust his beak forward from his perch and stared as fixedly as a bird of prey while she stopped about twenty feet short of the altar.

Monica hadn't been sure of what she would do when she got to the church. What was clear to her was that years of Episcopalian restraint were about to give way to a childhood of Mediterranean passion, a passion that only the being who was now on the receiving end knew anything about. She lifted the classic Italian index finger of accusation and pointed it at the altar, unable to speak while the finger silently jabbed forward several times. The finger acted like an old fashioned oil pump. When she was sufficiently primed, the well blew.

"Whadya doin' here!" she finally yelled. "Do you want me to do this job or not?! I know you don't give much of a rat's ass whether we're Episcopalians or Jews or Baptists or Hindus because your thoughts are *so far* above our thoughts and all that crap. But I kind of thought you'd at least like it if I did this—you know, just to help further your cause. But, whadya doin' here? I can't be a bishop if I'm a freak, can I?" The words had gushed out, and she only took a quick breath before continuing. "Couldn't you just tell me not to take the job? That would have been *fine* with me, honest! A simple "no" would have been *fine!* I try to listen, you know I try to listen—couldn't you just give me a less obvious sign—like not being voted in? Do you have any idea how this is gonna look to the members of this diocese? Do you even give a shit?"

She stopped, out of words only for a moment. The finger wasn't giving her argument the force she intended. She needed to kick something, throw something. She grabbed a dark blue hymnal from its wooden compartment on the back of a pew and heaved it in the direction of the altar. It opened as it flew, its pages flapping like wings helping to carry it. Narrowly missing the large Paschal candle in its stand on the left the book fell on a straight-backed chair against the wall of the sanctuary. She thought that felt pretty good, so she threw another and another, seizing hymnals and red prayer books all the way down one of the pews and pitching them in the direction of the altar. Some fell inside the sanctuary, some were a direct hit on the massive white marble table and one even struck the Sanctus bell on the floor and made it ring. But as her energy spent itself most of the books fell short of the altar rail.

Her hands were throbbing painfully now, and that quieted her down even more. She stopped for a moment listening to her breathing; then moving out from the pews, Monica climbed the three steps into the sanctuary and glared at the area in general. Her eyes finally rested on the clear glass sconce on the wall to the right with a candle that always burned, signifying the eternal presence of the Divine.

"Hah! I'll snuff you out. How do you like that?" She stumbled over the books through the doorway to the area just in back of the sanctuary where long-handled candle snuffers sat in a rack like billiard cues. Grabbing one of the snuffers she approached the sanctuary light and clamped the silver cup over the sconce, watching as the flame began to die. But when the light had shrunk down until there was only a yellow and blue glow at the base of its wick, she pulled the snuffer away and watched the candle spring to life again. There was such a creaturely aspect to the flame, she couldn't bring herself to kill it, and that took from her whatever fight had remained. When she spoke to the flame, it was with a quieter voice than before.

"You know, Dad, I've never questioned you before. Even the things that don't make sense. Cancer, palmetto bugs, my looks. Did you ever hear me complain that I never got to be the queen of the May Crowning? Have I ever pitied myself for not having the husband I wanted? Have I ever been bitter about people laughing at my looks behind my back? No." Monica stopped to wipe her nose with the tip of a red fuzzy finger, but she wasn't finished.

"You saw the pictures, Dad. All those gorgeous women, swooning in the arms of their confessors with the marks of the crucifixion on their hands and feet. Even St. Francis with his delicate beard. They were all so beautiful. And thin. They were really thin. Are you getting this? Are you picking up on the extreme dissimilarities here? Thin—fat. Beautiful—ugly. Look at me! Look at what you created! Do you really want one of your children to go around looking like a harpooned whale? What will it get you when they start laughing at me this time?"

Monica stopped again and the answering silence pounded on the ears of both mortal and devil.

"Look, I know it's absurd to make deals with you," she continued after a space. "I'm the first to tell people that. But I've pretty much towed the line, haven't I? I acknowledge that there's something of pride in all this bishop stuff, and I'm sorry about that, but I knew you could even use my pride to make something useful happen. I've played the fool to counteract the pride, Dad, but so far I've played the fool on my terms."

Monica lifted her hands and slowly peeled off the gloves. A trace of pink showed on the gauze bandages which grew redder and redder and she unwrapped them. The punctures still showed in her palms but they weren't bleeding right now. She raised her palms to the figure of the *Christus Rex* hanging on the back wall of the sanctuary.

"See, this is what I look like, with my terminally bad hair, and my too big face, and my excess blubber, overused, and my stigmata.

Some package, eh? Is this really what you want the world to see? A circus act of the crucifixion? Ladies and gentlemen, right here under the big tent, keep your eyes on ring three and see Monica the Clown in our very own passion play!"

Monica dropped to her knees before the cross and then was down full length on the floor, red palms pressed against red carpet. The tears that had been leaking out over the last few days finally came in a torrent that was forced from her eyes and throat and nose by her great sobs. For a long time she cried for herself, and for everything she thought she was in danger of losing—her life, her career, her faith, her place as a regular member of humanity. When the sobs finally died, Ferdy had to strain to hear her whisper her prayer into the carpeting.

"Won't you grant me just—a—little—dignity?"

Ferdy listened as hard as he could. He had never heard the Enemy speak before, but knew it sometimes happened, and if ever there was a time...he felt a filling up of the church with something other than sunlight. It was more like a slow pulse of air reaching into the tiniest crevice in the farthest reaches of the choir loft. He could feel the very walls strain with the same pressure that he could feel against his skin. And against his skin the pulse of air felt most like the word NO. He couldn't tell if it were his imagination or a door opening at the back to let in a draft of morning air. Whatever it was, Monica heard something like it, too. He could tell by her shudder, which turned into one last sob, which turned into a stillness.

The stillness turned into Melba McGregor, come to prepare the altar for morning mass, who turned on the sanctuary lights and saw the bishop lying face down on the floor.

"Oh, my God!" she screamed.

"Amen," muttered Monica, not looking up.

# Chapter Twelve
## In Which Adelaide Falls the First Time

One hour later and twenty six thousand feet over Lake Okeechobee in central Florida, God was speaking. Well, not precisely God. On a Delta flight headed to New York, Adelaide Siren tapped out his final monologue for "Sex and the Holy Trinity" on a lap top computer spanning her bony knees. God was saying:

God: And finally, how do I feel about sex? (pause, then sadly) It was just a gift, you know. Like food could have been created as some gray paste, but I thought of making it pleasurable for you. Same with sex. You had to reproduce yourselves, so why not make it fun? Just a little something to counterbalance all the pain you were going to feel trying to become like me. I never thought it would become such a big problem. (pause) You know, if I were The Enemy, here's what I would do. I would find the most trivial fault I could, something really venial, and convince you that it was by far The Most Significant Sin in the Entire World. Then, while you were obsessing about that sin, focusing inward, I could lead you into all the others while you weren't paying attention. I could churn your guilt until it foamed up and filled your mind, blocking out thoughts of anyone else. I could keep you up at night beating yourself up for yesterday's infidelities so you never remember to take out today's garbage for the person sleeping next to you. I could have you so busy worrying about whether your gay neighbor is going to influence your kid that you never notice the child living in the cardboard box on the next block. And I could turn you into one black hole of self-centeredness, forever falling in upon itself. And that, my children, is Hell. (pause) Sex. Come on, I dare you, ask me really important questions. Like how do I feel about not giving blood? How do I feel about corporate downsizing? How do I feel when you cut someone off in traffic? How do I feel when you don't have your cat neutered? How do I feel when you gossip and call it Christian concern? How do I feel when you use the copy machine at work to copy something personal? (voice rising) Isn't there anybody out there to ask me how I feel about that? (shouting) Hello?!

(He listens to the silence, then moves way downstage center and sinks to his haunches to get as close to the audience as possible)

God: Tell you what. I don't care if you have sex. Go home and have sex. Two, three times. With yourself or someone else. Either gender. I don't care. But when you do, you can do one thing for me. Ask yourself a question. It's the only question I care about, the only one that matters. Ask yourself (he pronounces each word carefully) Is-this-a-kind-thing? Is this the kindest thing I can do in this moment? Because that's a focus outward. Get it? It's what I've been trying to make you think of since I started this whole show. Forget the word Love. It's fallen into disrepair and confusion in this generation. Just be kind. Then you can fuck your brains out for all I care.

(Curtain)

    Over the final parenthesis Adelaide's little finger trembled, her mouth slightly open and breathing hard with effort. She felt her eyes grow wet with the emotion of the final birth push of the play. There it was, a part of her apart from her, saved to a disk rather than a crib, but just as certainly a child. Of all her children, this was the favored, her best. Without calling it so, this was the closest she ever came to love.
    It wasn't that she didn't recognize love. She'd been observing it and documenting it ever since she was a child, ever since she discovered she was a writer. Putting it into the mouths of a thousand characters. Take that elderly couple across the aisle. Adelaide found herself suddenly listening, changing to a fresh

screen on her computer and rapidly typing their dialogue as the woman nagged the man about his in-flight breakfast.

"Look at that pancakes and syrup. Why are you eating that?"

"Pancakes and syrup is what they gave me. What do you expect me to eat? The butter?"

"The butter would be better than the pancakes. Why have me fix you all those steaks for the Atkins diet and then you do this? Pancakes have all those carbohydrates. You'll go out of ketosis."

"Three weeks ago you didn't know a carbohydrate from a carburetor. Now I'm married to a goddam biochemist."

"You're losing weight aren't you? Stop whining."

"So, you want me to starve? Would that make you happy? You want me to pass out in front of the kids rather than go out of ketosis?"

"You could have eaten the sausage. The sausage is on the list."

"It looks like a poodle turd."

"It's on the list."

The man picked up the sausage with his fingers and poked it in his mouth, licking the greasy syrup off his thumb while he spoke. "There. I ate the sausage. Now will you shut up about the ketosis?"

"It's too late. You already ate the pancakes."

"Aaaaa," said the man, waving a hand in her direction as if she were a disagreeable smell.

Adelaide couldn't figure out whether the sound and gesture indicated one last weak defense or complete surrender. Whatever it was, the woman seemed content and withdrew her attack. After the stewardess picked up the remains of the offending breakfast the couple sat quietly, holding hands. Adelaide sighed contentedly and saved their conversation under AC.doc where she kept her aging couples. That was indeed the dialogue of love. Yep, she thought with a self-satisfied mental pat, she recognized love when she saw it.

She still remembered the first time she had observed it. Elena Garcia had invited her over to swim when she was in the first grade at St. Anthony's. They played Marco Polo until their toes bled from the marcasite on the pool floor, then put on some of Elena's heavy school socks and swam some more before they wore the bottoms out. As the late afternoon took the sharpness off the day's heat they sat at a shady picnic table on her back porch cramming their mouths full of Charles's Chips which they scooped from a huge brown can with water wrinkled fingers. Adelaide wondered if her own eyes were as red as Elena's and her lips as blue. If the girls were cold, they ignored it rather than stop their assault on the potato chips. Mrs. Garcia must have looked out a window and seen them shivering, though, because she bustled out clucking with two rainbow striped beach towels under her arm.

Adelaide was the first to have a towel draped around her shoulders; she could still remember the smell of fabric softener mixing with the sharpness of chlorine that clung inside her nose. Unfolding the other towel, and holding it out wide, Mrs. Garcia next swooped down on Elena as if she were going to smother her. Elena laughed and pretended to dodge the attack, but the towel and Mrs. Garcia's ample arms were around her in an instant. Adelaide started to laugh, too, but stopped when Mrs. Garcia and Elena stopped. She watched them for the long moment they spent, Elena smiling in her mother's arms. She thought it was the most interesting thing she'd seen in all her six years. Then Mrs. Garcia looked across the table and something made her give Adelaide a hug too.

She looked at her watch, noticed the white slivers forming over the pink part of her nails and began a quick manicure with her teeth. Nothing to do and one more hour left in the flight. This was why she hated planes; too much time for thinking. A brief spin in therapy at Joe's suggestion fifteen years ago had made her do all the thinking she could ever want to do.

Self-awareness was highly overrated. So what if she had been brought up in a non-nurturing home with benign neglect by parents who probably hated each other's guts though they never said one way or the other? So what? They were just plain mean. She was mean, too. It was a genetic thing she might as well accept.

She remembered the first time she recognized the meanness, too. Her grandparents on her mother's side had come down from Cleveland for a visit at Easter time when Adelaide was seven, and on Holy Week break from the third grade at St. Anthony's. Adelaide didn't like her grandpa Emery because he had a harsh too-deep voice and a dark bushy mustache that grew well over his upper lip so when he spoke it seemed only his lower jaw moved like a ventriloquist's dummy.

Her grandmother's name was Elizabeth, but Emery called her "Elsie." Gramma was huge, not with the welcoming, pillowy hugeness of some grammas, but with the shape and massiveness of a small refrigerator. Kissing her cool smooth cheek made Adelaide think of a refrigerator, too. It was hard to think of Gramma being budged against her will, let alone knocked down, so the whole family listened open-mouthed while Adelaide's father told his tale at Easter brunch.

"You should have seen it," her father said, spooning some fresh shaved horseradish onto the stuffed veal breast already on his plate. "Grampa was trying to figure out how to drive my car while Gramma was getting in on the passenger side. She had just opened the door, like this, " he made an elaborate sweep with his right hand, which was holding his fork. "Grampa accidentally threw the car into reverse, and it jumped backwards. The open car door caught Gramma and blam! she was down on the pavement before Grampa could stop it. I ran around the car to see if she was okay and she was just laying there on her back staring at the sky. Grampa leaned over across the passenger seat and yelled, 'Elsie! Get in the car!' So she did. She just got up and got in the car." Adelaide's father laughed with everyone else around the table, except for Gramma, who looked like she was trying to hurt him with her pale blue eyes.

"Elsie! Get in the car!" he repeated with his mouth full of veal breast, and everyone laughed louder, especially Adelaide's mother. She had hated her parents ever since they made her work in a factory so she could help send her oldest brother to medical school.

"Elsie! Get in the car!" he howled again, and laughed a speck of horseradish out his nose. The horseradish landed near Adelaide's right hand. She was careful not to jerk her hand away, but giggled along with everyone else, relieved that the focus was not on her.

Remembering her mother made Adelaide think about her death two years before. She still marveled that she had felt nothing at the time, no happiness, no grief, and that that was the first time she suspected she might have no feelings at all. Now she wondered about her father, and how much longer she would have to make her Wednesday visits. Age wasn't mellowing him; the older he got the meaner he got.

Fear suddenly shot through her with the familiar plunge in her gut which always signaled the descent of the plane. Although she had conquered her fear of flying some years before she had to be careful to sit on an aisle seat to avoid the feelings of vertigo that overtook her whenever she sensed height. She looked at her watch. Yes, one half hour before landing, as usual; the plane was obviously descending by its own will. Just one half hour and the thinking could stop. There would be something to do.

Across the way the man gripped his wife's hand a little tighter, holding onto his life. Adelaide stared at the dry liver spotted hand and was suddenly aware of the pressure of her blazer lapels on her nipples, rubbing ever so slightly through her thin t-shirt with the rise and fall of her chest as she breathed. Joe would be pleasantly surprised when she got home tonight. There was nothing sexier than a victorious woman, she had once read, and her clitoris nodded enthusiastically as she thought of her husband.

Now there was something to think on.

Even after thirty years, when most other couples had slipped into a companionable marital truce, she was still hot for Joe. Sure, for most of the week she was faithful to her work, but by Saturday afternoon, when she had shot her creative wad at the computer and there were no rehearsals to attend, she noticed the build up of steam that only he could release. Adelaide could never figure out if he was just naturally good at sex, or if she inspired him. All she knew was that her imagination could never beat his when it came to the erotic.

Each moment of lovemaking was an act of singular, messy, creative play. Sometimes they would undress without speaking on either side of the bed, watching each hidden part of skin reveal itself. Sometimes he would undress her while she was still at the computer and she would pretend to ignore him as long as she could. After decades of experimentation he could get around her body the way a blind man could get around his house, and after years of practice his big hands were deft with the front clasp of her bra. There was the time when he'd treated her like a pet from his grooming salon, sculpting her fur into some strange pattern with gentle fingers. There was the time he read passages from the Kama Sutra in his low hum voice while he traced over her body with a finger dipped in oil, noting each new erogenous zone indicated by an intake of breath, a tightening of her stomach, the slightest squirm. There was the time he teased her relentlessly with a silk scarf, never touching her with his hands and not allowing her to touch herself for release. There was the time they took a bottle of champagne into the shower and drank it while it mixed with the shower water and other things...

"Excuse me, ma'am, welcome to LaGuardia."

Adelaide's eyes refocused on the drab geometric design of the seat in front of her, then on the rest of the cabin of the plane. It was empty except for herself and the flight attendant and absolutely quiet except for the low hum of the plane's generators. She slowly pushed her mind away from the friendly vibration of the cabin and looked at the too-attractive young man standing over her.

"Have a good flight?" he asked, carefully not looking at the bits of fingernail clinging to her jeans.

Adelaide wondered if she had an after-sex glow about herself and made a mental note to somehow use the scene somewhere. After one false start at getting up, she remembered to unbuckle her seat belt and wove just a little unsteadily toward the exit with her lap top strung over her shoulder. A negative murmur answered the attendant's question about anything in the overhead. Her mind was someplace else now. She had become a huntress on the Serengeti, crouched in steely anticipation, her tail twitching and her carnivore's eyes focused on her prey.

Her prey's name was Harvey Kalman and his address on the Serengeti was 27 East 43rd Street. Her appointment was at 11:00.

Harvey sat behind a modest desk in a modest office. He had always considered it prudent not to show his clients how he spent the money he made off of them. Of course, after all the years he had known her, he considered Adelaide more of a friend than a client. And Adelaide's friendship had renovated his historic Connecticut home. So when she had told him she was more excited about this new play than any other she'd written, and wanted to deliver it in person, Harvey made the time.

"I wanted to watch your face while you were reading it," Adelaide explained, sitting low in her chair with her knees pressed against the top edge of his desk as if it stopped her from sliding off altogether.

Harvey scrolled rapidly down the screens of the computer before him, his too long legs occasionally pushing restlessly against the wood paneling underneath his desk like a veal calf in a stall. Not caring whether it made him self-conscious, Adelaide watched his face intently the entire time. She silently wagered that he was a pretty good poker player, but did notice that he didn't look up for some time after his eyes had finished darting right and left across the screens.

"Well. Del," he said, mouth slightly open, fingers patting his impeccably groomed white hair which, billowing out on the sides and indenting at the top where he was balding, gave the appearance of a meringue topping.

"It's different, isn't it? I knew you'd react this way." She let her spine relax against the chair for the first time since she sat down.

"Well. Del," he reiterated, and fiddled with a paper weight, moving it closer to his side of the desk. "Different. Ye-e-es. But, Del. Adelaide."

"What? What? Tell me what you think."

"Del, it's not funny." The words came out of his mouth reluctantly, like a bit of water splashing over a dam. He picked up a letter opener and put it in a drawer as he spoke.

"Oh, that. Maybe I should have warned you, but I wanted your honest first reaction. It's not funny because it's not a comedy. It's a drama."

"Jesus, Del, it's obscene." In his agony of not knowing what to say he seemed unable to say anything but what was on his mind. "You can't have God talking this way. It's disrespectful."

"What's disrespectful?"

"For one thing, God doesn't use the F-word."

"Harvey, this is theater, remember? It's a character. I invented him. And what is this with the 'F-word?' all of a sudden? You've got a mouth that would make, well, me blush sometimes."

"Me, okay, but not God."

"How do you know. Have you ever talked to him?"

"Don't forget, my people wrote the book on God. Literally. If anybody knows how God talks, I do."

"Tony Kushner got away with stuff like this."

"Not this. And don't forget Raleigh pulled back its funding from the state theater when they tried to produce 'Angels' there."

Adelaide lowered her knees and raised her elbows onto his desk. "Since when do you let North Carolina dictate taste? I want to be taken seriously, not just thought of as Adelaide Siren, the one who comes up with snappy lines. Look, I'm fifty, it's time I did something important, Harve, something that will make me remembered after I'm gone. I'm going for the Pulitzer here, and by the time I'm sixty-five I'm going to win the Nobel. No more comedies."

"But they give the Pulitzer for comedies...they do," he said, a whine creeping into his voice.

"I want to go international. I want to be translated," she said with reverence, as if she were talking about being assumed bodily into heaven.

When Harvey spoke again he tried to disguise the fact that he needed badly to clear his throat. "Sweetheart, dramas just ain't as marketable as comedies. When folks go to the theater these days they want to forget about Alzheimers disease and the cost of higher education, they want to laugh a little."

"What about Mamet? Talk about heavy, and he sells. Won a Pulitzer too."

"What about Simon?"

"I don't think he ever won a Pulitzer."

"Wait, I think he—shit, get off the Pulitzer thing. Simon makes a thousand times more money than Mamet or Kushner at the box office. You, why you're the female Simon."

"I want to be the female O'Neill."

"O'Neill doesn't pay."

"I'm not interested in the money."

"Well, everybody else is." There. He said it. Adelaide let the silence build until she had a sense of Harvey's heart rate increasing. She'd been in the theater long enough to know her timing.

"That's what the past twenty year's relationship amounts to?" she said, her breath pushing the words out. "Money?"

"Del, Adela, I love you. Even though you're a royal bitch sometimes I've loved you when no one else did because I've always thought that no one could write comedy unless they had some warmth somewhere inside them. But I'm giving you a businessman's opinion here. I don't think we're going to be able to find a producer for this."

"It'll play."

"It'll play at a college in repertory with Ionesco's *Rhinoceros*."

"That's really low, Harvey."

"Much as you hate hearing it, that's the truth." He leaned across the desk and covered her small hands with his like he was trying to keep a bird from flying away. The hands fluttered and twitched. "Del, you're a very funny person—a little prickly in person, maybe—but you write very funny things. Do what you're good at and I'll find you producers."

"I want the Pulitzer."

"Stop begging. Let's have lunch."

"Haven't got the time, have to find an agent." Nearly grazing his nose with the lid of the lap-top she snapped it shut and zipped it into its carrying case. With one last glance over her shoulder she walked out of the office while Harvey sat back, his whole body looking spent except for the pleading glimmer in his eyes.

Adelaide felt like a lemming discovering its destiny, that moment of shock when it sails over the abyss and finds there's no way but down. She walked blindly, feet finding their way out the front door and to the curb where she waited for a taxi to see her. This was the first time she had experienced any resistance to her work, and she wasn't prepared for it, especially right now, especially with this work. Her threat to Harvey about finding a new agent evaporated on the sidewalk. Even if she weren't totally immobilized she couldn't see herself approaching anyone else. What would she say when they asked what happened to Harvey? She pictured herself murmuring excuses about artistic differences through a dry mouth to suspicious eyebrows across a restaurant table. Her thoughts tumbled about like smooth stones in a fast river, constantly moving but going nowhere. Rejection. The word kept clicking in her mind in a fine syncopation with thoughts of finding a new agent, rejection, finding her own producer, rejection,

producing the play herself, rejection.
Rejection. Losing.
No. She turned around and looked over the heads of the lunchtime crowd on the sidewalk, up at the window on the fourth floor where she hoped Harvey was watching. She couldn't see him through the grimy glass, but imagined that he stood there gazing at her in anguish. Ignoring the glances of passersby she fixed her eyes on the window. She would give him one last chance to observe her agonized, rejected countenance, one shot of her suffering face to grind his guilt into his heart and make him come rushing downstairs pleading for—
Her eyes swerved to a decorative ledge on the floor above where she had been staring.
Adelaide closed her eyes and felt something under her heart surge, felt her thoughts flying up away from the pavement. She suddenly stood on her own wall, smelling her own hot summer sweat, sobbing in fear and frustration, her grimace pulling at the hair caught in tight wet braids. She fought back the sight of the small child reaching out, her fingers gripping and ungripping, gesturing for help that receded more and more with each moment, and such a simple help that would have erased her humiliation if only there hadn't been something to prove, godamnit, and was it ever really proven? The dizziness struck her, and her stomach churned with nausea as a black and white checkerboard pattern swelled on the inside of her eyelids. A step backwards off the curb brought her back as she fell against the fender of a parked car.
"Loser," she snarled, whether about Harvey or herself she wasn't sure. She turned to hail a taxi.

☿ ☿ ☿

While lizards dashed past her feet Adelaide lugged her computer and backpack up the front walk with Sisyphean effort. Except for moving mechanically when told to board the plane she had done nothing but stare the entire afternoon. Okay, so maybe she had overreacted. Life was not over, it was just that Harvey had taken her so completely off-guard. Her expectations had never been higher, and the reaction never so contrary to them. A good night's sleep and she would call him, talk some more, who knows, maybe he would even call her. Maybe there was a message waiting right now. She stood still, trying to summon a reason to go inside.

Joe opened the door and saw her standing there.

"I thought I heard you. Why aren't you coming in?" Without studying her eyes to determine her mood as he usually did, he grabbed her hand and propelled her into their bedroom, removing her backpack and computer strap from her shoulders as they moved. "Never mind, you have to see this. They just announced it before the commercial."

The small television on top of the highboy dresser was tuned in to the local evening news. Adelaide sat down on the edge of the bed without waking a large grey Persian cat nested in the rumpled covers. Figuring he'd ask about her day right after this, she stared at the television screen.

Maria Montez, the channel six anchor, began another story. "In local news tonight, Mysticism Hits Miami. Sources at Jackson Memorial Hospital have informed WMBR that the bishop of the Southeast Diocese of the Episcopal Church was admitted today for treatment and tests on large puncture wounds which have mysteriously appeared on her palms. Bishop—or as she is fondly known to people in her church, 'Mother'—Monica Laparro was found early this morning face down in front of the altar at the parish church, St. Steven's Cathedral, here in Miami."

The commentator's face changed to a shot of the church while the voice continued. "Paramedics rushed to the scene after a member of the church, Melba McGregor, called for emergency services."

The shot of the church turned into a shot of Melba McGregor slamming her front door as the voice continued. "Ms. McGregor was unavailable for comment, and physicians would not allow our reporter into the private room where the bishop is resting after receiving a pint of blood." The commentator's face appeared once more, serious with concern. "At first the bishop was thought to have been the victim of some bizarre attack by cult members, but sources close to her deny the rumor. To speculate on the real nature of Bishop Laparro's condition we have Dr. Nathanial Walker, a clinical psychologist as well as ordained minister, from the South Florida Theological Seminary." The camera moved out to encompass an edgy, petite man whose head seemed too small to contain all its degrees. The commentator smiled encouragingly. "So, Dr. Walker, just what do we have here?"

"Well, Maria, it's hard to say with assurance. What you've told me would indicate that Bishop Monica Laparro has received the Stigmata."

"How would you explain that word? Just what is a Stigmata?"

"Can you believe this? I can't believe this," said Joe over the voice of the professor who was explaining the process of crucifixion.

Not responding to Joe, Adelaide still stared at the television screen with her legs twined and her arms folded tightly against her as the professor went on.

"—makes sense. Although depictions of Jesus on the cross show him with the nails through his palms, forensic pathologists have determined that the tissues of his hands wouldn't have been strong enough to support his increasingly dead weight as he weakened. The nails would have ripped through the tissue right out between his fingers."

Maria's bright smile faded just a little. "My. But getting back to the Stigmata..."

"Over time since about the thirteenth century individuals who are known to be very saintly and who spend time contemplating the sufferings of Christ have acquired, as a mark of divine favor, some say, any or all of the marks of the crucifixion which I've just described. It's always the hands that are reported to receive the wounds rather than the wrists, which is interesting."

"And that's where Bishop Laparro's wounds are?"

"So I'm told. No one has mentioned anything about her feet or side yet."

Maria leaned forward conspiratorially as if to share a secret that would not be heard by thousands of television viewers. "Do you think Mother Laparro is a saint?"

"I've never met the bishop, and even if I did I don't believe I'm equipped to give an opinion on that."

If Maria was disappointed with that answer she didn't show it, but gave the doctor a 'job well done' smile. "Thank you, Dr.

Walker, for your time," and as the camera closed in for a tighter shot of her face, "A saint in our midst? Watch for Miami's intriguing answer to Mother Theresa. Coming next, Higher Property Taxes in the Gables..."

The phone rang. Joe, who had been standing by the bed watching the interview, picked it up from the nightstand.

"Hello? Oh, hi, hon. Sure did." He turned to Adelaide. "Palma wants to talk to you."

There was a second while Joe noticed that Adelaide's head was shaking in a mild tremor. He watched her as she reached out for the Persian cat sleeping next to her. Instinctively moving in that feeling of slow motion, which he regretted was considerably slower than most, he tossed the phone onto the bed and scrambled through the covers toward Adelaide. But he wasn't quick enough to stop her from snatching the cat from the bedcovers with two hands and lobbing it at the television screen. Too surprised to yowl, the creature rebounded and ran off.

Slightly shaken, he sat up and found the phone.

"Tell you what," he said into the receiver. "I'll have her call you back."

# Chapter Thirteen
## In Which Palma and Adelaide Visit the Sick

"I have work to do. I'm not going."

"Of course you are. She needs us."

"Did you hear that crap about Mother Theresa on the news? Monica's about to become internationally famous. Aborigines in the Australian outback will recognize her face. She doesn't need us."

Adelaide watched the cold espresso swirl down the kitchen drain. Even though they'd come as close to fighting last night as they ever did, Joe had still left the cup on her nightstand. Maybe it was understandable that he would object to her pitching the cat at the television in her fit of pique, especially since it was somebody else's cat and there was liability involved. But he had uncustomarily raised his voice, even if just a little. In return Adelaide had let fly with all the invective that had been building up in her since she left Harvey's office. She couldn't remember most of what she said, and wished she could forget the rest. Still floating up near the ceiling were the acrid words from the night before, words which she wished she could flick away with a towel like Joe did when something burned under the broiler and set off the smoke alarm. Pictures of her father saying such words to her mother clouded her mind. She picked up the dish towel from the counter to wipe her hands and pressed the dampened cloth against her forehead.

Palma sat at the kitchen table with a copy of The National Enquirer. The tabloid had moved fast, probably because their offices were just up the road, relatively speaking, in Lantana. The headline blared JESUS SPEAKS TO BISHOP THROUGH MIRACLE WOUNDS. In Rubinesque colors, Monica's face took up the whole cover. Her eyes bugged out at Adelaide and her smile seemed to beam a victory message. Her hands were upraised, palms showing, with an oozing red spot drawn in the center of each one. Only slightly less aggressive bulleted subheadlines trailed down the side of the page.

Top Experts Predict This Means Second Coming

Friends Cite Miraculous Healings From Holy Hands
Vatican Denies All Allegations

Some starlet and the hideous secret she hides from her brother was only an inset at the bottom.

"Those aren't even her hands. And look, her eyebrows are bigger than this," Adelaide said, tracing one with her thumb.

"I noticed that, too," said Palma. "They do terrific things with computers these days, don't they?"

"Yeah. Terrific. What is this "Friends Cite Miraculous Healings From Holy Hands?" What friends? Have you talked to these people?"

"Me talk with reporters from The National Enquirer?" Palma said.

Adelaide looked down at Palma who sat with her spine as perfectly perpendicular to the plane of the floor as a plumb line.

"Sorry. I'm not thinking straight this morning."

"Poor Monica."

"What?"

"This is so...distasteful. She must be absolutely humiliated."

"Oh, get off it, Palma. Monica is eating this up. She's probably the one who called the tabloid. What I'd like to know is how long this has been going on. I don't remember anything funny about her hands at your dinner party. Did you know about this?"

"No, but remember I told you she was wearing gloves when I saw her last? She must have been hiding her hands then, and she wouldn't tell me. Here we are, best friends, and I hear about it on the six o'clock news. That's so unlike her."

Adelaide waved a hand like she was shooing a mosquito. "Best friends...you have this idea about the three of us like we're still some adolescent three musketeers who share all our petty little joys and sorrows in the finest detail, sitting around saying 'and then he said, and then I said.' That was thirty years ago, Palma, and I'll bet things have happened that even you don't know about. Don't be so naive."

Palma eyes dropped away from Adelaide's face, but not before Adelaide could detect a flicker of anger there which made her own somehow less acute, as if she were ridding herself of rage by passing some of it on. *Now that's sharing,* Adelaide thought, and resented Palma a little for letting her do it.

When Palma's eyes came back up she seemed to have done something with the anger, gotten rid of it somehow. "You're a little more cranky than usual this morning," she said mildly. "Do you want to talk about it?"

"Ignore me. Joe barked at me last night for accidentally hurting one of his animals and this on top of that. Did you read the article?"

"It was embarrassing enough to buy it. I sent Estella Too out for it. Haven't actually opened it up yet."

Adelaide turned the pages of the tabloid before her feeling like a bomb expert searching for the fuse. She stopped when she saw a page with the headline "Mother Laparro Healed My Infirmity, Grateful Friend Affirms."

"Who is this friend?"

"I don't know. Come with me to the hospital and let's find out."

"I told you I'm really busy."

"Even if you don't care as a friend, you should care as a writer. When was the last time you saw a Stigmata?"

More because of guilt over her thrust at Palma than because of curiosity over Monica's hands, Adelaide agreed to go. She knew not to offer to drive—putting Palma in Adelaide's Volvo was kind of like putting the Lindisfarne Gospels in a library bookmobile, or John Gielgud in "Attack of the Killer Tomatoes." They rode in Palma's Mercedes. Adelaide sagged in the passenger seat, stunned at the change that twenty four hours of failure could make in a perfectly good attitude. She pulled a cigarette out of her blouse pocket where she always kept a couple for emergency purposes.

"Del, you know I don't like smoking in the car."

Adelaide bent over and pushed in the cigarette lighter. "Have mercy. I'm devastated here."

"Drama queen."

"Duh."

"Well at least crack the window and blow the smoke outside."

"This is impossible," Adelaide whined. "She couldn't have healed anyone. We're talking about Monica. Monica who we went to college with. Monica who drinks too much and tells us which priest got thrown out of his church for sleeping with parishioners. Monica who was rumored to have blown her way to her Master's in Divinity!"

"Del, you know better than that," Palma chided.

"Okay, slept her way."

Adelaide felt Palma's controlled silence which was always her tactic when someone got out of hand. *And I think I have no feelings,* thought Adelaide. *One of these days I'm going to get a rise out of Miss Congeniality.* She slumped in her own thoughts until Palma found a space in the hospital parking lot and the two walked up to the entrance portico.

A small crowd had gathered in front of the automatic doors, before which stood a proud security guard who looked like he was experiencing the finest hour of his career. The crowd, or rather, two camps with conflicting missions, let their placards intermingle. As the message on their signs indicated, one group represented the Spirit Fed Pentecostal Brotherhood. A member of the brotherhood stood on the fringe of the group lighting a cigarette while balancing in the crook of his arm a stick nailed to a droopy cardboard sign that read, "Beware the Catholic Anti-Christ!!!" Adelaide walked up to the man who turned to her with a grin lacking a right bicuspid.

"She's an Episcopalian, not a Catholic," Adelaide mentioned.

"Satan is Satan," replied the man, scratching his bristly cheek against the stick which supported his sign.

Less homogeneous than the brotherhood but just as intense was another group holding signs which were more supportive in tone, or at least more needy. Their slogans proclaimed, "Heal Us Mother Monica," and "Feel the Presence of the Lord." There were also a few with a less creative but equally enthusiastic "Halleluiah!" on them. As if trying to decide which camp they would join, both crowds eyed the two women as they passed.

With gentle persistence Palma led the way up to the substantial security guard who stood with his hands on his hips to make himself even wider.

"We're here to visit a patient," said Adelaide.

"Yeah, that's what they all say," snorted the guard.

"Excuse me," said Palma. "Do you really think I have anything to do with this rabble?"

The guard looked at her a moment, apparently immobilized by the use of the unfamiliar word "rabble," then let them pass. They walked past the gift and florist shop and on to the dark green marble visitor's desk where a woman dressed in a good suit was in quiet debate with the elderly volunteer behind the counter. Adelaide recognized the news commentator from the night before.

"Won't you please just call her and ask her? Or I could just talk to her over the phone right here," she was saying.

"No one admitted. That's the rule," the elderly lady said, her pink duckcloth jumper puffing.

Palma stepped up while Adelaide nudged the irritated reporter away.

"Hello, Ruth," Palma said. "How is funding for the neonatal facility coming along?"

The wrinkles in Ruth's face expanded in recognition of Palma then gathered back together in consternation at her question. "Hello, Palma, dear. I'm not on the committee and Marjorie likes to keep secrets too much. I have no idea what's going on."

"You should, having donated so much to it. Tell you what, if I find out anything I'll share, alright?"

"It's a deal," she gleamed, not hiding her delight at playing the role of conspirator. "Who are you here to see today?"

"My friend Monica. Monica Laparro."

The reporter ceased an annoyed shuffling and listened intently to the volunteer's next question.

"You're friends with that bishop? What do you know about what's going on? Does she really have that, you know, stigmata thing?"

All four women leaned forward together like a tulip closing its petals. "I don't know what's happening anymore than you do," Palma whispered. "But we're best friends from college and we want to find out if Monica is okay. This woman, too," indicating Adelaide.

The pink lady stiffened her upper lip and looked over the top of her glasses at Adelaide who nodded and muttered, "Best friends from college." Then the woman decided. "Well, since I know you, and all, I guess it's alright," she said to Palma. "Here are the passes." She stopped to write the floor and room number on the pass and handed it to Palma upside down so the reporter couldn't see. Undaunted, the reporter trailed them to the elevator, standing with them as they waited for a car to descend. "Excuse me, I'm Maria Montez from WMBR. Aren't you Adelaide Siren, the playwright?"

For the first time in twenty four hours Adelaide felt her mood rise a bit from its murky depth. She turned to the reporter and said, "Yes, I am—" but the door opened, Palma deftly pulled her inside and pressed the button for the fourth floor before any more could be said. Once arrived, Palma walked through the mint green halls as quickly as she could without drawing attention to herself, hunting for 431B. She had Adelaide, who was hanging back like a reluctant child, by the hand.

"But why did you—" Adelaide started for the third time since they got in the elevator.

"For the last time, we're not here about you."

As they followed the signs to 431B Adelaide amused herself by looking into the rooms they passed. Some of the doors to the rooms were closed with only a sign to look at, "Caution With Handling of Body Fluids." It made her aware of the hospital smell that was so typical she had almost failed to notice it—mucus, blood and urine, mixed with antiseptic solution. Through the smell floated a far off dinging of message bells that must have communicated something to those who knew the code. When she looked through the doors that were open she saw the same thing in almost every room. Elderly people on angled beds, bony knees poking up beneath the sheets, heads turned back so that their mouths were open. They all looked still, as if this were a place for the dead rather than the living. If the patient were a woman she was nearly always alone. If the person in bed were a man, there was always a bony woman, who looked much like the patient, sitting just as still beside the bed wearing a look of quiet resignation. *Would I sit next to Joe that way?* Adelaide thought, and trying to picture it, failed.

Palma, who must have been paying attention to where they were going, made an abrupt right turn and Adelaide suddenly found herself confronted by two Monicas. The first beamed at her from the cover of the tabloid laying at the foot of the bed. The other, even less attractive than the photo, beamed at her from a plump pillow at the other end. Her unrestrained breasts sagged over her sides beneath a hospital gown which matched the green walls while the oil in her unwashed hair made it jut out in more alarming angles than usual. And Adelaide made it a point to mention to her later that deep mauve lipstick was better than nothing. Then she noticed the bandaging around Monica's hands which left space for an intravenous needle capped at the end by a rubber stopper.

What Adelaide didn't see was Ferdy reclining on the seemingly empty bed at the other side of the room by the window. After watching at the church the aftermath of his attempts to assail her, he had struggled to enter her thoughts throughout the night but only succeeded in getting a second-hand buzz from the demerol they had given her. Too relaxed now to try to figure out how much progress he had made with her, he lazily toyed with the channel changer for the television attached to the wall at the foot of the bed. Even the sight of Palma only caused a mild stirring in his mellowed brain.

"Well, if it ain't the French Hens come to visit the sick," Monica grinned.

"Yeah, but we can't stay long because after this we still have to feed the hungry and clothe the naked," Adelaide said.

Monica laughed and waved the hand without the needle protruding from it at the only two chairs in the room. "Don't worry—it's just a flesh wound. Have a seat."

The visitors pulled the chairs closer to the bed, Palma on the left side closer to Monica's head, and Adelaide at the foot of the bed with her feet resting on the metal bar next to the chart.

"Love what you've done to your hair," started Adelaide, but no one laughed and she looked to Palma for help. Palma hadn't spoken since they entered the room. Monica looked half apologetic, and half like she was going to start giggling.

"Don't just stare at me, talk to me," she finally said. "I'm in a hospital bed, not a casket."

"When did it—" Palma said, and "Why didn't—" Adelaide said at the same time, and then both lapsed into silence once more.

"Okay, never mind, I'll start," Monica laughed. "Don't be embarassed, I seem to be having this effect on everyone—nurses, doctors—everyone moves around me as if they're afraid my hands are going to start a gregorian chant and they don't want to be there to hear it. To answer the question you meant to ask, Palma, it happened last Sunday, the morning after your dinner party—what day is today, anyway?"

"Friday," said Palma.

"Five days, it seems like forever. And to answer your question, Del, I think I was too embarassed to talk about it. I felt ashamed."

Adelaide shifted uncomfortably on the thinly padded seat of the chair, twisted around and looked at the television behind her. "Is that thing changing channels by itself?"

"I hadn't noticed. Do you want to turn it off?"

"Please. Where's the remote?"

The three women glanced around the room until Adelaide spotted the remote control at the edge of the tightly made empty bed on the other side of the room. In one swift move she was up grabbing the control, and the television screen went blank. She sat down again, and Ferdy watched her nibble at her lower lip, at a place that already looked redder and smoother than the rest like she'd been working on it before now. Her eyes were pointed in Monica's direction, but travelled in slow circles around her face rather than meeting the other woman's eyes straight on. She pulled the second cigarette out of her pocket.

"Del, No!" the two other women said sharply in unison, as if to a misbehaving dog.

She looked around the room quickly, shrugged, and started tapping the cigarette against the arm of the chair instead. "No matches. You know you don't need to talk about it now if you don't want to."

"Oh, but I do want to. The last five days have been so lonely and I was desperate to talk, to *show* you what was happening to me and ask you to help me figure out what it meant. Do you want to peek under the bandage?"

Palma ignored the offer, waved a finger over Monica's hand, indicating the stigmata with a gesture rather than the word. "That. Does it hurt?"

"Yes, with an aching pound like arthritis. Although sometimes less than others. Less when there's bleeding." Monica leaned towards Palma whose eyes had drifted to the window at the other side of the room when Monica mentioned bleeding. "Please don't stop, please keep asking me questions. It feels so good."

Palma struggled a moment, then, "What do the doctors say about it?"

"That was a trip. The paramedics wouldn't believe me when I told them I was praying face down in the church yesterday. They insisted I must have passed out and brought me here in an ambulance with lights and siren. Since then I've done MRI, serology tests, and had some sort of electronic sensor probe nosing around my hands like a robotic banana. Then there was a biopsy to see if this was just some sort of very distinctive staph infection. Between the physician and the psychologist who talked to me yesterday they've come up with something called hysterical purpurea. That means I'm bleeding because I'm nuts. They think I'm a bloody lunatic, I guess." Monica chuckled lightly, comfortably, as a grown-up would at some particularly childish misinterpretation of the scientific world.

"You're not crazy. You're the sanest person I've ever known," Palma said, glancing into the hallway as if she intended to tell someone out there. "But frankly, darling, this doesn't seem like something you'd do. You're so modern and I thought you rejected the Catholic church, and here you are, doing something positively Roman, and just a little morbid, if you don't mind my saying so."

"But I agree with you! The thought of walking around like some medieval throwback is embarassing, and if I had a choice you can bet I'd get rid of it. See, even I'm calling it 'It,' like it's some alien being fastened to my hands. It came without my asking for it, or wanting it, and hasn't gone away even though I've prayed for that to happen. And then something happened yesterday and I'm kind of resigned—more than resigned." Monica raised her hands and playfully made them into fists as much as the bandaging would allow. "What about you, Adelaide, got any good Stigmata jokes? I'm ready for you."

Palma winced at the word, but Adelaide just asked, "Why?"

"Why jokes, or why this?"

"Why this."

Monica looked at her in smiling seriousness. "Damned if I know," she said, and stared back at the woman staring at her. Then she closed her eyes as if Adelaide had won a point. When she opened them again she said, "That's not the way I wanted this to go. Listen to the dream I had the other night."

Adelaide groaned but Ferdy paid closer attention.

Monica pushed the button that made the back of the bed rise so she could talk from a more upright position. "Shut up a minute and listen," she said.

"A minute ago you wanted me to talk," Adelaide said. "What'll it be?"

Monica ignored her. "I can't remember too much of it, but I think I was in one of your plays, Del, and you were being a real bitch about my acting. I was burned by a fire, and there was this ugly little gargoyle creature who was in love with me."

Ferdy ran a claw from his beak over his low slung forehead to the fur on the back of his neck. *Among devils I'm not so bad looking*, he thought. *And look who's doing the judging.* Monica wasn't getting the dream right either. He wished he could jump in and help her explain what actually happened.

"It sounds like a horrible nightmare," Palma said.

"That was the funny thing. Some of it felt like a nightmare while it was happening, but some of it felt wonderful, and thinking about it afterwards, it felt like one of those dreams that's supposed to be a message." Her eyebrows drew together as if conferring while she struggled to recall the memories and articulate them at the same time. "You know, that demon telling me he loved me and then stabbing me—"

Palma looked at Adelaide although her question was directed at Monica. "A demon stabbed you?"

"I tell you it was pretty bizarre, but it was okay. Thinking about it now I figure it had something to do, okay listen to this, with the connection between wounding and love."

Ferdy felt his mind desperately scrambling to figure out Monica's. There was something in the connections Monica was making that made him vaguely uncomfortable.

"Oh, I know this is sounding crazy because I haven't had the time to think it all through yet, and with this feel-good stuff they have me on my brain is fuzzed."

"Well, either you're talking Jungian archetypes and you see yourself as a Christ figure or there's a little bit of sado-masochism creeping in here," Adelaide said with satisfaction. "Maybe you *are* nuts."

"Del!" Palma started, but Monica cut her off.

"I know what you're getting at, but forget the archetypes for a moment. The important thing was that I was on stage, you see, and everyone was able to see that I was wounded and bleeding. The main feeling I had was...shame, yeah, shame, that everyone could see me with these big gaping wounds. But then there was that creature who knew I was wounded but loved me anyway. Are you getting me now?"

Ferdy felt his pulse pounding in his throat and wondered how to shut up the woman in the other bed before some other immortal heard her. This assailing thing was all backfiring, and in a big way. Now she was saying that the part he played in her dream was significant. In a minute she would say that he, Ferdy himself, had inspired her to go public! What would Gregory do now?

"Okay, here's the point," Monica said, drawing up her knees and hugging them as if she were having trouble staying in the bed. "Having something like this, that everyone can see, it's almost like you're naked, like everything you are inside is exposed to anyone you see, like someone can look through the holes and see who you are. I started thinking about how no one could see me before, how I could keep my real self a secret, even from you two." Monica rubbed her feet under the sheets as if they itched to pace the room. "And then I got this idea that, you know, even between us, knowing each other so many years, it's like we keep these masks on. Look at us, we're supposed to be friends, and well, do you get it? The play I was in...Del's plays...the way we are with each other. And then my hands so honest. Doesn't any of this feel right?"

"I don't know about Palma, but I'm having trouble just making sentences out of what you're saying, let alone sense," returned Adelaide.

Palma stood up and busied herself pouring a glass of water from the plastic container on the tray next to Monica's bed. Monica let her do it even though she didn't want any water.

"It doesn't feel right to me," Palma finally said when the glass was filled and placed before Monica. "You make it sound like we're all phony. I don't play a part."

Adelaide snorted.

"See?" said Monica. "I am right, I'm just not saying it right. Palma, I'm not saying that you do it on purpose. But you have to admit there is a phoniness in how we all behave. Look at you. I know you feel like shit most of the time because you're so lonely and I—we just go on helping you pretend your life is perfect."

"She's got you there, darling," said Adelaide.

"And you, Del, look how you come to visit me and we both start in with the wisecracks, like we're in one of your plays. Maybe you should admit you've got hurts too, and maybe it's time we changed that so we don't just go toddering into our old age pretending that we're still college friends, repeating all those old stories endlessly to make us feel like we grew up smart enough, or good enough, or perfect enough to satisfy somebody else's expectations. Don't you see how important this is? It's like I've had this gigantic "AHA" experience. This is great stuff. This is the greatest —"

Now it was Adelaide's turn to stand. "You know what I always liked about you, Monica? No matter how deep you got into religion you never preached at us. Did I ever tell you how much sermons bore me?"

Monica swung the sheet back and flipped her legs over the side of the bed, without regard for the pearly rump she flashed at the others. She noticed that Adelaide had a sharper edge than usual today and attributed it to her own intensity. Adelaide never liked intensity. "Oh, Del, I don't mean to dump this on you so fast, I was just so excited—you've said yourself that I'm rarely guilty of original thought—that I couldn't wait to tell you, even if it bothers you at first."

Adelaide had moved closer to the open door of the hospital room, where Palma was already standing. "So who's bothered? This is not a new concept. We all went through the consciousness-raising in the seventies. Sure, we've all got troubles. I don't know about Palma, but I don't think I could take all of us regularly whining about them."

Monica raised her hands as if beckoning the other two women to come closer. "It's not just being honest about problems, it's being honest about every feeling. Like right now, see what's happening? You're both standing by the door like you want to leave, only you won't admit that I'm acting a little crazy and it's getting to you. On any other day Adelaide would say something clever, and Palma would give her gentle smile and I would laugh and you'd go away and there would be all kinds of things we wouldn't say. But today I'm not letting that happen."

"I don't understand—" Palma began, but Monica shook her head impatiently.

"This time don't leave," she begged. "Just once, tell me what you're thinking right now. Please. Even if you're thinking, 'Boy, that Monica is really an asshole.' Tell me an honest thing. Please."

Adelaide stepped further into the room. "There, happy now?" She turned to look at Palma who stood with one hand on the door handle, her purse over her shoulder, staring at Monica and Adelaide in turn as if by concentrating very hard she could control what her friends did next.

"Would you like to know what I'm thinking right now? Are you ready for this?" Adelaide walked closer to the bed and held onto the edge of the privacy curtain as if she expected the blast of her words might blow it away. "I'm thinking you're damn right we all cover up who we are. So I play a part, I wear a mask. Big deal. The question really is what makes you think you have the right to get under mine? Maybe I don't want you to know me, ever think of that? Who gave you the right to judge my honesty? And are you being *absolutely* honest right now or have you just switched to another role—like saint?"

With each question Monica's shoulder drooped a little more until Palma finally stepped in. "Come on, you two, I think we're all under some emotional strain and sometimes it's better not to talk, at least not right away. Maybe Monica's been through more than we can imagine, and she needs some rest."

As if Palma hadn't spoken Monica answered Adelaide's question. Her voice softened as if it could be a balm to Adelaide's harshness. "I didn't mean to sound that way. I love you and I want my love to be worthwhile. I don't want to just help you stay unhappy. Aren't we still friends?"

The corner of Adelaide's mouth twitched before hardening. "Sometimes people are friends for a long time because they just don't know how to stop."

There was a long silence while Adelaide stood like a long locked door. Palma struggled for her composure and walked briskly across the room, past Ferdy who watched her hips move with a rocking of his head like a metronome measuring their rhythm. The other two watched her, depending on her to supply the words that would take away what had just been said. Even Adelaide desperately wanted something to be said though nothing was coming into her own mind. With a cheerfulness that appeared only a little forced Palma looked out the window. "You can't see the crowds from here. We must be at the other side of the hospital. You should see them, Monica. From the signs they're carrying they either want you canonized or—"

"Fried," Adelaide suggested, and picked up the copy of the Enquirer. "It's probably because of this tabloid article. Maybe if you avoid contact with the news media it will all die down in a couple of days. There are always enough murders to get their attention."

"I've been thinking about that, too, and I'm not sure that's what's intended," said Monica hiding a sigh in the safer conversation. They were interrupted before Adelaide could ask what she meant.

A doctor young enough to be called son by any of the women entered the room briskly. He stopped, glanced at Palma and Adelaide, then back at Palma, then snapped into his role. "Good morning, Bishop Laparro."

"Good morning, Dr. Steele. These are my best friends Palma Blanco and Adelaide Siren. They don't have to leave, do they?"

"As a matter of fact, we were just—"

"Really, this will just take a moment," he said. "I wanted to tell you that the remaining results are in. Pathology reports no presence of infection, either bacterial or viral, so that rules out staph. For lack of a better explanation," here he smiled a small apologetic smile, "we're sticking with our original assessment of...of purpurea."

"Hysterical..."

"Ahem. Yes." He handed her two slips of paper. "This prescription will get you into the hospital wound center. The treatment will consist of oxygen rich whirlpool baths which we hope will heal the, um, ulcers. And this other prescription is a referral for," he carefully kept his eyes on Monica and away from the other two women who were staring at him intently, "a psychiatrist if you would like someone to talk to."

In the small ensuing silence a series of muffled "dings" out in the hallway were broken by an odd thippa-thippa sound followed by subdued scuffling, the sound of people trying not to make a ruckus. The four people and one demon simultaneously looked up, then out of the door, then down to watch a dove which had somehow gotten into the hospital, bounce against the door jamb, flap to the floor, and stroll in.

A tug of passion snapped Ferdy's attention away from the dove.

*Adelaide abruptly grabs the blanket off Monica's bed and slams the door of the room before the dove, or anyone else, can escape. Waving the blanket as if it were her own wings, she flies after the dove. First she climbs on Monica's bed and then leaps across the room to the one on which Ferdy rests as the bird flaps into the air. The bed's wheels go into motion, scooting her to the far wall, just missing Palma by the window who scrambles ungracefully out of the way just in time to avoid the crush of the metal frame. Adelaide pays no attention to Palma's shouts, the doctor's frenzied cautions, or Monica's laughter, but casts the blanket again and again at the dove flapping against the ceiling like a tuna escaping a fisherman's net. On the fourth try she catches the bird with a corner of the blanket and knocks it to the floor. In a moment, she is on the floor too, pinning down the blanket with her hands and knees over a tiny struggling lump.*

When Ferdy ceased focusing on Adelaide's mind he was more than a little shocked. While the others watched in stunned silence she was on the floor with the captured dove pinned under the blanket. This time it wasn't just imagination.

# Chapter Fourteen
## Palma

When Palma was upset she drove ten miles over the speed limit rather than her usual five. Her Mercedes screeled a bit as she hit the brakes on the smooth pavement of her driveway. She barely waited for the automatic door to clear the roof of her car before sliding into the garage. Estella Too must have sensed something was wrong because she was standing just inside the door as Palma entered.

"I was getting your lunch ready," she said, as if it were an excuse, as if she had been caught worrying.

Palma allowed the briefest scowl to flutter across her brow, so ephemeral that only a long time friend would notice it. "It has been a very hard morning." She examined her hands as she washed them at the kitchen sink. Then she sat down in the breakfast nook overlooking the back patio where Estella Too had set her white linen placemat and silverware.

"Tell me."

Palma talked as she picked through grilled eggplant and peppers sprinkled with crumbled gorgonzola cheese and capers, declining wine with the reminder that her personal trainer would arrive in an hour. The whole morning meeting with Adelaide and Monica had its replay. Estella Too was presented with every word and look, laid out like evidence before a judge, that Palma could remember or imagine. The duenna turned housekeeper made few comments, mostly clucking here and there in an encouraging and supportive way.

"And that wasn't the end of it. I had my appointment with the psychiatrist, you know."

"The new one? You liked him, didn't you?"

"I thought I did. But halfway through the session he started to cry. Just sat there, breaking down in front of me."

"*Madre de Dios.* About what?"

"He said he'd fallen in love with me. He offered to leave his wife and three children for me. He actually knelt in front of me, his hands waving weakly like a woman. It was horrible." Palma examined a bit of gorgonzola on her fork as if it had turned to a grub, and put the fork down. "I thought it was supposed to happen the other way, that the patient was supposed to fall in love with the doctor at some point. Transference or something."

Estella Too looked across the table at Palma with a mother's embrace in her eyes but only reached to cover the hand lying on the table with her own rough one.

Palma ignored her, thinking about how her tongue and jaw both felt so hard, like one stone encasing another. Marveling that she could turn to stone and no one would know. "Leave it alone, Estella," she finally sighed.

"No. No, I will not leave it alone. Remember the plates. Do you want me to get you the plates, Palma? I tell you it will work."

This made Palma smile again. "No, Estella, I will not break plates. Maybe that has worked for you, but you know that is not my style. I'm going to go get into my work-out clothes now. Thank you for the lunch, darling." She patted Estella Too's powdery cheek and slipped out of the kitchen, but not before turning around, her bright smile at odds with her next words.

"If it weren't for me, we probably wouldn't be friends anymore. I'm the glue that holds us all together, the telephoner, the food bringer, the one who organizes all the celebrations. Why do I do this? And why isn't anyone envious of me?"

# Chapter Fifteen
## Adelaide

Adelaide didn't realize her father had been in an actual brawl at the Veteran's of Foreign Wars Club until she arrived. The message on her answering machine that she heard after she got home from the hospital only said to come pick him up and they "wouldn't press charges." Now he was in her car, twisting a plastic bag he had remembered to grab off a bar stool before she took him away.

"What the hell happened?" she yelled, letting out the rest of the anger left over from the hospital.

"How many times I gotta tell you to watch your mouth, missy?" he yelled back, though not as loudly. Adelaide could tell he was far too pleased with himself to argue. "You know I'm not so old I can't give you the back of my hand. I can still fight back. Just ask Irwin Liptak."

"Look, Dad. I'm not in the mood to play about this. Now tell me what happened before I have you committed."

"My pop always told me, 'Don't let anybody kick you around. Anybody so much as looks at you funny, let 'em have it.' Boy, he would have been proud of me today."

"So who looked at you funny?" Adelaide couldn't believe she was asking this of a seventy-six year old man, and hated him for it, hated being compelled to be the other half of his conversation.

"Irwin Liptak, the Jew."

Luckily, they were stopped at a light so Adelaide was in no danger of ramming anyone when she groaned and leaned her forehead against the steering wheel. "Must you—"

"Everyday I have to listen about how he was in the 101st Airborne, how he saw so much more action than the rest of us. He talks about the Purple Heart like practically everybody didn't get the Purple Heart. I tell you, if I saw him pull up his shirt and show me his shrapnel wound once I saw it a hundred times. It's like he grew his belly as a monument to it."

"So you punched Irwin Liptak."

"Not exactly. It was more of reaching behind the bar for the seltzer hose and turning it on him. He tried to get a grip on the hose or my throat, I couldn't tell which, but I got him good before they stopped us. Lucky for him."

"You turned the seltzer hose on Irwin Liptak because he was showing you his shrapnel wound."

"Nah! I was defending Monica."

Adelaide suddenly yearned for a seltzer hose of her own, but she kept her hands clenched to the steering wheel and listened to herself go on as if she were reading a script. "What for?"

"I was talking about how I knew Monica because she was your friend and everybody was real impressed that I knew someone on the cover of the National Enquirer. But then that bastard Liptak got jealous that I had something that was bigger than his shrapnel wound and he made a joke, said what's the big deal about some shiksa with swiss cheese hands. I wasn't about to let some kike make jokes about a Catlic even if he is a war hero, and I told him so. Us Catlics have to stick together. So he showed me the finger. So I showed him all ten of mine, like this. And then he called me a Nazi, can you believe it? That's when I got him with the seltzer hose, right in his goddamn shrapnel wound. There's a Publix. Can we stop and get ice cream?"

"No, I'm in a rush."

After one more turn Adelaide noted with relief the low stucco wall flanked by rows of colladium that marked the entrance to her father's subdivision. This time more than any she couldn't wait to be rid of his presence. She pulled into the driveway before she faced him and spoke again, trying to keep her voice low.

"Next time I'm just going to let them take you to jail, got it?"

He grinned. "Got it." He gripped the bag he was holding in one hand, and the door latch with the other.

"What's in the bag?" She squinted through the thin plastic. "Is that a Hustler magazine? Where did you get that?"

"Hank gave it to me to borrow."

"Can you see well enough to read it?"

The way he smiled gave her a bitter taste along the sides of her tongue.

"Sure, only my left is totally gone. The right has enough left in it at least to make out shapes. Besides, I've seen this one before."

Her father pulled himself out of the car a little more slowly than he had the last time she gave him a ride. He used the top of the door to hoist himself up and gave a small airy grunt that made it look like an effort. As she watched, Adelaide felt something inside her head go soft, then hard again. Without saying good-bye she pulled out of the circular drive and forced herself to not look in the rearview mirror as he made his way into the house. She could picture him just the same, shuffling feet, elbows out like rudders, and his pause at the door as he felt for the keyhole. She wiped her mind clean and drove on.

# Chapter Sixteen
## In Which Monica Gets Called to Headquarters

Having stopped off at home to change into clerical garb after her release, Monica arrived at her office in the early afternoon to see the same commotion outside the cathedral that she had witnessed upon leaving the hospital. The crowd had merely switched venues and seemed to be heating up. She pulled into her usual space in the north parking lot without attracting attention only because everyone was focused on two other people. One was Gus, dressed in attractive slacks and a collared t-shirt, who stood on the steps leading up to the big red cathedral doors. He was talking animatedly to part of the group while pumping his legs up and down like a marionette. The other person Monica recognized was Melba McGregor, Generalissimo of the Altar Guild, who further away on the lawn with a rolled piece of cardboard in her hand was beating up a man.

Forgetting both her arthritis and her stigmata Monica threw her keys in her pocket, unhooked her seat belt and threw open the car door in one quick move. She dodged the sprinkler heads in the lawn as she ran in Melba's direction. Gus was autographing someone's placard as she sped by the steps.

"Look! There she is!" shouted one of the people whose attention had been diverted from Gus by the snaking moves of the woman in black.

"Melba! You stop that right now!" Monica yelled as she closed in on the woman. Distracted by the sound of her name, Melba stopped swiping at the man and turned to face Monica. Unable to check the forward momentum of her weight, Monica slapped into Melba's smaller but still considerable bulk with the smack of two bull seals fighting for territorial rights. The women bounced back from each other, momentarily dazed. Monica recovered first and knelt beside the whimpering man with thoughts of pastoral care barely edging out fear of a lawsuit.

"You're not hurt, are you?" she asked, trying to keep her voice positive.

With Monica shielding him from the angry, panting woman beyond, the man regained his spunk. "Satan," he said, albeit more softly than he might have dared to moments before. Melba menaced him once more and he clutched Monica to him for protection, apparently fearing Satan less.

"Melba, it's all right. You don't need to defend me. I'm a big girl."

"Defend you?" Melba repeated the words as if they were three day old sushi in her mouth. She pulled herself up with all the dignity that a woman with smeared lipstick can muster and glared at Monica who still knelt in the grass. "You're a disgrace to the Episcopal Church of the United States," she announced, then turned and stalked off in the direction of the office, discretely twitching her dress out of the wedgie created in the fracas.

Meanwhile, the crowd, that had hung back in anticipation of mayhem, surged forward. The first ones to reach Monica fingered her clothes and face as if they were already relics capable of miraculous healing. Gus battled his way through the group just as they were going for the cotton mittens the hospital had given her. He helped Monica to her feet and held off the crowd with the stick dislodged from the placard Melba had used as a weapon. The two backed off toward the office with the crowd advancing on them.

"Wait, Mother Monica, don't go," one heavy man in enormous shorts implored. "I have a condition."

"I'm so sorry," she said.

"Sorry? You're sorry? Sympathy I can get from my wife. I need healing."

Monica frowned at Gus and then they were into the office, locking the crowd outside.

"What did you tell them?"

"I just told them what you did for me. Just the simple truth. You healed me."

"The simple truth is that you're feeling better. You can walk without your canes. Once you get into miracles you're getting a lot more complicated. I didn't heal you."

"Yes, you did."

"No, I didn't."

"Yes you did."

Monica noticed over Gus's shoulder a young woman pressing her fingers and lips against the window screen outside. She snapped shut the verticle blinds in frustration and turned to see Sharon standing at her desk looking less self-possessed than usual. Stunned actually, even a little pale.

"I'm fed up. Let's get to business," she said sharply to the secretary, who jumped slightly. "Did I miss any important meetings yesterday?"

"Uh, there was one planned to go over the agenda of the Fall Diocesan Convention. I'll give you the notes I took. And I left your mail and messages on your desk." Sharon said all this without quite meeting Monica's eye and definitely avoiding Monica's hands. The older woman blew out her bad temper in a great breath and sucked compassion back in.

"I know how you feel," she said. "I feel the same way."

Monica pictured her energy leaking out and puddling behind her as she headed through the door of her office. The adrenaline surge of her battle with the crowd outside was followed by renewed fatigue from the strain of the hospital, and the reactions of her friends. She longed for the quiet and dark woodiness of her office, where there lingered the smell of a century of friendly old men.

Instead she encountered the mingling pungence of cheap perfume and body odor. Melba stood by her desk, arms crossed, with a judgmental scowl worthy of a Spanish inquisitor.

"Oh, please no," slipped out of Monica's mouth, then, "Melba, I'll be happy to talk to you about what's troubling you, but right now I have some things to catch up on. If you're not in crisis—"

"The whole church is in crisis," Melba snapped. "And you're not helping any!"

Monica would have preferred not to get trapped in this particular conversation but was too tired to fight it. "What have I done, Melba?"

"They're talking about reunification everywhere. Us and the Romans. And what do you do? You go traipsing around like some Catholic mystic. Where's your Anglican pride? Where's your Protestant heritage?"

"I don't have a Protestant heritage, Melba. I was born Catholic. Italian Catholic."

"You're a mistake, Bishop Laparro, that's what you are. They never should have elected you. They never should have let women into the priesthood. Hysterics, all of them."

Gus appeared suddenly at the open door. "Quick, Melba, someone in the sacristy spilled Kool-Ade on a chasuble."

Melba let fly her parting shot as she charged out of the office. "And they never should have revised the 1928 Prayer Book!"

With a conspiratorial wink, Gus closed the door leaving Monica finally alone. "Bitch," she muttered as her glance fell to her desk. She flipped through the little slips of pink paper in a pile before her, all headed "While you were out."

Call your mother.

Mrs. Ingeborg Swadin says she sees your face every time she opens the door of her microwave. Call her at 561-7628.

Call your mother.

Tommy Elkness wants to know if you're interested in a ghost writer to do your autobiography. Call at 587-3001.

Maria Montez wants to interview you for WRMB.

The Today Show wants to interview you.

PB Roxbury's office called. They would like to speak with you at your earliest convenience.

Cynthia Slome says that as a result of praying to you, her cat beat up the pitbull that attacked it.

Letterman wants to interview you.

Call your mother.

Monica held up her mittened hands cupped like weighing scales over the telephone. Roxbury. Mom. Roxbury. Mom. She dialed St. John Vianney Retirement Center first.

"Hey, Ma," trying to sound casual.

"Who's this?" At eighty-five her mother could be excused for not recognizing which of her seven children were calling.

"It's me, Monica."

"Oh, Monica. So what's going on?"

"What do you mean, Ma?" she evaded, trying to buy time.

"You always call once a day to check on me. You haven't called in three days."

"Things have just been so overwhelming, Ma, I guess I've let the time slip by. Phones work both ways, you know. You can call me anytime, not just wait until I call you."

"Well, I know you're busy. You're all so busy. Listen, Ja-Monica." For years her mother had been momentarily confused about which of the children she was speaking to, Jane, Theresa, Nick, or the other four. The family joked about the odd hybrid names that resulted.

"Yeah, Ma."

"I was talking to Father Kelly the other day about how you left the church. He said not to worry. He said the Catholic Church would probably absorb your church within the next few years. Then you'll be a Catholic again. I feel a lot better now."

"Well, that's great, Ma. I'm glad you're feeling better." Monica felt relieved too, at not having to explain her condition to her mother yet.

"Oh, and another thing."

"What's that?" said Monica, wary again.

"I won thirty dollars at Bingo yesterday night."

"Wow, Ma, that's terrific."

"Yeah. Well, I gotta go. I'm due at pool exercises."

"Talk to you tomorrow, Ma. Promise. Bye."

Monica never thought she'd have an appreciation for her mother's selective inattention to the world. When it came to marking the amount of time between phone calls her mother's mind worked with the precision of an atomic clock. But, luckily in this case, she was oblivious to most current events that didn't impinge directly on her life. After seven kids and a husband she could be excused for focusing on herself. Monica just hoped her next call would be as easy. Maybe the Presiding Bishop wanted to tell her he'd won the lottery. She put on her best ecclesiastical voice and practiced keeping it from cracking while she dialed.

"Hello, this is Bishop Monica Laparro. I have a message to call."

Long pause, then, "Hello, Bishop Laparro. Let me give you to the Administrative Deputy to the Presiding Bishop."

A rustling sound preceded the next voice she heard, like that of a squirrel in dry leaves. The Administrative Deputy Reverend Xiu was, as a matter of fact, very like an asian squirrel, small and quick. Whenever he appeared with the larger than life figure of the

Presiding Bishop some irreverent clergyman would comment about Rocky and Bullwinkle. The rustling sound continued, then stopped suddenly as if the squirrel found the nut it was looking for.

"Hello, Bishop Laparro."

"Reverend Xiu, how are you today?"

The Reverend Xiu's voice darted here and there, meaning changing in a flash and only hinting at commas. "Oh, very well, Bishop Laparro, very well, well, well as can be expected, so much going on all over the country, sometimes I don't know where to start when I come into the office in the morning, and," giving a high pitched chuckle, "I haven't seen the wood on my desk in weeks, if you know what I mean, how is your family?"

"I'm not married, Reverend Xiu, but my mother is alive and doing well, thank you. How is your family?"

"My wife is actually enjoying living in the City, but after two years I'm afraid the girls still are having trouble acclimating to their new social environment. Things were much different in Indianapolis, ah, thank you for asking." He paused, and Monica could feel him sitting up straighter, the phone clutched in both tiny hands; if he had whiskers they would be twitching.

"Reverend Xiu, um, I had a message to call your office."

"Ah, yes, you see the Presiding Bishop, we received a copy of the tabloid today which your picture, this really is you, yes? quite prominently displayed on the cover, Bishop Roxbury was unable to think of another time that a representative of the Episcopal Church was in a tabloid much less one of our bishops on the cover, of course the Pope gets a lot of press this way, remember that last article about him keeping the Anti-Christ chained in the Vatican basement," another high pitched chuckle, "not that I read it, my wife saw the headline in the grocery store, but not, not the Episcopal Church, are those really your hands?"

Monica found she had been holding her breath trying to keep up on the trail of his comments. Now she exhaled and said, "No, they aren't my hands."

She heard the Administrative Deputy exhale on his end of the line. "Ah, then the whole thing is one of those deplorable, but why pick on you, I wonder?"

"No, Reverend, actually the story is quite true. I'm just saying they dummied in someone else's hands and faked the stigmata on them."

"Oh. Oh, oh, oh, then I think we probably need to take some action, especially in light of the Presiding Bishop's upcoming visit with the Pope regarding long term reunification plans, very delicate time we're in right now, unfortunate time for publicity, of this nature, until you meet with, ah, people from this office, we request that you have no further conversations with, members of the press."

"I'm not sure that's what's intended," Monica said.

"Intended?"

Monica cradled the phone on her shoulder and held her mittened palms before her face as if straining to see through the white cotton. "I mean, why would someone paint a billboard and then not put it up?"

An alarmed rustling started again on the other end of the phone. "Bishop Laparro, Monica, I think the Presiding Bishop would agree that it's imperative, that you come up for a visit just as soon as you can get a flight, when, shall I tell him?"

"There are lots of flights between Miami and New York. I'll have my secretary get me on the earliest one possible."

"Grand. Have your secretary leave word with mine about your arrival time."

Monica felt her hands throb lightly as she hung up the phone. Was the pain and the bleeding some code, she wondered, that she hadn't learned to read yet? What would her hands say about Presiding Bishop Roxbury if they could talk? Hey, once you stepped outside the natural realm into the bizarre what was there to stop you? She tapped her thumb and fingers together in the universal gesture of talking.

"So hands, did you hear how nervous they are about me?"

"Sounds like headquarters is in a regular tizzy," they answered in a high pitched voice. "What are you going to do about it?"

"Oh, I don't know, hands. Maybe I'll show up and bleed all over the Presiding Bishop."

"Got a second idea?"

"Maybe I'd know what to do if I knew what you were for. What good are you, anyway?"

The hands were silent.

Gingerly resting her chin against the very edge of her palm Monica thought about what life had been like a week ago before she started talking to her hands. The future had seemed so clear. As if it were a reminder of common things, a formal invitation among her message slips and other mail grabbed her attention. The cottony fingertips of her gloves made it hard to open so she took them off, then managed to open the flap of the envelope without causing herself too much pain. It was the invitation to Palma's Spay Your Cat Gala just two weeks away. A week ago she would have thought of the party with a tingle of pride, picturing Palma introducing her as Bishop Laparro. Now she would see people looking at her and wonder what they saw. An icon? A freak?

With an impatient shake of her head Monica focused once more on the reality of her desk. She lined up the pink message slips across her desk like cards in a game of solitaire. Which one to call next? Closing her eyes, she picked one. It was the owner of the pit bull bashing cat. She crumpled the paper and tossed it in the basket under her desk. Try again. The second one was the message from the Today Show. Against the opinion of her friends, the orders of her boss, and her own reluctance, she knew. As she picked up the phone to dial she called out to her secretary.

"Sharon!" she shouted through her closed door. The door opened a crack and Sharon's face peered around the corner at her. "Would you please book me on the earliest flight to La Guardia? And Sharon?"

"Yes, ma'am?"

"Would you try very hard to act as if you didn't think I was about to fly out the window? I'd really appreciate being treated like just your average everyday bishop."

"Yes, ma'am." Sharon couldn't help but stare at the hand holding the telephone receiver; it showed a rosy pinkness coming through the white gauze. She gave a weak smile and disappeared.

# Chapter Seventeen
## In Which the Narrator Indulges in a Brief Description of Hell

The worst thing about Hell was that it lacked imagination. Other than that it had never been a bad place to live. Here is how Hell happened.

Angels had originally been created as mere functionaries, with jobs comparable to security guards, postmen, and theatrical choruses on earth. Most of them were contented, rejoiced even, in the roles they played in The Great Plan. They weren't sure what the plan was, exactly, but it had to do with God releasing her/himself through creation, then drawing him/herself back again. It was all very complicated and going to take a lot of time, but since angels didn't spend much of their existence in time they weren't concerned about that aspect. Most of them were never troubled by an original thought. It was only the mortal imagination of the Renaissance that glorified the spirit world, and a group of metaphysically inclined 18th century Brits that placed them above mortals. Consequently, if it weren't for the presence of God, heaven itself would be a pretty mundane place.

Shortly after the angels were created, one of them decided it could do better on its own. So it gathered together some like-minded spirits and headed off excitedly to a separate place which God obligingly created. Once ensconced there, the Devolvers, or "Devils" (a useful term to differentiate them from the spirits who chose to stay in heaven) were free to make of it whatever they chose. Unfortunately, lacking imagination, they couldn't think of anything really good despite their enthusiasm. So for thousands of millenia, Hell held about as much interest as a Montana laundromat on a quiet weekday. The devils just sat around and pretended to ponder ideas for improvements.

After several thousand more millennia one of them actually had an idea. His nickname was Bub. Bub suggested that the race of mortals that God (now termed the Enemy because they felt they had been somehow duped) had created was endued with that quality of imagination that Hell lacked. If they could encourage mortals to spend their eternity in Hell, who knew what charming innovations they might bring with them? Thus began the campaign to divert the earthly creatures from heaven, which the devils also hoped would piss off the Enemy who never paid them any attention let alone ever coming to visit.

The plan worked and it didn't.

Over the ages Hell was indeed able to attract a modest number of mortal inhabitants. But progress happened at an excruciatingly slow pace because of the nature of these mortals. It was a chicken and egg sort of thing. The kinds of people that Hell attracted were people who were attracted to nothing. These mortals all had one thing in common. They, like angels and devils, lacked imagination. Specifically, they couldn't imagine changing. They were all the sort of people who took, "You haven't changed a bit," as a complement. They rejected heaven when they found that it was a rigorous place where change was likely, even required. Instead, they brought themselves and their entire existence intact to Hell.

So the devils had their world evolve very slowly for better or worse by arriving souls who brought the baggage of their world with them. It was better than nothing. Hell had acquired beer by this means about four millenia ago, and the concept of slavery shortly before that. More recent additions had been latex prophylactics and managed health care (the latter for mortals who couldn't bear to part with their diseases).

Even so, Hell couldn't be said to be a precise duplication of earth. Given the kind of person who chose to go there, one would be hard pressed to find the unique, the newest, or even the slightly unusual. Hell was more of an echo of an echo of an echo of earth and decidedly behind the times as well.

# Chapter Eighteen
## In Which Ferdy Gets Called to Headquarters

On the day that Ferdy shuffled down the linoleum-floored hall looking for his supervisor's office, the part of Hell he visited was like an old movie—badly colorized.

The offices to his right and left had closed doors with names painted in black over opaque textured glass. He could hear voices coming through the transoms, saying things like, "I know I can crack this story, Chief, just give me a chance." The hall bustled with mortals, their skin unnaturally peachy, their clothes in varying shades of sepia, going about their business as they had on earth. They passed in and out of doors with differing degrees of vitality and ambition. Most of them carried papers of some sort on which they were intent. One of them zipped happily past Ferdy in a motorized wheelchair.

"Excuse me—"

The wheelchair didn't slow down. "Sorry, buddy. I'm on deadline. Major stress. Ask somebody else."

Ferdy looked at the names on the doors. Lots of insurance companies on this floor. That and the corporate office of one of Hell's several hundred newspapers. He walked in the door of a boating insurance company to see an owl-faced demon in slightly more modern surroundings than the hallway. Posters picturing mountaintops and rainbows which extolled the virtues of perseverance, teamwork, and a good attitude hung on the walls about him. Ferdy had spent so much time on earth he'd forgotten that rainbows were beige here.

"Hi, Frank."

"Ferdy? Son of a gun, boy, surprised to see you. I thought you'd been laid off eons ago."

"Uh, no, Frank, I'm still around. You happen to know where the Super's office is? I haven't been here in awhile. It's kind of confusing."

"Yeah, lots of changes going on here. Lots of progress. So you want—" here the demon either hiccupped or giggled, Ferdy couldn't tell which. "Just keep going down the hall. Last office."

Ferdy closed the door so that the peals of laughter within were muffled. He wondered what joke he wasn't getting this time. At the far end of the hall cigarette smoke issued from an open door. The smoke moved against the walls in the background. Hyper-aware of the scratch of his claws on the linoleum, he shuffled his way down to the door and stood just outside, hoping the smoke would clear enough so he could make sure this was the right office.

Whoever was smoking must have stopped momentarily because Ferdy began to make out items in the room. There were two leather chairs with metal arms facing a tired wooden desk. On a credenza by the right wall the slow paddles of a table fan played patty cake with a large fly while it shoved the smoke about the room. There was a black candlestick phone on the desk and a manual typewriter slightly to the right of it. One demon's claw stroked the keys, while another pulled a cigar out of a face that was slowly coming into focus through the haze.

"Is that you?" Ferdy asked.

"Look at the sign on the door," the voice behind the cigar said, slightly slurring the esses.

Ferdy obediently stepped back outside the office and looked at the front of the open door.

It said:

## GREGORY
## SUPERVISOR OF THE WESTERN HEMISPHERE
## NORTH OF THE EQUATOR

Ferdy stepped back around the door.

"Wanna cuppa joe?" Gregory said, now completely visible although a considerable amount of smoke still hung about the room.

"Sure, Gregory, a cup of...Joe would be fine."

Gregory creaked his chair around and shouted through the door off to the left which Ferdy hadn't seen before. "Hey, toots!"

A slight man with lips the thickness of a pencil line scuttled timidly out of the adjoining office.

"Coffee for my friend here. Make it black and make it snappy." The little man moved off as snappily as possible and returned with a mug of something which threw off a beige steam. He set it on the desk in front of Ferdy and scampered back into his own office as if there were something burning on a stove there. Gregory watched him go.

"So, nothing's perfect. I've requisitioned a broad who put up with sexual harassment but have to wait for the next busload of souls. Until then I'm stuck with the cockroach there. He was a file clerk with the Vermont Division of Motor Vehicles for forty-five years. So, Ferdy, baby," Gregory stretched and put his feet up on the desk. "Whaddya think?"

"Really impressive, Gregory, congratulations. And I like what you've done with the place."

"Early Sam Spade, they tell me."

"Who?"

"I guess it was impossible to brief you about everything. Never mind."

"Gregory, does this mean you're my supervisor?"

"I always said you had a brain. Even when everybody else said you were an idiot. You put two and two together faster than Noah. So why, I ask myself, why do I get stuck with constantly defending your screw-ups? That's why I've asked you to pay this little visit. So I can make some sense of what you're doing out there. So I can explain to the guy upstairs who I report to. So I can keep this nifty job. I tell the guy upstairs 'Ferdy must have a real good explanation for what's going on.' I'm sure you have a real good explanation, so shoot."

"Well, I..."

"Sit down, why don't you?"

Ferdy sat down in the leather chair on the right hand side of the desk, gripping his bony knees with growing apprehension. His chair was a good three inches lower than the one in which Gregory sat, so he was forced to look up to his former colleague in more ways than one. Gregory gazed at him as intently as anyone with white eyeballs can be said to gaze.

"We're waiting."

"Well, uh, two nights ago when I assailed her—"

"You what?"

"I assailed her, in her dreams."

"Why'd you do that?"

"You remember, that's what you told me—," the white eyeballs gleamed a warning which even Ferdy could read. "It seemed like a good idea at the time," he shifted. "But then I sort of. . .lost control of the dream."

"So it wasn't such a good idea after all, was it?"

"No, I guess not. The dream seemed to have pushed her into a confrontation with The Enemy and when it was over she'd given in and decided to go public." Ferdy suddenly remembered the moment he had felt the single word "no," that contact with The Enemy that filled the church and pressed softly against his own skin. He tucked the memory inside him like some guilty pleasure derived from a private nasty act. Rather than share the moment with Gregory he skipped to, "So now everyone's reacting. Her friends are either embarrassed or angry—"

"Who's angry?"

Ferdy described Adelaide's reaction to the dove in the hospital room. Gregory sat up with new interest. "Sounds like a situation with possibilities. Maybe we can use her. Hey, Insect!" he shouted again into the other office. The tiny man appeared, seemingly unruffled by the name, as if he'd been used to it for a long time. "Get me the file on Adelaide Siren." He turned back to Ferdy.

"I may have to get involved myself."

"Aw, no, Gregory, I can handle this. I swear I can get things back on track."

"Yeah? Like how? What're you gonna do now that your SIP is getting national attention? Start the paperwork for sainthood yourself?"

Ferdy was aware of a tremor appearing on the surface of the coffee he was holding. "Well, I. . .I think someone has to be dead first to start sainthood—"

Gregory bolted up from his leather chair and leaned over the desk far enough so that Ferdy could look deep into the twin pits of his upturned nostrils. "Hello! This is Gregory. This is Gregory being sarcastic. See Gregory being sarcastic, butthead?" His voice rose several decibels. "I asked you what are you going to do?"

"Well, I—"

Increased volume. "You already said that once. We're losing

daylight here and I got other managerial tasks. What are you going to do?"

"Uh—"

Gregory's scream sent shock waves that rippled the hair on Ferdy's stomach like an approaching storm waving a field of grain. "WHAT ARE YOU GOING TO DO?"

Ferdy drew the now rapidly vibrating coffee to his lips to buy a moment. Putting all his concentration into steadying his shaking claws he succeeded in sipping some of the brew into his beak without sloshing it over his pot belly. In a wish so fervent Monica might call it prayer, he wished he could be spirited away from this office to his little post as a gargoyle on Notre Dame, where everything had been so simple, where he didn't have a snarling supervisor inches away from his face who didn't let him think, let alone speak. He wished he had never heard of Monica Laparro or her world. At the very least, he wished Gregory's management training had included a little more creative problem solving.

As his concentration focused once more on the demon before him, his attention was suddenly drawn to a speck of gore hanging from one of Gregory's fangs. It fascinated him. He wondered what, or who, it might be.

The fang disappeared as Gregory whipped around to Insect who stood quietly holding a dossier. Ferdy looked up at the man as well and saw an ever so slight change in him. There was a faint twinkle in his eyes, and a whisper of a smile in the thin lips. Insect had been watching Ferdy's suffering, and it had pleased him. Gregory held out his claw and the man put the dossier into it. Then he stood quietly as before, only his eyes shifting back and forth between the two demons, watching what would happen next.

"Get the hell out of here," said Gregory. Insect left obediently. Gregory turned once more to Ferdy. He was softer now as he tossed the folder across the desk, and this frightened Ferdy even more. "Do you have this one?"

"Uh, sure, sure I do," said Ferdy, trying to sound certain.

"Have you read it?"

Clearly this was not a time to hedge. "No."

"May I suggest you check it out sometime when you're not too busy jerking off? Are you reading me?"

"Yeah. Sarcasm. I get you, Gregory."

"Call me Sir. And Ferdy?"

"Yeah, G-Sir?"

"This is your one and only warning. Next time I see you, if Monica Laparro is any closer to sainthood, we're talking disciplinary action, get it, buddy?" Gregory dug at his teeth with his pinky claw and dislodged the piece of gore that had held Ferdy's attention before. He put the claw between his lips and sucked at it with satisfaction. "We're talkin' layoff."

# Chapter Nineteen
## In Which Mortal Life Goes On, Incredibly

Over the two weeks following the appearance of Monica's face in the tabloids life went on in a more or less usual fashion the way it always does despite the tragedies and triumphs that seem to make it unique. Monica noticed that with time even miracles became just another part of daily life. Palma called to fuss about last minute arrangements for the Spay Your Cat Gala, and Joe wanted to know if she needed anything done at the new house. Monica hadn't spoken to Adelaide, but figured she'd be worrying about plot problems the way she always had. The stories surrounding Monica were still mentioned briefly in daily news broadcasts, although she was not, for the moment, the lead story. The local media covered residents of Miami, as well as points south into the Keys and north as far as Vero Beach, who reported miracles of cars starting without gas, holy statues skipping about living rooms, and children who did what they were told. All these reports came from people who were certain that Monica was somehow responsible.

Welcoming the normal feel of life, Monica jack-knifed into a sea of duties as bishop while flying to New York to placate Presiding Bishop Roxbury, scheduling an interview with the Today Show despite the Presiding Bishop's specific order not to, and fielding several dozen telephone calls a day from people wanting everything from healing to financial investment advice. Sharon, who in just a few days had come to accept Monica's condition as the norm, began to relax and was able to screen the calls with some degree of efficiency. With Sharon on guard, Monica was able to keep up with signing letters of canonical consent for the institution or resignation of other bishops, meeting with her deans and canons, discussing vocations with aspirants to the priesthood, talking finance with the property and loan committee, and even performing her first confirmation at the Church of the Intercession. In her business, as in Adelaide's, the show had to go on.

Her wounds didn't get any better or any worse, though now that they had made their presence known they seemed less inclined to bleed than before. Monica tried daily visits to the wound care center at Jackson Memorial Hospital, but gave up after a week when the medical staff reported no progress in healing. They showed her instead how to keep the wounds clean and how to dress them to prevent embarrassing seepage if they bled; they prescribed aspirin for mild pain and Tylenol with codeine when the throbbing kept her from sleep. Monica discovered that at the start of the new millennium the medical community dealt logically and calmly with stigmatas. No pageantry, no swooning, no awe. No wonder, she thought. Miracles had been replaced by the term "medical anomaly." That satisfied everyone, including Monica, who was simply glad not to have to make the trip to the wound center. It took too much of the time that she needed to give to her job.

Life had finally become normal for Gus as well. He was relatively happy in his new position as sexton to St. Stephen's Cathedral. He lived in a one-bedroom apartment on the cathedral property. Though he didn't have any of the qualities usually found in a sexton, like mechanical handiness, he was able to find people who did, and supervise them well. He was keeping the church, and himself, neat and clean. He was also filling out considerably and looked less like a praying mantis than he had the month before. Whenever Monica had a moment he talked with her about his past and inner healing kept pace with his outer improvements.

In the evenings Gus danced. He danced in his apartment to CDs played in a borrowed deck. He practiced all the steps he had ever learned, and repeated the fast and bouncy routine that had won him the gold medal at the Palm Beach Competition in 1992. For the slow songs he used a rocking chair to practice lifts that grew more fluid as his muscles strengthened, the chair rising up from the floor over his head in one slow sweep. He discovered the apartment was too small to attempt large moves without slamming into a wall. So after dark when the church property was deserted Gus leaped about the moon glowing lawn, breathlessly humming snatches of "Stardust," and rejoicing in his legs. The reason for these activities was not simply recreational; Gus was forming a secret plan, of which not even Monica was aware.

What Monica liked most about him was that he touched her. Although he was busy enough around the cathedral, he found moments to stop by and say hello. These moments always began or ended with Gus wrapping his arms around her in a friendly hug, or at least pausing with his hand on her shoulder or covering her hand with his own. She felt her spirit respond to his touch with a warmth that was nearly visceral and yet not sexual, and she was grateful. It was the only physical contact she knew in those days, what with everyone else trying their best to avoid touching her. She wondered sometimes if he was aware of the gift he was giving her but never thanked him for fear of losing the spontaneity of the act.

Sure, he still had a few minor drawbacks. One was his insistence that she had miraculously healed him. His interview with Maria Montez had kept the publicity simmering. Another unfortunate quality about Gus was his language. Where before he had been grumpy and rude, now he was cheerful and rude. Monica never knew when the Canon for Adult Education might pass through the office and hear Gus cheerfully chatting with Sharon about how "the fucking lawn had more bugs than a Hanoi whore's pussy." Monica would mutter something about vocational rehabilitation to the verbally assaulted cleric and hope for charity on his part.

The third, and possibly worst, drawback to Gus was that he teased Melba McGregor. Endlessly. Mercilessly. And he never failed to take her by surprise. On one morning just a few days after he had become the cathedral sexton, he was rearranging the microphone wiring behind the pulpit when he spotted her coming in the front door with a couple of large altar candles. He ducked down as she started up the nave and forced his voice into its deepest register, which years of Marlboro cigarettes had refined. In his best stained glass tones he said into the microphone, "Melba. Melba McGregor."

Melba stopped and gripped the candles tightly, while the echoes of her name drifted around and up into the vault.

"Who's there?" she asked timorously, her double chin slowly puffing like an alert frog.

"It's me. God," Gus continued. "I've been meaning to speak with you about the sacramental wine you use here." He moaned softly down the scale. "Oooooo-ooo-ooo-ooo..."

"Who IS that?" Melba demanded, angry at having been frightened.

"That's the Holy Ghost. He says the wine gives him agida."

An enraged Melba rushed the altar before Gus could leave the pulpit, and battered him with one of her candles before he could get to his feet. While he scrambled to safety out the side door a suppressed giggle from behind the sanctuary wall signaled a witness to her humiliation.

Melba blamed Monica for Gus. Actually, Melba blamed Monica for just about everything. Ever since Monica had been ordained things just hadn't been the same for her. The seams of the world that Melba had sewn for herself seemed to be unraveling daily. That world had always been controlled to her satisfaction, most of it with an accountant husband over whom she had held sway for forty-six years. How her husband felt about his own life became apparent when he developed lung cancer. Older parishioners still remembered how he had arrived at a Lenten pot luck dinner and gleefully sang his prognosis, "Too late to do anything, I'll be dead within the year!" Sure enough, even with Melba's relentless ministrations, which she enjoyed recounting to acquaintances at Episcopal Church Women meetings, Malcolm McGregor had departed from the world five years ago with what seemed to her an uncanny joy.

After his death Melba's attention had turned to Malcolm's old australian shepherd, Andy, whose hold on life was stronger than Malcolm's. Andy just kept getting fatter and fatter on the biscuits which Melba forced on him whenever he moved. She gave him one every time he barked and Andy got so sick of the biscuits after a time he seldom so much as whimpered. When Melba walked Andy the two of them waddled back and forth like twin metronomes.

But Andy wasn't enough to fill Melba's life after Malcolm. Although she had always been very involved in the Episcopal Church, she had stepped up her activities since his death. It was her church, after all. So protective of its traditions was she that any discussion of reunification with the Roman Catholic Church would set her snarling.

So they elected a bishop who was born Italian Catholic, who showed a decided lack of respect toward Melba, and to top it all off, had acquired the standard symbol of Catholic sainthood. It was no wonder Melba hated Monica.

Now Melba was not one to simply *bear* a grudge; she felt that a good grudge deserved more. Instead she nursed it, cultivated it with all the care given to an orchid grown in the hothouse of her mind. She fertilized it with repetition. While she sipped her tea in the evenings and stared unseeing at the Wheel of Fortune from a plaid Herculon recliner, her mind ran over grievances and events, recounting and embellishing, until the grudge's petals thickened into a heartier shrub that dropped toughened roots deeper and deeper. Within a short time she could feel a pleasant solidness in her chest where the roots passed through and a tightening in her gut where they twined and held. It was pleasure for her; she hadn't felt this way since Malcolm was alive.

But the pleasure had to be shared, and this proved to be a problem. Her minions would listen attentively while she railed against the bishop, but if they agreed with her she could tell it was half-hearted, and suspected it was just a result of her bullying. They didn't really hate the bishop the way she did. Nor was she able to convey her hatred to the bishop herself, though she used all her usual methods. Monica was terribly busy and, whether Melba was gossiping about her, being rude to her in a not-so-subtle way, or ignoring her altogether, Monica didn't seem to notice, let alone care.

This made the grudge grow so rapidly that in a short time it filled Melba completely and had no more room to grow. Melba thought she might burst if she couldn't get some sort of revenge against Monica, but every tactic in her arsenal had failed. In all her life she had never failed to intimidate a person enough to bring them under her control, until now. She considered trying sabotage, but missing wafers at Mass on Sunday or clipped candlewicks would only reflect badly on her. Besides, sabotage was childish. Ultimately, it was Melba's sheer glowering presence that had always been her most effective weapon. She thought that even the bishop would notice if she really turned up the heat.

So Melba became a stalker.

In a way it was a new, untried tactic, but Melba took to it with aplomb. All she had to do was position her presence wherever the bishop was, as often as possible. At every service in which Monica presided, Melba was there, sitting in the first pew where no other Episcopalian ever sat except at Christmas and Easter when the church was too full to avoid it. When Monica left her office Melba was sitting in the waiting room where she gave Sharon the willies. In the evenings Melba parked her Camry sedan in Monica's driveway, eyes fixed impassively on the house. But even to this there was no reaction. She wasn't sure if Monica ignored her or just never looked outside her front windows. Something more drastic was clearly called for.

On the fourth day of Melba's activity, Monica was seated in her office with a Baptist minister named Hobart Henry who felt called to be an Episcopal priest after hearing about her stigmata. In the midst of their discussion on infant baptism Brother Henry looked up at the jalousy window in the office. Monica saw him start and looked up too, at Melba McGregor's face staring back at her. Her small eyes were pressed into her face like tiny marbles, and her mouth, lips tightly together in the shape of an inverted U, looked as if it had been drawn messily with a sculpting knife. Monica eased herself from her desk and sidled up to the window while Hobart Henry gaped from the safety of his chair.

"Well, hello, Melba."

Melba remained mute.

"Is there something we can do for you?"

Melba did not voice a need.

"Well, then." She kept her eyes on Melba like a lizard gauging its distance from a cat. Hearing Gus's voice in the outer office she said his name as softly as she could and still be heard. He poked his head in the door.

"Yeah, hon?"

This time Monica ignored the term of endearment which she had repeatedly asked Gus to avoid around visitors. Still not taking her eyes off the face in the window she said, "Gus, Melba seems to be. . .stuck somehow. Can you help her out?"

She heard Gus duck back out the door and heard the outer office door open and slam shut. In a moment more he had rounded the corner of the office and was trying to shoo Melba as if she were a cow. He waved his arms furiously and shouted, "Go on. Get outta here!"

As Monica and her guest watched fascinated, Melba remained unshooable. Gus doubled the waving and raised his voice. He added jumping up and down. Melba held her ground. In one final effort Gus hauled back and whacked her on the backside. Her eyes flew open in surprise and she ran off shrieking, with Gus in loping pursuit. Monica returned to her desk.

"Sorry for the interruption. Now where were we?"

Hobart Henry forced his gaze from the now empty window. "Ah. I was just about to comment that this sort of decision takes a. . .lot of prayer. And that's what I'm going to do, Bishop Laparro. My wife and I are going to do some very hard praying." He got up to go, then paused at the door. "Do you think," he said, giving a vague gesture toward the window, "that it's. . .er. . .safe to go out there?"

"Oh, don't you worry about a thing, Brother Henry. Melba is just a little...eccentric. Quite, quite harmless."

He gave a wry smile and left.

"Quite," Monica said to herself, wondering if she believed it.

☿ ☿ ☿

After her hysterical capture of the dove in Monica's hospital room Adelaide avoided her friends and doubled her efforts at finding a producer for her show. Having relied on Harvey over the years she had few contacts in New York, but those that she had she called on. Every call ended with a promise to get together ringing hollow in her ears.

She couldn't understand what was happening. The play was slightly avant-guard, but a lot of crazier stuff had shown up on Broadway. And these days God had become a hot property. She had been doing her homework in order to pitch the show. There were three bestsellers currently on the market with divine themes, and seven shows in the new television season had at least one character who was an angel. Why not a play called "Sex and the Holy Trinity?" It didn't make sense. Brewing her third espresso one morning while she dragged on a cigarette through a mouth filled with jelly beans she had the eerie feeling that someone was manipulating her world. If she had believed in God she would have thought he was getting her back for her envy of Monica. *Okay, Bud,* she thought, *how about I play nice with Monica and you give me a producer for my show? No dice, huh? See, that's why I don't believe in you.*

The sound of the espresso pump brought her attention back but she flicked the off switch too late to prevent coffee from flowing over the edge of the regular sized coffee cup she used. She picked up the cup and threw a towel at the mess to sop it up. Forget the coffee, it was time to get back to the phone even though she dreaded it. Once New York contacts had been exhausted she had fallen back on major local production houses to launch the play.

She was running out of hope even there. One recent meeting with the artistic director at the Lanceley Regional Theater in Fort Lauderdale had been disastrous. Driving up to Lauderdale at the invitation of Roy Thurston, the director, she had found the theater in the downtown area to be agreeable enough, but everything broke down over lunch afterwards. They sat inside at Roseola's on Las Olas Boulevard pretending to be interested in salads made of lettuce in every color but green on plates the size of sun hats. Roy, a pale, slight man with receding blonde hair, shifted back and forth so much in his chair Adelaide surmised how the term "beside himself" had been coined. She in turn was doing her own dance, making an effort at being charming, trying her best, a part of her mind realized, to act as she thought Palma might. But now it was time to make the deal.

"Let me say again, Ms. Siren," Roy was saying again, "how honored I am that you're considering our theater for your pre-opening run."

Adelaide leaned intimately across the table, letting her fingertips rest in Roy's space, and smiled, more like Palma would smile, she hoped, and less like a predator.

"Well, if we're going to do this, Roy, the first thing you need to do is call me Del."

Roy gulped. "Del. Would you mind telling me about the play?" he added, and cowered slightly as if afraid the question was too presumptuous.

"Not at all. Roy, it's a departure from my usual comedies. The concept for this drama is the sexuality of God."

Roy forgot to fidget. "I'm sorry?"

"The sexual nature of God."

"You have a character named God and he has sex and it's a drama?"

"Something like that. You see, try as we might, we can't shake the puritanical attitude that God doesn't really like sex, but has to put up with it. Now I know you might be wondering why I'm not giving this to the Coconut Grove as I usually do, but their milieu doesn't extend any further than the frothy little Edward Albee properties. I'm looking for a theater with balls, Roy," (here she dropped her eyes briefly to that part of the table under which Roy's balls might be tightening in his trousers) "and I'm just beginning to think yours is the one."

"Did you happen to bring a copy of the play?" he said in an airy higher pitch like a man whose balls were being squeezed. Although most of his body had stopped moving about his fingers still scrabbled furtively at the tablecloth like a rock climber trying to gain a hold. "You know, Del, I'm not the sole decision maker at the theater when it comes to new productions." (and here he cleared his throat so that Del knew he was lying) "I'll have to present this to the board."

That was it. In the shock of realization that she'd lost him she had tried to adjust her glasses, discovered she wasn't wearing them, and stuck her thumb in her eye. He noticed. She could tell he was reading her as well as she was reading him, and it would be a waste of time to continue. All that remained was to get the check and escape leaving behind shreds of dignity and lettuce. While leaning down to get a copy of the play from the canvas backpack she used as a brief case she wiped her teary eye on the table cloth, then located the waiter and made a little check mark motion with her index finger.

To think she'd actually been flirting with the weasly little man! Adelaide shook her head as if that would dispel the humiliation burning there and took her weak espresso into her office.

*I don't care.*

*I really don't care.*

She had to stop thinking about this, just for a while. Maybe turn her attention to something more positive, like a new play. That was it, no fourth rate theatrical directors were going to get her down. Adelaide grabbed a lucky tie off the tie rack on the wall, and looped it around her forehead. She stretched out in her desk chair, her body at a forty-five degree angle.

Then she seized the Mickey Mouse cookie jar that Joe had bought during a rare weekend at Disney World. Mickey's torso was split at the top of his little black shorts and was filled with notes written on used envelopes, torn bits of theater programs, and the back of grocery lists in Joe's handwriting. She tossed a handful on the keyboard before her and opened them one by one.

They would all have happy endings, of course; all her plays had happy endings.

What could she have been thinking? With a dismissive hand she swept all the notes onto the floor beside her chair.

"Nothing is funny anymore," she said aloud.

Ferdy couldn't have agreed more. He had been hanging around Adelaide ever since his chewing out at headquarters. Now he glumly stretched out on the computer desk between Adelaide and the monitor. Dabbling in her thoughts had been no fun. For someone who wrote comedy this woman could be really depressing, and given his line of work, he knew depressing.

With a groan he felt her thoughts turn once again to Monica, and how Adelaide could beat her at the game that had started so long ago.

*Hacking her way through the dense underbrush of the Amazon jungle, Adelaide travels alone except for the news camera crew which had insisted on following her. She is resolute in her search for her friend, and neither tropical thunderstorms nor terribly large ugly spiders can halt her progress. After weeks of trudging she finally arrives at the clearing of the village the natives had told her about and with a sense of horror beyond words sees Monica, struggling desperately against a large group of very determined pygmies. . .the cameras start filming Monica. . .no that wouldn't do at all.*

*Adelaide alights from the train at the main station in Calcutta, hot, tired, and surrounded by beggars like small fish around chum. She hires a rickshaw and gives directions to the address given to her, which turns out to be a poor structure of sticks and tin graced by the term "hovel." Adelaide walks through the doorless entryway to find Monica on a filthy pallet, moaning, "Water. Water." Ignoring the bandaged stumps which Monica raises in both welcome and supplication, Adelaide takes the bottle of Perrier out of her backpack and presses it to Monica's rotting lips. As the last drops of water gurgle out of the bottle, Monica gives an echoing gurgle, gazes her gratitude at her old friend, and slumps. The camera crew captures the mourning in Adelaide's eyes as she emerges into the relentless sunlight outside the hovel. The beggars soberly link together and perform a solemn conga line through the cluster of shanties, while Adelaide talks to the press about her next play, "No, Calcutta"...hm.*

For the first time that morning Ferdy watched Adelaide smile. Mortals were truly awesome, cheering themselves up by imagining the death of a friend by a horrible disease. He found himself thinking that devils were kind of superfluous. There was plenty of evil in the human soul to get any job done that the Boss wanted. Ferdy just had to make sure it went in the right direction. He sat up, let his bony legs dangle over the edge of the desk while he studied Adelaide close-up. Could she kill? Did she have enough envy inside her to engineer a friend's death? Preposterous thought. But if she followed through on her wishings Monica would be a martyr and Ferdy would be last week's spinach dip as far as his continued existence was concerned. Right down the disposal—or Gregory's gullet. It would be Becket all over again. In the latter part of the twentieth century he couldn't quite picture Adelaide running Monica through with anything but words, but with this breed you never knew. Guarding Monica clearly meant keeping an eye on Adelaide too.

Adelaide's smile dropped as instantly as it had come. Her eyes closed and her hand went over them as if to hide an embarrassment from even herself.

"You're losing it, babe," she whispered. In the slight southern twang of Monica's voice, she said, "Have you seen Del lately?" Then she answered, in another voice that was remarkably like Palma's, "No, but I've been meaning to."

☿ ☿ ☿

These days Joe's business was off a bit. All the condominium dwelling dogs had gone north shortly after the spring solstice, like a canine version of migratory birds. Starting around mid-October they would begin their relentless return to Miami, crated on planes or sedated in the backseat of white cars. In preparation for their coming, hurricane shutters would disappear from the windows of their twenty story apartment buildings on the beach to be replaced, if you could see that high, by their little faces staring out to sea. Not as dramatic as the swallows of Capistrano, but just as sure a pattern of nature. Until the great condominium dog migration Joe had his usual clientele of year round house dwelling dogs. These dogs kept him busy for a good part of the day, but he still had several extra hours during the summer months. It gave him some extra time to read, which he liked, and to worry about Del, which he didn't.

"I wonder," Joe said to a Llasa Apso who sat on his lap in a canvas deck chair at the shop, "whether it would have been different if we'd had children. Maybe forcing the focus off ourselves would have made our lives different. Who knows, maybe Del's obsession with plays is just a drive to produce offspring." He stroked the silk of the dog's ear with a couple of sausage-like fingers. "You're a woman, Doctor Nelly, what do you think?" On hearing her name the Llasa responded by climbing up onto the shelf of Joe's belly and licking his nose. "Yeah, that's what they all tell me. Don't worry about it, it's a woman thing. But things around the house have changed, and I don't like it. She's home more, but she's edgy, she's lost her energy, and all she does is watch TV. We don't talk about it, but I know she's looking for news of Monica, and when she finds it she's worse than before."

Joe closed his eyes and felt a humming in his arms, a yearning to hold Adelaide until she was calm, the way he could calm an animal. But lately there was an invisible thorny field around her which kept him away. He kept trying to get through with offerings of food and occasional small animals, but nothing really worked and the lack of success was making him feel heavy inside and out. Something had to be done, some radical cure to snap her out of her obsession with Monica's condition.

After the Llasa's owner picked her up he made a few stops and headed home. There were still a good three hours of daylight left in the hot mid-summer day. The humidity assaulted him whenever he left air-conditioning, producing a sensation like breathing through warm wet cotton. The usual two p.m. thunderstorm had failed to materialize and that put the entire lower peninsula in a cranky mood. After being honked at constantly for driving too slowly Joe himself was as close to cranky as he ever got. He opened the front door almost wishing that Adelaide's Volvo had not been sitting in the driveway. The suit in the dry cleaner's bag which he carried felt like a weapon, or a shield.

"Hi, Del!" he cheerfully forced. "I'm home. Almost." Back out to the car again and returning with two plastic shopping bags. After depositing them in the kitchen he walked over to the door of her office but didn't go through, getting a feel for her mood while he leaned against the door jamb.

"I brought your favorite tonight."

"What's my favorite?"

Encouraged by a response he moved closer to her chair. "Cheese tortellini with pesto sauce."

Adelaide looked up from the computer with a half-smile that drew up one side of her face. Joe nearly leaned and kissed the corner of the smile but checked his downward swing. Still, the half-smile was so heartening he held out his hand to see if she would take it. "Come on, hava glassa wine."

"I thought cheese tortellini with pesto was your favorite," she said, but took the proffered hand.

He drew her into the kitchen and sat her at the table while he poured a glass of wine and began preparing the meal. "Oh, no, remember over at Palma's about a year and a half ago, maybe four boyfriends ago—"

"You mean the conductor?"

"...I don't think so. You were eating cheese tortellini with pesto and you practically came at the dinner table. You said, 'God, I love this stuff.'"

Adelaide sipped her white wine and let her fingers rest on the stem. Joe watched her visibly relax, and felt himself relax a little in response.

"You remember everything," she said. "You amaze me. But you have to admit 'I love this stuff' isn't the same as 'my favorite.' Tell you what. How about if I concede that it's one of my favorites?"

Joe paused from whisking the pesto in a saucepan and narrowed his eyes as if her question warranted focused consideration. "Okay, I can agree to that," he said soberly. He studied her a while longer, taking in the growing softness around her lips and the smoothing of the place above the bridge of her nose. "But if we're negotiating here I want something too."

"Not my virginity, you cad."

"Curses, foiled again," he said mildly. "Well, then, can we get a puppy?"

"Are you being serious?"

"No, just priming you. What I really want is for you to change your mind about not going to Palma's party next week."

"Joe, you know Monica's going to be there and I just don't want to see her right now. Or Palma either, for that matter."

He poured more wine for them both and joined her at the table while the water for the tortellini took its time to boil. "Hey, where's my butch wife who's not afraid of anybody?"

"I'm not afraid," she would have snapped it out, but the wine softened her voice, making her sound more like a child going into the haunted house ride at the carnival.

Joe thought, and started to chuckle. "Remember when you were telling Monica how to be more assertive, when she had to go before the. . .whatever that group is called she had to prove herself to before she could be a priest. . ." he started laughing harder with the recollection, "and she was so afraid because in those days everyone in the church was a man, and you told her. . .you told her. . ."

Adelaide nearly choked on her wine before she could tip the glass back, remembering too. "You mean when I told her she should strap a dildo to her forehead?"

Joe sucked his laugh in, making kind of a snocking sound. "I'll never forget the vision I had of Monica sitting before some committee of tight-assed clerics politely ignoring a huge pink pecker on her forehead dangling—"

"Oh, no!" Adelaide screamed, "No d-dangling. If she's going to be really assertive it has to be erect." She gasped for air. "One—one of those—those hard rubber jobs."

"All right," laughed Joe, holding the back of his hand against his forehead with the index finger pointing, "so jutting, how's that, jutting out from a piece of black elastic. And what was even funnier, I remember this look on her face—"

"Like she might consider it! We were all so crazy then you never knew."

Their eyes were shut and their mouths open, bodies rocking back and forth on the wooden captain's chairs with merriment. Their laughter bounced against the kitchen appliances and doubled with the echo. Reaching for the edge of the table to steady himself, Joe's hand jerked out and swiped at his wine glass which tipped and spilled. The sound of laughter slowly died in the house as Joe lurched for the dish towel and reached the wine before it reached the edge of the table. They both looked away embarrassed because they knew how precious the sound was, the sound of their laughing together, and these days how rare.

Joe finished preparing the pasta. They ate in silence, and later made unscheduled love in silence. Afterwards, when the glow of the bathroom light made Joe's semen shine like a snail's track across Adelaide's thigh, she agreed to go to the gala. Then she rolled to her side, trying to steady her breathing so Joe wouldn't hear the deep, long breaths that come with tears. He heard anyway, but let her be, felt the heaviness slowly seep back onto his own skin as he crawled out of bed to set up the morning espresso. He stood by the bed staring at her back, thinking how under the covers pulled up to her chin she was naked and sticky with him. For a moment a pain infused his heaviness and he welcomed the change. He allowed himself to think the words he never said because he was too afraid of the response, or lack of one. *I love you, I love you, I love you, I love you.*

☿ ☿ ☿

Palma grabbed a large topiary cat stuck in the grass of her backyard. The cat was stuck in a playful pose, down at the front with its back end stuck up in the air as if just having finished a leap. There were five cats like this, in various poses, secured to the lawn by metal poles.

"They look very nice," encouraged Estella Too, who stood by her side also surveying the backyard.

"Oh, I suppose it will be all right." She gave the cat a harder nudge to straighten it. "As long as those big fans don't blow them over. I keep wondering what logic lead me to decide to have a fundraiser off season, let alone require black tie in the middle of the summer?"

"In season you're busy with the opera and the heart association and Children's Home Society. Are Monica and Adelaide coming?"

"I'm afraid so, but I'm trying not to think about it. Every time I do I picture Del making a scene like in the hospital room and photographers from a tabloid getting a picture of Monica with me, and they'll catch me with shiny makeup and a sour look. How do they manage to make people look so bad in those things?"

"They probably touch up the photos. It makes the readers feel good to see glamorous people look ugly."

"It's a mess, that whole situation, and I don't know how to fix it." Palma continued her reconnaissance. Four days to go and things were shaping up nicely. The bare skeleton of the gala had already been set about. Folding tables and chairs placed comfortably for guests who wanted to sit. The frame for the white silk canopy over the buffet on the lawn sloping down to the lake behind her home. A stage for the dancers on this side of the pool.

That was a departure. She had intended to cover the pool as she usually did for fundraisers and use that for dancing. Her party consultant, though, Parties by Maxx, had been inspired recently by movies from the forties. Why not float a platform in the pool for the orchestra? It would be so dramatic with the pool lights shining up from beneath. Maxx had fairly drooled with enthusiasm while describing the vision it would create. And indeed, it promised to be spectacular. The platform was successfully in place already, anchored by ropes tied to concrete blocks which maintained its three foot distance from all sides of the pool. The platform was big enough to hold whatever size orchestra she chose, short of symphonic, and stable enough so the violin section wouldn't go overboard if the drummer stood up too fast.

"I could kill Maxx," she muttered, though loudly enough for Estella Too to hear.

"Still no progress on the band? Are you sure you don't want me to call my cousin Edoard?"

"Maxx was so adamant about that swing band. 'You have the floating stage,' he said. 'No rock and roll, no country, no latin, no classical, not even easy listening.' He was so definite, and we waited too long to find the right one, and now most of the bands have gone north for the summer. I'll be lucky to get a—a kazoo player with a hare lip."

"Something will happen. It always does," Estella Too philosophized as she stared at the platform. She stared harder. "What is that thing in the center?"

"What?"

"See in the center of the platform, that little flat thing?"

Palma walked over the grey flagstone patio to the pool and nimbly leapt across the three feet of water. She bent down at its center and picked up the small plastic case. "It's a cassette tape," she called to Estella who remained on the patio. "And it has a label on it that says. . ." without the glasses she seldom wore, her eyes narrowed to focus. "It says, 'Play me, sugar babe.'"

Estella Too's brows shot up as she bustled closer to the pool. "Sugar babe? Who could have gotten onto the grounds to put this here without your permission? The devil. . ."

Palma sprang back onto the patio and made a few mental connections as she patted Estella Too's hand. "Or maybe an angel. Maybe an orchestra angel. Let's hear what's on it."

# Chapter Twenty
## In Which Mortal Life Doesn't Go On

Except for the soft drink cans spread through the house there was no sign that a film crew had been at Monica's house most of the afternoon. Now she sat exhausted on the edge of her bed, looking past herself in the dresser mirror while cold green washcloths draped over her hot bare shoulders. She felt like a tired frog surfacing in a lily pond. The nice young man from The Today Show had been very kind, and understood why she had to have the interview at home rather than on diocesan property. She owed some respect to the Presiding Bishop's wishes, and even agreed with him that a shot of her unbandaged hands elevating the consecrated host lacked taste. They could get an establishing shot of St. Stephen's if they wanted; freedom of the press and all that. The interview and shoot had taken five hours, from which she was told there would be edited a seven minute segment. All this for seven minutes? she had asked, and was told that she was getting as a bank robbery.

The nice young man had asked if she had friends who could be interviewed. Monica thought of Palma, then Adelaide, and said no.

But she was going to the ball tonight. She might be a stigmatic, but she wasn't tired enough to play the hermit. Besides, she had sent Gus out to hunt for a set of evening gloves and wouldn't dream of wasting them. Rising to go into the bathroom Monica eyed the popsicle stick crucifix on the wall.

"Say," she said, "If you're in the mood for miracles, how about finishing this menopause thing, huh?" And not really anticipating a response, concluded, "Be that way." She shed her warming terry cloth lily pads in the bathroom sink and pulled up the straps of her slip. A little powder, a little lipstick...

A knock at the door.

That couldn't be Adelaide and Joe, she thought. While they often used to pick her up for this sort of thing, they hadn't talked in two weeks. Monica pulled on her chenille peacock robe hoping she wouldn't start sweating again and went to open the front door.

She didn't use the peep hole. She would open the door no matter what the person on the other side looked like, anyhow.

On her front porch was an attractive middle-aged man with greying hair, silver blue eyes, and just enough grin to give him a devilish air. He was dressed in a tuxedo that quietly respected his tall, lean form. Before Monica could speak he said in a deep gravelly voice that made her stomach twitter delightedly, "Your escort service is here."

"I'm sorry," she began, then stopped and squinted, having left her glasses in the bathroom. "Gus, is that you?"

"Damn right it is."

"You're absolutely gorgeous!"

"Fuckin' A," he agreed.

"I don't understand. I'm sorry," she repeated, "please come on in. What is this all about?" As she fluttered and spoke he moved into her living room, not with the self-concious stiffness of a man who is unaccustomed to formal wear, but with the grace and fluidity of a ballerina strolling on the beach in nothing but her own skin. He sat down on the tropical bird couch and hoisted his right ankle casually onto his left knee.

"I'm taking you to the party tonight. Get dressed. Look out," he commented softly, "you're about to get blood on your robe."

Monica's naked hands flew up in embarrassment as she grabbed a towel from the kitchen pass-through. But the embarrassment passed quickly into a rush of love for this man who spoke so casually about her wounds. No shock, no evasion, as if he were an old buddy telling her she had spinach in her teeth. Twenty minutes later they were in her car on the way to Palma's, with Gus driving. Her hands were bandaged and hidden in the black satin evening gloves, resting on the lap of her floor length purple gown. The dress nicely accentuated her love handles and matched her favorite dream catcher earrings. Monica thought of one small problem.

"Gus."

"Hm."

"Did you buy a ticket for this shindig?"

"No. I figured I'd use yours. No one would dare accuse a bishop of party crashing."

"I see."

☿ ☿ ☿

The first thing to hit the guests at Palma's gala as the valet attendant opened the car door was the aroma of night blooming jasmine. A Floridian can stop noticing the smell of salt after living on the coast for many years but despite its tiny, delicate petals, jasmine is too bold to ever be ignored. Banks of it ran beside the broad stone path that lead around the side of the house to the patio area. The sprays of white flowers tumbled down over their hedges like a light southern snow.

Joe followed Adelaide along the path as they were directed, knowing that inside the house Estella Too would be clucking and gesturing at the servers. The backyard was breathtaking, even if it wasn't Palma's best effort. A white canopy glowed in the early evening light, its silk billowed by a mild breeze. The same soft fabric spread over the tables and chairs dotting the grass. As he stepped onto the grass Joe nearly bumped into a topiary cat the size of goat that was stopped in mid-frolic. But it was the smells that really took his attention, the jasmine being only a prelude to entice him in. All of the women, and most of the men, moved about with their own distinct scents like giant gaudy flowers. Like being in a tropical botanic garden where the flowers could move. He wondered if the women there knew each other by their smells, as dogs did. The evening had cooled into the lower eighties but the lingering heat blended with sippings of summer wine had warmed the scents until they rose off the skin. As he watched a woman in a gown the color of lemon cream lean intimately into a conversation, he imagined he could feel her perfume rising against his cheek like that of a blossom screaming for pollination.

The smell of food intruded delightfully when a server passed by with trays of rumaki and crab stuffed mushroom caps. He had magically appeared just as Joe selected two glasses of champagne from another passing tray. Joe fought the urge to grab the hors d'oeuvres tray and instead lifted one skewer. There were more substantial snacks on a side table featuring an ice sculpture of a cat sitting before its food dish. With an exchange of nods, Joe ambled over to the table. Adelaide's nod meant, "Go on, I'm fine here."

Joe's nod meant, "I'll bring you something."

The ice food dish before the ice cat was filled with red caviar. One of the guests standing beside the cat introduced himself, Joe marveling that he was able to shake hands while holding a champagne glass in one hand and a caviar-smeared cracker in the other. Certainly an accomplished buffet grazer.

"Lovely surroundings, aren't they?" said the man, portly like Joe, but not as tall.

"Palma certainly knows how to do this," Joe agreed, focused on the table, strategizing how to most efficiently load the very small plate he picked from a stack.

There was a pause while Joe felt the man forming the expected question.

"So," said the man, "What do you do?"

As always, Joe resisted the urge to say, "about what?" Instead, "I'm an animal groomer."

"An animal groomer. Well." Even as Joe decided to pile one plate with just cold shrimp he could feel the man beside him doing a quick calculation, matching him up on a table of professions and their average gross incomes, as if he were being qualified for a mortgage loan. The portly man soon drifted away.

A voice somewhere off by the pool said loudly enough so that as many as possible could hear his joke, "So how many cats can you get spayed for a hundred bucks? I want to make sure I'm getting my money's worth!" Simultaneously Joe noticed a quick movement close to the grass on his right. Something ran under the white cloth covering the hors d'oeuvres table. Thinking rat, he cautiously lifted the cloth with the toe of his shoe and glanced down. A small black cat stopped licking the stray roe off its paw and stared imperiously at Joe. As if the single black cat created an epiphany for him, Joe could suddenly see at least a dozen cats in the yard. Most of them were wandering, or lounging about the lawn away from the guests, though one black tabby with a white muzzle kept trying to snatch the pate from an elderly woman seated in a wheel chair. Another cat, of a marmalade hue, cocked its tail and looked like it was rubbing against someone, though nothing was there that mortal eyes could see. Its cry penetrated the air with, "YODEE, YODEE, YODEE" in a steady flow until one of the servers picked up the offending animal and put it in the house where Joe could still see it pacing in front of the plate glass door wiping a trail of mucus from its nose onto the glass. Palma really did know how to do it, he thought.

Then he spotted her. Palma was standing just on the other side of the pool. A twenty piece swing band, all dressed in white like the rest of the decorations, was playing at full tilt on a platform in the water; she was just visible between the gleam of two trumpets easing through "Blue Lagoon." The conductor wielded a baton with his right hand while his left elbow supported his horn in Dorsey fashion. A few beats and glides of the baton, then Joe watched the conductor's attention diverted by an arriving couple. With an upswing of his baton the conductor waved to a tall man standing at the patio entrance with Monica and gave a slight bow. Scanning the crowd for a glimpse of Adelaide, Joe spotted her standing near, almost against, the side of the house, her beige pantsuit blending chameleon-like with the wall. He knew she had seen Monica and kept his own eyes fixed on her in case she signaled to him.

Nobody but Joe, and maybe Adelaide, noticed an uncustomary hesitation in Monica. Just a pause, an intake of breath, and then like an engaging eggplant in her purple gown she burst upon the party. A passing champagne tray provided her with a glass which she held high, saying in a voice loud enough to be heard over 200 chattering voices, "TO PALMA BLANCO. ANDREW LLOYD WEBER WOULD BE PROUD!"

Laughter rippled appreciatively across the crowd, and carried Palma to where Monica stood. While conversations resumed, glances followed her and discretely watched the progress of the greeting. Not only was their friendship famous in Palma's set, but Monica's recent celebrity made her a curiosity even in a crowd of celebrities. The two knew they were being watched, and played their usual parts.

"I know, I know," Palma giggled, responding to some old in-joke. "I laughed, I cried—"

"It was better than Cats!" Monica reached out to touch one of Palma's earrings, a spray of wire filaments each ending in a tiny diamond. "Love your earrings."

"And yours!" Palma said vaguely to the dream catchers which

rested against Monica's cheeks. Her twinkling glance shifted to Gus.

"You'll remember Augustine Thomas."

The twinkle blinked out briefly while Palma unsuccessfully tried to remember where she had met this attractive man. No matter. The twinkle returned as she made a quick deduction worthy of Sherlock Holmes and responded obliquely, "Of course. That church function..."

Gus didn't even answer. He was busy assessing the dancing capabilities of her dress with the skill of a physicist calculating a space shot. A white Versace gown held up on one shoulder with a brooch to match her earrings, clinging around the curve of her bottom and easing out gently from there to the ground. Arms and legs unrestricted. Circumference of hem roughly seventy-two inches. Shoes with straps.

"Dance?" he interrupted. Before she could answer he tucked his right arm around her waist, cupped her hand in his and stepped her effortlessly between the tables to the dance floor. The band switched from "Pennsylvania Six Five Hundred" to "The Best Things Happen While You're Dancing." In the center of the dance floor he stood still a moment, holding her, looking off over her shoulder as if he had no interest in her, only in where to enter the music. Uncomfortable with the pause, she began the usual conversation that was part of her social dancing.

"I've forgotten how long you've known Monica."

Gus closed his eyes briefly. "Sssh," more of a soft release of air than an actual hushing. He finally took a long stride into her with his left leg that established his command over her body. Her right leg instinctively, submissively moved away from his and her eyes flashed with surprise at his aggression. His torso, firm and straight, pressed unyielding against hers so that they moved as one while their arms and legs slid in mirror images. Once around the dance floor in a slow box step, turning, turning. She missed a step and he swayed back and forth gently, still with the music while he place his right hand between them, his pinky and thumb connecting the same spot in their midsections.

"Feel my diaphragm," he whispered.

He ignored her look and concentrated on the rhythm hidden in the melody. Within the course of a single pattern he could tell how much dancing she'd had. Cotillion, and never a real partner. That was fine. She was up on the balls of her feet and knew the slow, slow, quick quick routine. With his three fingers pressed against her back precisely ten inches above her pelvic girdle and his diaphragm sending messages to hers she was no longer Palma Blanco. She was an instrument to be played.

A wink at the conductor seguéd the music into a rhumba. Nothing too exotic, just something to get her tuned up. He kept her close at first, with simple steps, letting her feel the confident control of his body over hers, enjoying the natural roll of her hips with the rhythm. He felt her chin touch his chest and nearly lost concentration. Releasing his hold on her back he gave her a gentle turn with his left arm, pushing her out and bringing her back to his body in one fluid motion, facing her away from him while his fingers lightly played across her abdomen. Once more out, then back, and he stepped directly into her, placing his right thigh between hers for balance. He swept her body slowly in a low arc from right to left, then brought her back up to him on the last notes of the song without retracting his thigh, maintaining his control.

Palma, on the other hand, for the first time in her life had no control at all. She couldn't recall when the fox trot had ended and the rhumba began, or that her hips had rocked back and forth obediently to Gus's silent command. All she knew was that she had never felt quite this way before. It was like a vibrating forty-five degree ski slope fifteen hundred feet glider through the Grand Canyon sex on a cloud champagne marijuana high (even though she couldn't be sure about that last bit because she'd never smoked marijuana). It was the most perfect she'd ever felt, though she could take no responsibility for it. Other men she had known were eager to please her, to give her whatever she wanted. This one seemed not only to know what he wanted, but to be able to take it from her, delighting her in the process. Yes, there was something of aggression in it. Like a patient coming up from a delightful dose of sodium pentathol she struggled weakly for her voice.

"It feels like you're teaching me, but by-passing my brain and teaching my body," she murmured, half to herself.

Gus cleared his throat, preparing to keep the huskiness of emotion out of his voice. "Pay attention. There will be an exam."

"Written?" she said coyly.

"Oral."

Another part of her body leaped into the dance, already drunken with melody and movement. Her heart beat against his chest and she was unable to consider how she appeared, standing so close to this man without a note of music in the air.

Meanwhile another, uninvited heart, was beating behind the jasmine bushes as Melba McGregor peered through the shrubbery. Even though she didn't think she'd have the courage to actually crash the party, she was dressed in her Sunday best just in case. A pattern of yellow squares over a sky blue nylon shirt dress with a wide skirt and narrow belt. She had walked up the driveway following the sound of the music, glanced at the bored valet to see if she was noticed and quickly turned right behind the bushes lining the path. There she stood, searching for Monica, her arms thrust through the scratchy bush to open a viewing space. Unlike Gus, she had no plan for this evening, but her stalking had become a habit that she couldn't quite shake no matter how dreary, or in this case, how uncomfortable it might be. Not that she wanted to stop, she thought. Sooner or later her efforts would have some effect, would make Monica feel... ashamed...or...just real bad...or something...something that would make her make things the way they were before. Before all this blood and...*sex*. The word popped inadvertently into her mind as she spotted Gus and Palma on the dance floor.

*Sex,* thought Ferdy, also watching the dancers. He was sitting in a patio chair beside a woman whose hair and mouth were both held in tight lines. He had arrived with Adelaide and Joe, had no idea that Melba was behind the bushes, and was currently more interested in screwing Palma than in watching over Monica. Interested. That put it mildly. He felt his groin tingle as he pictured the spot between them where Palma's pelvis pressed unavoidably against Gus's trouser fly. Ferdy cradled his throbbing member in his left claw. Trying to get to Palma through the Yorkshire Terrier had been a long shot; certainly he would have a better chance with Gus.

"So what do you think?" he said to the tight woman beside him who was, blessedly, oblivious to the presence of a very erect demon. "Should I fuck her or should I do my job?" He marked the presence of Joe by the food table, Monica picking her way over the grass to Adelaide, and the cat calling "YODEE" to him from behind the sliding glass door. "Everybody seems okay, for the time being, everyone getting what they want. Except that Yody cat, who apparently wants me." He contemplated his hard-on again. Figuring it would be more responsive than the woman beside him, he spoke to his penis this time. "Well, you don't have to tell me what you want. It's always plain and simple for you, isn't it?" The penis gave an enthusiastic throb, while the music and the chatter and the perfumed summer air enticed him. "It's not so simple for me," said Ferdy. "Sometimes I don't know what I want." There was something about the mortal world that drew you in if you stayed too long, he thought. A seductive current that had something to do with so many complicated things. Acting like the person you wanted to be, for instance. They did that a lot, and sometimes it worked. Then there were things like giving and getting and how it was hard to tell the difference between them. He remembered, still with sadness, Yves's gentle conversation on the parapet of Notre Dame. He recalled Joe's ministrations to him in the tub at the grooming salon. And that made him think of Monica carefully bathing a man who disgusted her. Ferdy looked at the marmalade Yody cat pacing back and forth inside the house, yearning for him. Back and forth, back and forth, caught wanting behind the glass. Like himself, Ferdy thought, caught on his side of eternity watching the mortal world and wanting...wanting what?

And that made him think of Gregory. His penis drooped.

"You're right again, old buddy," said Ferdy to the penis. "Fucking is safer than thinking any time." He rose from the chair, flew to the dance floor, and slipped into Gus who felt nothing but a pleasant tingling just under his skull which he attributed to his pleasure in conquering Palma. Ferdy adjusted to his new space, thinking it was certainly a better fit than the Yorkie. He thrilled to the feeling of Palma melting into him, could sense her warm breath against the side of his neck while they swayed to a slow tune. He wondered where her bedroom was. If he tried to take her here he'd be stopped by a dozen party guests and even Palma, ready for seduction as she was, might conceivably object.

"Okay, let's see what this baby can do," he said to himself, and revved the gears for a test drive. First he pumped Gus's heart, sending extra blood through arteries down to the organ that needed it most. Then he concentrated on the valve that would close off the veins to keep Gus's penis engorged. He had been checking out the condition of his prostate when it suddenly seemed that a lot of time had gone by. Ferdy flexed a bit. Nothing was happening. He checked the blood flow. Sure enough, millions of corpuscles were bustling their way southward. He flexed again. Gus was about as stiff as a raw oyster. Ferdy cranked hard. The oyster stirred, then nestled back into its cotton shell. The realization hit him like a snoot full of brimstone.

"Shit," he said, throwing his small body against the walls inside Gus, and "Shit, shit, shit, shit, SHIT!"

The last "shit" was strong enough to be voluble, though Palma couldn't quite make out what Gus said. Gus cleared his throat and tried not to think about whether the heavy smoking and drinking he had done in the last few years were creating a permanent condition. The band started up again, and they began a slow tango.

"...sex," Adelaide was saying to Monica, who had joined her by the side of the house while Gus danced with Palma.

"I know, I can't decide either whether it's dancing or foreplay," Monica responded, watching them. "Maybe he'll do me next. Where is that hors d'oeuvres tray? Servers are like cops. Never around when you need them. What is Palma serving? I hope it's not the clams casino, they tend to get rubbery soon after they come out of the oven so they're not good being carried around outside like this. Oh, there's one. Yoo-hoo. Over here. No, that's okay. We'll take the whole thing. You can go get another one, can't you? It'll be safe on this table. Leave a few napkins, too. Okay. This one looks like a rumaki—you got your chicken liver, you got your water chestnut, you got your strip of bacon all skewered together. Yep, definitely a rumaki. Want a rumaki, Del?"

"No, thanks."

"Well, there's other stuff here, too. Some sort of deep fried thing." Monica bit into the end and watched a glob of melted cheese drop to the bosom of her purple gown. "Oh, wouldn't you know it, I wonder if champagne works as well as seltzer water is supposed to." She wiped away the excess cheese with a finger, then dipped her napkin into her glass and began rubbing furiously at the pale yellow spot on the purple fabric. She continued speaking as she cleaned, "Look at her, she's like you, she never seems to age. She doesn't even have those little jowly things yet. And the skin under her arms doesn't sway with the rest of her body. Looks like when she danced at her wedding. God, how long ago was that? Has it been twenty years?" As she spoke Monica realized she was babbling, but the icy calm she felt from Adelaide put her on edge.

She was tired from the events of the day, and she was edgy, and she was beginning to regret coming to the party at all.

For Adelaide the calm exterior wasn't coming easy, even after the champagne. She was having more trouble maintaining control than she thought she would. She acknowledged to herself that she was acting like a sullen child. Monica wasn't really to blame for her recent theatrical set-back. But then Monica was here and Monica was somebody she could hurt as much as she was hurting. All she had to do is wander through the conversation until she discovered Monica's current weakness, and attack it. The word "wicked" appeared on the slate of her mind, and she thought it odd that such an archaic term was still so descriptive. Yes, she was being wicked, and if she wanted to stop, it seemed she couldn't. It was hard to tell. She disguised the dampness of her eyes in the glint of the setting sun against her glasses and answered Monica's question about Palma's wedding.

"I never make an effort to remember weddings. I prefer funerals. They're so much more definite."

A month before Monica would have retorted and they would have both laughed. Tonight there was something in Adelaide's tone that made her respond, "You're not serious?" as if to a new acquaintance.

"Serious? Of course not," said Adelaide lightly, hiding her bitterness. "I'm never serious. I don't do drama, remember?."

Monica's next question was unexpected. "Besides, there's Joe, isn't there?"

Adelaide was thrown off balance, and felt the puzzlement show in her face. "What about Joe?"

"You can't be totally down on marriage with a man like Joe in your life. Isn't it funny that Palma, who deserves so much, is the one who's looking for love, but you're the one who found it?"

Adelaide's head gave a slight jerk. Whether or not Monica was the one doing the attacking, that's what it felt like despite the fact that she had said it mildly and was still rubbing at the spot on her dress as if she were only paying half-attention.

"Shit, Monica, are you still on that?" Adelaide snapped.

"On what?"

"On that 'let's open up our hearts and be honest with each other' kick. Jesus, Monica, give it up. No, on second thought—" Adelaide saw a couple sitting at one of the lawn tables very nearby, looking at each other without speaking. She could tell it was because they were listening to her conversation. Clutching the edge of Monica's evening glove, Adelaide pulled her away from the crowd, closer to the night blooming jasmine bushes. The waves of her anger were so strong Adelaide thought she could see the bush trembling at her approach.

"Let's get real honest. How about we just cut through all the crap and say you've won," Adelaide said, almost in a whisper.

"What are you talking about?" said Monica, matching her whisper.

"I'd say that divine favor in the form of miracles beats out any number of little statuettes and framed pieces of paper. So let's say that you've won and be done with it."

Monica's eyes softened to tears as her understanding grew. "Is that what's been bothering you? Oh, Del, I don't want to beat you. I don't even want to play. I stopped playing years ago. I'm not jealous of you."

Adelaide couldn't listen. Instead she was hearing every conversation that she'd had in her mind over recent weeks. Now the words of those conversations were coming out whether or not Monica knew her part. "Bullshit. And the word is 'envious.' You've always been envious of me. Of my fame. Admit it. It was a big deal when you became a priest, but that got old after a while so you had to become a bishop. But that wasn't even big enough.

Do you realize you got that stigmata thing the day after I told you I was up for my fifth Tony?" Her whispering increased its force until it became a scream that only Monica could hear. "So don't tell me you're not playing! You're playing, all right!"

Monica's hand came up to touch Adelaide's, but Adelaide's hand went up at the same time to take another slug of champagne. No contact was made. That seemed to be all it took to ignite Monica's own anger. When she spoke her voice matched Adelaide's.

"All these years you've been taking that competition stuff this seriously?" she scream- whispered back. "You're out of your mind." While Monica filled her lungs Adelaide waited to see if there would be another blast, and there was. "But if you really want to know, yes, I am jealous, or envious, or whatever you want to call it. You want to know of what?"

"Hah! I knew it. Go ahead and say it." Adelaide snarled.

"Not your money, or your fame. I envy you Joe."

"JOE!"

The night blooming jasmine bush beside them emitted a heightened perfume, as if something was heating it up.

"Yes, Joe! All my life I've gone to dinner parties alone and I see the two of you there and I've watched how hard he loves you and how you never care."

"Of course I care! Joe has everything he wants," Adelaide said, hating herself for suddenly being on the defensive.

"But you never really give him you, you know what I mean? You hide your love as if it's something to be ashamed of. I know it's there, Del, we all do, no matter how hard you try to cover it up with snappy dialogue. Joe knows you have love inside you and that's why he keeps loving you, hoping that someday you'll let it out and discover it's for him."

Adelaide opened her lips to speak, but because she couldn't think of anything to say Monica was allowed to fumble on with her thoughts.

"I don't care if this sounds like a sermon. Maybe a sermon is what you need. Don't you realize how much he adores you, like a god, and that espresso he makes you every morning, like, like a sacrament to show his love. And all my life I've wished someone would love me that way. But it doesn't seem to matter how great a personality you have. I kind of think you need ankles and maybe even a waist to have a man like that fall in love with you."

Monica's words had turned pleading, with all the anger gone, but they still felt to Adelaide like a hammer on stone. Adelaide set her teeth against the impact as she taunted, "You don't need a man, remember? You've got God. Isn't God enough for you?"

The jasmine bush shook as if in response to her anger.

"Well, I tell you, Del," Monica whispered, the screaming part of her voice replaced by weariness. "Sometimes you just want somebody with skin on them."

"Well, God knows Joe's got enough skin to go around. Tell you what, I'll loan him to you."

"If only you could."

It wasn't so much the words as the way Monica's face changed when she said them. Adelaide knew what love looked like. This time it looked stricken. A wave of sadness washed away any anger she had felt a moment ago.

"My God, Monica. How long?"

"As long as I can remember."

The next thing Monica saw was Adelaide's face, her parted lips suddenly gaping wide in surprise. The last thing Adelaide saw was a large angry woman pounding toward them with a shriek like an eagle protecting its nest. The woman was waving the nest over her head which Adelaide later recalled was actually one of the topiary cats. Monica turned to see what Adelaide saw and took the first blow from the cat bush full in her face.

"Melba!" she screamed as she stumbled backwards.

"Fornicator!" screamed Melba in return and hit her again with the cat.

The absurd sight of Monica being whipped by a blowsy woman with a bush in the shape of a cat dispelled Adelaide's immobilized shock and made her laugh with relief. The attacking woman was able to keep Monica off balance, but didn't seem to be inflicting any real damage. The rest of the crowd was unabashedly stunned at the sight of the bishop being set upon. More than one glass dropped while minds checked their memories for the more obscure rules of etiquette. Did one try to separate three women who were apparently brawling or politely pretend it wasn't happening and allow them to duke it out?

As for the band, it had seen entire wedding parties erupt into free-for-alls with a three tiered cake turned into a ballistic missile; this was nothing, comparatively speaking. Though aware of the brouhaha they neither dropped a beat nor missed a note. The only creatures completely oblivious to the battle were the yody cat which had slipped out a side door of the house and was sniffing around the patio for Ferdy, and Ferdy himself, who was still concentrating on giving Gus an erection even as Gus's attention reluctantly turned to the noise by the shrubbery.

Melba hacked at Monica with the cat, raising it up over her right shoulder and bringing it down quickly in diagonal blows across Monica's body before she could regain her balance enough to fight back or run. Half-blinded by her rage, Melba was barely aware that she was backing Monica in the direction of the swimming pool. She seemed unaware of the people watching, of Adelaide pulling at her skirt, of the yody cat approaching her feet. She was simply lost in striking at Monica, at everything Monica was and stood for, and even at her own Malcolm who had the audacity to die.

Then the four things happened. If any single thing hadn't happened the result might have been different.

If.

Monica's heel slipped against the concrete lip of the pool and she started to topple over slowly, waving her arms like she was attempting to fly. A swipe of the topiary cat caught Monica's dream catcher earrings onto the chicken wire form of the bush. Melba found her follow-through abruptly halted and tried unsuccessfully to pull the cat away. At that moment the yody cat passed between them, intent on its own mission. Melba snagged the cat on her instep and tripped forward, her slick nylon skirt slipping out of Adelaide's hands.

Melba, Monica, the shrubbery and the yody cat all went into the pool, striking the platform as they went. The platform swayed and dipped sharply at one end so that the whole drum set toppled into the water. The music stopped on a single note as the musicians lept to safety like rats in formal attire. The folding chairs on which they had been sitting were scattered over the platform and into the pool, becoming lodged in the three foot space between the platform and the Italian-tiled ledge. Even the conductor had no courageous notion of going down with the ship. He grabbed his horn tighter and hopped the short distance to the patio. The twenty or so members of the band jumping out of the pool collided with the guests who had now rushed toward it, unable to contain themselves any longer. The drummer cursed at the sight of his cymbals lying at the bottom of the deep end. Two of the musicians had gone into the water in the shallow end and drippingly ascended the tiled steps to freedom. The trombone player started to sob. In all the scramble to avoid being thrown back in, no one noticed that Melba and Monica, not to mention the shrubbery and the yody cat, hadn't surfaced.

The three creatures and the one plant were wedged under the platform, out of sight from the shuffling mob. Melba had cracked her temple against the corner of the platform as she fell in and was now sucking water into her lungs. Monica struggled against Melba's weight and the shrubbery attached like vicious seaweed to her ear. Trying to move purposefully while her thoughts flew towards panic. *Oh, no, you can't mean, why this way, you can't, you... You...* In her frantic desire for release she hardly noticed the yody cat's own hysterical claws ripping through her long dress in a feline frenzy to escape. Monica hadn't had time to take a breath before she went under. Within thirty seconds of her struggle her lungs felt like they might burst, and within a minute the pain in her chest grew so unbearable she longed to pass beyond it, wherever that lead.

Her last mortal thought was oddly detached and observant, as if she were watching rather than participating; how strange that her lungs felt like bursting when they didn't have anything in them. Then something adjusted in her mind like a capsule breaking and the pain passed into a calm tickled around the edges with euphoria. It felt good to breath again. Blackness followed as her brain briskly went about its business of shutdown.

As the pandemonium intensified Ferdy's attention finally turned from Gus's impotence. All three made their way from the dance floor and met Joe at the edge of a crowd of black-jacketed guests giving aid and comfort to white-jacketed musicians while the women clustered to one side shouting advice like a Greek chorus. Joe spotted Adelaide a short distance from the side of the pool and forced his way to her.

Adelaide was laughing. "I tell you, this was worth anything," she said when she saw him. "I have to remember this whole scene. It's only too bad I do plays and not movies. I wish you could have seen Monica—" here she started to make hacking motions with a large bulky object but was too weak with laughter. "Oh, God, I think I'm going to wet my pants."

Joe smiled. "Is Monica okay? Where is she?"

"Bishop Laparro?" said Adelaide, adopting a British accent. "Oh, I do believe the Anglican Bishop Laparro might have fallen into the swimming pool. I missed that part. She's probably over there in that group that's acting like a Red Cross contingent."

As the mortals maneuvered around the edge of the pool Ferdy hung back, held in place by a feeling of dread that washed up from his bowels in one long slow pound. He knew it was useless to look over by the pool. If he needed confirmation of his fears it came a moment later with the loud-voiced man saying, "Look at this, this water looks like it's turning pink. Doesn't this water look pink to you?" Then he watched Adelaide jump in the pool, heard her roaring with a voice outside her own, but one more real than any voice she had ever used, "Help me! Help me somebody!" and saw her tugging on a handful of something purple.

# Part Two
# Saints Above

# Chapter One
## In Which Monica, Melba, Ferdy, and the Yody Cat Find Out What Comes Next

Hoping that he was wrong, and not wanting to know, Ferdy's beak nevertheless turned upwards. There he was surprised to see not only Monica, but Melba and the yody cat surveying the commotion from above as if they were helium balloons at a parade. Monica spotted Ferdy, looked a little startled to have made eye contact, but then waved at him to join them.

Ferdy flew up to the floating women and watched with them as Monica's friends twenty feet below frantically grabbed chairs out of the pool and shouted to one another to move the platform. Adelaide had managed to free Monica's body but was still shouting sobs while she cupped her hand over her friend's shredded ear where the dream catcher earring had pulled away. Palma was gone, probably to call an ambulance.

The yody cat drifted over to Ferdy and snuggled down on his back between his wings.

"I love you," said the cat, apparently uninterested in human tragedy. "I want you to be a part of me. I want to eat you."

"You'll have to get in line," said Ferdy. "Just stay quiet for a bit while I sort this out." He turned to Monica. "What happened?" he asked. Of course he knew what had happened. What had happened was that he had failed to guard Monica properly, lost her, and was now going to have to face some pretty ghastly music. He wished demons could throw up because he really wanted to. Then he looked at Monica looking at him for the first time and thought the words "lost her" but in a different way. After this he would never see her again. Like Yves. His now familiar sadness welled up inside him and the indescribable feeling of wanting, not only her, but something she had, blotted out his dread of the certain reckoning he faced back at headquarters.

"Huh?" he said, aware that Monica had spoken.

Monica pointed at a scowling Melba. "It all happened too fast to be sure," she repeated, "but I think she might have killed me."

"You're dying. I'm so sorry. It was all my fault," he said quietly.

"I think it was really an accident."

"No, I'm to blame."

"Hush for a moment," she interrupted, "my life is starting to flash before my eyes." She gazed into space with the intensity of someone watching *Gone With the Wind* for the first time. Then she turned to look at him again. "And you're in it. Who are you?"

Ferdy put out his claw. "I'm telling you, I'm the one who caused all this," he said mournfully as Monica held out her hand. "I wish—"

Before he could make his wish the watery evening light surrounding them solidified and formed a funnel which moved in a circle around them as if the light were not light, but substance.

"Hold on!' Ferdy shouted. Monica clenched his claw tighter in her hand and grabbed Melba who had been pretending to ignore them. Holding together, with the yody cat riding Ferdy as if he were a sled, they slipped down a long tunnel of light. The light sparkled and as they moved faster the sparkles turned into sharp lines that pointed them in the only direction there was. Monica marveled that her only sensation of movement was what she saw. There was no wind in her face and her dress, now quite dry, did not whip against her legs. There wasn't an uncomfortable feeling in her stomach that you would expect from a roller coaster ride like this one, either. Though the tunnel may have been long, Monica had no sense of duration and felt no hurry to reach the end. Being in whatever moment this was suddenly felt just fine.

The trip went on for so long that Monica was able to question Ferdy about what he might know. While they traveled Ferdy told her about his involvement in her life. Where he had been for the past six hundred years, how his people had identified her as a Saint in Progress (she laughed at that), how he had been assigned to guard her until she could be gotten off that track, and how he had failed miserably.

"What do you mean off the track?"

"Most mortals have moments of saintliness, those times when they focus outward instead of on themselves. That's when they give a beggar some change or even risk their lives for another soul. Sometimes it lasts a second and sometimes it lasts years. But one of the qualities of mortals is that they lack staying power. There have been very few people who managed to be saintly for the seventy or so years they had in time. Saintly enough to be recognized for it, that is."

"I guess you're right. There've been billions of people who have lived and died, but only a few made it into Fox's Book of Saints and Martyrs. Ah."

Ferdy winced at the word. "You got it."

"You mean I'm a martyr?"

"You died saintly, and it's all my fault. Just like Becket," he groaned.

"Thomas a Becket? You guarded Thomas a Becket?"

"You know him?"

"Sure. He was the Archbishop of Canterbury. I saw the movie. Anyway, Peter O'Toole says, 'Will no one rid me of this man?' and three of his henchman go to the cathedral early in the morning when they know Richard Burton is going to be saying mass and they stab him at the altar. Great movie."

Understanding enough of what she said Ferdy replied, "Yeah, I never saw those guys coming. Seems like I'm always busy jerking off in one way or another at the critical moment. Well, this time I don't think I'm going to get gargoyle duty."

Monica gave his claw a reassuring squeeze. "You never know. Maybe things will turn out fine."

"You haven't met my boss."

"And you haven't met mine." Monica looked at the needles of light up ahead and pointed out a variation, as if they were bending. "What happens now?" she asked.

"I don't know, I've never come this way before."

When they got closer they could see that the tunnel separated and veered off in two separate directions. If they continued straight ahead they would shoot off into blackness and who knew what else. A decision had to be made, and quickly. Melba spoke for the first time.

"Left turn!" she shouted as they reached the fork and jerked the others after her. Without having been warned the yody cat flew off

Ferdy's back and he quickly lost sight of it catapulting down the tunnel to the right.

This part of the tunnel looked the same but was shorter. After a brief trip at the same speed they found themselves in a quiet vestibule, a reception area with comfortable couches and wax plants with dark dusty leaves. Paintings on black velvet decorated the walls. Except for that, everything was pretty—

"Beige," thought Monica and wistfully remembered her own couch at home with the flying macaws. She felt disoriented. Not dizzy, or uncomfortable, but as if she had fallen asleep during mass and woken up in the middle of her own sermon. She struggled to get her psychic bearings and meld the individual events, starting with Melba smacking her with the topiary cat, into a sequence that made sense.

"Herculon," Melba grunted, stroking one of the couches as she settled into it.

A girl in her twenties sat at the reception desk wearing a polyester jacket opened over a tube top. Monica approached her. The girl looked up from her September 1972 copy of Vogue.

"May I help you?"

"Well, yes, I suppose so. I'm just not sure what it is you can help us with," said Monica.

"Oh, don't worry," responded the girl cheerfully. "Someone will be with you in a minute for intake and signing of releases. Just sit tight. It may be your first time but we know what we're doing."

Monica had her doubts as she joined the other two on the lobby couch. None of this fit her idea of where she wanted to be. For one thing, she hadn't imagined anything so bureaucratic as filling out forms and she wondered what she would do if she didn't quite fit in. Melba looked comfortable enough, but this little leathery guy with the beak and wings, this Ferdy, looked absolutely despondent, she thought. His skinny shoulders were hunched over and he hardly thought to pull his wings away when she sat down on one. Whole patches of feathers were missing from the wings, and Monica could see through to where the skin showed beneath. Despite the fact that he was even less attractive than their surroundings she still managed to return his weak smile. As a priest she had seen a lot worse than Ferdy.

The aggressive rap of stiletto heels on linoleum signaled the arrival of someone new. Another woman with an expertly sculpted beehive hairdo and glasses decorated with tiny rhinestones stopped before them. She sat down in an armchair near the couches, smoothed her crisp white lab coat over her knees and introduced herself with a broad but professional smile.

"Hi. I'm Patty Yollie, and I'm here to do your intake. Did you have an easy trip? Is there anything I can get for you?" She half listened as they murmured something positive to the first question and negative to the second. "Excellent. All righty, let's begin with you." She indicated Melba with her eyes and flipped through several hundred sheets of paper attached to the clip board on her lap.

"This shouldn't take too long. Name?"

"Melba Mary McGregor."

Patty carefully printed the name on one of the pages. "Excellent. Well, that's about it. If you'll just sign here we'll get you started with initiation processes." She watched Melba sign her name. "Excellent. I think you'll like the person we've selected as your mentor," she said, standing and beckoning Melba to do the same. "If you'll just go down that hallway to the left, where I came from, you'll receive your initiation kit and be directed to your mentor's office. By the way, what kinds of work are you interested in taking up here?"

"Do you have an altar guild?" Melba asked. "I'm the head of the altar guild."

"Absolutely. I bet you'll find our altar guild just like yours. Not a speck of difference. Lots of silver that needs polishing, though," Patty said with a sly wink.

Melba shivered with delight. "Are there many other members of the guild?"

"Absolutely. Tons. Just tons. They could use some strong leadership."

Patty pointed again down the hall and Melba nearly started off, then stopped again. "You know my husband, Malcolm McGregor?"

Patty's smile stiffened into a tool prodding Melba to move on. "Sorry. Haven't heard of him. Ask around, though. I'm only in charge of female intake."

Melba moved off down the hall muttering something about wanting to take care of poor old Malcolm again.

The two remaining on the couch waited as Patty took the forms with Melba's name to the girl at the reception desk and told her to make three mimeographs for the record room files. Then she turned her attention to Monica.

"Name?"

"Could I say something?" Monica asked.

"Absolutely."

"Mimeographs went out forty years ago, along with wax plants."

"You see," Patty said in a gush of exuberance, "That's just the kind of progressive thinking we're looking for here. Management tends to move very slowly." She whispered behind her well-manicured hand. "There's some that say we're still in the dark ages. You look like the sort that will contribute lots of forward thinking ideas. Are you a secretary in an office? We have a tremendous need for secretaries."

"I'm an Episcopal bishop."

Patty blinked away a flicker of disappointment. "Oh. Excellent. You've made a marvelous choice, coming here. I'm sure you'll find lots to keep you busy. Receptions, committee meetings, general conventions to lead. You'll probably want to meet the priests who are here from. . .of what diocese are you the bishop?"

"Diocese of Southeast Florida. My name is Monica Laparro, and something doesn't feel quite right. Is this really death? Or could it possibly be near-death? I've heard of things like that happening."

Patty put out a hand as if to touch Monica's, then drew it away again. "Oh, darlin', no, I'm sorry, you have indeed 'bought the farm' as they say. No going back. As for not feeling quite right, that's to be expected. You may have been through the most traumatic event since your birth, and I come barreling in asking you all these questions and shuffling you off as if you were here to have your teeth cleaned. Of course it will take a while to get acclimated. Absolutely. Take all the time you need. We have nothing but time. No one wants to make it difficult for you." Her tone grew confiding again. "You know, I'm a social worker. I just love being needed, I love that people who have problems can say Patty I need you, and talk to me and get comfort from me. When I came here I was delighted to find out that I could go on being needed forever. I can just go on and on and on helping people cope with their troubles. It's wonderful, isn't it? I guess you and I are sort of in the same business, making people feel better."

"I never saw it quite like that," Monica said. "Sometimes I suppose I make people feel worse."

"How awful. But don't worry. You're here now, and our responsibility, yours and mine, is to help everyone be satisfied with themselves, just the way they are. Accepting yourself. That's the key to eternal happiness." Patty pressed her lips together and gave her beehive an impatient little shake. "But listen to me, the old social worker counseling you. That's up to your mentor." She flipped through the stack of forms that would become Monica's. "What did you say your name was?"

Monica wasn't reassured by Patty's speech. If anything she felt agitated. Her hands began to throb. She rose from the couch and tried not to pace, just pressing her feet into the linoleum and her palms against her thighs. "What about Melba?"

"Who?"

"Melba McGregor, the woman you "took in" just before me. Will she stay the same forever, too?"

"Absolutely," said Patty cheerfully. "She'll just become more and more Melba McGregorish for all eternity."

Monica thought about that a moment.

"I don't like it."

"I beg your pardon?"

"I don't like it. I don't like the idea of her becoming more herself."

Patty's relentless smile finally faded. "Well, of course, you don't absolutely have to stay here. You're free to go at any time. We have an enormous waiting list, but I understand that not everyone can accept who they are." Her eyes warmed again with sympathy. "But talk to me. Tell me how you came to be here."

"Melba McGregor kind of killed me."

"Kind of?"

"I don't think she really meant to, or maybe not. She definitely meant to hit me with a topiary cat, but we both fell into a swimming pool and drowned."

"That's too bad. How do you feel about her?"

"I guess a feeling of resentment would be right about now, but it seems useless considering the finality of the situation."

"You're right, it's over and done with, isn't it? No reason to hold a grudge, unless you really want to, unless that's part of who you are. Why did she kill you?"

"I'm not sure, but I think it had something to do with...if it's still there. I don't know how these things happen." Monica stripped off her evening gloves, peeking under the gauze patches to see if the holes might have disappeared at her death. Not only were they there; they began to drip through the bandaging onto the linoleum. The receptionist leaned over the counter of her desk like a rubber necker at a seven car pile up with possible decapitations.

"Oh, dear," Monica said. "I'm making a mess. If you have a paper towel I'll clean it up."

Ferdy looked up at Patty and spoke for the first time since his arrival. "Does the word 'martyr' mean anything to you?" he mourned.

Patty's composure dropped to the floor and mingled there for a moment with Monica's blood. She left so fast Monica and Ferdy nearly didn't see her turn to go, but only heard the stiletto heels receding into the distance from which they had come along with a quavering, "Stay right there."

"She's right, you know," Ferdy said to Monica in the same dolorous tone, his body nearly folded in two with fear and dejection.

"Some of it sounded half right," Monica admitted, "but I kept getting confused about which half. I had trouble with a lot of what she said."

"I'm talking about you being able to leave. You don't have to stay here and I think," he added, lifting his head to look down the hallway where Patty had gone, "that it would be a good idea if you left real soon. All you have to do is decide to change your place and it happens."

Monica watched Ferdy lean down to grab one of his oversized feet and draw it up to his beak. A black tongue something like a bird's, short and thick, came out and hunted curiously between his toes.

"Why are you doing that?"

His tongue paused its search. "Because I'm scared shitless. I always do this when I'm scared or nervous. Does it bother you?"

"No. Does this bother you?" She indicated her hands which were seeping onto her dress, the blood turning the purple fabric black. She held them over her lap to keep the blood from getting on the couch. The receptionist had gone back to her reading without offering to bring a paper towel.

Ferdy shook his head and went back to the comfort of his toes. That left Monica to her thoughts. The silence didn't last long before she spoke again.

"So this is hell."

Ferdy looked up at her. "I'd really like it if you left now."

"Why? I just got here. You know, people spend a lot of their lives wondering what this place is like, and here I am. Kind of a let-down, I must say. No fire, no torture, and the only devil I see is really kind of, well, sweet."

Ferdy made a hiccupping sound and his dark beak seemed to redden a little. Monica leaned over to see his face and wondered if the glistening she saw in his eyes were tears.

"I didn't want you to die," he muttered around his big toe. "I liked watching the way you were around people. I liked what you did with Gus. It was, you know, hopeful that you could change such a loser. If you had lived maybe you could, um, change more."

"You sure don't sound like any devil I've ever dreamed of," Monica said gently. Ferdy didn't respond. "What about you?" she said, after a long pause.

"Huh?"

"Are you allowed to leave?"

"I have no other place to go that isn't here," Ferdy said.

"Are you sure, Ferdy? Are you absolutely sure?"

"P-please. Please go now. I don't want you to see."

Ferdy's voice held such a hollow core of horror that Monica swallowed once before forcing a lightness into her voice. "No, I think I just might stick around a little."

Monica put her bloody hand on Ferdy's slobbery foot. Neither of them flinched.

That is, neither of them flinched until they heard a shout down the hall followed by hysterical laughter. The laughter grew the way the sound of Patty's heels had faded. Then Monica saw a pale grey-skinned demon (she was getting the picture now) far more grotesque than Ferdy and twice as tall. Even though Monica could see his open mouth and hear the laughter coming from him, the lack of pigment in his eyes kept the laugh from showing there and turned the sound ugly. He was naked except for a plastic lobster bib tied around his neck. The bib was white with a bug-eyed grinning crustacean raising one claw as if beckoning the observer to eat him. It was the bib that the demon seemed to think was funny.

Disgust and fear rose up inside of Monica, and mingled with the waves of terror coming off of Ferdy. She felt the muscles in her legs tighten as if she would leap up despite herself. Then she felt Ferdy's foot trembling under her hand. She patted it softly and held her ground. After all, she half-reasoned, half-hoped, having already died, what's the worst that could happen?

The demon stopped before them, coyly raised the bib over his face and lowered it slowly until it covered his pig nose so only his white eyes showed over the edge.

"Peek-a-boo," he said, and started laughing again.

"Hi, Gregory—Sir," Ferdy said, the trembling turning to an all-out shake.

"Well, isn't this cute," Gregory responded, letting the bib drop to his chest. "Isn't this just the most sweetums thing imaginable. Instead of you protecting Saint Monica here, she's protecting you. I knew you wouldn't get it right, you jerk-off, you miserable excuse for a corporate functionary." He did a little hopping dance around the vestibule singing, "Ferdy's a jerk-off, Ferdy's a jerk-off." Then he stopped and said soberly, in his best Bogartese, "So, Alonzo, you've come back. Now you're going to get what you've got coming. Your walking papers, Alonzo. We won't be needing your services anymore." This set him off laughing again.

"Excuse me," Monica interrupted. "But I think I could—"

"Shut up," Gregory merely snarled without looking at her.

Ferdy stood up from the couch and looked up at Gregory towering over him. Through chattering beak he said, "No, Greg.

Gregory. Sir. Oh, please, everything just went a little wrong. I should never have been given this assignment anyway. I'm just a miserable worm good for nothing but gargoyle duty. A worm—see these arms and legs? I don't deserve them. Please just send me back there to the cathedral and I'll stay forever, I promise," the last word trailed off into a whine and then into a choking sob.

"You know, you do look a little like a worm," Gregory said. "Can you act like a worm?"

Without a pause Ferdy fell to his face and squirmed on his belly in terror before the other demon. Unable to look and unable to look away, Monica watched while something in her heart clicked and broke beyond tears.

"Not bad," Gregory said. "But you know, I always wondered if worms can talk. What does a worm sound like?"

Ferdy made a noise mixed of moaning, the bark of a seal and something that sounded like "please."

"That's good, that's really good." Gregory stopped laughing. "Well, it's lay-off time, old buddy. I was always told I shouldn't play with my food."

Gregory started to grow until his back touched the ceiling of the lobby and he was forced to bend over. Like an earthquake gash his mouth ripped open, revealing yellow root-like teeth. His now gigantic claws reached down to surround Ferdy's tiny body. Watching the demon fill the room pressed Monica into the couch as if she were in the grip of a G force. She felt powerless to move, powerless to even close her eyes against what was about to happen. Not the least of her horror was her vague awareness of the receptionist at the desk who went on blandly reading her beauty magazine as if this were just another day at the office.

"Wait," Ferdy gasped, his breath pressed out of his lungs under the pressure of Gregory's clutch. "Gregory—I thought we were friends!"

Gregory paused, but only to comment, "What can I say. Power corrupts." Then his jagged maw descended in a slow smiling way over Ferdy, his lips jutting out and engulfing the smaller demon to the waist.

Monica could hear Ferdy's scream inside the huge mouth and watched his feet, lifted off the floor, waving frantically. She heard an echoing scream and realized it was her own. Hardly conscious of what she was doing, and having no idea of doing any real good, she stood and grasped Gregory's leg with two bare hands. It was as large as a tree trunk and smooth as a snake. Her hands slid down over the smoothness, trying to catch hold of him, and only leaving a trail of blood down his calf. She stopped at his ankle and held on, knowing as she did that it was a futile act.

The next moment she heard Gregory's gasp from high above her and looked up. He had stopped his lips from encroaching over the rest of Ferdy's body. His white eyes turned their attention first to Monica, then to the bloody streak on his leg. Monica watched his eyes and mouth slowly begin to widen until she could see Ferdy's head again. Ferdy's pulsing scream, much louder now, was surpassed by a lower pitched roar from Gregory that rolled around the ceiling and made the wax plants vibrate. Even the receptionist looked up.

Gregory released Ferdy and grabbed his own leg as it if had just been caught in a bear trap. Screaming with pain he tried to brush the blood away with his claws. Monica smelled something like a steak broiling. As Gregory rapidly shrunk to his normal six-foot size he rushed about the room, still howling, wiping his hands against his chest uselessly until he fell against the wall where he rubbed his body desperately, trying to rid himself of the searing blood.

"Okay, I'm out of here," Monica squeaked. She turned to Ferdy who had slumped weakly to his knees before her, beak chattering, shiny with Gregory's saliva. "Come with me."

"Where? Where can I go? There's no place I can go!" he cried hoarsely.

"From here, nowhere but up, I guess," she answered, her hands stroking his slimy head in an effort to calm him even though she wanted nothing more at the moment than to run.

Ferdy spread his claws as if to truly show himself to her. He kept his head bent and said without lifting his eyes, "Look at me. Can't you see what I am? Don't you get it? I can't go there."

Monica knelt before him and said, a little more sternly, "You might be right. It just seems like being laid-off in hell is a good definition of nothing to lose. Come with me."

"They don't take devils."

"Why not? I hear they take murderers and thieves. Hell, my boss says they'll take anybody and be glad to have them." Monica took his outstretched claws in her hands and brought them together, her voice taking on a softer tone, trying to hide the urgency she felt as she glanced at Gregory still caught in his throes of pain. "So what if it's never been done before—just think, you might start a trend, a regular migration from hell. Who knows, Ferdy, maybe you'll get rejected, but maybe you'll be a hero."

"I don't want to be a hero," whispered Ferdy in the smallest voice that could still be heard. "I just want somebody to accept me."

"I know just the guy to do that, sugar, and it's a whole lot better than accepting yourself. Take a chance with old Mother Monica. Come with me."

Ferdy's eyes blinked up into her own for only a moment but she took that as assent. Monica turned to the receptionist.

"Come with me."

The girl looked up and scoffed.

"Are you crazy? Where else can I get a job where I get to sit around and read magazines all day?" She snapped her gum for effect and tucked her head back down to an article about Twiggy's theatrical comeback.

Monica grasped Ferdy's claws tighter. "What do I do?"

"Just want," Ferdy said.

"All right, but you have to want too."

Down went Ferdy's head in a half-nod. Monica took one last look at the whimpering Gregory pounding his whole body against the wall like a berserk sumo wrestler and wanted with all her will.

# Chapter Two
## In Which There is Granting and Yielding

They had been back in the light tunnel for some time. Monica's heart, that had been pounding furiously from her encounter with Gregory, calmed to a slower beat. There was nothing to be frightened of here.

She had time to think, and thought about her death. How amazing it was that she felt no regrets, no sorrow for her own demise, no sense of loss of either world or friends or family. She thought of her mother mourning her and felt a sympathy akin to that of a grown-up comforting a small child who has lost a favorite toy, the grown-up knowing that the toy will soon lose its importance. Maybe later she would have time and then she would miss people. But the concept of time itself was growing a little hazy, and she was already thinking of the creatures of life as if they were a different class of being from herself, in a different plane of existence.

She still held Ferdy's claw in her hand and could feel his tension through it. As the light grew even brighter she could feel his pulse race. She hoped she hadn't given him the wrong advice. "Fear not," she said, with mock solemnity, and watched him simply close his eyes in response and allow himself to be swept along.

Amid the points of light streaming towards them in the distance, Monica thought she detected something that was not light. It looked a little like a thin snowman, white body topped with a white head. The closer they got the more she could see it was a real man, or whatever creatures were called in this place. He was a little old, a little stooped, a little balding, with a radiant smile that matched the glow about him. Monica thought of what she had heard about meeting old friends and family at this point, but as they flew close it was Ferdy who seemed to know the man.

"Yves!" he screamed in happy surprise, as if he and the man were long-lost comrades.

"*Monsieur Chimiere!*" Yves yelled, and received Ferdy who flew into his arms like a forward pass. "Phew! *Mon cher* Spitting

Gargoyle, you smell like Jonah, and you're twice as sticky."

"How did you—why at—" Ferdy stuttered, and then, "You know me."

"Of course I know you. We were friends for over thirty years, *non*? When I knew you were coming I asked to be assigned as your guide."

"I figured you'd be here, but I didn't think—is that what you do here? You're a guide?"

"For now. But, *Monsieur Chimiere*, we are being rude to this incredibly vivacious woman, and that is against the *Code Napoleon*." He turned to Monica and offered his hand.

"Really glad to meet you," she said. "Ferdy could use a friend here."

"Ah, but I sense that you are his friend too," responded Yves. "You brought him here."

"That reminds me," interrupted Ferdy, with a furrow appearing just above his beak. "Yves. I kind of feel responsible about you getting killed. It seems like everyone I love ends up getting killed."

Yves waved away Ferdy's apology and said, "Well, if I am going to be your guide we should get started. This way." And tucking Ferdy comfortably underneath his elbow like a football, he flew off in the direction they had been traveling, Monica following, deeper into the light.

Gradually their forward motion slowed until they found themselves gently floating in a brilliant sunrise. Not blinding like one reflected in a clear sea, but softened and colored as if strained through clouds streaming off a mountain top. Monica felt herself merging with the sunrise. The light seeped into her heart, warming it, making it pliant, preparing it to listen. She lifted her hands and spread her fingers, wanting to absorb the sunlight through her whole body. It was then she noticed that her wounds were healed. No blood, not even a scar to show what had happened.

She heard words which she imagined to be coming from her own heart, one word repeated over and over again, and the word was "glory."

There was another sound that came to her as if echoing off some distant hill. She had to strain to hear it at first, but as it grew clearer and clearer she heard something like a good hard rain on the pavement, then something like trumpets and drums, then something like the audience at one of Del's plays.

The sound was laughter.

This wasn't just your everyday party-going-on laughter, either. Not a discreet chuckle, or satiric smirk. Not even a banana peel guffaw at someone else's expense. This was loud, unabashed good-humor-take-the-ache-out-of-your-gut laughter. The kind that Monica had most often known sitting around a table long ago with her best friends when they had just discovered who they really were, and with tears streaming down their faces loved each other, and themselves, anyway.

Movement around her seized her attention. The rays of the sunrise began to undulate as if the light was a living thing. Indeed, it was. She could pick out faces and bodies of creatures who appeared out of the light and then disappeared back into it. Mortal faces and powerful bodies but without any discernible gender, size, or coloring that usually characterizes the mortal figure. Mortals without the details. She could see wings, too, twice the size of the bodies, wings that reflected the light gaily, and made the creatures look like a whole herd of romping Pegasus. Monica saw Ferdy strain against Yves's arm as if yearning to join these angels at their play, but Yves gripped him a little tighter.

"Not yet, *Monsieur Chimiere,* it is better to be invited."

Finally, they arrived at what seemed to be the source of the light. Monica and Yves, with Ferdy still held by the old man, settled down to stand on ground that could be felt but not seen. The source of the light in which the creatures played, and which had formed the tunnel through which they had traveled, was not itself light.

It was most, Monica thought, like a big white lap.

*Giant knees.*

And on the knees there purred the now sleeping marmalade yody cat. The lap was in the center of what she might remember later as a throne, though there was nothing splendid or remarkable about it. She watched Yves put Ferdy down. Actually, she watched Yves peel a reluctant Ferdy off his arm and give him a mild shove toward the knees.

"Can you stay with me?" said Ferdy to Yves.

"Not for this part, *Monsieur Chimiere*. But we will meet again."

Then he was gone, leaving Monica and Ferdy to gaze at the knees like small expectant children. After a moment Monica heard a voice; or perhaps it was more like feeling words in her softened heart.

-*Welcome home.* And directed at Ferdy, *Are you here to stay?*

She felt answering words coming from the tiny demon. "I'd like to, Sir. Ma'am. But you know what I am. I'm not sure you'd want me."

-*I know that you are my creature. You must remember that you are not a judge. Come up.*

"You have no idea where I've been and what I've done. Shouldn't I at least go somewhere and wash up first—"

-*Ferdinand, I said 'come up.' Your response is either yes or no. I wait.*

Without stalling a second more, Ferdy crawled up into the big lap, looking at the yody cat as if thinking he was expected to curl up on the other knee. Despite any intention he may have had of maintaining a respectful formality, with the instinct of a trusting child he put his arms around the being.

And snuggled.

It didn't matter that Monica had recently died, or that she had fought with a devil in hell, or that she was in the presence of the divine. The sight of these two ancient beings, one perfect and the other flawed, uniting in love, gave her a thrill greater than any she had known. She imagined the beginning time, a glorious birth, before the death of hell had moldered Ferdy's body and soul. And as she watched him weep, she felt his joy.

-*I've been waiting for your return so long. Would you like to be re-created as you once were? Can you change?*

Ferdy's eyes flashed and his head nodded eagerly as if he understood precisely what the voice meant. The other creatures who had been frolicking nearby suddenly stopped and assembled in long rows near the throne as if they understood, too, and prepared to celebrate a sacred ritual. One by one down the line they soared soundlessly upwards, carrying the light with them, and formed a winged dome that hovered high above the heads of the three below. The creatures in the dome continued to move, weaving in and out among each other so that they became a dancing canopy of awe-full synchronicity. The brushes of a million wings against one another sounded like the whish of silk on silk, the music of a pale percussion.

Monica watched the pulsing sky-wide display for a long moment, then turned her attention to Ferdy once more. He had gotten down from the giant lap and stood facing it, so that she could only see his back. His feet were planted wide apart and he lifted out his arms and his poor shabby wings in one slow stretch. While Monica watched he stretched out farther and farther, until his arms and legs and wings had all doubled their length. His form morphed before her into one of godlike proportions. Dark brown muscle rippled on his shoulders and calves. His tiny claws spread far apart and grew into strong, reaching hands modeled by a renaissance artist. Most glorious of all were his wings, transformed from scrappy appendages to a mighty span with shining ebony feathers. He stood there for a long while, arms and wings still outstretched, while the canopy fluttered in soft applause. She heard his voice saying just as softly, "Thank you."

After the applause had died Monica watched the powerful neck slowly turn his face to her. Ferdy's leathery beak and beady eyes were gone. In their place was a finely crafted dark face with large brown eyes and full sensuous mouth. The donkey ears had shrunk back leaving a head worthy of African mythology. Ferdy flashed the stunned Monica a joyous smile which still conveyed a healthy dash of impishness. In the next moment the tips of his wings rose so quickly straight over his head that she gasped in surprise. When they came down his body soared up to the canopy in one smooth rocket glide. There he stayed, leaving Monica alone before the throne.

Caught in the splendor of his triumph she hopped up and down, spread her arms wide and said, "Oh, oh, do me now, do me!"

She felt a gentle chuckle in her heart.

-*Why? This is how I created you. Do you criticize the work of my hand?*

"Oh, no, no criticism here," said Monica, trying to keep the disappointment out of her voice. "I just thought you might make me, you know, beautiful."

-*My child, angels take great stock in uniformity so I give it to them. But mortals—that's where I exercise my real creativity. I think you are beautiful, perfect, just the way you are. My image and likeness, you see.*

"Of course," said Monica, agreeably, though wondering for a flash about the job he did on Palma. "I didn't mean to presume..."

*-Besides, it's time to talk.*

Of all the words Monica could have imagined hearing on her entry into heaven, "we need to talk" would probably have been the least expected, and the least desirable. Caught up short with surprise and a sudden consciousness of the possible gravity of her situation, she found herself first sinking to her knees, then lying face down before the throne. Behind her closed eyes she felt her life passing before her senses once more, but in a different way. There seemed to be a focus on specific events to make a point, or rather, establish a case.

She saw herself kneeling before Gus, bathing his sores.

She saw herself telling that six foot tall construction worker holding the bat that his wife would be leaving with her.

She smelled the pungent mixture of fresh stuffing and old urine in a soup kitchen on a Thanksgiving Day.

She felt the papery chill of old hands on hers as she administered the chalice in a hospital room.

Over and over again she heard herself speak life-giving words in a room full of death.

She saw herself praying, in thanksgiving and supplication.

And through it all she felt the words of a greater one than she,

*-Well done, good and faithful servant.*

But there was more.

She also saw those times when, greedy for attention, she hungrily grabbed the focus of a crowd away from a lesser mortal with her sheer presence.

She saw her impatience with Sharon, and Melba, and everyone else who got in the way of her doing her job, without ever noticing that they *were* her job.

She felt the small inner scorn at those who could not be good as easily as she.

She passed by countless hands up-stretched on the other side of the communion rail and doled out the consecrated bread noting each time she had wearily ignored the dirty cuffs, the bitten nails, the trembling fingers, the bruised wrists.

She heard herself baiting Adelaide, striking at her most vulnerable spot under the guise of friendship.

Her last act on earth an argument with Del. . .Monica lifted her head slightly.

"I'm sorry."

*-I know. Come up.*

Feeling washed with complete and eternal forgiveness in the words 'come up,' Monica scrambled onto the lap unhindered by any trace of her arthritis. She felt herself enfolded in strong arms and sighed as contentedly as a five year old child whose daddy has come home.

"This is—"

*-Heavenly?*

"Yes."

*-Well, don't let the lap fool you. I'm not Santa Claus. Instead, I'm going to tell you what I want.*

"You know I'll do anything you ask. Anything at all. Anything."

*-It's Del.*

"I don't think I can help you there."

*-She's written a play about me.*

"I'm sure she meant no disrespect."

*-It's not a very good play, but she has an uncanny knowledge of me. Nevertheless, she continues resisting me. No matter who I've put in her life to love her, she has never learned to love back. It puts a great strain on her soul.*

"We've been friends for thirty years and I've never been able to change that—maybe just the opposite. Maybe I'm not the best person for the job. The envy thing, you know."

*-You'll find her greatly changed.*

"Find her? You mean I have to go back? I don't want to go back. I could really get to like it here."

*-It's not exactly going back, more like running in tandem.*

"Are you saying I'm going back as a spirit, to be like a guardian angel for Del?"

*-No, that will be Ferdinand's job.*

As if hearing himself summoned, a dark streak cut back against the dome and lighted before the throne. When Ferdy heard that he was to accompany Monica, his wings fluttered with pleasure. On hearing a second command, his eyes flew open with surprise, then slammed shut.

"I don't think I can do that. There was this problem—"

*-I know, but don't worry. You have my power now. Monica?*

"Yes?"

*-It will be your job to guard Ferdinand.*

# Chapter Three
## In Which Adelaide Is Not The Same

Adelaide stared at her computer screen, a blank grayness except for the blinking cursor. The cursor was designed to tell her where she was on the page, and the cursor was rhythmically reminding her she was nowhere. This despite her wearing her lucky writing shirt with Jane Austen's face on the front, and her most lucky writing cap, a purple one with the words Waste Management stitched into the front. Since none of her lucky writing ties had worked over the past several weeks she had switched to the big guns. But even these weren't helping her get any words onto the screen. She couldn't count on anything anymore except the beat of the damn cursor. Cursor. Cursor. Curser.

Another day at the office.

The blinking made her think again of the rhythmic flashes of the society reporter's camera beating at the back of her eyes while they pulled Monica's body out of Palma's swimming pool. That hadn't been easy, what with Melba's soggy body, and the platform in the way, and the chairs, and the topiary cat, and the real one, its claws tangled in Monica's dress. On her belly were deep scratches, their ridges swelled with water.

Like another voice outside her, she could hear herself shrieking to the paramedics as they worked on Monica. "It's been less than four minutes, hasn't it? Less than four minutes so you can bring her back, right? I know it's been—Oh, please!" She was just getting in the way, she knew that, but had resisted Joe's trying to lead her away just the same. "It's just a stupid mistake, stupid, stupid," she panted to the people standing around, who didn't pay attention to her, but only to the young man in blue shirt and pants. He thumped and blew at Monica, trying to make her body work again.

"Stupid, stupid, stupid," she said in time with the cursor, and felt the sound of her voice dissolve the knot at the back of her throat into tears. They, the tears, were her only relief these days.

They, and the cigarettes she smoked more than usual, and the video she would look at later. For now she sat, as she had been sitting for four weeks, arms wrapped around her body and legs intertwined with themselves, wanting to write.

If she could only write, she could stop the pain. That's how it had always been, but for the first time in her life the writing didn't come, the writing felt like a anesthetic withheld by a cruel surgeon. She blew her nose in Jane Austen's face.

No one knew about the argument between Monica and Adelaide, no one knew how Adelaide had goaded Monica into saying what she said just before Melba McGregor had attacked. Adelaide was sure that her words had incited Melba's rage. She determined never to tell anyone what she had done, and throughout the days following Monica's death, no one seemed to suspect.

The funeral had been at St. Stephen's Cathedral just one month ago. In response to dictates from headquarters the dean had tried to keep the funeral from being a media event, but without luck. Reporters stood in the aisles frowning into their digital cameras. Giving up trying to find chairs for everyone, the ushers ended up leaving the doors open for the overflow.

Palma sat next to Gus, wrapped in her usual stoicism, but gently patted his hand while he wept. Joe was by Adelaide's side in the last pew. She couldn't seem to make herself come in any further than that.

Presiding Bishop Roxbury had declined to attend, sending only his regrets. "So soon after her ordination," he lamented.

No one mentioned Monica's stigmata. Not even Palma, who gave the eulogy because Adelaide would have drawn too much celebrity attention. Adelaide thought again of Monica's body, her hands hanging limply by her side with the gloves gone. Everyone thought she must have ripped them off trying to fight her way from the pool. The fingertips were raw, but there were no wounds in her palms. It was as if the marks had never been there at all.

Palma, who would have had a reception at her house after the funeral, was loath to gather friends where they could see her swimming pool. Instead, she, Gus, Adelaide, and Joe left the cemetery immediately after the interment and collected somberly in the restaurant off the lobby of the Delano Hotel. They sat at a cherry wood table decorated with a spray of live orchids, while discrete waiters hovered nearby. The restaurant was Palma's choice.

"I just don't understand why you avoided it," Adelaide said, heading off in a different direction from whatever they had been talking about. She was half-way through her first bloody mary. She could tell that Joe noted the uncustomary hard liquor before noon but was grateful that he said nothing.

"Avoided what?" asked Palma.

"The stigmata, for God's sake. How could you say nothing about it?"

"That's what the dean asked me to do. It was only appropriate."

Adelaide rolled her eyes. "Oh, well that explains everything."

"Besides, what would I have said? By the time of the funeral there was nothing to talk about. It's gone. Del, you can't be sure it ever was. Did you ever see it? I didn't. I think we should just forget about it. I think we should focus on thirty years of friendship, and the fact that Monica is in heaven, and not focus on the possibility of some freakish, lurid—"

"Great words for a second language," Adelaide observed, trying to keep a light tone in her dry mouth.

"I saw it," said Gus, who had been sitting quietly with Joe listening to the women talk. "No, Adelaide's right, she had 'em all right. Holes right through the center of her palm, that bled sometimes, and gave her a lot of pain. I was there when it first happened, didn't give a flying fuck about her at the time, of course, but afterwards. . ."

Even absorbed in what Gus was saying, Adelaide instinctively glanced at Palma to see the effect of Gus's language. In the past that would have been enough to eliminate a suitor. But if Gus's vulgarity made Palma recoil mildly, Gus seemed to not. . .well, give a flying fuck what she thought. It took all the fun out.

". . .afterwards I cared. I cared." Gus's face gave a little twist and turned quickly toward the plate glass window overlooking the pool shimmering with the noon heat. When he turned back he was in control. "But I agree with Palma. Monica was a special person with or without those things. She never wanted that stigmata and never needed it to make her extraordinary. I'll always remember her for the things she said and did. For what she did for me." He nearly lost his fight against tears on the last line, and wiped his nose on his napkin. Palma didn't flinch, but placed her hand over the hand that covered the napkin.

Adelaide suddenly hated listening to Gus talk about Monica. Hearing him say her name sent tiny electric shocks down the side of her face. Whether it was because she was jealous of her friendship or whether she hated herself for knowing less about Monica in her last days than Gus did, she couldn't tell and didn't bother to assess. She could feel Joe tensing slightly beside her, as if he could feel her coiling to strike.

"So how long did you know Monica?" she said mildly enough, but Joe squirmed anyway.

"Not long, a coupla months."

"Seems like an incredibly assured analysis for only knowing someone a 'cup-la' months, Gus." Joe reached out his foot and tapped Adelaide's gently under the table but she was in no mood for restraint. Her head snapped impatiently in his direction. "Did you want something?" she shot at him, and snapped just as impatiently back to the other man. "So. . .Gus. . .on a scale of one to ten just how extraordinary would you say she was?"

"What I meant was—"

"You know. . .Gus. . .everyone else at this table has been friends with Monica for over thirty years. Can you imagine being friends for thirty years? I think that any one of us with advanced Alzheimers would be a better judge of what Monica Laparro deserves to be remembered for. You should count yourself lucky just to be sitting at this ta—"

"Del," Palma whispered.

"Look, hon," said Gus, calmly leaning forward over the table onto his elbows. "I don't know you, and I don't know much about you except that you've written some funny plays." Adelaide winced, and Gus continued with his index finger lazily raised from his glass of iced tea to point in her direction. "I never even saw you until the night Monica died and you were standing by the pool while she was—" he stopped. "I don't know you and this may just be your way of dealing with pain. I'm sorry if you're hurting, but you can stay off my back. I wasn't responsible for her death so do somebody else."

"I hate when this happens at funerals," Palma sighed dismally. "Shall we ask for the menu?" .

Adelaide watched Joe nod at Palma as if they were communicating around her and felt the unanimous disapproval of her behavior. She felt suddenly deflated by what she heard as Gus's accusation but tried to keep up her front.

"What are you insinuating?" Adelaide asked, with a nerve twitching slightly in her left eyelid. She pushed her chair out from the table a bit.

"About what?" Gus responded.

"Are you suggesting I was responsible for Monica's death? Are you suggesting I was responsible for Monica's death?" Each word rose in pitch and volume until people dining at nearby tables began to glance in their direction. Adelaide saw Palma fix her best "DO SOMETHING" stare at Joe. He swallowed and rose from the table.

"Let's go, Del," he said.

"All I want to know is—"

From behind her chair he put his hands gently under her elbows and raised her to her feet. Pale and suddenly, totally exhausted, she allowed Joe to guide her. She fixed one stricken look on Gus before Joe lead her away.

"Well, I wasn't."

*Methinks thou did protest too much,* she recalled now. She missed the ashtray at her left and jabbed out her cigarette on the tile windowsill instead. If her smoking in the house bothered Joe's allergies these days he never said so. She reached by habit and felt the dish of peanuts and jelly beans. They must have been there a long time. The peanuts were oozing out their oil and the jelly beans stuck everything together so that the dish contained a single mass of sweet and salt. Rather than expending the effort to pry anything loose she moved instead to her espresso cup and tilted it to see nothing but the dried crema encrusting the inside.

The coffee made her think of another cup, full and cold, sitting on her bedside table. Since Monica's death she had neglected to throw out Joe's morning offering. He had taken to removing it himself when he got home from work, but doggedly continued to make it each morning just the same.

Thinking of Joe made her think of her last words to Monica. *Why not give him a hand job?*
*NO—stop the thought. Think of something else.* She looked at the clock at the bottom right hand of her computer screen as it clicked on 4:30 p.m. She and the cursor had been blinking at each other for about seven and a half hours.

*On the other hand, what the hell.* Joe would be home in another half hour, so she had just that much time to give into what she had come to think of as her 'little compulsion.' She hit the ashtray square in the middle this time, rose and walked resolutely into the bedroom. The blinds stayed shut in here so the room was cool and dusky as a shaded wood. It smelled fresher, too, since she didn't smoke in the bedroom.

The video tape was harder to find than usual. She looked impatiently under magazines on her nightstand, nearly upsetting Joe's espresso, and scanned the bookshelves against the wall where she had found it once before. The desperation of an addict whose need is becoming dangerous welled up in her viscera. There was no coincidence that she finally found the tape at the bottom of Joe's underwear drawer, only half covered by his big white socks to make its presence there look accidental.

Joe had caught her watching it often enough to understand the obsession. She knew he kept hiding it to prevent her from watching. She knew he was probably right, but slipped the video from its casing and inserted it into the player anyway. Then she sat on the edge of the bed and groped for the remote control among the rumpled sheets. Pressed rewind. A few seconds of buzzing whir were followed by a moment of static and fuzz, then:

"Welcome back to the Today Show. We traveled to Miami, Florida, to visit a fascinating woman with a physical condition fairly unique in this century, let alone in the modern world today. Mother Monica Laparro, Episcopal Bishop of the Southeast Diocese of Florida, carries The Stigmata."

The camera panned over the inside of Monica's house while the voice explained the word that so many newscasters had used in the time just before and after her death.

As she did every time she watched the tape, Adelaide held the remote control in both hands and stared intently at the screen as if she were a detective searching for clues. She never listened to the commentary. She was studying Monica's things.

Each time the camera passed a familiar object, her flamingo coffee mug, or the popsicle stick crucifix hanging on her bedroom wall, Adelaide paused the tape and gazed, remembering what it was that made the object Monica's. She had taken as much as an hour to get through the four minute segment in this way. Today she stopped for a few minutes at the rocking chair Monica had impulsively purchased from the front of a Cracker Barrel restaurant on her way back from a conference center outside Hendersonville, North Carolina. Adelaide remembered the name of the town because it was right next to Flat Rock, a small theatrical enclave. Closing her eyes for a moment she recalled rocking and laughing in the chair while Monica told her and Palma the story about stuffing the chair into the hatch of her '82 Civic. Rocking back and forth a little now, Adelaide summoned the vision of Monica waiting out a Florida thunderstorm under an overpass on the turnpike so the rocker wouldn't get wet. There was something in the story about six bikers in chains and leather who had also chosen the overpass for a shelter. What a story it had been. Adelaide had said something funny about the crazy chances Monica took and made them all laugh harder. But she couldn't remember now what she had said and she couldn't remember what had happened with the bikers. She only remembered the laughter.

But remembering the Monica she knew wasn't the main reason for watching the tape. Pressing the forward button, she let the video run until the cameras rested on Monica from the waist up. In the background was her ridiculous bird couch, the green macaws rising up behind her as if her sitting there had startled them. Monica was talking about her experience, her argument with God, and the subsequent assurance that signs were meant to be seen. The interviewer's voice announced that with the help of satellites the whole world was about to be edified by the sight of her wounds on network television, but Adelaide wasn't interested in seeing the stigmata again.

She paused the tape where she'd been pausing it every day for the last month, in the frame just before the camera moved down to Monica's hands, when Monica might have thought the camera was already off her face. In that second, in the last glimpse of Monica's face before she showed her hands, Adelaide studied the look that broke her heart freshly every day.

The inside edge of Monica's heavy brows dipped ever so slightly downward. One corner of her mouth extended out as if it were trying to force her to smile. And her eyes looked to the left and down as if she had discovered something embarrassing on her coffee table that everyone might see.

No one else but Adelaide would be able to read the look. She knew its meaning because she had been reading that face for over thirty years. She knew when Monica was bored and when she was high on nothing but an idea. She knew the spark of fire in Monica's otherwise jovial eye when Adelaide sunk a barb too deep, and the triumphant set of her lips when Monica scored in her own rhetorical assault.

In this face frozen on the television screen Adelaide read feelings of uncertainty, and vulnerability, and the shyness of the younger woman she hadn't seen for years. This was the face from before they had set out to conquer their worlds. Before she learned how to use that preposterous grin. In recent years this face had appeared so seldom and flown so fast that even Adelaide at her most observant would miss it. The child within her friend.

From the first time she saw it on film, Adelaide had decided the face was that of a saint, and the thought made her feel like shit. These days, feeling like shit was an improvement in her attitude.

"Hey, Del."

She pressed the rewind button and looked up, realizing that was the second time Joe had spoken. He stood at the door of their room holding a basset hound puppy and waving the entertainment section of The Herald. By not coming in the room he could pretend the tape didn't exist and that their old life still did.

"Rough day?" she said, forcing her voice up at the end to sound like a question.

The click of the rewind stopping was his cue to enter. He punched the off button on the television to stop the sound of static.

"Got bit by a new schnauzer. Other than that not bad. You?"

"Can't imagine any dog biting you."

"I was surprised too. . ." He tossed the newspaper on the bed. "Wasserstein's new play closed already. Kind of early, wouldn't you say?"

"Whose hush puppy?"

"This is Werther. His owner didn't have time to pick him up today. Thought he might be fun to have around." Joe sat Werther on the bed next to Adelaide where the dog looked up at her through lugubrious eyes, then lowered his already wrinkled face onto his paws. They both looked at Werther, then at each other. "Guess not," he said.

Joe took off his shirt, redolent of flea dip, and tossed it into the corner he used as the laundry basket. The he sat down next to Adelaide with Werther moping between them and waited, gently forcing his presence on her until she had to speak.

"This dog's pretty depressed," she said finally.

"Down in the dumps, I'd say," he said.

"Mmm, you can see it in his eyes. The way his lower lids sag."

"Those eyes tear my heart out."

"What d'you think's eating at him?"

"Some metaphysical angst known only to his breed, maybe."

"Ah, *Weltschmerz.*"

"*Gesundheit.*"

"So you figure there wouldn't be any real therapeutic benefit in having him talk about it?"

"Benefit to Werther? Nah, I don't think so. . .of course, it could be something else."

"What's that?"

"He may be in love with a critter from the shop, but that would be unfortunate."

"Why? Who?"

"An arrogant Siamese who finds him much too baggy to be desirable."

Adelaide let her fingers play over the bumpiness of Werther's head, ignoring Joe's careful glance. She knew he wasn't just gauging her mood. Ever since she'd thrown the cat at the television he'd kept an eye on her with animals brought from the shop. But her petting was just something to put in the space left by the sudden silence between them. Once even the petting didn't seem to be enough anymore, Adelaide said, "Joe, I know what you're trying to do even if young Werther here doesn't have a clue."

"I just thought—"

"You don't have to say what you thought. I know—"

Joe stood up, rather abruptly for Joe, and interrupted her. "Del, I know you know what I'm thinking." Unzipping his trousers and talking while kicking off them and his shoes, he stood at the end of the bed in white socks and briefs while he continued. "I know you're so smart you know everything there is to know about me and I wouldn't have to say another word for the rest of my life and that we'd get along fine with no change and no surprises."

Adelaide's hand stopped in mid-pat over Werther's back. She had never known Joe to use such a long sentence, and it stunned her. Joe seemed stunned too, and stood quietly in his underwear for a long moment. But the sentence must have opened a door that he decided to step through. He went on, a little more haltingly this time.

"But. . .you know, Del, sometimes. . .just sometimes it would feel good to say things anyway. Even if you already knew what I was going to say. Sometimes I have this fantasy of myself giving an opinion about one of your plays and your stopping to jot it down so you don't forget to use it. Or I picture myself being part of a real conversation with your friends, not just speaking the lines you expect me to say. I'm not complaining, mind you, and maybe it's a crazy idea, this speaking business, but I think it would feel good. . . just to hear what comes from me, and just to watch you listen, and maybe even react."

Joe picked up the floppy basset in both hands and slung him carefully over his left shoulder as he would carry a baby. The dog scuffled for a toe-hold on the man's belly until Joe propped Werther's bottom securely on a bent forearm. Facing in the opposite direction Werther could not see Adelaide's open-mouthed reaction even if he wanted to. While Adelaide dug in her mind for an uncharacteristically illusive response, Joe continued.

"And who knows? At some point in the distant future, I may even say something you don't expect."

He moved to the nightstand and picked up her espresso cup with his free right hand while Adelaide watched him. She was searching his words for a subtext, but could find none. There was no anger, or harshness in what he said, just words laid out for her that she could take or leave. In twenty-five years she had never heard him say so many words at one time, let alone say something that surprised her, let alone tell her how he felt.

First there had been Monica's face, and now Joe. All the world seemed to be shifting, taking another form. For every person she knew, another was being revealed. Maybe she was cracking, or life was cracking, or this thing that was cracking around her had never been real life at all.

She even wondered whether there might be another person inside of her who she didn't know, and thought what that person might be like. Would she be a better Del than the one the world saw? What would that person say to Joe right now?

All these thoughts had blown through her mind in only an instant after Joe's last words, and he was still standing, a little fearfully, before her as if anticipating a response. Swallowing something close to fear herself, her eyes moved to the tiny cup and saucer nearly lost in his hand. Her mouth opened, and she heard herself say, "You know, you could stop that if you wanted."

Joe followed her eyes to the cup. "This? No. I don't think so."

"I have to tell you, I don't drink it. I haven't drunk it in ten years. It's always cold by the time I get up. You don't have to do it."

"I know all that."

"Then why do you do it?"

"You already know why."

Adelaide leaned forward on the bed toward the strange man wearing only his underwear and holding a basset hound and a cup of cold espresso. She wasn't positively sure she knew why this man fixed his offering every day for ten years even though she never took it. But the other person inside her had a suspicion, and the other person was more tenacious. She wanted to bring the man of many words back into the room even if she didn't know what she would do with him. Who knew? Maybe there would be a dialogue between the people inside them and they would go somewhere deep in their secret selves. Though the outer Del felt like she was exposing her throat to a strange animal she heard herself speak again.

"Tell me," the person inside her invited him breathlessly. "Tell me about why you do this."

Joe studied her for a moment, appearing to her as if he glimpsed the other person in her words and decided it was safe.

"Because I love you," he said, as matter-of-factly as he could, and without waiting for a response this time, carried the cup into the kitchen as if it weren't the holy grail.

With a great rush in her head Adelaide felt herself standing on her ledge looking far below into a dizzying bottomless depth. In the midst of a hot wind that threatened her balance, the person inside her gave a crazy yell of "Dive!" and pushed at her back till her bare toes curled over the edge and her fingertips screamed for some surface to cling to. She shut her eyes and forced herself backwards on the ledge, knowing that there she would be safe. Only after the final echo of Joe's last words retreated into her unconscious was she able to open her eyes and take control of her mind again.

*That's it?* Adelaide thought lightly, ignoring the final tiny shaft of pain that cut through her, wrenching her again from the other self she had just discovered. *Is that our deepest secret?*

And deeper inside her than she knew, a voice too hidden for even her to hear admitted that had been a close one.

# Chapter Four
## In Which Monica and Ferdy Begin Their Guarding

"Are you sure you don't remember anything about Adelaide on a ledge?" said Ferdy. He and Monica, unbeknownst to Adelaide, were riding in the backseat of her Volvo. "It seemed more significant to her, more frightening, than just a passing fantasy." He stopped preening one of his new wings—he was doing that a lot lately—and half turned to Monica. "Should we worry about suicide? That would be a problem."

Monica snorted. She was inexplicably pleased that she could still do things like snort after death, or at least have the illusion that she could do them.

"Adelaide kill herself? Not a chance. Until all this business happened with me, she's had one success after another in her life like a roller coaster ride that only goes up. I wish I could have seen what you were seeing."

"Yeah, well, it's a trait we angels have," Ferdy said. "It's handy, but trust me. You wouldn't want to see some of the stuff I've seen. You mortals can be pretty bizarre."

Unsavory thoughts of Ferdy's legs protruding from Gregory's mouth flashed through Monica's mind, but she decided not to start a discussion on the nature of the bizarre.

"Tell me, Ferdy," she said instead. "How is it that I can snap my fingers, like this," she demonstrated the click of her thumb against her second finger, "and hear it, when both my fingers and my ears are buried in a box on the other side of town?"

Ferdy only leaned forward and stared at the back of Adelaide's ponytail as if it were a rope he could use to haul himself into the inside of her mind. "How should I know?" he said. "Stay on task."

"You're a fine one to be reminding me of focus," she retorted. "Okay, Ferdinand, let's stay focused. Tell me, if you can get inside Adelaide's brain, why can't you read any deeper than her imaginings? Why don't you know why she's thinking about a ledge?"

His chin tucked down, Ferdy cast her a sadly shy look which reminded her of the broken devil she had first met in the vestibule of hell. "I was never a very good devil, you know. Now I'm probably a mediocre angel. Maybe with time and help I'll be one of those guys who make major announcements and stuff, who get written about, but for now I've got serious limitations. Remember, I didn't know Melba McGregor was hiding behind that hedge until she came running out. And I can't tell you where we're going now."

Monica patted his hand without comment while it finally occurred to her that two rookies had been sent on this mission to help Adelaide. *Worse—I'm still trying to get used to being a spirit, and my partner has an inferiority complex.* Could she trust that they would do the right things? It would seem that you had to have as much faith when you were dead as you did when you were alive. Hoping that Ferdy hadn't been reading her thoughts she snapped her fingers again.

"Hah!" she said. "I do. I know where we're going. Number one, we're on the road to her father's house. And," she added, "Number two, I bet I could even tell you what's going to happen there. What a team we are, eh?"

"What's going to happen there?"

"Del will ask him how he's doing, and write out a weekly check for the person who comes in to take care of him. She'll put the check under a paperweight on the buffet, but not before they argue."

"About what?"

"I don't know, the times I've gone there with her I can't even remember what they argued about. I just know one starts to pick at the other, then the other picks back, then she leaves. She's never liked her father, but I could never get her to talk much about him, or the rest of her family for that matter. See, what did I tell you?"

On cue, Adelaide turned off Federal Highway just at that moment. Two more turns brought them to Malaga Lane and halfway down the street her car crunched onto the gravel of her father's driveway. She didn't bother to park under the shade of the banyan tree. Likely her visit would be brief. With a little grunting sound of "Mmm" as if her body were too heavy for the action,

Adelaide turned off the ignition and got out of the car. The three went inside the house though Adelaide stopped to slowly unlock the front door first. It was because they were inside first that Ferdy was able to murmur, "Oh, shit," and Monica was able to say, "Ferdy, don't let her come in!" before Adelaide was hit by the stench of her father's body.

The sight of him, still, his staring eyes and mouth slightly open, had less of an impact than the one hundred ninety-five pounds of bad hamburger smell that drove her backwards out of the door. Before she knew what was happening she was in the driveway again as if the smell had the force of a bomb blast. She covered her mouth with her hands and blew out hard, trying to force all of the odor back out her nose. With difficulty because she was beginning to shake, she opened the passenger door with the keys still jingling in her hand and dove into the glove compartment. Ferdy and Monica found her muttering even while she was still dialing 911 on her cell phone.

"Bastard, bastard," she was muttering, in a controlled enough way; but by the time the line opened her teeth were chattering so badly she had to struggle to repeat herself three or four times before she could make the operator understand what had happened.

"Hello, my father is de-my fa-de-my father-he's...yes, that's right. Okay, 388 Malaga Lane...okay...okay...Del...Adelaide Siren... No, that was Neil Simon." She closed the phone and sagged against the side of the car not caring that the hot metal burned uncomfortably through her jeans. Only when she took her shower that night would Joe point out the burns in the shape of the Big Dipper that her back pocket fasteners had made on her bottom. On the front seat of the car where she had thrown it, the black plastic casing of the phone, wet with the sweat of her palm, dried swiftly. October in Florida was still a hot part of the year, made even hotter by the general feeling that this was supposed to be autumn. Shivering in the heat, Adelaide stared at the still open front door as if she were guarding the entrance to hell.

Monica stood by helplessly. All her efforts to take her friend in her arms went unnoticed. "She can't feel me. Can't you do something?" she said to Ferdy. He shook his head and stared at

Adelaide with sad eyes for a moment, then shrugged.

"Well, maybe one thing," he admitted, and slammed the front door so the smell wouldn't reach her.

Adelaide jumped and instinctively looked around searching for what made the door close. She could detect no breeze in the hot, humid air, let alone a gust strong enough to slam a door. Back to the door went her eyes and stayed there perfectly still, as if her father's ghost might have done it, as if that horrible thing inside might move without her willing it to stay put until help arrived.

It was only much later, when the paramedics had brought the body bag out of the house and driven it off in the ambulance, when Joe had eased Adelaide into his own car and gone, followed by Palma in the Volvo, that Ferdy and Monica spoke again.

"I'm sorry there was nothing I could do," said Ferdy. "Even if I was capable of intervening, I wouldn't because this is part of the plan. Devils try to upset the plan, but Angels respect it."

"You mean there's a plan?"

"Oh, there's a plan all right."

"Then why haven't you told me?"

"Because I don't know what it is."

"Then how do you know that Del's father's death is part of the plan?"

"Everything is."

"Then why aren't you told in advance? Wait," said Monica, in some exasperation. "I feel like we're looping here."

"I'll try to explain. First of all, the plan is so complex, that just hearing it would make your brain implode. Second, it changes moment by moment, depending on the actions that everyone takes, like a chess game, so even if you knew the plan at any one point, it would be obsolete within seconds."

"I don't think I like being part of a chess game. It makes it sound like we're all pawns."

"No, it's not that way at all. Picture a billion billion chess pieces, each with the capability of moving itself. It's different, see? The pieces move themselves, and every time a piece moves, the plan has to change. Got it?"

"Check, mate," Monica answered, hardly understanding at all.

# Chapter Five
## In Which Adelaide Feels Hopeful

Adelaide had decided to have her father's remains cremated. She didn't know what to do with his ashes, but the folks at the Gilead Funeral Home told her she did not have to worry about that immediately. They would take care of the cremation and she could decide what to do with the ashes later.

With the absence of a body she had a reason to skip the ceremony of a formal wake, but allowed Joe to arrange a brief funeral mass at St. Jude's in Coral Gables. A good-sized group of people gathered afterwards in the living room of her father's house for a reception. Joe introduced her to a few of his customers, but most of the guests were connected to the theater in one way or another. Harvey Kalman had sent the centerpiece that decorated the table with the deli platters. With the way their last visit had gone, and the fact that she hadn't spoken to him since, the flowers seemed like a flag of truce. Harvey had probably been afraid to show up.

"I still don't understand why you had to have it here," Margie was saying pleasantly. "You could have had it at your place."

"I don't have things at my place," Adelaide said, matching her sister's tone. They stood smiling at each other like family joined in sorrow, speaking lightly so that a person couldn't tell they hated each other even if that person was helping themselves to cold cuts from the table nearby. No one would even guess they were sisters. Dark and petite, Margie formed a contrast to Adelaide's tall fairness; their penchant for wearing discount store clothing was the only thing that tied their looks together.

"It still smells," Margie said, putting her hand gently on Adelaide's shoulder in a gesture of comfort and looking suspiciously at the dingy brown drapes on the living room windows as if they harbored the smell.

Adelaide took a good sniff at the surrounding air and shook her head. "You have no idea," she smiled. She didn't admit to her sister that she would not be having anything to eat at her father's funeral reception; indeed, that she had not been able to even look at a piece of beef since his death.

"I'd think you would have enough sense to be more discrete. Look at his chair over there—is that a stain?" Margie went on relentlessly. "How embarrassing."

"Shut up about that, you'll draw attention to it," said Adelaide, smiling and cocking her head as if Margie had said something warm and funny. Luckily, sounds of a child shouting, "MARCO!" and another responding as noisily, "POLO!" from the backyard took Margie's attention away.

"Joe shouldn't have let them go in the pool. This is their grandfather's funeral, for pete's sake."

"Leave them alone," replied Adelaide. "They'll have plenty of time for funerals."

"I'll go tell them to be quieter," Margie said, not moving.

"Oh, why. Who cares? Do you really want to impress any of these people?" Adelaide said, but walked away herself into the kitchen where the window over the sink looked onto the back patio. Sitting by the side of the pool, Joe was watching Margie's children jump in and out of the water in a game of tag for two. The boy's eyes were shut tight as he blindly hunted for his sister; the girl's bathing suit top sagged half-way to her waist, exposing nothing but two pink buttons on her chest. The children were so young you couldn't tell a difference between the boy's shout and the girl's. Joe laughed with the children and called the game like a referee from his patio chair. *That's what he would have looked like as a father,* she thought, and felt her heart give another one of those odd twists that she'd been feeling lately. Watching her niece run on the coping of the pool gave her another twist, a memory she pushed away as hard as she could before it drew her further down than she could bear to go today. She wanted to be up when Palma finally arrived so she could talk about her idea.

She was almost grateful for Margie's sudden presence at her side; it stopped her from feeling any more.

"So you'll handle everything?" Margie was repeating herself now. They had gone over this when they discovered that their father hadn't left a will.

"Yes, Marge, I'll handle everything even though you're the

oldest because I live here and so and so and so." She was glad the conversation had at least turned into a non-combative avenue so she continued along it. "I'll put the house up for sale, and deal with the probate, and make sure the pool man comes around."

"Because you might not care about the money, no reason why you should, you've got enough and you never spend any, but you know my situation is different." She waved her hand at the scene through the window, at her children absorbed in their game, as if the cost of two from birth through college was a figure Adelaide knew well.

Another sound, this time back at the front of the house, allowed Adelaide to escape again. She had never remembered being so consistently grateful for interruptions. Maybe it was Palma. "Sounds like more people have come. I'll go greet them," Adelaide said.

"Since when are you the gracious one? And who are all these people anyway? I can't imagine Dad having friends."

"They didn't know Dad—they're theater people. They think I'm mourning."

The two had stopped at the doorway to the kitchen, momentarily caught in time by that familiar space, pausing cautiously as they had so often when they were children looking out at grown-up company.

"Don't be so crass," Margie whispered, peeking around her sister's shoulder.

"What crass? Because I'm not feeling sorry he's gone?" Adelaide said.

"Of course you're sorry."

"No I'm not."

"You're heartless."

"So what else is new?" Adelaide turned around to look at her sister with real interest. "Did you get a heart out of all this? Are you really sorry he's dead?" Her jaw tightened and her gaze pierced her sister's eyes. "Tell me quick."

Margie's eyes flew wide in a flash and then fixed on a spot somewhere to the right of Adelaide's chin. "Well, yes, yes I am most definitely sorry."

"Yeah, you look it," said Adelaide after the briefest appraisal, and turned to the group of five men, all in their late seventies, who had just arrived and crowded uncertainly inside the front door on the small square of tile that passed for a foyer. "Ah, the VFW contingent has arrived," she said, with a light sneer. "Bring out more food."

"What's VFW?"

"Veterans of Foreign Wars. It was his local hang-out."

"Oh, God, do you think they know? They look like they know."

"I'll bet they know every detail, and if they don't know it they're here to find out."

She walked up to the cluster and shook each hand solemnly.

"Hi, I'm Adelaide, his daughter. This is my sister Margie. She'll share tender and poignant memories about our father with you."

Margie stepped up and shook hands too. "Please forgive my sister, gentlemen. You know how funerals cause some people to act out."

While four of the men stood silently, composing their faces into something suitably funereal, the one holding a half-smoked cigar detached himself from the group and planted himself before Adelaide. He was the hairiest one in the group, with a Einsteinian coif that seemed to have taken up so much of his growing energy that he had none left for height. He tilted his mane back until he could look Adelaide in the eye.

"I'm Irwin Liptak."

"I remember you," she said. "The one with the shrapnel wound."

Irwin pulled his banlon shirt out of his plaid sans-a-belt trousers and showed her a pattern of scars, one like a deep crater and a few more superficial, on the side of his expansive belly. "I got this with the one hundred and first airborne division," he said, plugging the very wet end of the cigar into his mouth, more to get it out of the way than to draw on it, and pointing with his second finger to the scars. "I just want you to know I don't care how he died. Your father had no respect for these scars even though he was a veteran himself. That's why even though you're his daughter I'm here to tell you he was a no-good son of a bitch bastard—and anti-semitic to boot."

Adelaide looked over Irwin's head at the rest of the VFW contingent. They were gazing at her in apparent horror, but she could see an interested shine in every eye, like people watching a fresh motor vehicle accident. She put on the same smile she had been using with Margie.

"Have some turkey?" she said, gesturing to the table against the back wall of the room.

"Sure," said Irwin, and led his forces in an assault on the Publix platters.

"Now I know why you serve food at these things," Adelaide commented thoughtfully.

"I cried," Margie was at her elbow again, persisting.

"What are you talking about now?"

"When I found out Dad was dead, I cried. Just ask Bill. He'll tell you." Margie blinked rapidly several times and rubbed her eyes. "Look at me, I'm crying now."

The doorbell rang.

*This is a tight show,* thought Adelaide with relief as she opened the door. "Palma! Darling! Late as usual—no that's okay. It's really good to see you," she said, and meant it.

Palma drew her friend into her arms in a soothing hug while male heads from five decades turned to look with interest.

"I'm so sorry," Palma said.

"Oh, that's all right," Adelaide muttered. Trying to hide her embarrassment at the sympathy, she cast around in her mind for a line and could only come up with a used one. "Give me a good funeral over a wedding any day, I always say. They're so much more definite."

Palma only frowned. "And so soon after—what were the circumstances?"

Adelaide glanced at Margie who was staring in horror at the buffet. The VFW group had paused from their grazing and were watching her, waiting for the answer to Palma's question, all of them grinning broadly.

"Heart attack," she said, a little too loudly. "But forget that now. I want to talk to you. Just the two of us," she said, more in Margie's direction, and drew the surprised woman down the hall and into the master bedroom.

They sat down on the edge of a queen-size bed covered with an olive green bedspread that had once sported ridges of chenille running in curves all over it. Over the years the chenille had worn off in so many places that most of the curves were dead-ends, like in a maze.

Adelaide took a deep breath and began, "I've figured out what to do about Monica."

Palma touched her arm so lightly she could hardly feel it. "I didn't know there was something to be done about Monica."

"I'm going to have her be made a saint."

Palma watched Adelaide's face as if waiting for more, but the other woman sat very still, watching back with more than usual intensity, waiting for a response. The response was cautious.

"I didn't know it was that easy. And she's not even a Catholic... wasn't...when she died, at least."

"I've already researched it. The Episcopal church does make saints. They just haven't been real public about it because they don't want to seem too Catholic. But now with both sides talking reunification, I'll just bet the Episcopalians would like a new saint to wave at the Pope as an indication of good faith. Will you help me?"

With a physical hum running just under her skin, it seemed to take all of Adelaide's energy to sit still on the bed, her fingers working with their own agenda on the chenille spread. As if she felt the vibration and expected her friend might fly around the room at any time, Palma held on to her arm. Her next words came out in a 'put the gun down' kind of tone.

"But, Del, I need to understand why you want to have Monica made a saint, when you have never, as long as I've known you, seemed to have any faith in spiritual things. What does it matter to you?"

Adelaide gave a small jolt as if her vibration had intensified. She tried to keep her own voice calm to not alarm Palma. "It's...it's not for me I'm doing it, it's because I think Monica should be a saint and you and I are the only ones who can recognize it. I've already decided, Palma, I'm calling that head bishop tomorrow. That seems like a good place to start, he's met me, you know. I'm going to make an appointment to see him, in New York, and I want you to come with me."

"Why do you want me?"

As if sitting still were suddenly unbearable, Adelaide stood up from the bed, but stayed close enough to it so she could pick at the chenille cover.

"Del?"

She didn't look at Palma when she said, "Because these people will be hard-line religious, and I don't want to say or do anything inappropriate." When she looked up she was biting the inside of her upper lip. "You always say the right things and I need you to keep me in line so I don't do anything obnoxious."

Palma was up and had Adelaide in her arms before the other woman had time to flinch. Against the side of her cheek Adelaide could feel her friend's soft voice.

"You miss her. You try not to act as if you do, but you do. Oh, Del, I miss her too."

She felt the twist in her heart again and drew her chest away from Palma's, hoping that would ease the pain. It did, but the lump in her throat, the one that could only be washed away by crying, was back again. She wanted to push Palma away, but somehow couldn't. It was that person inside of her, she thought, the other person wouldn't push away.

"Please, Palma," she was able to beg and hoped what was in her voice sounded like a laugh, "Anything but sympathy, please. I can't take it."

The bedroom door flew open and Margie stood pale on the threshold, white knuckling the doorknob. Adelaide was grateful for her interruption this time. It made stepping back from Palma's embrace possible.

"Jeez, Marge, can't you leave me alone for three minutes?" she said, nonetheless.

"You've got to come out there and do something!" Margie insisted.

"There are two more party platters in the refrigerator, and Dad had a couple bottles of cheap scotch hidden under the kitchen sink. Put that out."

"It's not that. This is serious. They're..." here she looked at Palma and dropped her voice to a whisper, "They're talking."

"Oh, shit, well, come on in and just ignore them, Margie. As long as one person knew we probably couldn't keep it a secret forever."

Palma's curiosity overrode her discretion for once. "What in heaven's name are you talking about? What secret?"

"Del...there's—" whined Margie.

"Just hold on a second, Marge. Palma can know this." Adelaide leaned against the dresser and went over the coroner's report.

Dad had indeed suffered a heart attack, that much was true.

What everyone had not known was that the attack came while he was masturbating with a gallon of vanilla ice cream.

"I was so shocked at finding his body I didn't notice his pants were pulled down, let alone the half-empty container next to his recliner. They tested the dried white stuff pooled around his genitals and found out it wasn't just an inordinate amount of cum."

Margie closed her eyes and took a deep breath. "Thank you for not sparing us the details," she said, and to Palma, "Notice how she can't just say seminal fluid? Now will you—"

"But how...?" said Palma, thinking hard.

"God, Palma, do I have to draw pictures?" Adelaide pantomimed scooping something with her hand, then rubbing it up and down a pole.

"Now will you come *do* something?" Margie had trouble keeping her voice low in her exasperation. "Those gross old men out there are making jokes about a whole new meaning for the term 'cold-cocked.'"

Adelaide laughed. "You have to admit that's pretty funny."

"All right, miss comedy writer, you want funny?" Margie was suddenly calmer, almost smiling. "There's a young strange man talking to them, and asking questions, and he's holding a tape recorder. Doesn't that make you laugh your socks off?"

That did it. Adelaide pushed past her sister and ran down the hall, followed by the others, but they weren't quick enough to stop the stranger who had mingled with the rest of the guests and caught the story of their father's macabre death on tape.

And that's how Adelaide finally got into the National Enquirer and evened at least that score with Monica.

# Chapter Six
## In Which Del Goes Ahead With Her Plan

Two weeks later, while waiting with Palma in the room outside Cardinal Victor Parelli's office, Adelaide busily worked on biting the inside of her left cheek. There had been a slight set-back and she was only here by default. True to her plan, she had tried to get a meeting with the Episcopal Presiding Bishop, but apparently the presiding bishop's wife was in the habit of reading the National Enquirer and the story of her father's death had been in the last issue. He would have nothing to do with Adelaide Siren, no matter how virtuous her intentions. She had slight hopes that this meeting would be better, partly because the Cardinal had at least granted an interview, partly because she heard Parelli liked the theater, and partly because she had taken the trouble to dress in a suit and pumps. For the moment there was nothing else to do but work on the inside of her mouth. She had to hold her lips rigidly to the right side of her face to get at the tender lining of her cheek.

Palma, sitting in the comfortable leather chair beside her, nudged her gently and whispered, "Stop that."

"Stop what?"

"Biting the inside of your mouth. It makes you look like you've had a stroke."

"Good. I can go in his office like this, then drop my lips in place and you can jump up and down and shout, 'Look! It's a miracle!' That should impress him."

"Does everything that happens have to be like one of your comedies?"

Adelaide pretended to tap a cigar and did a bad Groucho Marx impression, "Consider the alternative."

Palma rolled her eyes and pretended to tap her own cigar. "That's the silliest thing I ever hoid," she said, in a slightly better imitation.

Adelaide closed her mouth on what she was going to say next and speculatively considered her friend. "Are you going around with that crude asshole who rapped my knuckles at Monica's funeral?" she concluded.

"Yeah. I mean yes. But he's not—"

"I like him. Did you do it yet?"

Palma sighed, only half-contented. Having gained Gus the same night she lost Monica had been so wrenching that she felt her life was divided in two that evening. As if a great hand had dashed across time a wide strip of red paint that she could never cross back over. Life on this side of the line was going to be different, she felt, and was thrilled to realize she could make it whatever she wanted, starting with herself. At first she had fallen in love with the dancing. Whenever Gus whisked her around a dance floor until her skirt swayed like a living thing she felt the same as the night they had met. Then it got better. He had taught her how to eat wings and beer without noticing the orange grease that ran down her fingers. They had had whole dates at the local Blockbuster video store, where they went to pick out a movie, wandering through the aisles pointing out their favorites to each other, and then leaving two hours later without a tape. He had taught her how to leap on benches in the middle of the Lincoln Road Mall and not care if anyone was watching, and how to lie down on the beach at night to watch the stars and not care about getting sand in her hair.

Most importantly, he had taught her about how everyone had wounds and how it was only a human condition, and not a shame, because no one was perfect.

With all this, she still fretted. From the first she had been more than ready to invite him into her bed. Yet whenever she tried to lead the conversation in a direction that would make him ask the right question, he glanced away and changed the subject, leaving Palma for the first time doubting herself, and his feelings for her. She wanted to talk to Adelaide about it, but for the first time felt an odd loyalty toward Gus that prevented her from discussing their sex life, or lack thereof.

Fortunately for Palma, they were interrupted by a youngish woman for whom the term "colleen" was created. Her exuberant red hair framed a flawlessly complexioned face needing no other adornment than her green eyes. The contours of a well-tailored jacket over a long flowered skirt covered and revealed her slim hips.

"Cardinal Parelli will see you now," she said in a voice with a blush of the old sod. She lead them through her office into a magnificent oak-paneled room whose size and furnishings did justice to the legends of ecclesiastical grandeur. Adelaide had one moment to note the buddy shot on the wall of a man in a red cassock standing beside Pope John Paul II before the cardinal himself hefted his girth from behind a mahogany claw foot desk and strode the considerable length of the room to greet them, his outstretched hand and booming voice preceding him.

"Ms. Siren, I can't tell you how thrilled I am to meet you. I've seen all your plays."

"Which ones?" asked Adelaide.

"I did say all, didn't I? And before we discuss them. . ." he released Adelaide's hand from his sure grasp and turned to Palma as if she were an amoretto truffle.

"I'd like you to meet Palma Blanco, Cardinal Parelli—she's a Catholic," Adelaide added, as if that explained her presence.

"How do you do, Your Excellency."

"Enchanted." The Cardinal held onto Palma's hand a moment longer as he turned back to Adelaide with a wink. "And you? Aren't you a Catholic?" Without waiting for an answer he released Palma and turned to the lass still hovering in the doorway. "I think I can be trusted alone with these ladies, Sister Joan."

At hearing her name, Adelaide's eyes and brows reflectively parted company while Parelli continued his low clucking.

"Perhaps we could use some coffee," he looked at his watch, "or a cocktail? No? Well then, come. Come sit," and he directed them to a grouping of cornflower blue moire wing backs clustered snootily on one side of the office. His wisp of white hair topped by the red satin skull cap against the dark blue of the chair created a patriotic allusion. Adelaide wouldn't have been surprised if that, like everything the cardinal did, was by design.

"I could see by your reaction you are surprised Joan is a nun," he said to Adelaide once they had settled down. "Forgive me, but one doesn't rise to be a cardinal without being able to read every nuance of body language. Working in the Church hierarchy is still very much like dealing with a renaissance court. There are friends and enemies and one must know which is which so as to use both to their best advantage. As for Sister Joan, we have Vatican II to thank for releasing her from that habit and rolling asexual walk that justifiably used to liken the poor creatures to penguins. In all the clamoring for reformation of the church people don't seem to notice that we already have. Reformed, that is, if you don't count the unfortunate hold-up with birth control and married priests. I'm getting more annulments through than I used to, at least. This is what reformed looks like. Mind if I smoke?" He leaned over to the dark Queen Anne table between them and opened a box inlaid with five different colors of wood. "Cigars, yes, but I don't think you'll find these objectionable. May I offer you one? The slim ones are rather nice. A friend brought them back from the Bahamas, but swore up and down they weren't Cuban imports. My eyes are no longer good enough to read the little sticker on them. Could you imagine the scandal of contraband in the cardinal's chambers? Why, I could get written up in the tabloids."

Adelaide's eyes flared at his last remark and fixed on his to see if he was teasing her. She detected nothing but the same benign twinkle she had seen when they arrived. He was right; he was very good. He lit her cigar with accustomed expertise and took a sensual pull off his own before he continued with that same style that approached unctuousness without actually sliming over the edge. The cigars gave off an aroma like incense at a high mass.

"Now forgive me for chattering and tell me what you wanted to talk to me about that you couldn't reveal over the telephone? Are you doing research for a play?"

"Cardinal Parelli," Adelaide began, expecting him to invite her to call him Victor, which he did not. "I have been doing some research, but not for a play. I've read that you had started the process for having someone made, declared, I'm not sure what you'd call it, a saint."

Adelaide's own vocation made her no slouch at reading body language and she noted the Cardinal's dazzling smile stiffen for a moment even though he carefully controlled the light in his eyes.

"Ah, you know about Frank—my own Santa Francisco," he responded in a voice one peg softer than before.

"Yes, Brother Francis D'Angelo. Can you tell me how

successful you were with the process, and how one begins?"

"You must know, to begin with, that *we* don't 'make saints.' Saints are made by the grace of God, and occasionally His Holy Father the Pope will recognize infallibly that this is so. Brother Francis D'Angelo is a saint in heaven. I am personally convinced of that. Convincing the Holy See is a much more laborious project."

"What convinces you that Brother Francis is a saint? What was your experience of him?"

"A saint is someone who lives his or her life in such a way as to show the world that this is how Christ would live if he were here today. It is a life that one can point to and say, 'This, this is what is meant by the gospels. Live this way.'" The Cardinal rose and moved to a table on the other side of the room. With his thoughts engaged in his saint he shed his earlier hearty image and allowed his walk to betray his age. He opened a drawer in the table and removed a book which he brought back to show the women. "You see, here is his St. Joseph's Missal. He always carried it with him when I was in seminary." Adelaide took the small book and felt the pages swollen with use. "See, there is an inscription inside," Parelli continued. "He left the missal to me. It is my relic—remembrance—of him."

"To my best student," Adelaide read. "What did he teach?"

"He taught Greek. And through that language he taught us to see the gospels as the earliest church saw them, in their true Platonic context of the golden mean in their expression of the kingdom of God. In his analysis, the 'fullness of time' was one in which Greek philosophy was allowed to spread on Roman roads by the Jewish race, and could only have been divinely engineered. A 'brilliant' man if that word hasn't been worn down to nothing. This man would be a saint for the intellectuals; we haven't had one of those since the time of Aquinas, and never an American one."

"Respectfully, sir, haven't there been other intellectual Catholics, just a few?"

Happily the Cardinal was past the age of taking himself, or his saint, too seriously. He chuckled at Adelaide's remark and went on. "Of course, of course, but that's only part of it. I wouldn't want you to think that Brother Francis's only grace lay in snobbish erudition. In his spare time he started a literacy program for the homeless. I remember an eighty-five year old man who died blissfully happy, finally able to read. I watched Brother Francis administer the Sacrament of Extreme Unction while the fellow clutched a copy of *Green Eggs and Ham* to his breast." Cardinal Parelli let his eyes shine with the tears that old men can't control. "I could go on."

"So if I. . .how did you actually begin the process for official sainthood?"

"How much do you want to know?"

"Everything."

"You're making me get my exercise today, aren't you," he said, with a return to joviality, and rose once more to fetch another book, or rather two large typewritten tomes bound in cardboard covers by heavy metal clamps. "This is called a *positio*. It is 1,500 pages covering Francis D'Angelo, with all the details of his life and virtues. Three people, lead by another brother at St. Vincent de Paul Seminary in Boynton Beach, where Brother Francis taught, spent five years locating and interviewing over 200 people from fellow clergy to any surviving family members. With time, labor, travel, printing costs the last estimate came to over $23,000 in expense and we've only just begun. By the time we reach the elaborate canonization ceremony in Rome we may end up spending as much as a quarter of a million dollars. Some of the funds have come out of my own pocket and others have been received through the fund raising done by those in charge of publicity."

"What publicity?"

"The publicity needed to achieve the next step. You thought this little *positio* was all that was needed?" He flipped open one of the books and removed a small card. "See, this is Brother Francis's prayer card. Color printing on this heavy stock is quite expensive these days. Here is his picture on the front, and a prayer to him on back. You look surprised. Have you forgotten that we pray to the saints to intercede for us?"

Palma smiled and Adelaide glanced down. "I had forgotten that part."

"What else have you forgotten, my dear?"

"What is the purpose of the publicity?"

"To foster prayer to the saint so that the necessary miracles can be documented."

"You have to have miracles?"

"Oh, yes. You used to need three miracles just to get any one's attention, but the rules have relaxed somewhat. Now you only need one for beatification, and one more for full canonization. That's the next document we'll be working on, a description of miracles claimed. It's a tricky process and it's taking time, but once we have assurance of a miracle the document is blessedly shorter than the *positio*. Then the whole thing goes to the Congregation for the Causes of Saints at the Vatican and sits there until someone has the time to read it. I'm afraid I'm leaving information out but I hope you understand the overview."

Adelaide was too engrossed in her topic to comment. She pressed relentlessly on. "What kind of miracles are you waiting for?"

"Physical healing is usually the one given the most credence by those at the top."

Adelaide's glance at Palma communicated *Gus* and was answered with a nod. If Parelli noticed their exchange, he ignored it. "We're waiting for someone to surface who can claim physical healing by praying exclusively to Brother Francis. It sometimes takes a while. You have to find a terribly ill person who has enough faith in your saint to risk praying to him alone, without sneaking in a petition to some established heavy weight. There are alternatives to healing miracles, it's true. Sometimes the initial miracle can be the incorruptibility of the corpse, but that didn't work for us. We had Francis dug up a while back and there was nothing left, unlike Cardinal John Neumann who was disinterred a month after his funeral in 1860—for identification purposes—and found to be virtually intact."

Another wordless conversation between Adelaide and Palma, this time with Palma showing some small sign of alarm. She relaxed when Adelaide changed the subject.

"Cardinal Parelli, how long has Francis D'Angelo been dead? And how long have you been engaged in this process?"

"Let's see. I believe we're somewhere in the thirty-first year."

Adelaide's breath left her in one dejected blast. "Thirty-one years? I have to move things along a lot faster than that. I could be dead before this is finished!"

The cardinal chuckled again and looked at her with new interest. "That's the whole point, my dear. Again, the old rule used to be that you had to wait fifty years before you could even begin the process. That's to assure that cases aren't built on a mere temporary local celebrity. The Vatican wants to know that your saint has a certain universality and staying power, and not just some current caché. Unlike the church, which espouses inclusivity, the brotherhood/sisterhood of saints is quite the exclusive clique. The whole juridical process—the Informative Phase, the Judgment of Orthodoxy, the Roman Phase, the preparation of the brief against which the Promoter of the Faith, or Devil's Advocate, subsequently argues—this is designed to discourage all but the most tenacious. Don't look so disappointed. You young people have no patience these days, always wanting immediate gratification. But now you have told me the reason for your visit. You are asking me all these questions because you have a candidate of your own in mind. Tell me about your saint."

"Well, she was murdered," Adelaide began, leading with what she figured was her most compelling fact.

She figured right; Cardinal Parelli stopped puffing on his cigar, clearly impressed. "Murdered. Do you mean martyred? Because if it is true martyrdom, you are in a completely different ball park. That omits the necessity of the first miracle. If your case proves martyrdom, and I must stress that means dying for The Faith in capital letters and not for human justice or politics, then you could go straight to beatification. Still a lengthy process, you understand, but doable within the course of a century or so. Then you would be able to pray to Blessed—what is her name?"

Adelaide paused, prepared to gauge his guarded response. But it didn't take a genius to interpret the body language when she said Monica's name. He choked on his cigar.

"Are you talking about that Episcopalian bishop who was supposed to have the stigmata? She's not even a Catholic—"

This part was going faster than she anticipated and she was losing control of the interview. Feeling like she was on a submarine on a forty-five degree angle with the warning whoop sounding and the captain yelling, "Damage Control!!" over the loudspeakers, Adelaide jumped in with the argument she had prepared.

"Oh, but Cardinal Parelli, the ordination of Monica Laparro could be the act that finally unifies the Roman and Anglican churches. Listen to me for a moment. Please," she insisted, as the man shifted uncomfortably in his chair and she sat on the edge of hers. "Here you have a woman, raised in the Catholic church, and loving its traditions, who because of an intense call to the priestly vocation has no choice but to join the Episcopal church. She serves long and well, rising to the rank of bishop not through political wile. . ." here she noticed the cardinal's buttocks shift again and cursed her lack of diplomacy, "astuteness, rather, but against all odds, given her eccentric, flamboyant style which is totally out of keeping with the straight-laced-stiff-upper-lip Anglicans. As you know, they aren't called God's Frozen Chosen for nothing. Anyway, she is elevated, nearly miraculously I might add, to a high position by virtue of her joy in life and joy in God, and shortly after her ordination as bishop God visibly shows his own joy in her by visiting upon her the marks of the crucifixion. Several weeks later she dies, struck down by one of her own parishioners who object to the stigmata on the grounds that it's *too Catholic*. I ask you, Cardinal Parelli," she sank back into her chair like a defense attorney exhausted by her final peroration, "what more do you need to declare someone a martyr to the faith?"

It was a good monologue, and a better delivery. Parelli looked at her kindly, but she could see the conversation had turned. The mild light that had been in his eyes earlier had grown crisper. She feared this was not going to end the way she had planned.

"A very compelling argument," he said, as one who is not convinced, "and one which I assume you have already presented to some official high in the Episcopal Church."

"No, Presiding Bishop Roxbury refused to see me," she answered honestly, but didn't explain that it was probably because of her recent notoriety.

"I know him. Well, he probably wouldn't have bought it either. I don't think the Episcopal Church is even making saints anymore and that's good. It was getting ridiculous there for a while. We were canonizing people they martyred and they were canonizing people we martyred. We're still having trouble sorting out the sixteenth century British saints, figuring out who belongs to what church tradi—."

"About Monica Laparro," she said, not bothering to hide her impatience.

The Cardinal placed his cigar in a huge murano ashtray as a firmer indication that he intended to bring the meeting to closure. "My dear Ms. Siren, we can only become so reformed. There have to be some rules for the Church to go by, and one of them is that the saint must be an orthodox Catholic. You cannot ask the Holy Father to declare someone a saint when that person has rejected his authority and the very dogma upon which a canonization is based." He frowned at the half finished cigar sending a lazy feather of smoke between them. "It would be like putting Fidel Castro on the board of IBM."

"I won't give up on this."

"I admire your fortitude; but give up on this."

Adelaide felt her gut burn and her breathing quicken. Her mouth opened without knowing what was going to come out. "Look," she started, her head tucking down so she could see the cardinal over the top of her glasses.

"Del," inserted Palma quickly, "I think we have enough information for now. Cardinal Parelli has told us so much, don't you agree?"

The Cardinal must have noticed the interplay between the two women, saw the two wills locked together silently in his peaceful office. He gentled his tone.

"Remember, Ms. Siren, I told you a person doesn't need to be publicly declared a saint in order to be one in the eyes of God. . . and in yours. If you believe Monica Laparro is a saint, then pray to her to ask God for whatever you desire. If she is a saint God will listen tenderly to her. I pray to Brother Francis with his missal in my hands. I advise you to do the same. Find your own relic and pray."

# Chapter Seven
## In Which Adelaide Begins Her Final Descent

Palma and Adelaide sat in the back booth of the Calle Ocho restaurant. Between her thoughts of the conversation with Parelli, Adelaide stared at the gaudy mural that stretched along the whole side wall of the restaurant. A street scene somewhere in Cuba, presumably, with pink stucco buildings and vendors selling vegetables with colors not found in actual nature. In her current mood she pictured what she would have put in its place. A view of Guantanamo Bay, maybe, with barbed wire fences and gun turrets. A *trompe d'oeil* boatload of refugees paddling out of the wall. Adelaide also thought about Palma stooping to come into a joint like this. She figured Gus must be having a terribly positive influence on her friend.

But mostly her thoughts wove in and out of the rigorous process of saint-making and the difficulties attendant in getting Monica her halo.

Monica was sitting next to Palma marveling that Ferdy, not taking up actual space, could lounge on the table top without getting in the way of the plates of *lechon asado* set before the mortal women. For herself, she wasn't yet completely comfortable about being spirit and tended to stay very still as if, lacking the usual boundaries of skin, she might fragment and fly off in a hundred different directions.

"So how do you think it's going so far?" she asked the only being in the room who could hear her.

"Not good," Ferdy said, frowning. "But that could be good. We'll just have to wait and see."

"We do an awful lot of waiting and seeing. Are you absolutely positive that's all we're supposed to do?"

"Right. We just guard Del. Guardian angel—get it?"

"This is going to get boring fast."

"That's why angels are assigned to do it. We don't bore easily."

"So why am I here at all? Besides being told to guard you, I don't know what I'm supposed to do."

"Just wait till the right moment."

"But how will you know when the right moment comes? And how will you know what to do?" she asked, still hoping for a different answer than she had received the other times she'd asked the question.

Ferdy frowned again, and this time there was such uncertainty in the eyes under the furrowed brow that Monica added, "Never mind, we'll figure it out."

Ferdy crossed his long legs and leaned over to stare into Adelaide's misted eyes. "Do you think she'll pray like the cardinal told her?"

"Nah. You've seen her. She doesn't actually believe in any of this. She's only doing it because she thinks with me as a saint I'll be more famous than her and it will make up for me dying. She puts a lot of stock in public recognition." She sniffed at the food and remembered a time when the smell of marinated pork and onions had allure. "I guess we all do. . .did."

"Shh," Ferdy said, with his eyes still on Adelaide.

"I don't know what to do next," said Adelaide. She wasn't exactly eating her lunch, but rather shifting the sauteed onions about on her plate with her fork and now and then spearing a plaintain as if it were a cardinal's cap.

"First you should eat," Palma said. "You're getting too thin. I can see your collarbone and you have those dark circles you get under your eyes when you lose weight in your face. Second, you should forget about this canonization business and get back to your life. You've got the Nobel Prize to win, remember?"

Adelaide sniffed to corral the tears threatening to escape from her nose to her upper lip, but failed to hide altogether a stricken look that made Palma add, "Sorry."

When Adelaide spoke it was with a mighty control, not daring more than a halting whisper, but needing just the same to finally release the words aloud.

"Don't. . . remind me. I keep thinking. . .the wrong person died. I should have. . .have been the one. She was so good."

Palma put her own fork down and drew a breath; she seemed to be making a choice of responses. "Oh, please," she said briskly, without another trace of sympathy, "you should be honest with yourself about why you're doing all this to begin with."

"I told you. It's because she was so good."

"That's a crock of shit," Palma said. "Maybe I'm losing patience in my old age but it's getting hard for me to watch you play out this charade of sainthood."

"This is not a charade," Adelaide insisted, with what she hoped was a final backhand to her wet nose. "Everything I'm doing is in good faith. All right, maybe I don't believe the life after death stuff, let alone the voodoo business of saints obediently trundling off our requests to some higher being, but that doesn't mean Monica can't be honored as a saint in someone else's eyes even if I think she's dead and gone and that's that. And stop talking like Gus."

Palma ignored her last remark and stubbornly held on to the point. "Did you hear the sorts of things that Cardinal Parelli was saying? Spending a quarter of a million dollars—"

"I have the money."

"And he said no church will touch her case—"

"Like I said, I have the money."

"So you're going to buy her sainthood? What about getting sick people to pray to her so you can rack up your miracles?"

"I won't have to if I can prove martyrdom."

"Digging up her body for mercy's sake, to see if it's rotten, I knew you were thinking about that. This is—"

"For identification purposes, he said."

"—insane, Del. And I know why you're doing it even if you don't want to admit it."

That stopped her. "Oh, really?" she said lamely.

Palma released her usually erect posture and slumped wearily down in the booth until she could rest her shoes on Adelaide's seat across from her. "She's dead. And if I know Monica she has no interest in being painted on a holy card, because she knows how stupid she looked in those bishop's robes that make her look like a giant beetle. This isn't about her—it's about you."

Adelaide felt her defenses rise. "You know, maybe Gus hasn't been such a good influence on you after all. Maybe you think this 'she stoops to conquer crap' elevates you somehow. Look at how you're talking. Look how you're sitting. What is this, plebian chic?"

"You sit this way all the time."

"Yeah, but when I do it it's part of my character, eccentric. When you do it it's just faux low-class. Pretending to be like your boyfriend."

Palma took her feet off the booth and leaned far across the table on her elbows to be sure that Adelaide could hear her say quietly, "You will not speak that way about Gus ever again—got it?"

Adelaide gave up the pretense of eating and put down her fork. "Palma, it just isn't like you."

There was no other sound than Adelaide's words, but it was as if the click of a trigger had sounded at the OK Corral. Palma's eyes narrowed into brittle slivers like glass shards.

"How the hell would you know?" she said cooly, and in the space filled by Adelaide's surprise she went on. "So that's how to get your attention. Drop out of the character you've written for me. Oh, I know it well and I'm well equipped to play it. I'm always in good taste, never one to argue, or confront. I always left that to you and Monica because voicing opinions wasn't part of the character you created for me in our little play. God forbid I should say what I'm thinking."

"Oh, oh, this looks like it's spinning into some dangerous territory," said Ferdy. "What do you think?"

"I thought I was rather grand," Monica answered.

"What?"

"Palma said I looked like a giant beetle in my vestments. I'm a little disappointed at how your best friends talk about you after you've gone."

"Don't sweat it. They probably talked that way about you while you were alive. Now pay attention."

Adelaide's mouth had opened to retort but the change she saw in Palma had taken her by surprise and put her timing slightly off. Palma was able to go on without interruption.

"I've always kept my mouth shut and figured it was between the two of you, you with your petty envy of Monica. For what? Because it was real envy, or because you could use that emotion to manipulate yourself and drive your work, but always using Monica. And she knew it was happening and pressed your button just often enough to perpetuate it. Maybe she was even flattered that you considered her competition. It was part of the dynamic that kept us together so I never tried to stop it because I was just glad we were together. Sure, the repartee was kind of exciting and a little sick, what the two of you did to each other over the past thirty years, while we were all toasting to The French Hen Society and talking about our affection for one another."

"Is that really how it was?" asked Ferdy.

Monica grimaced. "Yeah, I guess so. Looks like Palma knew us better than we knew ourselves. Or I knew but wouldn't admit it. At least I have a chance to make amends now. To clean up this mess before it's too late."

"From the look on Adelaide's face it may be too late now. And Palma's not even finished."

She nearly was. "Now something has happened and you feel responsible somehow that Monica died and that's finally jogged something else besides envy in you—not affection, maybe, but something. And I think I know what it is. I think you're pursuing this saint business for no other reason than to get rid of your own guilt. The only thing I don't know is why—what did you do the night of Monica's death to make you feel so guilty?"

Palma's words felt like a finger jabbing Adelaide hard somewhere in an unprotected core part of her being. She hated her friend in that moment. Wrapping her sarcasm about her for protection she lashed back.

"So that's your opinion, is it? Now you know why no one has ever asked you for it."

Palma only smiled, obviously basking in the gratifying power of a direct hit.

"*Su abuela,*" she hissed complacently.

There is no rage greater than that created by certain knowledge that your adversary knows they've won. Adelaide sat in stunned silence for a moment, shocked that Palma had been the one to put her into words. Then she picked up the lime on her plate that had been congealing the fat from the pork around it. She squeezed the lime once, hard, in Palma's direction, so that the lime juice and pork fat sprayed on the woman's pumpkin colored silk blouse.

"Forgive me if I don't do food fights," said Palma. "There are limits to how low-class I can be." She got up and threw her napkin on the table without bothering to daub her blouse with it, and turned to leave. Three steps away she stopped, turned again, and walked back to the table, tears and anger both struggling for a hold on her face.

"On second thought," she sobbed, "let me leave you with the tip." She lifted the edge of Adelaide's plate with her index finger so that it up-ended into her lap. Then she left.

"You go, girl," said Ferdy admiringly and hopped off the table to go with her.

"Wait," said Monica, forcing her attention away from Adelaide who sat with fingers laced on the table top, doing nothing but stare at the bottom of the plate in her lap while the marinade ran down her stockings into her pumps. "Where are you going? I thought we were supposed to guard Del."

"I'll leave her with you. It's easy, just stay by her. I'm sure Palma will go to Gus for comfort and I think I may come in handy."

"What do you have to do with Palma?" Monica sputtered. "My friend looks like she's going into crisis!"

"Direct orders, Madam. And this I know I can do."

Ferdy winked and saluted before disappearing altogether, leaving Monica to watch helplessly as Adelaide tried not to cry in public. With a holding of breath and wrenching in her heart she willed the haycocks of her hydrodynamic system to stay shut. But the river was too much for the dam, and she finally gave into it and heaved great sobs into her napkin while the waiter lurked in consternation over the yet unpaid check. Along with the sobs Adelaide barely heard herself speaking. Even Monica could barely hear.

"Why do I say these things?" she heard someone inside her whisper. "Why can't I just keep my fucking mouth shut sometimes?"

"I'm so sorry for the part I played," Monica mourned.

"No one is acting as they should," Adelaide whispered through her tears.

"Or maybe because I died they're finally acting like themselves," Monica said, staring at her joyless friend across a greater gulf than death could create.

# Chapter Eight
## Palma and Gus...and Ferdy

Unlike Adelaide, Palma held her own tears until she reached the safety of her car parked out front. Then she let them flow, and as with most people, once started, she cried for everything. She cried for the stricken look she'd caught on Adelaide's face, and for the shame of her angry reaction. She cried for the loss of Monica who would have quietly listened to her talk about what had just happened. She cried for the perfectly flawed, wasted years of her own loneliness.

And she cried about Gus, for both the acceptance she'd found in him, and the nagging worry of her unfulfilled desire. She thought again about how she would come home from a night of dancing with her inner thighs aching, with her wet panties cooling in the evening breeze as she spread her legs apart while they kissed goodnight at her door. He was the only man she'd ever known who hadn't grown erect at the slightest brush of her breath on his cheek.

*Damn it! Is it a moral thing with him? Am I losing it? Am I getting older and losing my attraction?*

She didn't want it to be this way, she didn't want to be alone anymore. But today seemed an appropriate day to find out the worst, so she took the turn at the Arthur Godfrey Causeway that would take her to St. Stephen's.

Palma parked close to where Gus stood talking to another man next to a van with Fernandez Roofing painted on the side. If he noticed the grease on the front of her blouse or the mascara streaked in diagonal lines from the corners of her eyes he gave no indication as she walked by him into the empty church. She sat in a pew all the way at the back waiting for him, thinking of her questions, steeling herself for his answers. One thing she knew, he wouldn't be cruel; she felt she could count on that.

Within a few minutes she heard the large door creak open behind her and felt the vibration of Gus's presence. He settled down next to her, put his left hand over hers where it rested on the wooden pew.

"Del?" he asked.

She nodded and started to cry again.

They sat in silence for a few moments, and when Palma's sobs had subsided Gus pointed with his free hand up into the rafters of the cathedral.

"Can you see up there, one. . .two. . .the fifth beam from the altar? You can see the stain on the plaster around it where the leak is. There's been a steady drip every time it rains so that the pew directly underneath is stained too. Beautiful old church, but boy, is it in bad shape. I can't fault it, though. Reminds me too much of me."

Palma let herself relax into the safety of small things. "How is it here since...since Monica?"

"Business as usual. Since there was no suffragan bishop to step in, the canon for the ordinary has taken over the administrative stuff until we can complete the search process for another bishop. Canon McNeely is no bigger asshole than anyone else. That's okay," he went on, as if responding to a third person in their conversation. "Monica said once there were assholes in paradise. I kind of like the way that sounds."

"We've been through such craziness, Gus, and everything feels like it's fallen apart because of it. I think about how my life used to be, fussing over whether this Versace gown went with that David Yurman necklace as if my survival depended on it. Since I've found...well, just lately, I don't know what's important anymore. Or maybe what's important now is different from before. I just don't know. I want to know what's right, and do I sound nuts?"

Even while she was saying the words, Palma listened to herself, to the way she could stumble and stutter through her thoughts while he listened as if she could go on forever in this way and he would still be willing to listen. She felt her gut torn between the comfortable, accepting feel of his presence and the fear that it wouldn't last, that this talk might lead them to the end.

There was a pause while Gus silently encouraged her to go on, and when she didn't he picked up the thread himself. Like her he was facing towards the altar so their eyes didn't meet as he spoke.

"If you're nuts, I am too. I know how you feel." Gus closed

his eyes to imagine what it was like. "Okay, let me see how this sounds. Let's say there's this snake—"

"What?" said Palma, giggling in spite of her mood.

"No, stay with me here. The snake gets too big for its skin, see, so it shucks it off and then it's crawling around in a new skin, kind of tender and smooth. That's what I feel like now. Only I'm afraid that this new skin is too soft against all the underbrush I have to crawl through. You know, what if it's not tough enough to protect me in the world that I know. That's scary, because I've seen what the world is like. It can beat you up. So I'm scared. I haven't been this scared since I stood up to hear the verdict at my court martial."

There was a silence. They had gone over his past, her past, in such loving detail that he would know the silence wasn't caused by his mention of it. He had said his fill for the moment and would wait for her to fill the silence, or not. Palma took a deep breath and plunged into what she knew might be her own sentencing. "What happens next?" she asked.

"I've been giving that a lot of thought, and figured that I would wait until we had a new bishop in place here, and then I would ask him if I might apply for entrance into seminary."

No matter how well she thought she had prepared herself for this Palma pulled her hand from under his as she felt her scalp at the back of her head burn with the shock of losing him. "You want to become a priest?"

"I know what you're thinking. I'm getting on in years and it seems a little late to find a job as somebody's assistant. But I've heard of people who've done it later in life than this." He looked at her with a weak smile. "Or do you think they'll reject me because of my record?"

Palma turned to face Gus on the pew and heard herself say, "No, that's not what I thought at all. I thought you might want to marry me." They were not the words she would have planned and she sucked her breath in rapidly as if she might take the words back in as well. But they floated in the silence between them and all she could do was search his face for the reaction.

Gus squeezed his eyes shut again and said simply, on a held note, "Oh." His bottom lashes dampened, and when he opened his eyes again they were wet. He placed his hands carefully, one on each knee. He could feel her beginning to tremble beside him, and concentrated on his hands in order to still the tremor in his own voice. Now he would have to tell her the rest, how the medication hadn't worked, how he was not good for more than dancing. And he knew that took away his right to tell her how much he loved her.

"Palma...sweetheart...you know how I was talking about those faulty beams in the rafters, and how this church reminded me a lot of me..."

On the word "me" Ferdy flew in through the stained glass window depicting St. Paul being knocked off his horse on the way to Damascus. He heard Gus's next words.

"...but there's something else I have to tell you that—"

Ferdy guessed what that was going to be from the stricken looks on their faces. He knew there was no time to waste in priming the pump or Gus would botch things for all three of them. It would be wrenching for Gus, but if he finished that sentence...

Gus's body jerked to one side and his eyes suddenly flew wide.

"Oh my God!" he gasped.

"What's wrong?" Palma reached for him, thinking that a heart attack wouldn't be surprising the way life had been going.

Gus's hands lifted from off his knees. In the crotch of his light weight work pants he could see a mighty bulge easily recognizable even after all the years of absence. Palma saw it too.

"Oh my God," she repeated.

One of Melba's former minions entered the sanctuary to change the altar candles. Looking happier these days, she waved gaily to the couple praying at the back of the church. Gus waved back, knowing that she wouldn't be able to see Palma's hand which had crept with a will of its own to cover his still growing erection.

"We could go to my place," she said, breathily, while smiling and nodding at the altar guild lady.

"We shouldn't take the chance of waiting—my place is closer," Gus said, with the same cheerful smile. But his eyes were solemn as he looked into hers. "I could be married while I'm in seminary. Could you take to being a poor priest's wife?"

"Fuckin' A," Palma said.

# Chapter Nine
## In Which Ferdy Makes Matters Worse

Ferdy swaggered into Adelaide's bedroom as she was lacing up her boots on the side of the unmade bed. Monica turned to eye Ferdy like a suspicious wife whose husband has arrived home three hours late.

"Where have you been?" she asked from the other side of the bed where she leaned against the corduroy backrest. "Don't you realize I'm new at all this?"

"I had to help Gus out. He needed a jump-start. I think he'll be all right from here on."

Monica looked at him for a long moment and then blinked. "On second thought, I don't think I want to hear about it."

"How long has she been crying?"

"On and off all afternoon."

Now it was Ferdy's turn to stare. "Why do they do it?"

"You mean cry? It's a way of expressing pain...no, of easing it."

"It looks like it hurts."

"Well, it does. But it feels good too. Is it making you sad?"

Ferdy looked up as if he had been somewhere else. "Uh, no. I was thinking how things might be different if devils could cry."

Monica got off the bed and took his arm. "Ferdy, just waiting around like this is agony, and I've been thinking. I've always found out ways to fix things, that's my nature, and I've never been one of those people who kept all the rules. Maybe that's a fault that I should work on now that I'm living this other life, but I just can't stand around any more. I have to do something."

"Like what?"

"I don't know!" Monica nearly shouted her exasperation. "Look at me, I'm a spirit. I can't talk to her, I can't touch her, I don't know what I can make happen. And I sure wasn't expecting this much frustration after my death," she ended, her voice softening a little as she noticed Ferdy's downcast look. "I'm sorry, I just heard things were supposed to get a little easier on the other side."

Ferdy's only response was to sit on the bed and reach for his foot, but they were all interrupted by the front doorbell.

Adelaide quickly blew her nose, and glanced at her eyes in the mirror over the living room buffet on her way to the door. "Forgot your key again?" she said as she opened it.

"Trick or Treat!" shouted two furry creatures standing on the front step, both about three feet tall, paper bags held open as far as their tiny arms could reach. With the light from the front hall the white part of their plush costumes gleamed just enough to make them visible. The white fake fur was dotted with uneven black spots that made them look like a pair of Jersey cows.

Adelaide stood staring longer than their four year old patience could endure.

"We're one hundred and one Dalmations!" one of them shouted even more loudly than before as if she thought Adelaide might be hard of hearing. The other one nodded vigorously in case it was only Adelaide's ignorance of what they were portraying that had momentarily stunned her. But when they thrust the bags at her once more, Adelaide still didn't react.

"It's Halloween," came a man's voice from down by the sidewalk; the voice had an edge to it that made it sound like it was really saying, "It's Halloween, you big jerk."

Adelaide slowly looked into the darkness from where the voice had come.

"I didn't know," she said, in a voice mixing annoyance with defeat. "I haven't got anything."

"C'mon, kids," the man's voice said.

One Dalmatian immediately disappeared down the path while the other gazed at her. "You didn't know," said a tiny voice behind the mask, a voice which sounded like the creature's tiny heart was breaking for her. "Everybody knows." It turned and trudged slowly down to the sidewalk, it's polka dotted tail swinging wearily in time to its step as if the creature had learned something sad about the world in that moment.

Adelaide shut the door, re-opened it, then shut it again a little harder than she meant to. She patted the pockets of her jeans. Not finding there what she was looking for she went back to the bedroom and picked up her suit jacket from the floor. The pork marinade had dried to a white film on the navy blue crepe and she had to pick a piece of onion off the pocket before she could stick her hand inside and pull out her keys.

"She going somewhere? Where is she going now?" Ferdy asked.

"The out-of-town run of her new play is opening tonight. I saw her leave a note for Joe on the refrigerator to meet her there," Monica answered.

"She wears jeans and a t-shirt to her own opening night?"

"It's part of what she does. She acts like she doesn't care. You know, come to think of it, this is a little peculiar. Joe should have been here by now. He always goes to opening nights with her."

Ferdy's wings fluttered the way some people squirm when they're having an idea. "How would she feel if Joe didn't show up? Would it bother her?"

"A lot, I think. And tonight it could be especially bad. Palma and I always went, too, and I think the odds are good that Palma won't be there tonight. She'll be all alone."

Ferdy pulled himself up with the forced resolve of one who might be making a big mistake but is going ahead anyway. "Look, Monica, I think I've got an idea."

"Is it part of the plan?"

"Could be, but I have to warn you. Throughout most of my existence I've been a devil. All I'm really good at right now is making trouble, and I think I know how to make things worse for Adelaide. But that could be good. Sometimes, making things worse is just the thing you need for things to get better. Are you understanding me?"

Monica nodded slowly. "No," she said.

"Will you trust me?"

"What have we got to lose?"

"Adelaide."

Adelaide was again moving toward the front door. She had started making soft little humming noises to herself, sort of a "Mm...mm," as if there were a disagreement going on inside her head. The humming sound and her progress to the door were interrupted by the telephone. She hesitated, then stopped at the kitchen and picked the phone off the wall.

"Joe, is that you?" she said, by way of greeting, and without waiting for an answer, "Where are you?"

She heard nothing but the sound of heavy breathing.

"Harvey, stop screwing around. I haven't got the time. I have an opening in half an hour."

"Jeez, and no sense of humor. Got just a minute? Listen, your guilt trip has been working real good. I just wanted to tell you I had lunch today with a guy who I think will do your play, you know, the drammer? I told him all about it, and warned that it could be worse than "Angels" and even if it could play in the city it won't make money on the road and he just said, 'What the hell, it's not theater until men with guns show up.' What a guy, huh? I think he heard that in some college appreciation class. Maybe he's a lapsed Catholic. So you want me to set up a get-together for the three of us?"

Despite her hurry to leave Adelaide let a little silence go while ten or twelve responses fought for dominance in her brain. One finally slipped out between her teeth. "That's real nice, Harve, going to bat for me when you didn't feel good about the project."

"It was the least I could do."

"No, Harvey, the least you could have done was to take it seriously in the first place. The least you could have done was to put out your feelers before I embarrassed myself all over the country."

"What?"

"Because you turned me down everyone else got scared off. I couldn't have run this play at the Dania Community Theater during the summer. And the funniest thing about it, you know what the funniest thing about it is?"

"What, Del?"

"I don't even give a rat's ass anymore, you son of a bitch bastard!" she shouted into the phone. "Because of you I've killed my two best friends and I don't give a shit about anything! You hear that, Harvey? I had friends! People who loved Adelaide Siren and I killed them!" She slammed the phone down and ignored it when it rang again. Turned off the speaker so she couldn't hear the message. She spoke to the message machine that was trying to deliver.

"Mm...I don't care. I *really* don't care."

Wondering what it was that she didn't care about, she started crying again as she opened the front door.

There was a UPS delivery man standing in it.

"Package for Adelaide Simon," he said.

"I'm in a big hurry," she said.

As if he hadn't heard her, the man placidly wrote a number on the list attached to his clipboard and handed it to Adelaide, who signed with his grimy ball point pen on the line where he pointed. After tucking the clipboard under his arm he leaned down and lifted a small cardboard package the size of a shoe box which had been resting near his foot.

"Here you go. Have a good evening." He turned and climbed into the brown truck parked just at the end of the sidewalk.

"It's Siren," she called after his retreating back. Rather than taking the time to put the box inside the house, Adelaide picked up the package and carried it to the car. She was tossing the box into the passenger seat when she noticed for the first time the sender's name above a Handle With Care stamp—Gilead Funeral Home.

There was a small shock of recognition as she followed through on the toss, the box leaving her fingers and landing half tilted on its side against the handle of the passenger door. Gilead had told her they would be sending her father's ashes after the cremation. She had never stopped to think how they would be sent. She gingerly righted the box on the seat beside her. Funny, she thought, how there was no getting rid of anyone she hated, while everyone she loved..."mm," she said, silencing the other person's words which were not her own. After three tries she successfully got the key in the ignition and started the car.

Monica watched her drive off. "Ferdy, I'm having second thoughts about making things worse for Del. I mean, look at her. She's just about hit bottom."

"'Just about' usually isn't good enough." Ferdy clutched Monica's rounded shoulders and straightened them up. "Monica, stay with her at the play. Stay with her no matter what. I'm going to find Joe and start making trouble."

"I just don't like this. Let's come up with a different plan."

"I don't have a different plan. Besides, it's already happening. That last caller was Joe."

# Chapter Ten
## And Worse

Joe hung up the phone behind the customer counter at the Dog's Day Salon. He was worried that Adelaide wouldn't get the message that he would meet her at the theater, but if Buford's owner would just show up within the next fifteen minutes he figured he'd make it into his seat just before the curtain went up. After a questioning look, she would settle against him and take his hand as if he were the one with the opening night trembles.

Buford was a greater challenge. A Himalayan cat with a coat too dense to comb, he'd needed to be shaved from the neck down. Now Buford sat in a holding cage, implacably furious, fixing a laser glare on Joe.

While he waited, Joe alternately cleaned up the place and talked baby talk to Buford, who paffed and spit unappreciatively whenever Joe drew near. The cat did his best to act like a lion, but with his bulgy eyes and flattened nose he came across more like an irate owl.

Once the towels were in the wash and the shaver was cleaned of cat fur and put away, Joe pulled up one of the canvas chairs in front of Buford's cage and lowered his body heavily into it. He rubbed his beefy hand over his face, letting the roughness of his five o'clock stubble revive him. Hefting wet fifty pound dogs in and out of the tub was hard work and he could feel himself getting older and wearier sometimes when the day was done. Being with someone who was hurt and angry tired him out, too. Like this cat, he meant. He gazed at Buford from under eyelids heavy with sadness, rubbed his stubble again and then took a swipe at his eyes. He opened his mouth to speak, wondering what would come out, but certain it wouldn't be baby talk.

The shop door shut loudly.

"Sorry, Mummy's late!"

Joe rose from his chair while Buford growled and paced his cage.

Charlotte Sulzyki bustled up to them. Charlotte was one of those incredibly small women who compensate by acting big. Her feet fell on the linoleum of the shop as if she were carrying one-hundred and eighty pounds of weight rather than ninety-seven. She invaded Joe's personal space and belly-laughed up at him when she saw the cat.

"Buford, you're a scream!" she screamed. "What's Daddy going to say when he sees you all naked, huh? Is he ready to go? What's the charge—besides indecent exposure?" She laughed again.

Joe tried to make his laugh as big as hers and put the safety of the customer service counter between them while he wrote up her bill. Then they moved to the cage where Joe undid the latch and reached in. Buford backed up with a hiss, apparently wondering what else Joe was going to remove from his body.

"Here, let me," Charlotte said. "Buford's always a good kitty for me, aren't you Buf? Buf-meister, you old pusser-face, you." Joe couldn't imagine Buford ever being a good kitty but stepped aside anyway. It was Charlotte's turn to reach into the cage and, moving naturally faster than Joe, she was able to seize the recalcitrant animal and drag him out, holding his hind legs so he couldn't use his claws on her.

"Don't you have a carrier?" Joe asked. "How about I give you a cloth bag? They feel secure when you bag them, sometimes. Won't he get into trouble on the ride home?"

"Nah, Buford's different. He likes the car. We'll be just fine." Charlotte walked to the door, and opened it with her left hand, where Buford sniffed the freedom of the evening air. With only one hand to hold him, the tiny Charlotte was no match for Buford. He dug his claws through her silk shirt just above the waistband of her size one jeans and used her bottom rib for a springboard as she reflexively loosed her grip. Charlotte and Joe both watched a golden streak fly across the darkened street and through an alley on the opposite side.

Charlotte streaked after Buford so quickly that within seconds Joe had lost them both. He fished his keys out of his pocket as he padded back to the shop, hurriedly locked the door and jumped into his car parked along the curb outside, thinking to pull around the block and track Buford down that way.

Buford easily outdistanced his mistress and stopped near a tiled fountain surrounded by hibiscus plants in a small park several blocks away. He lapped some of the water and let his heart slow down while he contemplated what revenge to take on Charlotte and that man who had turned him into a clown.

"Psst! Buford," a voice said nearby.

Buford started, what remained of his fur rising along the ridge of his backbone. He was surprised that he hadn't sensed the presence of someone before they spoke, until he saw the angel sitting on the other side of the fountain. Angels could sneak up on you that way.

"Who are you?" he asked.

"Name's Ferdy."

"Angels don't visit Miami very often. My name is Buford. I'm pleased to meet you but rather embarrassed given my current condition."

"Why? What's wrong?"

Buford scoffed. "I'm sure you're being polite, but you must be aware that my breed has much longer fur than this. I was taken to shop today by my Charlotte Woman where this was done to me. Now, lacking all trust in my feeder I simply don't know what to do next." He sat back on his haunches and lifted a hind paw to dig in his ear.

"If you ask me I think the look is really kind of macho. With all your fur bunched up around your face you look a little, you know, like a male lion."

"That's very kind of you, but I want to look like a Himalayan. The fact remains that I was shaved against my will and I'm outraged and won't go home with Charlotte Woman again. So don't think you're going to convince me that it's the right thing to do and I'd better be good if I want to go to cat heaven. I'm not some kitten you can coax."

"*Au contraire,* Your Bufordness. I'm here to tempt you into quite the opposite. I want you to run away—at least for an hour or so."

"How is this? Are you a danger to me? Are you really a devil in disguise?" Buford looked a little disappointed that he was not going to be coaxed after all.

"No. Once I was an angel in disguise but that's all changed now. I could tell you about it if you like—"

There weren't many cats who could claim to have their personal angel, and Buford seemed gratified to finally be exalted as he deserved. He walked carefully around the sides of the fountain until he reached Ferdy, rubbed against him to mark him as his own and purred low, "No, let me tell you *my* story—"

They lifted up their heads simultaneously as they heard the stompings of Charlotte Sulzyki at the entrance to the park.

"Good enough," said Ferdy. "But first. . ." with an elegant sweep of his hand he silently beckoned Buford to follow him further into the deepening night.

# Chapter Eleven
## And Worse

Adelaide slumped into her lucky seat at the end of row R just as the lights came down. She had avoided most of the well-wishers this way and, with the play beginning, didn't have time to look at the three empty seats next to hers. Jake, the director, had seen her coming in through the back, though, and even in the shadows of the wings she could see him cock his head to the side and frown as if knowing that things weren't right with her. But he hadn't said anything, as if he figured it had something to do with the show and preferred not to know. For her part she had managed to squeeze a "Hello, Jake," from between lips that would have stayed silent if they were any tighter.

She slid down until her tail bone came to a stop a few inches from the edge of the seat, and balanced her knees against the seat in front of her. This is how she always watched a play, or rather, watched the audience to determine where they were caught up in the action, and where they were let down. She didn't need to take any notes; she remembered every detail and would go home immediately after the show to rewrite.

But not this night. The empty seats to her left were louder than the nearly constant laughter of the full house. The seats weren't talking to her, though. They were talking to that other woman inside her, the woman who she had discovered a few weeks ago when Joe had told her he loved her. Now that she was still, and sitting in the dark with nothing to occupy her, the voice was stronger than it had been when it was speaking just words now and then. Joe had never missed an opening before, the empty seats were saying to the woman inside, and she had never thought about it. The woman inside her answered that it was kind of like breathing, you never noticed it unless you needed it. Adelaide was suddenly aware that only the very top of her lungs was expanding with each breath she took. *He's never missed one of my openings before,* the woman inside her said, *and now just when I'm feeling so alone—*

A rush of anger gagged the voice. Adelaide took her damp rag into her imagination and wiped those words off the slate of her mind. *You are alone,* she fought back. *That's who you are. Now get over it.* Friendship, love, it was all an illusion. Joe was probably off somewhere with some. . .*dog,* she fumed, with the simmering rage of a wife contemplating a mistress. He didn't care about her anymore than, than she cared about anyone. How could she have let her guard down like this? Let herself be seduced into feeling connected? The only thing she could count on was herself.

Her memory flashed a scene in the house where she grew up. She was fourteen and passing through the living room where her parents watched the television from twin recliners. On the television was a movie with a dinner party in it.

"Why don't we ever do that?" said her mother. "Why don't we make some friends?"

"We're not the kind of people who have friends," said her father.

They continued watching the movie and Adelaide went out.

And being the best. That was the other reality she could deal with.

The sight of the curtain at intermission made her angrier. She had been so lost in her thoughts that she didn't even notice the lights had gone up until people wanting to exit her row got piled up at her knees. Keeping her eyes down to avoid compliments from anyone who recognized her she rolled out of her chair without comment and headed for the front lobby door. Once outside, she lit a cigarette and walked around the corner of the building where it was quiet. She was staring so hard in the direction of the parking lot that she didn't notice Jake come up behind her and jumped when he said, "Boo! Looks like tonight had no effect on the house," he added, allowing himself a wide grin while he looked like what he really wanted to do was roll on the ground like a triumphant chipmunk.

"What do you mean?"

"Halloween, you know. Didn't you know it was Halloween?"

"No. Are you happy with it?"

"Happy?" Jake looked so full of emotion that the only truly appropriate expression of it would be to explode the top of his head. He settled for "Ecstatic! Rick upstaged himself a couple of times, and Betsy's moving a little woodenly, but that's because she's not used to the changes we made in the set yesterday. Give her another night to play with it and she'll be fine. Do you want to come backstage?"

"Ah, no. Just tell them they're all doing a great job."

"Fab! Then I'll see you at the opening night party."

"Yes. No. Look, Jake, I'm not feeling so well."

"I thought you looked a little off. Is Joe all right?"

"If I'm not there don't take it personally, okay?"

"Sure, Adelaide."

She glanced at her watch and forced herself to comment. "Oh, the first act ran over by five minutes."

"So what do you want me to do? Hold up the Don't Laugh sign?" He winked and was gone.

As the lights blinked through the lobby windows and Joe still hadn't arrived Adelaide's thoughts vacillated between rage and the image of Joe's Mazda broad-sided by a Cadillac crashing the red light on Almera Avenue. That turn light was never long enough and tourists always thought they could run it. Joe drove as slowly as he walked and maybe he hadn't cleared the intersection in time. Visions invaded her of his bloody head hanging over the steering wheel while she beat him with the seat belt he had neglected to buckle. So what? So what if something had happened to him? Heading back into the theater she left her cigarette to glow in the grass like a beacon sending out her message.

*I don't care.*
*I don't care.*
*I don't care.*

She was so intent on not caring that she didn't see the second act any more than she saw the first.

☿ ☿ ☿

*I don't care.*

The words comforted her and kept the other woman quiet. She was still thinking them when she pulled into the driveway and saw Joe's car safely parked there, without the driver's side smashed in and no trace of blood anywhere. The vision of the accident on

Almera Ave was replaced by the vision of being stood up for a dog.

Stifling the voice inside her which said her actions were highly incongruent with not caring, Adelaide charged through the front door like Medea looking for the kids. She found Joe in the kitchen, still dressed in his work clothes, suspending the box of Coco Puffs over a bowl of ice cream. He stood still, staring at her in alarm, blurting out what he would not have said if he weren't so surprised.

"Del, what's wrong? You look like you've been crying."

"What, because my eyes are all red and swollen? Nah, no crying here. I've just developed a sudden allergy to Coco Puffs! Give me those!" Adelaide grabbed the cereal box from Joe's still upraised hand and emptied it on the kitchen floor before Joe could stop her. Avoiding the lighted cigarette in her hand, he tried to take her wrists and pull her to him but she wrenched away and buried the cigarette so deep in his ice cream it didn't have a chance to sizzle.

"Okay, calm down," he spoke to her as if she were a high strung breed. "I take it you're angry I wasn't at the play. See, there was—"

"Brilliant deduction, Watson. So tell me, was I stood up for a matched set of Pekingnese or just a fucking box of Coco Puffs?"

Adelaide could see something like a light wash over Joe's face. He smiled broadly. "You thought I stood you up? You really wanted me to be there."

Joe was smiling and she was hurting. A hot blush rushed up her neck and spread over the top of her head. Adelaide was suddenly aware of a little corner in her brain. It sat at the base of her skull just to the right of her spine. It started to pulse slightly as if it wanted to escape the bone that trapped it. In that little corner of Adelaide's mind the other woman's voice piped up, stronger than it had ever been. It was saying *don't go there*. She heard the voice, and felt the danger of going there but she was hurting and Joe was smiling and her mouth was running on a different part of her mind. That part was saying that Joe was the last person making her hurt and if she killed him she wouldn't hurt anymore.

"Oh, don't get me wrong," she started, knowing this part wouldn't take long. "It's not as if I care, or anything."

"What then?" he said, clearly lost in the delight of having been missed "You wanted me to be there. You've never said—"

"But it's not as if I love you, Joe."

Vestiges of his smile hung on stubbornly as her words found their mark in his eyes. What was happening was just so unexpected that his whole face refused to catch up with the idea, leaving the corners of his mouth turned up and the bottom edge of his front teeth peeking out between still taut lips. But where his face couldn't register her meaning, his mind could. She may never have told him she loved him, but she'd never told him she didn't, either. He had known her well, and he would realize what she was doing. There may have been a time, long ago, when he would have fought her, but he knew her now and would know this was not a battle he could win. He stood, swaying a little unsteadily, with his smile traces, looking a bit like a drunk who couldn't find his car.

Adelaide might not have said more if Joe hadn't continued to stand there with his smile. She felt like someone who has delivered a fatal blow and watches, uncertain what to do next, while their opponent struggles to stay on his feet. With her own energy seeping away, she mumbled a coup de grace.

"It's not as if I ever loved you."

His smile faded into a pale sadness. Joe crunched across the kitchen floor in his bare feet and left a brown cereal trail on the dining room carpet which Adelaide followed into the living room. She found him collapsed into himself on the couch like one of the helium balloons the day after Macy's parade. Adelaide watched him hurting, and the watching released something, as if some of her own pain had been transferred to him. There was nothing left in her but a warm pulsing in her legs, like the timbers of a burned house just after the fire has gone out.

"Why are you telling me this?" he said, finally.

Adelaide groaned inwardly with the effort she was not expecting to make. This was taking more words than she had anticipated.

"Because it's true," she slurred.

"I know," he said, finally. "But I figured that was all right because you didn't love anyone else either."

"No."

"So I was waiting."

Each word she heard and spoke were painful as if the woman inside her head beat against the base of her skull, but each word got her closer to the end so she was able to force herself to say,

"Waiting for what?"

"I don't know. I guess I should go now."

Those abrupt words in Joe's quiet, steady voice sucked any remaining heat from her and left her ice. It was finished. The other woman in the farthest corner of her mind burst her bonds and screamed "I'm sorry!" over and over again, but the sound, more air than sound really, that came from Adelaide's mouth was "Yes."

Joe pushed himself off the couch, went back into the kitchen and slipped into his loafers without bothering to brush the brown crumbs off his feet. He turned back before going out the door and spoke calmly, but the last word twisted in his throat.

"I'll be at the shop."

Adelaide watched the door shut from the front hall and thought, *There. That's the last of them. Now I can't ever be hurt again because I've done all the hurting first and there's no one left. And I don't care.* She looked around at the part of the house she could see from where she stood. The mismatched furniture, the few knick-knacks they had collected, even the spots in the carpeting threw memories of the last thirty years at her. *That conversation only lasted two minutes at the most. It takes an incredibly short time to destroy a marriage. An audience would never believe it.*

She cautiously searched her mind, trying to avoid any backlash from the other woman while she wondered what she was feeling. Was the hurting gone now? Was there a peace beginning? She thought so until she turned one corner in her mind and found instead something that felt like howling.

Like a shrieking in the darkness of her soul, in the silence of the empty house the howl was the only thing she could hear. It blossomed up from the base of her spine growing in power until it spread across her face hunting for her mouth, hunting for release. She felt some senseless fear of what might happen if the sound escaped her lips. Her jaw tightened and her mouth twisted to get rid of the creeping howl but she couldn't twist her mouth hard enough to drive the sound back to that part of her brain where it had come from.

*It would be a very bad thing,* she thought, flooded with the sudden horror that felt like an insanity, *if the howling never stopped.*

Adelaide forced herself to move, anything to escape the sound that filled her. She dragged her feet step by step until she could feel the spilled cereal underfoot on the kitchen floor. Then she felt them on her knees. Then on her face. Putting out her tongue, she touched it to one of the unsmashed Coco Puffs, pulled it into her mouth and rolled its sweetness around, thinking of Joe. She turned over on the cereal and sat up against the cupboard under the sink with her legs stuck out in front of her. There was only one person left to help her escape the howl that still threatened to emerge from her mouth. He was in the front seat of her car, waiting patiently for her.

Monica came back into the house, having tried to stop Joe from leaving and only watching helplessly as his car drove through her.

"Why did I ever let you start this!" she wailed. "I had no idea she was going to kick Joe out of the house! Oh, Del, you big ass!" Monica tried to pluck a Coco Puff off Adelaide's right cheek even though she knew it was useless to try. She plopped down onto the floor with her legs stuck out before her like Adelaide's. "I had no idea it would get to this, or I would never have let you—"

Ferdy looked like the child who broke the window, and said a little defensively, "I told you I knew how to cause trouble. This is what it looks like. What did you expect?"

"I didn't expect you to destroy their marriage. I didn't expect you to hurt Joe like that."

"Now just wait a minute, I didn't hurt Joe, she did."

"Oh, what difference does it make. Now what?"

"What do you mean, now what?"

"What's the rest of your plan?"

"That's it. She gets so unhappy she asks for help. You know, prayer. All mortals pray when they've hit the bottom; either that or kill themselves. But you said Del wouldn't kill herself, so as soon as she prays we're home."

"That was your plan? To get Del to pray? Oh, Ferdy, why didn't you tell me. Del's not going to pray, she's never going to pray."

"How do you know?" he said, his voice getting smaller as he watched her walk back and forth through the front hall.

While Monica paced, Adelaide rose from the floor and began to search around the kitchen, then the living room. She finally discovered what she was looking for, her car keys, which were still in her left hand. She stared at them for a moment as if they had appeared magically, then started out the door.

Monica and Ferdy had nothing to do but follow.

# Chapter Twelve
## In Which Everyone Goes Into the Pool Again

They followed Adelaide to her father's house on Malaga Lane. The house was dark inside but a timer kept the porch light on all night and illuminated the shiny For Sale sign on the front lawn near the banyan tree. Adelaide got out of the car, started to walk toward the house, then doubled back. Unlocking the passenger door, she reached inside and lifted out the box with her father's ashes in it. Then she continued, not to the front door, but around the side of the house. Ferdy shot Monica a puzzled look, but Monica only shrugged, equally puzzled, and kept following.

There was a light in the backyard, too. This one was motion sensitive and came on brightly when Adelaide stepped onto the patio surrounding the pool. It flooded the whole patio area and suffused the water in the pool with a glow that reflected back onto Adelaide's face. The weather-worn PVC furniture that had been there during the funeral was gone, leaving just the flatness of the water, the brown chattahoochee patio surface, and the dark lawn stretching to a wooden fence at the edge of the property.

Adelaide set the box down on the white coping of the pool and stood beside it as if it were her father, live and whole, standing beside her, both of them facing the still water. Except for occasional bursts of canned laughter coming faintly from a television somewhere on the other side of the wooden fence, there was absolute silence all around.

"What's she doing?" Ferdy asked Monica in a golf tournament whisper.

"How should I know? I was going to ask you the same thing," returned Monica in the same whisper.

"You're her friend. I figured you would know."

"Well I don't. She never talks much about her family. Everything with Del is, you know, one-liners. We knew she wasn't close to her family, but she always talked about them in a joking kind of way when she talked about them at all. You know, 'you'll never believe what Dad said now,' sort of thing. She made us laugh at them."

Ferdy was gazing so intently at Adelaide gazing at the pool that Monica was sure he wasn't listening to her.

"What's going on? Are you noticing something?" she said, tugging on his wing.

Ferdy turned and looked at her with unseeing eyes, then focused. "Uh, I was just going into her imagination to see what she's thinking."

"What do you see?"

"A little girl, it looks like Adelaide as a little girl. This could be a memory of something real."

Monica tugged harder. "Show me, Ferdy. Make me be able to see. Maybe I'll understand."

"I'm not sure you can do this, but we can try." Ferdy stood Monica before him, facing Adelaide. He placed his hands over her ears and his chin on the top of her head, holding her perfectly still in a soft vise. "Stay absolutely still. Hold your hands away from your body. Don't hear or breathe. Separate your teeth and keep your tongue suspended so it doesn't feel your mouth. Now see..."

*A cloudless blue sky, as deep a blue as the water in the pool beneath, arches overhead as if its only purpose is to provide a canopy for the children's party. Presents wrapped in a calliope of patterns, with ribbons slipping in curls off their sides, are stacked on a glass top patio table under the back awning of the house. In a matching chair next to the table sits a man of about thirty-five, sipping on a canned beer, and looking like his position is assigned rather than chosen. Except for under the awning where it's shady, the light is everywhere, making the stucco walls of the house white hot, and shooting through the stirring water like electric shocks busily creating life in some primordial sea.*

*There is life in the sea. Twelve little girls, all of them somewhere around the age of eight, churn the water with their swimming and splashing. Two of them hold onto the silver handgrip on the stairs in the shallow end as they giggle and whisper. Two others are fighting to pull the other under in the deep end and look like they might end up in real battle.*

*Del sits on the side of the pool, her feet dangling into the water, lazily bumping her heels against the marcite. Her wet pony tail hangs off the back of her head; it's about as big around as a plump pencil. She smiles with half-closed eyes, like a queen aware of her subjects' pleasure without actually paying attention to it. Then her eyes open and she shouts:*

*"Hey, everybody, come here! I have an idea."*

*The others gather round her feet with the expectant thrill of those who are accustomed to her ideas.*

*"Let's pretend," she begins, and the girls exchange glances full of anticipation. "Let's pretend that we're all mermaids. We're mermaid sisters and we've all been captured in big fishing nets by the king's fisherman."*

*Del stops but the little girls stay silent, some holding their breath. They know there's more.*

*"We have to perform, with swimming and stuff, for the king. . .and his son. . .and, whoever performs the best is going to be chosen by the prince. . .as his favorite mermaid. And that will be really good because the prince is very handsome and will love his mermaid very much. He'll come into the pool and swim with her. . .and give her beautiful tops to wear to cover her. . .you know. . ."*

*The other little girls swim away shrieking with laughter at her allusion to breasts. Del doesn't have to show them how to swim with their ankles crossed and their feet curved like fins. They've played at mermaids for as long as they could swim. Now they leap and dive through the water, shooting from side to side with unsynchronized gaiety, performing  extravagant maneuvers for the imaginary prince. Del has slipped into the pool too, and cavorts like a dolphin among them. She looks shyly toward the man watching them.*

*"Dad, will you be the judge?" she asks. Her voice is more hesitant than before, and when he dismisses her with a wave of his hand, she doesn't beg.*

*One of the mermaids, an impish child with dark curls, struggles up the steps in the shallow end, and managing to keep her ankles crossed, dives back in.*

*"No diving from the shallow end!" shouts the man, doing the job he is meant to do.*

*The girls are obedient, but they can't take the chance that the prince will choose the impish child with the dark curls. Laughingly, they all struggle up the stairs or heave themselves over the side of the pool, and flop their way like seals to the deep end.*

*All except Del. She sits on the stairs at the shallow end watching, still with a smile, but a smaller one than before.*

*"C'mon, Del!" the others shout as they line up for their turns.*

*"No, I have to judge who dives best!" she shouts back.*

*One by one they slice through the water or crash into it, depending on how well they can dive. Once they are all in the water again, they gather around Del.*

"You have to go, now!" the impish child declares.

"Yeah! Yeah!" the others echo one another. "Show us how you walk like a mermaid!"

Del pauses, then gives in. She hops up one step at a time, carefully keeping her ankles crossed and her knees tight together. All the length of the side of the pool she rocks back and forth on the sides of her feet which are turned out as far as they can go. She looks terribly malformed, like a child with two club-feet, but the children see a mermaid princess.

She gets to the deep end and stands, barely balancing, with her toes brushing the edge of the coping.

"This mermaid does it differently," she announces. "She jumps in, in a real fancy way."

"No! We want to see how your flippers go in last!" shouts the impish child, and the others pick up the call. "No! No! You have to dive, like the rest of us," they shout, and quickly turn their call into a challenge. "Dive, Del! Dive, Del! Dive, Del!"

Del stares at the wildly chanting crowd below her feet. The girls in the shallow end are jumping up and down, making waves, while the ones in the deeper end who can't touch bottom are smacking the surface of the water with their palms. When she is grown she will remember this moment and think of its gladiatorial nature, but at eight years old she only feels the shame of being the one girl who's afraid to dive.

Her arms are raised straight in front of her in the ready position when she thinks of one possibility. Still keeping her mermaid tail in place she turns the top of her thin body to the man in the chair under the awning. He has been watching the scene, has his eyes fixed on Del now as he takes another sip of his beer. Arms upraised, the tips of Del's fingers stretch out to him in quiet supplication. She tests a shy smile. This has never worked before, but she is still young enough to think it might. She hasn't come to the age where she doesn't try to win him and pretends she doesn't care. No one in the pool can tell that she is pleading for him to save her. The girls are so caught up in the chant which has now become merely, "Del! Del! Del!" that they don't see the communication between the father and daughter.

They don't see him stand up, tuck his chin down and shake his lowered head as if his team had just lost, turn his back and go inside the house, letting the screen door close slowly on its spring behind him.

But Del sees. She can feel her father's disgust at her failure slam at her from across the yard and she forgets the other children are there. She screams *after the retreating back of her father.*

*"Wait, Dad! Come back! I can do this! I swear I can do this!" She forgets that she is standing with her arms out in front of her and her legs twisted absurdly around each other. When she is grown and can't sleep she will occasionally remember herself, standing in such a preposterous pose on the side of the pool, and grimace at how foolish she must have looked. "DAD!" She screams again, partly in anguish and partly in rage, but her father doesn't come back.*

*The children in the pool fall slowly silent, look away from her and at one another.*

Forgetting what she was and what she was going to, Monica rushed to the little girl at the edge of the pool and tried to take her into an embrace which neither phantom could feel. Still, she kept crooning to the young Adelaide as if she could be heard.

"Oh, Del, Del, you don't have to do it, he doesn't matter. Del, you didn't have to do anything—nothing matters that much."

She looked up at the real Adelaide still standing by the side of the patio and thought for a moment that she was watching and listening. But then she saw that the woman's eyes were still turned inward to the imagination which had created the children in the pool. When she looked back at her side the imaginary child was gone and the next moment Adelaide was moving off around the side of the house, her father's ashes tucked under her arm.

# CHAPTER THIRTEEN
## In Which Estella Too Takes the Stage

Estella Too concentrated on the beat of the rhumba music as she tried out new steps Gus had shown her. She was using the stereo system in the living room since Palma had called to say she wouldn't be home tonight. The last of the tricker treaters had appeared hours ago but the sugar high she got from the leftover Milky Ways had her up dancing even though it was nearly midnight.

She held a CD at arm's length as she danced, practicing her sultry stare at the singer's face smiling from the CD cover through his cigarette smoke. Her ample hips rolled into the rhythm. Her right arm shot into the air and came down again slowly, her fingers fluttering seductively between her wrinkly breasts. A glass of second best wine lay half empty on the cherry sideboard, the rim of the glass slashed with a streak of her favorite burgundy lipstick.

Partly out of habit from her years as Palma's duenna and partly out of her strict religious upbringing, Estella Too had never approved of Palma's affairs. She especially hadn't approved of Gus with his crude ways and lack of social status, not to mention lack of funds. Still, when he grabbed her one night in the kitchen and forced her to tango the entire distance of the counter top she began to understand his allure. And when she suddenly found herself dipped within three inches of the surface of the tile floor, her powerless body supported in Gus's confident arms she succumbed to the philosophy, *Well, as long as she's happy...*

A shriek from the backyard brought Estella Too abruptly out of her music. She flicked off the stereo and stood trembling while she tried to sort out logic from fear. *It can't be burglars. Burglars sneak up on you. Unless they are clumsy burglars and trip over a sprinkler head.* She moved out of the light and away from the sliding glass doors leading to the backyard. Standing in the entrance to the kitchen she peeked around the door jamb, squinting to see movement in the darkness outside. *Carajo! Where is the security guard? The alarm isn't on yet. Are all the doors locked?* Against her will, her imagination summoned a black-clad figure at the sliding glass doors and her ears strained to hear the squeak of a glass cutter.

Nothing. She stood several minutes trying to keep her breathing as still as possible, but neither heard nor saw anything else. As the minutes passed her courage grew until she finally reached to her right on the kitchen wall for the backyard flood lights and boldly threw them on. Then she looked outside again.

Still nothing. *Was it a neighbor? An animal?* The light flooding the backyard made her braver and she slid open the door to have a look around. Everything was still. Everything except a small sound, like a roach on a newspaper, coming from the swimming pool. The pool light had gone on with the rest of the area and she walked across the patio to the edge and looked in.

"Mrs. Siren, what are you doing down there?"

Adelaide rose painfully to her hands and knees at the bottom of the empty pool. "I was taking the backyard tour of Miami and fell in," she said, weakly.

"The pool was drained after Bishop Laparro's death."

"Really?"

"Here. Let me help you out." Estella Too waddled to the steps at the shallow end, but Adelaide stopped her mid-way down.

"No, I don't think so."

"Eh?"

"I think I'll just stay here, thank you." Adelaide grimaced as she probed her knees with her index finger. Apparently satisfied that nothing was broken despite the pain, she crawled further into the deep end and retrieved the battered brown package which had been hiding in the shadows where the pool beam didn't reach.

"Are you hurt? Should I dial nine-one-one?"

Adelaide took a mental inventory. "No, nothing hurts too badly. I just stepped off the edge. It's not like I dove in or anything."

"Palma isn't here tonight."

"Ah."

Estella Too paused to see what would happen next. Nothing did. "You can't just stay at the bottom of the pool."

"Why not? I like it here." She collapsed down onto the tiles and lay on her back gazing into the night sky with the package cradled in her arms. "You know, with the pool light shining over your head you can't see as many stars."

"Do you want me to call Palma?"

"No! I don't know. I guess not."

"Mrs. Siren, are you drunk?"

"No."

That ended all the possibilities for questions and actions that Estella Too could conceive. Then she thought of one more.

"Would you like to be?"

Since there was no answer, Estella Too went back into the house. She got the second best wine from the cherry sideboard and collected two art deco plastic wine glasses that Palma used poolside. On second thought, she went into the pantry and tucked another bottle of wine under her arm. When she returned to the patio Adelaide was still down in the pool, but had crawled to one side and was sitting with her back against the wall at the five foot depth.

Estella Too stepped into the pool and filled a glass for Adelaide which she set beside her. Then she settled comfortably on a step and poured a glass for herself. Neither spoke, but Adelaide lifted the glass and sipped at it like a hurt child sips hot chocolate, cupping it in both hands as if to feel its warmth.

They sat that way for some time, silently sipping wine, while Estella Too kept watch. The sky was clear and lit by a full moon grown smaller on the back side of its nightly path. The smell of jasmine, not as pungent now as in the summer, was still strong enough to melt in the aroma of the wine. Estella Too could see a slow change in Adelaide's face as the wine took effect. It was melting whatever stone she carried in her gut. The wine was having an effect on the housekeeper as well. She dropped her usual deference and spoke as an equal. As a mother.

"Now tell me why you don't want me to call Palma."

"Because she hates me."

"Palma hates you? Why do you think that?"

"You see it was this lechon asado and stepped out of character all because of that damn stigmata thing and before you knew it it was 'th-th-fbt' all over her pumpkin blouse." Adelaide weakly brought her fingers together as if she were squeezing something between them.

"I see," said Estella Too, hardly seeing at all, wondering what could have brought Adelaide to this degree of inarticulation.

"And then I was furious with Joe because he didn't get into an accident and miss my opening, and how could he do such a thing? I told myself I didn't care but Estella Too how could he?"

"He should have had the manners to crash into the concrete divider on I-95 at least."

Estella Too watched Adelaide nod vigorously and thought maybe it wasn't important that she didn't understand a thing the other woman was saying.

"Then he left me."

That she understood. "What!? 'Left you' as in, leave you? Oh, Del, that's impossible. Joe would never leave you."

"I made it happen, Estella Too. I was a bitch—much worse than usual."

"You were cruel to Joe. Oh, Del."

"Everything was so good, life was so good before Monica. . . before she. . ." Adelaide threw herself face down on the tiles and sobbed as if she intended to fill the pool with her tears. Estella Too went to her then, sat down and cradled Adelaide's head in her apron. She had never seen Adelaide act like a child before, but was willing to comfort her as a child. She stroked her hair, half of which had escaped the bonds of a denim scrunchie, and brushed away some dark brown crumbs without asking what they were.

"Was life good, Del? Tell me. Maybe it was not so good."

"I never used to cry this much. I never cried at all."

"That doesn't mean that everything was good, *pauvrecita,* that just means you didn't feel enough of the pain."

"What pain? What pain was there?"

"Yours. Others."

"Oh, God, Estella Too, you're not going to lecture me, are you?" Adelaide tried to roll off the woman's lap but found herself pinned down with surprising strength.

"Call it what you want, but if you think you might like to try another alternative besides suicide. . ." here Adelaide winced, "you might do worse than listen to an old housekeeper." Adelaide winced again, but allowed her to continue. "It has been many years now since I have watched you, and Palma, and Monica, grow up as friends. You became so accustomed to me in the background that I disappeared from you—"

"You ne—"

Estella Too placed a finger on Adelaide's lips. "—and I accepted that as my proper role." As she continued to speak, she let her tone soften like a gentle surgeon who sought to hurt as little as possible, but who would perform the surgery nonetheless. "While no one noticed me I watched and listened to the thousands of conversations between the three of you and the people in your lives. There was Monica, who wanted to be so good. And my Palma, wanting to be perfect, and wondering why all the lovers who came through this house never made her happy. And you. . . you. You couldn't leave your writing at home, you seemed to live inside your plays all the time, afraid to come out and be with real people. You saddened me most of all."

"I don't want anyone to feel sorry for me."

"I think you do, or you would not be here."

Adelaide nodded, subdued by her fall and the wine and the crying, and seduced by the strokings of Estella Too's dry hand. A night breeze had snuck into the pool and mingled with the old woman's hand, making it feel as if the breeze had fingers. Other than Joe, she never remembered being stroked like this before, and thought *Is this what a mother feels like?* She responded to the other woman's honesty with her own.

"I've always been alone," she said. "Even with Palma and Monica I used to have this feeling of watching them be friends, of darting into their conversations with a line or two, and darting back out again. It didn't bother me, because that's the way I had always been, watching other people love each other. I can't imagine why people want to be around me."

"Well, most of the time when you are not feeling sorry for yourself you are fun. And then, maybe it's because you don't hide yourself as well as you think you do. Maybe they can see that when you are being harsh you are only like a small dog, showing its teeth to protect itself, but too comical to be very scary. Maybe the people who love you are smarter than you after all."

Adelaide groaned and shut her eyes to block out the memory of

Joe's face just an hour before. "Oh my God, Joe. I hurt him so much, Estella Too, and I didn't mean to."

"Of course you did."

"Well, yes I did, but it was to keep from being hurt myself."

"It didn't work very well, did it." Estella Too kept stroking as she sighed. "Joe is the one I've watched the most because he never noticed. He was always too busy watching you. Ah, Del, I have never seen such love of a man for a woman. I could have wished that Palma and Monica had found such men. I could have wished a man like that for myself."

"So the one who couldn't appreciate love got the most. Sounds like a play, only not one of mine. I only do plays with happy endings."

"This is not a tragedy. Joe's love is too strong for you to destroy. The merest nod from you will bring him back home."

"For what? So I can hold him away from myself until we die? I won't do that to him anymore."

"And by rejecting him you will sacrifice any hope of your own happiness. How noble. It sounds like even now you are competing with Monica, trying to be a martyr. I think you would say 'beating her at her own game?'" Adelaide's head gave a little twitch as if thinking to draw away from Estella Too's hand but not willing to succeed. Estella Too went on. "But there is another way."

"What way?"

"You could begin to love him back."

"I've told you I can't, Estella Too. I don't know how. With everything else I've learned I missed that lesson and the feeling just doesn't come to me."

"That may be true, although it may also be that you have hidden the feeling because it scares you. But not having a feeling doesn't have to stop you. In a sermon I once heard a priest say that love is not a feeling, but an act. You could do something. What would one of your characters do to show love? You could pray to know what act to perform to show love to Joe."

"If you know so much about me, you know I don't believe in all that."

Estella Too paused for such a long time that Adelaide feared the other woman had given up, that the conversation was over. She didn't want that, and was grateful when Estella Too went on.

"In the theater you have a phrase for what happens when the audience can watch people wandering about on a small stage and picture the whole world, yes?"

"Yeah. It's called a 'suspension of disbelief.'"

"Maybe for a little while you could do that. Doubt your unbelief and pretend. Theater is all pretending, is it not?"

"I don't know...I've always been proud of being honest, at least."

Estella Too ignored her last remark which made Adelaide think that honesty was not a terribly important virtue. "When I need a favor, I always pray to St. Jude, myself. In Colombia people like me never approach El Hefe, the head of the town. We always go through the middle man who carries our message to the leader who decides to grant our wish. That's what the saints are for. They are our middle men who petition God for us. Some think it is ridiculous, even blasphemous. But that is the custom."

Adelaide's thoughts turned to her discussion with Cardinal Parelli earlier in the day. Had so much really happened in less than twenty-four hours?

"Monica," she said.

"What about Monica?"

"I know for certain that Monica exists. Existed."

With the empathy that comes between two people talking outside at midnight, Estella Too seemed to understand. "Not official, but perhaps Monica," she said. "Wait here." She took the cardboard box from under Adelaide's hand and placed it underneath her head. Then she rose from the cold tiles with some difficulty, using the side of the pool for balance, and walked out of the pool and into the house.

When she returned, she took Adelaide's hand and laid something that was at once soft and prickly in it. Adelaide sat up and, leaning on one elbow, looked in her hand. The feathers were stuck together from being wet and the wires were bent so that the shape was no longer as round as it had been, but Monica's dream catcher earrings were still recognizable.

"They were found in the filter and Palma kept them as a remembrance. She loved Monica very much," Estella Too said, her voice catching. "And Monica, like you and Palma, was my child."

"A relic," said Adelaide.

"If you wish."

Adelaide rose to her feet, her body heavy with aching inside and out. "I guess I'm going now."

Estella Too picked up the brown package and only glanced at it curiously before handing it to Adelaide without commenting about it. "I don't think you should go. I don't think you should be alone tonight. Why not stay here?"

"No, I need to go."

"Are you going home?"

"I don't know," said Adelaide, thinking that was at least a difference from 'I don't care.'" Her father's ashes and Monica's earrings. Even unaware of Monica and Ferdy's constant presence, for a person who was traveling alone it seemed she was carrying a lot of baggage.

☿ ☿ ☿

"That was remarkable," Monica said, recalling the conversation at the pool as they followed Adelaide to wherever she was going next. "I was never able to talk to Adelaide the way Estella Too did tonight."

"I'd bet Adelaide was never ready to talk that way until tonight," said Ferdy as he appeared with Monica in the backseat of Adelaide's car. "She's on the verge of prayer, I can feel it. Everything that has happened to her brought her to it. Maybe my plan wasn't so bad after all, huh?"

If Monica thought *What plan?,* she kept it to herself and hoped Ferdy wasn't looking.

# Chapter Fourteen
## All Saints Day

One a.m. at South Beach on any typical Friday night was wake-up time. Reggae and rock usually blew out of the open doors of bars and revelers danced on the sidewalks among the tables of late diners at outdoor cafes. But on this Friday night the party gears were several notches higher. The music was louder and activity verged on the hysterical. People were dressed in crazier costumes than usual, or dressed in nearly nothing. Men shouted commands to women on the balconies facing the street, and cheered when the women obligingly raised their tank tops.

Weaving her way between a woman wearing only a black half slip and bra, and a Dorothy from Oz with wisps of hair from her wig caught in her mustache, even in her preoccupation Adelaide could not fail to be aware that this was Halloween.

Barely avoiding the cruisers whose attention was not on their driving, she crossed the street where there was a wide plaza and a concrete wall separating it from the beach. Here the pounding of the surf could just be heard over the vibration of the crowd. Adelaide didn't follow the wall down the plaza looking for the path that broke through it, but swung her legs over the concrete and dropped onto the sand. There was a sand sculptor who had just finished creating a large castle. He was lighting sterno beacons and placing them carefully in the turrets and courtyards of the castle. The bottom half of a plastic bleach bottle sat to his right, with a few dollars in the bottom. As Adelaide passed him she turned around and looked toward the people and buildings behind her. The glow from the neon lights flowed upward, paling the night sky and making everything invisible except the full moon and a stubborn Venus.

Over the water was different. The moon behind her lit the small whitecaps at her feet, but farther out only the lights from a few freighters and a marker buoy or two competed with the stars. With the blackness of the water reaching up into the blackness of the sky, the stars were the only way of telling where the horizon started. The tide was coming in, consuming a little more of the sand with each wave, slow but absolutely powerful.

Adelaide sat down cross-legged in the sand at a safe enough distance from the water's edge where she could only feel a mist from the breakers on her cheeks. She placed before her the earrings and the box of ashes like food at a picnic, and looked at them as if deciding what to eat first.

That she was here to make a choice was clear. She held the earrings in her palm and stroked the feathers with her thumb. "Monica," she said aloud, as if she were beginning a conversation, then she stopped, embarrassed. She knew that choosing the earrings meant choosing change. It would mean letting that other woman out, and maybe the other woman would rule her. Who would she be then? She looked inside her mind, deep into its core, and imagined the bit of bone behind which the other woman was waiting, maybe had always waited, the woman she had even hidden from Estella Too. The bone had been blasted by this day, and further chipped away by Estella Too's words. But the barrier was strong and she was suddenly very tired.

"Is she about to pray, Ferdy? That's what we're waiting for, right?" said Monica. The two spirits were standing a little way off, down where the water would have rushed in around their feet if they had any.

Ferdy narrowed his eyes in concentration. "Her thoughts are rushing around so much I'm having trouble tracking her. Stones, and a prisoner, it's nothing I can make sense of. Ashes." He gulped loudly enough for Monica to hear him over the breakers. "This could be a bad thing."

Adelaide placed the earrings carefully on her knee so they wouldn't get lost in the sand, and turned her attention to the brown package. She pulled off the tape and rolled it into a sticky ball which she tossed in the sand beside her. The cardboard cover opened to reveal a black enameled box in the shape of a cube. The box was sealed tightly with shrink wrap, but it only took a few scratches with her car key to break through the plastic. The wind caught the shrink wrap and sent it rolling down the beach. Letting her hand hover uncertainly over the box for only a moment,

Adelaide pried off the top portion of the cube which was loosely pressure fitted to the bottom.

The breeze lightly stirred the ashes inside without blowing any out of the box. Adelaide studied them; with only the light of the moon to see by, she thought they were fine, the particles so fine they almost looked like a light paste. It was only when she dipped the tip of her finger in the ash that she could feel the small chunks of bone that hadn't completely burned to dust. The ashes on her finger were a light gray and stuck to her like a second skin.

This was her other choice, she knew. She could stay the way she was, which was very much like her father, and become more and more him for the rest of her life. This was the easier way, because she was accustomed to the part.

A play of the moon on the moving water made her look up. With the variations of light and dark it was easy to imagine the form of her father hovering over the water, darkness on darkness, only his eyes glowing white where two stars shown through. She imagined what he would say.

*Your mother and I didn't get to go to college.*
*We worked for you and your sister so that you could have everything.*
*We expect a lot from you.*
*Don't let us down.*

"I don't want to be a winner anymore, Dad," she murmured, as if trying out the words to see how they felt. "It makes me tired."

*You're a fighter, just like me.*
*You are who you are.*
*Nothing can change that.*
*People don't change.*

"What's happening now?" said Monica, but Ferdy only stared over the water, open mouthed.

"Just like you," Adelaide whispered. Her fingers dipped into the ash until they were covered all the way down to where her palm started. Still watching the phantom she had created as if it were a mirror to guide her, she pulled her hand down the side of her face leaving a streak of ash. Again and again, she dipped into the box and spread the particles over her face like grease paint until she was completely gray. Even her eyelids were coated and bits of ash clung to her lashes.

"Del, stop!" Monica shouted, but her friend went on. "What about the earrings?" she said to Ferdy. "Make her remember the earrings!"

"I can't make her do anything," said Ferdy, with the increasing sadness of unavoidable doom. "She has to come to it on her own."

But Adelaide had already risen from the sand, carrying the box with the remaining ashes but leaving the earrings to flutter helplessly like wounded birds behind her as she walked closer to the water. Monica tried to block the way but each time she stepped in her path Adelaide walked through her in a way that looked like a pattern from a ghostly square dance. By the time Monica gave it up as useless Adelaide was up to her knees.

"Ferdy, I have to talk to her!" Monica yelled. "Help me talk to her."

"You can't. You're dead and you can't communicate with her."

"I have to get to her somehow."

"It's a rule that can't be broken."

The waves washed thinly over the sand and the high tide made it so shallow that Adelaide was now twenty feet into the water without it reaching her waist. But she kept going. Monica threw herself at the other woman's body again and again but it made no difference. She stopped, and had one last desperate thought.

"Ferdy, can you talk to her?"

"It's been done before, but not by me."

"What about when you appeared in my dream, you were talking to me then, I could see you, oh, please, please think."

"That was assailing and I screwed it up. This would be an awake assailing and who knows what I'll do this time? I could destroy her. I could turn her into a blithering idiot or make her disintegrate."

"So it's better if she drowns? Please try. I have to get a message to her. Thirty seconds, that's all I'm asking for. You go in, you tell her what I tell you, you come out."

"What if I fail?"

"Oh, for God's sake, what if you don't try?"

Ferdy shook his head hard enough to shake the memories away. "Monica, look what I've brought her to already. Becket, Yves, you, and now her. Haven't I done enough damage for one eternity?"

Monica heard the failure in the twist of his voice. She reached up and grabbed his face between her hands as if he were a kid. "Remember what you said about the plan, Ferdy, that it changes all the time. Even if assailing her isn't part of the plan right now, if you do it, maybe it will be." Monica shook his jaw with one hand and gave his face a light slap with the other. "Oh, Ferdy, I don't know if what I just said makes sense, but we don't have a lot of time to talk about it."

Ferdy looked into Monica's brown eyes with his own, leaned forward and kissed her forehead. Then he stepped in front of Adelaide, spread his wings and reached out to cover her face with his strong hands to shield her from himself.

In the next second she felt a soft pounding that didn't come from the surf or the music far behind her. The pounding increased its beat and intensity until it ripped open a gash in her world as if it were trying to escape. All the stars joined together and sent their bright heart into her core and she watched her own body light up the space around her. The beach was gone, and the water, and the night. It was just her and the figure of a black winged man standing between herself and where she had been going. He emitted a brightness in sympathy with her own and she saw beams shooting from her arms and chest meeting and mingling with his own until they were joined by a bridge of light across the surface of the water. Her heart filled her chest so that her lungs had no space to draw breath. She stared and held her breath and felt the beat of her hear replace the pounding in her mind. She thought would scream, but couldn't. She thought she would die and wondered why she didn't.

"FEAR NOT," a voice boomed.

She heard the words, and even in her shock wondered that the voice was neither male nor female but some other. She waited because she could do nothing else.

The creature appeared to do the same. Or was it listening? He glanced to his right as if there were another person standing beside him, giving instructions. She thought she heard him say, "So far, so good." Then he focused on her again.

"I BRING YOU TIDINGS—" he began in a somber tone, then shrugged his shoulders, and suddenly sounded matter-of-fact, like a next door neighbor come to discuss the shared hedges. "Hey, look, I—we—just have to have a talk with you."

After the first wave of electric shock had driven through her body Adelaide felt, hardly in control, but somehow all right with being out of it. Even though she tingled with anticipation, a feeling of ease enveloped her, as if she were surrounded by a soft invisible blanket on a cold night. She found it easy to speak since her mouth was open already.

"Are you an angel?" she asked.

The being stood a little straighter. "Well, yes, yes I am."

"Who's we?" and her own voice sounded oddly unlike hers.

"We?"

"You said 'we' have to talk."

"It's, well, it's Monica. Monica is here with me." The angel glanced to his right again, and Adelaide looked too, but saw only more of the blinding light that surrounded them both. "You won't be able to see her, because that's the rule. But she has a message she insists I give you."

"That sounds like Monica, ordering angels around. But how do I know you're not just a part of my imagination, like, like my father over there somewhere." Adelaide looked but couldn't see his blackness through the surrounding light.

"Oh, but I am part of your imagination," Ferdy said with a wide smile, more comfortable now that his appearance hadn't ripped Adelaide apart. "And your imagination is more true than anything. That's where the real things are."

Adelaide was quiet at that, but felt a stirring deep within her mind. It began as a pleasant tickling around the bone that trapped the other women at the base of her brain. It felt like something warm was sloshing onto the bone, like her brain was bleeding and the blood was melting the bone. She tilted her head back to feel more of the sensation, then cocked it sideways and watched an ephemeral form emerge from her side. The form wavered, then slowly gained in substance until it stood like another person beside her, separate, but just like her. Two Adelaides stood in the water, held in the grip of the angel light, both of them quite real. The difference between them was that the other Adelaide's face was not covered with ashes, but gleamed cleanly in the light.

Ferdy noted the second Adelaide without surprise and addressed her.

"Monica says to tell you that she loves you. That she always has, no matter what, and that she always will, no matter what. She's sorry that she never said it quite like that while she lived."

Adelaide felt the sea push at the back of her eyes, but knew that tears considered themselves too small a thing for this moment. She turned her gray-streaked face to the other woman who spoke for her.

"We receive the message. Is that all?" the other woman asked with dignity, as if she were a queen receiving an ambassador.

The angel paused to listen, then went on. "No, she wants you to know that, if everything that happened, her life, her wounds, her death, were for the sake of your loving, she gives it all gladly."

Adelaide shook her grimy face and shouted, "No, I refuse to take that. I don't want her death, she can have it back. I don't want to take responsibility for her death."

Without comment the other Adelaide looked at the angel for his response. Ferdy pulled himself up with a dignity of his own. The drama he had created in this glowing circle was having an effect on him as well. As if suddenly reminded that he was playing the role of the angel, he forgot the things he couldn't do, the things he feared to do, and rose to the part. Ferdy threw his arms and his wings wide. His strong voice made the light throb and a spirit flooded him with assurance and words that had never been inside him before.

"You can't take responsibility for her death. *You* had nothing to do with it. It was a gift and it can't be given back. The gift is given." Ferdy lifted his head until from his face there shone a beam that reached far up into the heavens as he finished in a mighty voice, "THE PALACE WALLS HAVE BEEN BREACHED BY THE ONSLAUGHT OF LOVE AND YOUR KINGDOM IS CONQUORED. I HAVE DELIVERED THE MESSAGE AND REQUIRE YOUR SURRENDER."

Forgetting that she was waist deep in the ocean, Adelaide fell to her knees and in doing so dropped out of the mystical bond that tied her to the immortal. She came up with a choke, and blew the water out of her nose before struggling back to the shore. The incoming tide was licking at the dream catcher earrings. The sight of the earrings made her look at the open box she still clutched in one arm, and the sight of the box made her look out over the water again. Still hovering over the surf was the dark figure of her father. She looked into its star eyes and wanted with all her heart whatever she was destined to want, whatever was most natural for her humanity to want, and heard herself say, "I don't want to be like you, Dad. I want to be like someone who loves me."

Over went the box of ashes, spinning upside down in her hands, and pouring its contents in a stream over the incoming tide. The particles floated there in a filmy mass until a second wave covered them and took them out to sea. Leaving only the two white stars that were its eyes, the figure disappeared.

With a triumphant laugh, Ferdy made one pass over the beach and alighted beside Monica. "Did you see that?!" he whooped, and strutted before her in the sand. "Would you say that was angel action, or what?"

"You were terrific!" Monica grinned and hugged him, but still looked expectantly at Adelaide watching the ashes being carried out to sea. Ferdy jabbed his forefinger at the wave that carried the ashes and answered her question before she asked it. "Now that," he said, "that's a prayer. Let's go."

He grabbed Monica before she had time to respond, flung her on his back and soared home to deliver Adelaide's prayer where the answer was, as always, yes.

The boy and girl looking for a place to make love watched Adelaide cackling on her knees; they decided she was in no danger and passed by, ascribing her laughter to drunkenness. For her part, she gradually took in her surroundings and her condition. The partying was still at fever pitch across the street, her face itched with human ashes that hadn't altogether washed off with her dunking, she was soaked with sea water, and she held a pair of dream catcher earrings in her hand like they were the winning lottery ticket.

And she was overwhelmed with a feeling of love.

It felt as if laughter had been imprisoned in her heart, but had finally been freed and poured out of its cell with an almost pain that was the greatest pleasure she had ever known. It felt as if she were a bell tower and all the bells there were pealing different notes of joy! joy! joy! in celebration of laughter's release.

She wondered what next. Something had to come next. She felt she had to use up the feeling in order to hold onto it. Estella Too had said something about an act, and certainly this feeling, this vision which was too real to doubt, deserved some act to mark it in the same way that statues are raised to commemorate great events. She rose once more, feeling lighter now that she had set free her other self, and went off to discover what action was appropriate for this night.

# Chapter Fifteen
## The Last Miracle

Adelaide drove away from the loud hilarity of South Beach and into the peacefulness of the residential area beyond. Cool breezes whispered a promise of winter through the darkness. One house she passed already anticipated Christmas, with a string of red lights candy caning a palm tree in the blending of Rockwell and Gauguin that characterized Floridian tropic denial.

The red lights burst into her consciousness much more vividly than she ever remembered any lights before. As a matter of fact, she realized all her senses had sharpened. Adelaide was intensely aware of the sand rubbing into the grooves of the gas pedal under her bare foot. Driving inland, she could smell the ocean salt more clearly now than when she was at the beach. Her headlights caught a raw egg smashed by some reveler in the street and she chuckled with delight at having noticed it. *What else have I been missing?* she wondered. *What else will I find?*

Adelaide didn't know where she was going, except that she sought an act, some symbol, that would preserve forever the delicious pang of joy she had felt kneeling at the beach. As if answering a question, looming up before her like a cliff in the darkness was Monica's Cathedral. She didn't think of it by its name—*what was it? Ah, there's the sign.* St. Stephen's. With the words *paying a visit* in her head, though to whom at this hour she couldn't imagine, she parked the car and tried, against all odds, the front door.

It opened.

The only light in the church came from a single white candle hanging in a glass sconce against the back wall behind the altar. Any other light snuck in from the setting moon through the stained glass windows causing a pulsing warmth that made the church feel like a living thing. The smell of candle wax and old fabric filled the vault. In the narthex she passed a Sunday School display of drawings pinned to a moveable bulletin board above which hung a banner proclaiming "All Saints." She could just make out crude cartoon faces with great staring eyes and wide grins, and names like St. Fred and St. Valerie written beneath. Their striped t-shirts and collared blouses abutted anachronistic halos.

Adelaide bowed to the bulletin board and placed the palms of her hands against the pictures. Her sensitive fingers could feel the innocent pleasure of the children and the good love of the parents behind them. The pang of joy shot through her arms and stoked her heart until she thought again that she must act or burst.

She faced the nave. The altar gleamed pure in the light of the sanctuary candle and she wanted to go there, but hesitated, aware of her state of disrepair. Pulling up the edge of her still damp t-shirt she wiped away at the grime on her face. She didn't want to track sand up the aisle either.

With a glance around her to confirm that she was alone she drew the t-shirt over her head and used it to wipe her feet. She looked at the altar again with the t-shirt in her hand. The act presented itself. She was a dramatist, after all, and this scene called for a ridiculously solemn pageantry.

As she walked down the center aisle between the pews that guarded her way like sentinels, she stepped out of her sodden jeans and shed her underclothes in a path as if she were going to a lover.

She felt herself shedding something else, too. The cage in which she had kept her laughter, her love and her soul, and which had sprung its lock at the beach now dropped to pieces on the floor. The restraint of a lifetime, the tightness of love withheld, fell away and left her soul fleshly naked and fully alive for the first time.

Standing before the altar she laughed softly at her own drama. The laugh magnified and echoed through the space of the great hall and made her think of music. Music made her think of dancing. If she was crazy, then let it be so; it would be the madness of the mystics.

Clumsily shy at first, then less self-consciously as the dance became all, she gave her performance around the sanctuary, skipping over prayer books and embroidered kneelers in her way. Her pale skin gleamed in the sanctuary light, the pang of joy came strong and sure, and hung with her as if it planned to stay.

Somewhere in the rafters she caught movement. On another

night, in another life, she might have been afraid, but tonight she welcomed whatever it was as a friend and kept on dancing.

The movement swooped down to the sanctuary. The only way she could see it was in how the light around it changed. In glimpses of darkness and sparkles of light she watched the thing step in time with her and felt an echo of her laughter coming from where it had been.

She imagined the spirit, if that was what it was, matching her nakedness with its own and flinging its arms and legs about in a mirror image of hers. She wondered if it was the same spirit she had seen at the beach. Tomorrow she might be sane again but she hoped not.

Lifting her head as she twirled behind the altar she spied the *Christus Rex* hanging over her. Carved from rose marble, the proud-faced man was dressed in kingly robes with arms outspread, not in the agony of crucifixion but in expectation of embrace, not sinking powerlessly into death but rising in triumph.

Her dancing slowed as she recalled her vision on the beach and she thought she might return to this thought again. But for now there was another act taking shape in her mind and at least for tonight she was letting grace lead her.

She walked back down the aisle putting on her clothes as she had dropped them, said "thank you" to the unlocked door, and left.

☿ ☿ ☿

Adelaide wasn't much good around the kitchen, but she knew how to make espresso.

She pressed the on switch to warm up the Krupps and compared its amber light to the candle in the church sanctuary. She twisted the heavy metal basket off its holder and rinsed out the grounds from a lifetime ago. Even here her pageant continued and she spooned the fresh coffee into the container with the solemnity of a ritual. After twisting the basket back into place she looked around for a cup. Not the usual one—not tonight.

She pulled a kitchen chair up to the cupboard which was too out of the way to keep anything useful in. She opened the door and rattled pieces of odd china which had somehow insinuated themselves into her life, looking for love the way things do.

There it was. A Bavarian demitasse cup ringed with violets whose little gold feet resting on its saucer made it look like a child dressed in its mother's high heels. And even further back, a Chinese lacquered tray too small to be good for serving anything—except a single cup of espresso.

She stepped down and placed the cup and saucer on the tray, drawing back to gauge the effect. The lavender flowers clashed miserably with the red dragon on the tray, she decided. Dragons and violets. Together in time, perhaps, but in this kingdom they needed something to separate them.

Adelaide didn't bother to look in the cupboards for doilies. She had never been a doily sort of woman. But she got a blue paper cocktail napkin out of the pantry and carefully folded it in half five times.

The kitchen scissors were in the junk drawer next to the stove. Cautiously at first, with the unfamiliarity of adulthood, then with the greater abandon of a child, she carved shapes into the napkin. Halves of diamonds and hearts, circles until there was more emptiness than paper. Careful not to tear the paper, she gingerly pulled the napkin apart and placed her homemade doily on the tray with the saucer on top.

*There,* she thought, using the word as an expression of the ultimate in human satisfaction. The pang of joy hit her again. *Over a paper doily—imagine that.*

She found half a lime in the refrigerator, just beginning to dry out where it had been cut, its peel drawing away from the pulp like the lips of a child wearing wax teeth. She cut a rectangular sliver into the other side where it was still moist. That went into the bottom of the cup.

The espresso machine's warm-up light blinked its readiness to begin. She tilted the china cup under the drip basket—it's feet made it almost too tall to fit—and pressed the on switch. In the quietness of the house the machine's pump roared self-importantly.

Twenty-seconds. She cautiously pulled the cup away and placed it back on its saucer. A bit of Seran wrap tight over the top would keep the heat in for the short drive.

She stepped back one more time to admire her work. A word

that Palma would have used came to mind. *Regalo*.

Gift. One received and now one to give.

She picked up her keys and balanced the Chinese tray in one hand as she opened and shut the front door, leaving it unlocked. Doors were not meant to be locked tonight. A hibiscus bush on the way to the car offered a gaudy yellow bloom for decoration.

☿ ☿ ☿

Luckily the drive was too short for her to practice much what she would say. She eased into a parking space outside the Dog's Day Salon, miraculously not spilling a drop of the espresso. A light inside the shop beamed hopefully through the blinds on the glass front door, making her stop to wonder what would have happened if the place had been dark.

The thought replaced her joy with a tiny pang of fear, and after having acted with such determination to this point she now stood before the door silently, a little shyly. She raised her bare foot and kicked at the door, making the blinds rattle softly.

In a moment the door unlocked and there was Joe, holding it open with his body. Without speaking he slowly examined her, from her wet hair hanging in long globs, a remnant of some gray dust at her temples, clothes stiffened with water, down to naked feet with a hint of beach sand encrusted around her toenails. Then his eyes traveled back up to the tray she held before her and paused on each aspect of it as if he were reading an important letter. Adelaide waited patiently for him to be done. When he was finished, he looked into her eyes.

She looked down first. "Your servant, Mr. Mangiameli," she said, solemnly lifting both hands before him with her offering.

"Thank you, Mrs. Mangiameli," he said, responding as solemnly to her gift as she offered it, holding out his own hands to cup hers, melding his symbol with hers.

She let out her breath, only now aware that she had been holding it. "Hey," she tried to sound casual, but her voice kept strangling in her throat and it made her quip sound poignant, "Don't think I'm going to do this every morning."

"I wouldn't imagine it," he smiled.

"Joe," she said, giving up her final pretense, "I'm so sorry...I—"

Joe lifted a finger to stroke her upper lip, but she caught the finger in her free hand and held it. "No, you have to let me say this."

He nodded his permission.

"I love you...and...even though I can't always promise—"

"Shut up, Adelaide," Joe said and drew her through the doorway.

Rebecca McEldowney has worked as an actress, theatrical director, and forensic science acquisitions editor for a major reference publisher. She obtained her MA in creative writing from Florida Atlantic University under the direction of Johnny Payne, author of the bestselling *Voice and Style*. She has been the recipient of the Florida Stonzek Award for best new play (*Abandon All Hope: A Comedy*), has participated in the Sewanee Writer's Workshop, and has been an invited speaker at the Arizona Mystery Writer's meeting. McEldowney lives in Tucson with Casper, Raven, and her husband Fred Masterman, an author and retired Episcopal priest.

## About Windstorm Creative
## and our Readers' Club

Windstorm Creative was founded in 1989 to create a publishing house with author-centric ethics and cutting-edge, risk-taking innovation. Windstorm is now a company of more than ten divisions with international distribution channels that allow us to sell our books both inside the traditional systems and outside these paradigms, capitalizing on more direct delivery and non-traditional markets. As a result, our books can be found in grocery superstores as well as your favorite neighborhood bookstore, and dozens of other outlets on and off the Internet.

Windstorm is an independent press with the synergy and branding of a corporate publisher and an author royalty that's easily twice their best offer. We have continued to minimize returns without decreasing sales by publishing books that are timeless, as opposed to timely, and never back-listing.

Windstorm is constantly changing, improving, and growing. We are driven by the needs of our authors – hailing from ten different countries – and the vision of our critically-acclaimed staff. All of our books are created with the strictest of environmental protections in mind. Our approach to no-waste, no-hazard, in-house production, and stringent out-source scrutiny, assures that our goals are met whether books are printed at our own facility or an outside press.

Because of these precautions, our books cost more. And though we know that our readers support our efforts, we also understand that a few dollars can add up. This is why we began our Readers' Club. Visit our webcenter and take 20% off every title, every day. No strings. No fine print.

While you're at our site, preview or request the first chapter of any of our titles, free of charge.

Thank you for supporting an independent press.

www.windstormcreative.com
and click on Shop
See next page for fiction titles by Windstorm.

## Rebecca McEldowney

Guardian Devils (Rebecca McEldowney)
Manual for Normal (Rebecca McEldowney)
Soul of Flesh (Rebecca McEldowney)

## If you like the work of Rebecca McEldowney, we recommend Gregg Fecchak

Bad Apple Jack (Gregg Fedchak)
The Broccoli Eaters (Gregg Fedchak)
Love Among the Tomatoes (Gregg Fedchak)

### Other excellent fiction

1001 Nights Exotica (Cris DiMarco)
1002 Nights Exotica (Cris DiMarco)
The Big Five-O Cafe (James Wolfe)
Bones Become Flowers (Jess Mowry)
Breed of a Different Kind (Walt Larson)
Crossing the Center Line (Jackie Calhoun)
False Harbor (Michael Donnelley)
Gathering in the Mist (David Bromden)
Heir Unapparent (John Harrison)
The Jamais Vu Papers (Wim Coleman and Pat Perrin)
Judah's Luck (Walt Larson)
The Junk Lottery (Adelaide Getty)
Little Balls, Big Dreams (James Wolfe)
On a Bus to St. Cloud (Patrick Brassell)
The Sitka Incident (Walt Larson)
Soldier in a Shallow Grave (Gerald Cline)
Storm on the Docks (Walt Larson)
Strong Medicine (Walt Larson)
Visibility (Cris DiMarco)
Willy Charles, Esq. (Walt Larson)